Some Other Place. The Right Place.

By the Author

The Cherry Pit (1965)

Lightning Bug (1970)

Some Other Place. The Right Place. (1972)

The Architecture of the Arkansas Ozarks (1975)

Let Us Build Us a City (1986)

The Cockroaches of Stay More (1989)

The Choiring of the Trees (1991)

Ekaterina (1993)

Butterfly Weed (1996)

When Angels Rest (1998)

Thirteen Albatrosses (or, Falling Off the Mountain) (2002)

With (2004)

Donald Harington

Some other Place. The Right Place.

amazon encore

Text copyright ©1972 Donald Harington
All rights reserved.
Printed in the United States of America.

Published by AmazonEncore
P.O. Box 400818
Las Vegas, NV 89140

ISBN-13: **9781612181073**
ISBN-10: **1612181074**

This book is for
Diana
...and also for Day,
in memory of Daniel

Then death, so call'd, is but old matter dress'd
In some new figure, and a varied vest:
Thus all things are but alter'd, nothing dies;
And here and there the unbodied spirit flies....
From tenement to tenement though toss'd,
The soul is still the same, the figure only lost:
And as the soften'd wax new seals receives,
This face assumes, and that impression leaves;
Now call'd by one, now by another name;
The form is only changed, the wax is still the same.
So death, so call'd, can but the form deface,
The immortal soul flies out in empty space;
To seek her fortune in some other place.

> Ovid, *Metamorphoses*
> In the John Dryden translation

I'd like to get away from earth awhile
And then come back to it and begin over.
May no fate willfully misunderstand me
And half grant what I wish and snatch me away
Not to return. Earth's the right place for love....

> Frost, "Birches"

Movements

Overture

"All my towns are fallen...."
—*Montross*

One

Diana Stoving Accidentally Sees Something That Interests Her

Back out of all this now too much for us, as the poet Frost once began a piece called "Directive," there is a town that is no more a town (there are, in fact, *four* of them, and in driving downstate after leaving one of them, to get to some other place, she passed one of those temporary red cardboard signs which proclaim "Frost Heaves," and not having seen one before, and it being one of the states in which the poet had spent his last years, she thought it was some snide commentary about him, like the graffiti that insinuate, "Nixon Sucks," and pointing this out to her companion, or consort, she wondered aloud if the poet's regurgitation was his reaction to their story. Her companion, or consort, did not seem to get it...perhaps because he was dead).

But to begin at the beginning, or at least, since this may be thought of as a narrative account without any conventional beginning at all, for reasons that will appear, once it is *started* if not *begun*, this now-too-much-for-us of which the poet speaks: the day that the wobbly Wheel of Fortune, out of alignment, needing a retread, needing in fact a whole front-end job, happened to cross the paths of the hero and heroine, who could and might never have met.

Mid-June. Her new Porsche 911E, blood red, fate swift, had hit a pothole on a decrepit section of the Garden State Parkway, and Diana Stoving, 21, a graduate the week before of Sarah Lawrence (major: dance), had been required to proceed slowly and with many

3

vibrations to the nearest exit, at East Paterson, and there scan a yellow pages in search of the nearest Porsche dealer, P.F. Gillihan, Inc. of Garfield, N.J.

Quivering with her car into the Garfield dealer's shop, she learned that her left shock was fouled up and would have to be replaced. She was asked if she could leave it. Diana explained that she was just passing through, with her passenger, Susan Trombley, 22, also just graduated from Sarah Lawrence (major: printmaking), and was on her way to Susan's home in Ardmore, Pennsylvania, for the weekend. The service manager pointed out that while a shock replacement is ordinarily the work of inside an hour, they were temporarily out-of-stock, or rather, not-yet-in-stock, of that particular part. When Diana and Susan looked dismayed and each groaned, the service manager said that he could send a boy some other place to locate one, if they wanted to wait, and they said please do.

It was already well into the afternoon, and Diana and Susan, sitting and waiting in the dealer's showroom, wondered how far it was to the other place, and how long it would take the boy to get there and back with the part, and what means of travel he was using. They smoked cigarettes and had soft drinks from the dealer's dispenser. Susan had a candy bar, as well, and thumbed through several back issues of *Road and Track*, indifferently. From the table Diana picked up a copy of the local newspaper and read the funnies and "Dear Abby," reading aloud an item from the latter for Susan's amusement, but the circumstances being what they were, Susan was not amused. She had arranged dates for the evening, with two particularly promising men recently graduated from Princeton, and home seemed a long way off.

"Why don't you phone," Diana suggested, "and tell them we might just be late? Your folks, I mean."

"*They*," said Susan, a bit archly, "don't even know we're coming. But maybe I should try to reach Larry. At least to find out what he has in mind. What if he has tickets for a play in Philadelphia or something?"

"What if?" said Diana, who was beginning to resent Susan's

tacit grudge. It wasn't *her* fault the pothole was waiting there in the road.

"Okay," said Susan. "I will." She went into the dealer's office to borrow a phone.

Diana resumed looking at the local newspaper, a thin daily with a neighborhood slant and too much regional coverage of golden wedding anniversaries, Elks' meetings, church socials, and recent college and high school graduates. She read what little national news there was; then, because there was absolutely nothing else to do, she began reading the local news. Good grief, *New Jersey*! of all places to be stuck in.

She found herself doggedly reading a "local interest" article entitled, "E. Passaic Man Reveals Age Regression Experiments." Suddenly her apathy took flight of her.

If she had not been on the right place of the Garden State Parkway that particular afternoon, if the pothole had likewise not been there, if her Porsche 911E had not hurt its shock, if she had not been required to locate this dealer, if the dealer had not been out of stock, if she had not had to wait, if she had not picked up this newspaper, if she had not begun reading it practically column by column, then she would never, never have

Two

Some New Jersey Newspaperwoman Has Written an Article of Interest

By Patricia Klumpe, Roving Reporter. Are you skeptical of age regression? Do you know what age regression is? I've just had the unsettling

experience of spending an afternoon with etaoin shrdlu 2 col. p. 8
ETAOIN SHRDLU ington Road, East Passaic.

Mr. Sedgely, a teacher of English at East Passaic High School, has spent his off moments during the past three years delving into the mysteries of this phenomenon, with uncanny results.

Sedgely has met with some controversy at East Passaic High School, where he recruits "subjects" from among his students. A few parents have complained about the propriety of his experiments, but John B. Pitts, principal of the school, feels that "it's all a lot of harmless foofaraw."

Several of Sedgely's students have been age-regressed by him, under hypnosis, not only back to early childhood, but also, supposedly, to their previous incarnations! One eighteen-year-old East Passaic senior, for example, told under hypnosis of being born in 1880 in Connecticut as one "Daniel Lyam Montross," who later traveled to the south and west and met a violent end in the 1950s.

Although Sedgely has been unable to verify any of the facts about his subjects' previous "existences," he feels confident that with enough time and research, it might be possible to trace the "life" of such persons as "Montross."

In another case, that of a seventeen-year-old girl who under hypnosis claims to be the wife of Thomas Jefferson, it has been possible for Sedgely to check the facts and ascertain that the girl, who knows little about Jefferson, much less his wife, has a truly remarkable knowledge about them while under hypnosis.

"Make no mistake," Sedgely declares, "we are on to something."

Three

Diana Stoving Changes Her Mind

"You look like you've seen a ghost," said Susan, returning from her telephone call. Funny that she should have phrased it that way, for it *was* a ghost Diana had seen. "What're you reading?" Susan asked.

Diana folded the paper and put it down. "Nothing," she said. "Just some story about an accident."

"Well," said Susan. "Is my face red. I talked to Larry, and told him we're stranded in this awful Jersey town, and guess what, he and his friend were going to take us to dinner at Three Wells and then to, you haven't seen it, have you, the new Truffaut movie. So bye-bye lovely evening." Susan stamped her foot and added, Oh shit.

"Why don't you take a bus?" Diana suggested.

"Ha! Why didn't we take a bus in the first place, instead of risking our necks in that…that be*yooty-full* new—"

"I drove over that hole on purpose, you see," Diana said, "so I could get out of sitting through a Truffaut movie with a blind date from Princeton who will go into the army as a second lieutenant and spend the next year writing me tragic letters from Vietnam and—"

"Oh, you're a scream, Diana Stoving," Susan said, "and I think I will." She screamed a small scream.

"Seriously, Suke," Diana said, "why don't you take a bus? There's still time."

"You keep saying why don't *I* take a bus. Not *we* but I. What about you?"

"I'll stay with my poor maimed car," Diana declared.

"All night probably," Susan said.

"All night then."

"You don't really want to go with me. You never did." Susan's right eye filled up and a teardrop hung precariously on the edge of the lower lid. "School's all out, all over, and there won't be any more. Any more." The drop teetered off the edge and rolled an inch down her cheek. "And there's nothing to do but have a good time, and I thought you would, if you went with me. So that's why I asked you. And that's why I asked Larry to ask his friend. So now what?"

"I'm sorry," Diana said. "I guess I shouldn't have said I would, to begin with."

"So now what? What are you going to do? You can't go back to Bronxville. They gave us our parchments and kicked us out forever."

"Maybe I'll go home too," Diana said.

"To *Arkansas*?" Susan said. "After all the times you've bad-mouthed that place to me?"

"Well, maybe then I'll go into New York and try out with Merce Cunningham, after all."

"You're a mixed-up kid, you are," Susan said. Diana made no reply to that, and after pacing the floor for a moment Susan said to the floor, "But what about *me*?"

"Take a bus," Diana suggested.

Four
An Interesting Hypnotist Is Visited

Susan Trombley took a bus home to Ardmore, Pennsylvania, arriving in time to shower and change and call a girlfriend to substitute for Diana as a date for Larry's friend. When I located her the following spring, nine months later, working as a typist in a Philadelphia law firm, she told me, "Well, if you mean was I the last of her friends to see her after graduation, I guess maybe I was. She took my luggage out of her car and even rode with me in a taxi to this bus station, in Clifton, I think it was, and told the taxi to wait, so she could ride back to that Porsche dealer and wait for her car to be repaired. She told me she might go home, meaning Little Rock, or she might go into New York to audition with a dance group. But I just *know* she didn't really want to do either one. Poor Diana. Maybe she *did* go into New York and maybe she got mixed up with some hippies and got murdered, for all I know. She was always an odd one. We were roommates the last year at Sarah Lawrence, and she was always doing funny little things, like—"

Like asking the Porsche dealer how to get to East Passaic. He, not the dealer actually, but the service manager, who had been kind enough to stay overtime and replace the shock absorber himself, finishing the job at half past six and declining her offer of a handsome tip, replied to her question by asking out of curiosity if she knew anybody in East Passaic. "Not yet," she said. But he got a map from the front office and traced the route for her. It wasn't far. A mile to Passaic, another mile to East Passaic. There she stopped at a telephone booth and consulted the directory, under S, for Sedgely. There was only one, a P.D. Sedgely, at 1244 Wallington Road. She thought of phoning, but decided to go there instead, and stopped at a Mobil station to ask directions.

It was a suburban community, of middle and lower-middle income families, identical to hundreds that speckle the flats amidst industries in that area. The Sedgely bungalow, save for its individual shade of gray paint, was the quintuplet of four other development houses on the block. Price Delmer Sedgely, "Del" to his few acquaintances on the faculty of East Passaic High School, lives there alone, as Diana discovered.

Ringing his doorbell, she was more than uneasy; she was queasy, and nearly frightened. She did not know what to expect, and thus prepared herself for the worst: a goateed Mephistopheles in a black cape, with a wand, who, like Mandrake, the only other hypnotist she had ever heard of or read about (in the funnies, long nearly forgotten, of her childhood), might put her into a helpless trance merely by gesturing.

She was surprised, then, to see that P.D. Sedgely looked like a high school English teacher, which he is. He is the epitome of the career high school English teacher: middle-aged, graying, dandruffed, bespectacled (steel rims), thin, a bit stooped. And it was he, not she, who was really nervous. He did not open the door fully but only a foot or so. One of his hands held the door ready to slam shut while the other hand tremblingly brushed supper crumbs from his mouth as he asked, "What do you want?"

"I'm sorry to disturb you," she said, for she could plainly see that he was disturbed. "I would like very much to talk with you."

"What about?" he asked, sizing her up. "Are you a reporter?"

Diana had not given any thought to what she would *be*, to him, beyond determining that she should not tell the man who she really was or what her interest in the matter was. Now his question provided her with a mask, although in her driving clothes—polo shirt and blue jeans—she knew she did not much look like a reporter. "Yes," she said.

"There's been too much publicity already," Mr. Sedgely declared. "I don't want any more." He started to close the door.

"Please," she said quickly. "I'm not going to print anything about *you*. I'd only like to ask a few questions about your patient, I mean, your *subject*, the one who is, uh, connected…with Daniel Lyam Montross."

The man hesitated. Then he said, "Well, come on in," and held the door open for her. She followed him into his living room, which was furnished in nondescript New Jersey taste. There were few books—mostly textbooks—in his bookcase. There was nothing in the room to indicate that he was a hypnotist. "Sit down," he offered, and she sat in an overstuffed modern armchair not of recent manufacture. "I was just finishing my supper," he said.

"Please don't let me keep you," she said, and realized that she had not eaten yet herself.

"That's all right," he said. "I'm ready for my coffee. Would you like a cup?"

The June evening was too warm, for her, for coffee. She shook her head, but then she said, "If I could have it iced."

"Iced?" he said, pausing in mid-turn.

"Yes. Like iced tea."

"Oh." Clearly he had never tried it himself. "All right. How much cream? How much sugar?"

"None, thank you."

While he was out of the room she turned her head and read the titles on the spines of the few books in his bookcase. There was nothing about hypnotism, nothing about age regression, not even *The Search for Bridey Murphy*. There was only one book which might be about reincarnation: *Many Lifetimes*, by Kelsey and Grant. She got up and removed it from the case and began flipping through it, but then she considered that her host might think it rude of her to pry uninvited into his library, so she put it back and returned to her chair just as he reentered the room.

He gave her the iced coffee—not in an iced tea glass, as she had expected, but merely in a coffee cup with two or three ice cubes thrown in. It was still warm, and the ice was quickly melting. He sat down with his coffee on the sofa across from her, and took a sip, and sighed, and said, "You wouldn't believe all the trouble I've had today, on account of that piece in the paper. I guess you saw the piece."

"Yes," she acknowledged.

"Parents calling me up," he said. "And kids. But that isn't as bad as the nuts and crackpots, and people wanting me to find out for them who they were. One fellow offered me a hundred dollars to mesmerize him—that's the word he used, *mesmerize*—and find out who he was in his previous incarnation."

"You didn't accept?" she asked.

"Of course not," he said. "I refuse to commercialize, to allow any taint of money to…. Besides, the man was probably hoping to find that he'd been Napoleon Bonaparte or Jesus Christ himself, and he would have been disappointed to discover that perhaps he was just some lowly peon or stableboy or something."

Diana decided that Mr. Sedgely, because of his sincerity, his manner, even the look in his eyes, was not himself a nut or crackpot. So she asked him, bluntly, "Do you honestly believe in reincarnation?"

"No," he said. "Not quite yet, at least. There is too little proof, at this stage, for me to accept reincarnation without question. I like to think of myself as a scientist, young lady. Scientists are, *must be*, constantly skeptical. And of all phenomena susceptible to proof, reincarnation must be the most difficult to prove. But I'm trying. *We're* trying. I'm not alone in this thing, you know. What most people don't realize is that there are quite a number of scientists, all over the globe, who are actively engaged in this quest."

Diana, satisfied, at least, that she was not dealing with an absolute absurdity, said, "I wonder if I might be able to meet the boy who…who apparently is…the reincarnation of Daniel Lyam Montross."

"Sure," the man said. "That's Day Whittacker, he lives not far from here. I could call and ask him to come over."

"If it's all the same," she said, "I wonder if you could simply tell me where he lives, and let me go and talk with him." The man looked at her strangely, and she added, with a smile, "Just to be scientific. So that he isn't under your influence when I'm talking with him."

Mr. Sedgely laughed. "I see. Well, yes, but I'm afraid he couldn't tell you much about his previous life unless he's under hypnosis."

"You mean he doesn't know he was Montross when he's awake?"

"'Awake' isn't actually the word, because, you see, the hypnotic state isn't sleep in the conventional sense. Actually, in fact, it's a heightened form of consciousness, even beyond 'wakefulness.'"

"Still," she said, "I would like to meet him, alone. I mean, maybe later I would like to see him hypnotized." At this stage in her adventure, Diana only wanted to *look* at the person, she was only curious to see what he looked like. "May I have his address?"

"All right," Mr. Sedgely agreed. "Are you on foot? No? Well, I'll tell you how to drive there."

Five
Day Whittacker Is Met

Day Whittacker was not at home. His mother said that he had gone to a Boy Scout meeting, but would soon return, and invited Diana to come in and wait, but Diana said she would come back later. Then she drove into Passaic in search of dinner. She would have preferred a good restaurant but was not dressed for it and did not want to get her luggage out and change in her car or in a service station rest room, so she stopped at a roadside diner and ate with truckers, who ogled her and made remarks among themselves. Her meal was veal cutlet, not poorly cooked, and she had a beer with it, and rather enjoyed the informal atmosphere of the place, and the experience of eating alone, both in sharp contrast to the dining hall of Sarah Lawrence. She began to feel actually adventurous, instead of bored, for the first time in a good long while. What will he look like? she wondered, and tried to visualize a typical New Jersey high school senior. What will I say to him? or ask of him? She was not exactly on pins and needles, but the idea of meeting somebody who was the reincarnation of somebody else disquieted her who was so quiet. She was not unmindful of what a silly situation it was, of how ludicrous, how fantastically *chimerical* it was, but she did not at all regret giving up the trip to Ardmore with Susan, which would have been merely a duplication of many ways she had wasted her time. While she ate her dessert, a lemon meringue pie not poorly cooked, she thought about some of the questions she might ask the boy. *I will really have to grill him*, she determined.

But as it turned out, she herself was submitted to a grilling. When she returned to the Whittacker home, which was another ranch-style bungalow of the same anonymous kind as Mr. Sedgely's, she discovered that the son had still not returned from his Boy Scout meeting, and was once again invited to come in and wait for him. Mrs. Whittacker was a flighty woman in her late thirties, who offered

Diana coffee and then, when that was refused (because Diana decided against asking to have it iced), offered a "highball." For Diana, it was an old-fashioned term and she could not remember exactly what a highball was, nor what it contained. She said a glass of water would do her fine, and Mrs. Whittacker brought it to her, along with a glass of what appeared to be iced coffee for herself, and they sat in the living room. "What kind of car is that you're driving?" Mrs. Whittacker asked, and when Diana told her, she said, "I've never heard of that kind before. Are you from New York?" Diana said she was not from New York City. "But you have New York plates on your car?" Mrs. Whittacker said. Diana explained that that was because she had purchased her car in New York. "Are you in school?" Mrs. Whittacker asked, and Diana said no, she recently graduated. "Where from?" Mrs. Whittacker asked, and Diana told her Sarah Lawrence. "Isn't that one of those ritzy high-tone places?" the woman wanted to know, and Diana agreed that it had a reputation for being rather high-toned. "You must be pretty well off, and with a car like that?" the woman had a habit of making questions out of declarative statements, so Diana felt some response was required, and modestly nodded her head. "What does your father do?" the woman asked, and Diana said he was in insurance. "My husband," Mrs. Whittacker said, "is in chemistry?" again making a question of a declaration and thus requiring some response from Diana, who asked if he were a chemist and was told no, he was a "sales engineer" for a chemical firm in Passaic. "How old are you?" Mrs. Whittacker asked and Diana told her twenty-one and fought down the impulse to ask her how old *she* was. "You're a very, *very* pretty girl?" Mrs. Whittacker said, and Diana didn't know how to answer that question except to say thank you. "Is your hair natural?" the woman asked, and Diana confessed that although she was a natural blonde she did resort to a rinse occasionally to lighten it a bit. "How long have you known Day?" Mrs. Whittacker asked, and Diana said "What?" and then said oh, she didn't know him at all and was just going to meet him for the first time. "What was it you wished to see him about?" Mrs. Whittacker asked in a suspicious tone. Diana wondered if she would jeopardize her chances if she admitted that it concerned the boy's relations with Mr. Sedgely.

Perhaps the woman did not like Mr. Sedgely, or did not approve of her son being used as a subject in age regression experiments. But Diana, thinking quickly, could not conceive a ready pretext. What did she know about the boy other than that he was a high school senior? Perhaps that was sufficient. So she told Mrs. Whittacker that she was a researcher from *Life* magazine and they were doing an article on a cross section of this year's crop of high school graduates, and that Day Whittacker's name had been chosen at random. Mrs. Whittacker, swallowing it, brightened. "Do you want to run some pictures of him when he was a baby? We have lots." Diana said that wasn't exactly the idea. Mrs. Whittacker protested, "But *Life* always runs everybody's baby pictures? You don't want to see his baby pictures?" Diana decided that she didn't mind; in fact, she was curious to see what he looked like even as a baby, so the woman hauled out the family album and put it in Diana's lap. She explained, "He's an only child, that's why we have so many of him?" and Diana nodded and glanced through the pages of his baby pictures. He looked like a baby. That was all. As much like Winston Churchill as like Daniel Lyam Montross, and she had never seen any baby pictures of the latter. But the pictures progressed from babyhood through childhood; the baby crawled, then teetered, then walked, and stood squinting in the bright sun with the photographer's shadow thrown across his tummy. A thin lad, towheaded, still too unformed to resemble anybody in particular. Diana flipped quickly through the album, and the boy grew up, and up and up. *He's tall*, Diana remarked and Mrs. Whittacker said, "Oh, yes, he's past six feet now?" Diana tapped one of the pictures with her fingernail and asked if it were a fairly typical recent picture, that is, did he look like that? and Mrs. Whittacker said, "Well, he looks a lot better than that, but yes, it's a recent picture, just last Christmas?" Diana studied it.

Diana looked at her wristwatch and said, "I'm sorry, but I can't stay much longer...."

Mrs. Whittacker patted her shoulder and said, "Now you just sit right there and I'll have him here in a minute?" and she quickly left the room. Diana heard her telephoning, in the hallway. "You said you'd be home by nine! What in heck are you doing? Huh, well tell him to finish his own bandage, and get yourself right home! There's a lady here from *Life* magazine wants to see you! You hear me! I'm not kidding you! *Life* magazine! You get yourself right home!" She hung up and returned to the living room, saying to Diana, "Don't you worry, he'll come through that doorway in two shakes of a dead lamb's tail?" Diana thanked her. While they waited, the woman recited a number of boastings about her son, his grades in school, his character, the fact that he was an Eagle Scout with forty thousand merit badges and all kinds of decorations, was also in the choir at church, and was going to be one of the head counselors at Scout camp this summer.

Mrs. Whittacker cocked her ear, hearing footsteps on the front walk, and stood up, saying, "And here he is! In person!" She made a dramatic sweeping gesture with her arm at the doorway, as the door opened and Day Whittacker came into the room.

Diana stood up also, to meet him.

He was not dressed in a Scout uniform, but simply in a white teeshirt, faded blue jeans, and loafers without socks. Although tall, he was very thin, and his clothes hung from him as if draped on a wire frame. His hair was not long, except a lock in front which seemed to be trying to hide what was actually a handsome face. He looked at his mother uncertainly, then briefly at Diana and then down at his shoes; he twisted his ankles sideways, standing on the sides of his feet so that his loafers came partly off.

"Day," the woman said, "this is Miss—." She turned to Diana and said, "I didn't even get your name?"

"Diana Stoving," she said and extended her hand to Day.

He gave her hand one quick and limp pump, withdrawing his hand and sticking it into his pocket. "I'm pleased to meet you," he said to the rug.

"Sit down, sit down," Mrs. Whittacker said to both of them, and pushed them toward separate chairs, where they sat. Then she herself sat down between them and said to Diana, "Now you just ask him anything you want to?"

Diana wondered how to get rid of the mother politely. She searched in her purse for a pencil or pen and a scrap of paper, to pretend that she was taking notes during the interview. She found an old ballpoint which she knew was dry of ink, but no paper except for an envelope, which however she took out and held in one palm beneath the useless ballpoint. "Now," she said, and decided she would ask a few simple questions and then get out of there, "what we're interested in, at *Life*, is the opinion of American high school graduates on a few topics, such as Vietnam. What is your own position, Mr. Whittacker, on the war?"

"He hasn't had his physical yet," Mrs. Whittacker said, "but I can tell you he will be proud to serve, like anybody else."

Diana gave the woman an annoyed look, with a polite question, "Would you mind?"

"Mind what?" Mrs. Whittacker asked.

"I would very much like to get *his* answers."

"Oh. Okay. Don't mind me. You tell her, Day. Open your mouth so she can hear you say something."

"I haven't had my physical yet, as she says," the young man said to Diana. The volume of his voice was so low that Diana had to lean closer. "If I pass it, and get inducted, I'll probably immolate myself."

Mrs. Whittacker nudged Diana and said, "Told you he was smart, didn't I? Uses all those big words!"

Diana caught the trace of a smile on the son's face and gave him a trace from her own. "Your immolation, Mr. Whittacker," she asked, "will it take the form of the usual pyrotechnics, that is, incineration?"

"Pyrotechnic in the figurative sense of a spectacular display," he said, "but not of combustion."

"My, my," said Mrs. Whittacker. "He'll be an officer, I'll bet?"

"What is your opinion of student unrest on the college campuses?" she asked, in further parody of an interview.

"I haven't given it much thought," he said, "because I'm not going to college."

"He is too!" Mrs. Whittacker said. "Don't you print that. He is too going, but he just hasn't made up his mind which college. His father and I intend to see to it that he goes. Day, you watch what you tell her! Hear me? This is going to be in *Life* magazine, and you think I want my friends to know you're a drop-out or something?"

Diana was thoroughly annoyed by the woman's presence, and wanted to get away from here as soon as she could. But she was attracted to the son and still wanted to talk with him in some other place, without the mother present. She had an inspiration: "I wonder," she said to him, "if I might have a look at your environment—the high school and the places where the students congregate, and that sort of thing. I have a car."

"It's too dark to see anything," Mrs. Whittacker said, "but we can show you all the local spots in pictures in Day's yearbook from the high school. Day, where did you put that yearbook?"

Diana sighed. She despaired of further ruses; she did not see how it might be possible to get him away from his mother. She even considered blurting out her true reason for being here, but decided against it.

She squandered another fifteen minutes of her time looking at pictures in the high school yearbook, asking a few polite questions and making a few polite remarks, and stifling several yawns. Then she told them that she had been happy to meet them, and told Day Whittacker that she would write to him if she needed to know anything else.

She stood up to go.

"You're not going to take any pictures?" Mrs. Whittacker asked.

"Our photographer does that," she said. "He might come later." She shook hands with both of them, and said, "Thank you very much, and good night."

She left their house and walked to her car. She turned and gave their house a long look, then got into her car and started the engine. She pushed the stick into gear.

Day Whittacker leapt from the steps of his house and ran to her car and around it to her open window and leaned his arms on the roof of the car and looked in at her. "My mother's a pill," he said. "I'm sorry. If you want me to, I'll be glad to show you the high school and some other places, even if they're in the dark."

"That's all right," she said, and then she said, "I don't care about the high school. I'm not really from *Life* magazine. I just wanted to talk with you."

"Oh?" he said, and removed his arms from the top of her car. "What about?"

"Do you know me?" she asked.

"Should I?" he asked.

"I don't know," she said. "Do I look at all familiar to you?"

He scrutinized her carefully. "You remind me of this movie starlet, I can't remember her name." He looked at her car, the redness of it, the sweep of its lines. "You aren't her?" he said. "I mean, you aren't a movie star?"

"No," she said. And then she told him. "I'm the granddaughter of Daniel Lyam Montross."

Six

Diana Stoving Receives
an Opportunity to Query the Subject

"I can't remember what she said her name was?" Mrs. Whittacker told me in the spring of the following year, "but that sounds like it, Diana Stoving? Anyway, she said she was from *Life* magazine, so maybe she's not the party you had in mind? But, yes, she was here just a day or two before poor Day disappeared, so maybe there's some connection? He ran out of the house after she left, and he didn't get back in until sometime after midnight, but when I asked him where he'd been he said he had to go back to the Scout meeting? I believed him at the time? I didn't think to make any connection with her being here? I didn't see her again? When Day disappeared, I thought it was just another case of a crazy kid running off from home? I told his father, I said to him, 'You just wait, and Day will come back when the Scout camp is over'? But maybe if you ever find her, she can tell you what became of him? I don't think, I certainly don't think he would have harmed her? He was a gentle boy, such a kind and decent boy…?"

It was nearly eleven o'clock when Diana knocked at Mr. Sedgely's door, not using the doorbell because it might startle him more if he were asleep, as seemed likely because the lights were all off except for one which might be in the bathroom. While she waited to see if there was any response to the knock, she turned to Day and said, "I would rather you didn't tell him. Let's just pretend that I'm a historian or something, with some knowledge about Montross, and if he can arrange it so that I can ask you questions while you're under. Just to check a few things, you see." She waited, and knocked again. "I feel foolish," she admitted. "Maybe we ought to come back tomorrow."

Lights went on within the living room, and the front door opened to reveal Mr. Sedgely in his bathrobe. "Hullo," he said, rubbing his eyes beneath his spectacles; Diana realized how much Day resembled him, as if they were father and son. "Hullo, Day," he said. "And Miss Stoving. Don't tell me, let me guess why you've come." He ushered them in, and closed the door.

Putting Day "under," as Diana discovered, was quick, nearly effortless, little more than switching an imaginary switch. Mr. Sedgely corrected her: "Not under," he said in a whisper. "Over. Above. Beyond." Then he said, "Don't be deceived by the quickness of it. In the beginning, it takes ten or fifteen minutes to put the subject into a deep trance. But Day is an old hand at this."

Day was sprawled limply and comfortably in the overstuffed armchair, his eyes closed, with Diana and Mr. Sedgely both sitting near him to one side.

Mr. Sedgely addressed Day, in a slow, even, somnolent voice: "You are going to go back, 'way back, back beyond your birth. On the count of three, you will be back fifty years. One…going back… two…'way back…*three.*"

Diana perceived no visible change in the boy's expression.

"Now," Mr. Sedgely said to him, "there will be another voice here, you will hear a voice other than my own, this other voice will ask you questions, and you will answer these questions." He turned to Diana and whispered, "All right. Go ahead."

Diana had her first question ready, but her voice broke as she began to ask it. She cleared her throat gently and tried again:

Where were you born?

There was no immediate answer. The gaps which Diana was to perceive between her questions and his answers led her to suspect that he was taking time to fabricate a reply. A few seconds passed, then his voice, which seemed not unlike his own voice, said

Dudleytown, Connecticut.

In what year?

————**I don't remember. Seventy-nine, eighty. Eighteen hundred and eighty.**

How long did you live in Dudleytown?

————**Until I was fifteen.**

Why did you leave?

————**Wanted to. I. I reckon. No opportunity there. And fought. Jared Story and Ferrenzo Allyn. Renz like to kilt me.**

In what year did you go to Arkansas?

————

Although she waited a minute or longer, and repeated her question, there was no answer. Mr. Sedgely leaned over and whispered to her, "Perhaps he's not there yet. I sent him back to around 1920. If it were later than that, he wouldn't know. I'll move him." He said to Day, "You are going up through time, thirty years, it will be thirty years later." To Diana he said, "Now ask him again."

In what year did you go to Arkansas?

————**Eighteen or nineteen years ago....**

What year was that?

————**Thirty-one, I reckon.** His voice seemed to have changed.

Where are you now? What is the name of the town?

————**Don't live in town.**

No? Then what is the name of the county?

————Isaac, it is.

Diana realized that she was beginning to breathe hard and audibly. She put her hand on her chest and took a deep breath, then asked her next question:

What is the name of the nearest town? Where do you do your shopping or trading?

————**I don't do any shopping or trading.**

But what is the name of the county seat? Do you know the name of the seat of Isaac County?

————**That would be Jessup.**

Diana gave Mr. Sedgely a stare and shook her head. She was shaking her head in incredulity that he should know this, but Mr. Sedgely thought she was denying the accuracy of the answers she was getting, and he spread his hands and shrugged. Diana fought to control her voice for the next question

What is your wife's name?

————**Haven't got one.**

What? You don't have a wife?

No.

Diana looked at Mr. Sedgely again and he leaned toward her and whispered, "Maybe he isn't married yet. I'll move—"

"No," Diana said. "He has to have a wife. Unless…" She asked another question:

Were you ever married?

No.

But haven't you ever fathered any children?

She waited a full minute and then asked again:

Didn't you ever father a child?

————**Yes, once, maybe.**

How long ago was this?

————**Oh, twenty years or more, back in Carolina.**

Carolina?

Yes.

What was it, a boy or a girl?

————**It was a girl.**

Where is she now?

————I don't rightly know, sister, tell you the truth. She left me.

Diana leaned toward Mr. Sedgely and asked, "Could you move him up again?"

"How far?" Mr. Sedgely wanted to know.

"Well—" Diana said, trying to calculate.

"How about up to the day of his death?" Mr. Sedgely suggested. "That's customary."

"Well—" she was reluctant and nervous. "All right."

Mr. Sedgely said to Day, "Now it is later, you will go on, you are going on until your last day on earth. This is the last day you live on earth." To Diana he whispered, "Ask him what you like."

She asked:

Did you ever find your daughter?

Sure did. And hers too.

What is your daughter's name?

Annie.

Where is she?

Out there.

Out where?

Somewhere. I don't know. Just out there.

What is she doing?

Looking for me, I suppose.

Why is she looking for you?

Because I've got her little girl.

Diana closed her eyes and slowly inhaled. Exhaling, and opening her eyes, she asked:

Why do you have her?

I intend to bring her up right.

How old is she?

Reckon near about three or so.

Can she talk?

Some.

Diana was firing the questions rapidly now.

Is she there with you right now?

Yes.

Ask her what her name is.

She says it's "Dinah."

What is she doing?

Just sitting on a rock.

Is she frightened?

Not a bit. She's laughing.

What are you going to do with her?

Already told you. I'm going to bring her up right.

What do you mean by "right"?

To give her a self of her own. To teach her how to read nature. To show her how to feel, and how to keep her mind away when it's not wanted. To protect her from—Hark!

For the first time the boy's immobile face registered an emotion, an expression of intense concentration. His eyes remained closed, but suddenly his brow twisted, his mouth twisted, and a low moan came from him.

Ow!

he said, and clutched his shoulder with his hand.

Winged me!

"Stop it," Diana said to Mr. Sedgely. "That's enough! Wake him up!"

"I can't, just yet," Mr. Sedgely said, "but I'll do this:

"It's later now, you feel no pain, it's later, an hour later now, and you feel no pain."

Then Mr. Sedgely asked him:

Where are you?

Floating.

Can you see yourself? Mr. Sedgely asked him. Where is your body?

Flat out on the ground.

Does your body feel anything?

Nothing.

Are there people there?

Yes. Officers, deputies, state troopers.

What are they doing?

Just standing around, looking at my body.

Is the little girl still there?

No. They've taken her away.

What are you going to do now?

Hang around and watch them bury me.

Then what?

I don't know. Maybe I'd like to come again.

"Any more questions, Miss Stoving? Anything else you'd like to ask?"

"No. Not now."

"Very well." He turned to Day and said, "Then on the count of three, you will be back to the present time. One…two…three."

Day opened his eyes and smiled and said "Hi" at her and then he looked at Mr. Sedgely and asked, "What time is it?"

"Fifteen after twelve," Mr. Sedgely said.

"My gosh," Day said. "I've got to get home. I'll catch heck from my mother."

"I'll drive you," Diana offered.

Seven

A Conversation Is Had,
Which Diana Finds Interesting

"I saw them only once after that," Mr. Sedgely related, when I questioned him in March of the following year. "It was the next afternoon. They came together, and she asked me to teach her how to hypnotize. I told her, of course, that hypnosis was not easy to learn, and, since she seemed to be impatient, it was certainly nothing she could learn in one quick lesson. But—and I assure you I did this without any inkling of what ultimate use she may have made of it—I told her that if it was simply a matter of putting Day into a trance, I could condition him through posthypnotic suggestion to go into a trance any time she simply said, 'Go to sleep, Day.' I made sure that he himself agreed to that, and then I gave him the posthypnotic suggestion, and invited them to keep in touch, but that was the last I saw of them. I must confess, sir, that I was very curious, and hoped they would keep me informed of their further researches. Imagine my disappointment when I never saw either of them again. Blame me, if you wish, for having rediscovered Montross in the first place in the person of Day Whittacker, but I can hardly be blamed for whatever two impetuous young people take it upon themselves to do with their lives."

Diana, after spending the night restlessly in a Passaic motel, kept her rendezvous with Day Whittacker the next morning—away from his home, away from his mother, at a park overlooking the Passaic River. Before meeting him, however, she visited several service stations until she found a road map of Connecticut. But she couldn't locate Dudleytown on it. She then went to the Passaic Public Library and asked to consult some detailed atlases of Connecticut. Again she found no Dudleytown. She was unable, after her sleepless night, to accept without much skepticism the information she had learned from Day during his trance of the previous evening. Although he had revealed facts which only her grandfather could have known, she was far from being a gullible girl.

So when she met Day in the park later that morning, the first thing she said to him was, "There is no Dudleytown in Connecticut," and the second thing she said was, "When were you last in Arkansas?"

He responded to these in reverse order. "I've never been west of Washington, D.C....if you can call that west." Then he asked, "And what is this Dudleytown?"

"You don't know?" she said. "Don't you remember anything you said last night?"

"I never remember. I was 'unconscious' in a way, you know."

"Aren't you ever...*aware*, consciously I mean, of being Daniel Lyam Montross?"

"Oh, occasionally he talks to me."

"*Talks to you?*" she said. "How can he *talk* to you if he's supposed to *be* you?"

"Well, I don't know, I guess it's like, you know, somebody talking to himself, only with him it's more like he's my father or someone, giving me advice."

"What does he say?"

"It's…it's…well, a lot of the stuff he says seems like platitudes. 'Happy are they who've lost their expectation, for they shall not be disappointed,' and 'Wretched are they who want more than they have, for the one is never equal to the other.' Stuff like that. But sometimes he kind of lapses into this country dialect and says things like, 'A perkin's not for jerkin but for ferkin.' What does *that* mean?"

"Well—" Diana hesitated, and giggled.

Day blushed deeply and said, almost inaudibly, apologetically, "Uh, I thought I didn't know what that meant, but maybe…." He quickly substituted another example: "When I was at the senior prom, a few weeks ago, he seemed to be there with me, and he was disgusted, or maybe *I* was disgusted and thought it was him, but anyway, when I was looking at all the girls and trying to decide which one of them to ask for a dance—I can't dance, anyway—I heard him say, 'The topwaters are a-shoaling but n'er a hoss in sight.' I didn't know what that meant, either, but somehow I had the idea that *he* didn't consider any of those girls worth dancing with."

"Day," she asked, "do you honestly believe in all this? Do you really think you're…well, *possessed?*"

He opened his palms and pushed them up to the level of his shoulders as if he were raising a weight. "I don't know," he said. "But sometimes I'm awfully uncomfortable about it. I won't say scared, but close to it—no, not even that, because it's as if he were protecting me, you know? And let me tell you about something else: last fall I had this little hickey on my finger here"—he showed her the side of his right index finger—"a wart, I guess it was, and I had had it for several months and couldn't get rid of it, once I even cut it off but it came back. Well, one night last fall I was lying in bed at night, before going to sleep—at least I was certain that I hadn't fallen asleep yet, although it did seem sort of like a dream—but anyway I had my eyes open, and I saw...I know you'll think this sounds crazy, but I saw *him*, Daniel Lyam Montross, sort of lift himself up out of my body and sit on the edge of the bed. Then he spat on his fingertip, and rubbed it around and around on my wart, saying, 'What I see increase, What I rub decrease,' then he lay back into me and I went to sleep. The next morning the wart was gone. Not a trace of it, not even a scar. See?" He thrust the finger right under her nose and looked at her as if defying her to find any trace of a former excrescence. "And that's not all he did for me," Day said.

"But I wonder," Diana said. "If reincarnation, or possession, or whatever it is, is an actual fact, why did he choose *you?*"

Day laughed. "It *is* strange, isn't it? that I'm not like him much at all. From what I gather, Montross was a big, brawling sort of man, always in and out of trouble. We've discussed this in the group—Mr. Sedgely's group—and it might have something to do with karma. Do you know what *karma* is? No? Well, the Indians—the Indians of India, that is, the Hindus and Buddhists, who believe in reincarnation like it was a simple fact of life—they think that what you do in this life is going to determine the kind of life you'll have next time around. What it boils down to is that Montross is being punished, you might say"—Day laughed again, self-consciously—"for the wrongdoing of his life, by being forced to be me. He had no choice. He didn't choose me. He was...*sentenced* to be me, condemned to be me. I am his damnation!"

Diana laughed too. "It's so fantastic," she said. "To think that you might be my grandfather...."

"Did you know him well?" Day asked.

"Barely. I was only three years old when he was...when he died, and I have just a vague memory of him. My family never once mentioned him. He has always been a figure of mystery to me."

"So now you want to know the truth?" he asked.

"Yes. It's incredible, but some of the things you said last night...I don't see how you could have known them, unless...unless you were reading my mind. I would much sooner believe in telepathy than I would believe in reincarnation."

"Me too," he admitted. "But you don't think I would be deliberately hoaxing you…?"

"No, but…" she said. "Other things…for instance, there is no Dudleytown in Connecticut."

"What is Dudleytown supposed to be?"

"That is where you—or *he*—was born."

"How do you know it doesn't exist?" he asked.

"I checked several maps."

"Old maps or recent maps?" he said. "What if it once existed, and doesn't, any more?"

"That's possible, I suppose…."

"One of the things he said to me, once," Day declared, "was this: 'All my towns are fallen.' That's what he said, like a lament, like he wanted my sympathy. 'All my towns are fallen.'"

Eight

Two Impetuous Young People Take It upon Themselves to Do Something

Dudleytown does, in fact, exist, though fallen. It waited for them. Even though it has not appeared on any map for seventy years, and then appeared only under the last of its fragmentary cognomens, Owlsbury, it is still there.

Driving northeast out of New York on Interstate 95 the next morning, Sunday, the middle of June, Diana noticed that her passenger was chewing at a hangnail on one finger. "Nervous?" she asked him.

He stopped chewing at it and dropped his hand to his lap. "Not about that," he said. "I was just thinking: right about this time

I'm supposed to be standing in my robe in the choir of East Passaic Methodist Church." In an excellent tenor, he roared:

> *What a friend we have in Jesus!*
> *All our sins and griefs to bear...*

"I'll probably be excommunicated or something," he said. "If not that, my parents will do something punitive, like cutting off my allowance or forbidding me to go to Scout camp this summer." He began chewing his hangnail again. "I've never done anything like this before."

She saw that he was genuinely nervous. "Go to sleep, Day," she said. And he did, at once.

She left him like that until they had crossed the state line into Connecticut. After slowing down for a toll booth and tossing a quarter into the hopper, then resuming speed, she said, "You are going to go back, oh, eighty years, until you are a boy, back home in Dudleytown, Connecticut." She tested him: "Are you there?"

He nodded.

"Well then," she said. "Where is Dudleytown? What part of Connecticut is it in?"

He took a long moment before replying. **"The country part."** The voice was high, thin.

"Which section of the state?" she asked. "East, west, south ...?" Again she had to wait for his answer, which was, **"Par'me, teacher, please, I dunno."**

She sighed. "How old are you, anyway?" she asked.

"Nine, ma'rm," he said.

"Oh," she said. "Then you are going to become older, you are older now, you are...fifteen. You are fifteen years old now. What section of Connecticut is Dudleytown in?"

"The hill country, ma'rm," he replied. The voice was deeper, older. "That would be the western part, would it?" she asked.

"Yes, ma'rm."

"What is the nearest city?"

"Never been there, ma'rm."

"The nearest village, then?"

"That would be Cornwall Bridge, ma'rm."

"Good." She reached into the glove compartment and drew out her road map. Driving with one hand, she unfolded the map and consulted the index of towns, and found Cornwall Bridge, on U.S. Route 7, in the northwestern part of the state. "Which direction from Cornwall Bridge is Dudleytown?" she asked.

He thought a moment, then said, **"To the east, ma'rm."**

"How far?"

"Just a few furlongs up the sound end of Coltsfoot Mountain, ma'rm."

"All right, Day, you can wake up."

He did not wake.

"Wake up, Day!" she said loudly to him. Suddenly she realized that although Mr. Sedgely had given her such a simple formula for putting Day into a trance, he had not bothered to tell her how to get him *out* of a trance, nor had she thought to ask. She slapped herself on the brow. Thinking of rumors she had heard about the danger of a badly hypnotized person sleeping forever, she drove the car off onto the shoulder of the turnpike and stopped. She turned off the ignition. She stared at Day. "Wake up, Day, please," she said. Lightly she slapped his cheeks. He did not wake. She lifted one of his eyelids and looked at his eye. It stared unseeingly at her; when she released the eyelid it snapped back over the eyeball, covering it again. She shook his shoulder. "Wake up! Wake up!" she pled.

A cruiser pulled in behind her and a Connecticut state trooper got out and approached her. "Having trouble?" he asked.

She tried her best to sound calm. "No, we were just resting."

"No place for that," he said. "Stop only at the rest areas."

"All right," she said and started the ignition. "I'm sorry."

The officer was staring at Day. "Your friend all right?" he asked.

"Yes, he's just sleeping one off," she said, trying to sound cool. She drove away.

She decided that she had better stop at the first telephone and try to reach Mr. Sedgely and ask him how to waken Day. She didn't want to bother Mr. Sedgely again, though; and what if Mr. Sedgely told her she would have to bring Day back to his house and let him do it? She couldn't do that; if she turned around and went all the way back she would never get started again. "Oh, Day, damn you, wake up!" she said.

Then while she was puzzling over what might possibly be done, it occurred to her that she had not moved him back in time to the present before trying to wake him. She had left him stranded in 1895.

"Day—" she began but then she realized that that, too, was stupid: to be calling him Day. He was not Day. "Daniel," she said, "you are going to move through time all the way back to the present. I will count to three and then it will be the present again, and you will be Day again, and you will wake up. One," she said. Then she said, "Two." She took a deep breath and said, "Three."

His eyes popped open. "Stop," he said. "Turn around. I want to go back."

"Why? What's wrong?"

"I'm worried," he said. "Please. Let's go back."

"Maybe you're just unsettled," she said, "because I did a bad job of trying to bring you back from your trance. Maybe it was just a bad trip."

"I'm sorry I changed my mind, but—"

"Let's stop for lunch," she suggested.

She drove off the turnpike at the first FOOD sign and found a diner in Darien. But when they were seated inside, and she asked him what he wanted for lunch, he said he wasn't hungry.

"Oh, I'll bet you are, too," she said. "I'm going to have a cheeseburger. Don't you want one too? And a milkshake?"

Very quietly he announced, "I didn't bring any money."

"Silly!" she said. "This is on me."

"You have money?" he said.

"Of course."

He stared at her for a while with what seemed to be a kind of frown. She wondered if it seriously bothered him to be dependent on her. At length he made a wry smile and said, "In that case, and this being Sunday, I'll have the roast beef dinner."

"Sure," she said. "Anything you like."

But during the meal, he did not talk at all.

She waited until he was finished, hoping that such a heavy meal would soothe him, then she asked, gently, "What frightened you?"

"Not *me*, I guess," he replied. "*Him.*"

"I should think he wasn't the sort of person to scare easily."

Day seemed abstracted, as if listening, not to her. Then he said, "'There's not ever any going back,'" and "'All the bridges are burnt.'"

"Is that what he says?" she asked.

Day nodded.

"Then tell him—" she began, but did not finish. She felt ridiculous; she was not even certain that messages could be relayed in that fashion. "Let's go," she said. She paid the check and they went out and got into the Porsche. Before she started the motor, she said to him, "It's *your* body. He can't tell you what not to do. And you're just as excited and eager as I am, aren't you?" She waited, then asked again, "Aren't you?"

"Oh yes," he admitted.

Nine

Finding Dudleytown Proves to Be Difficult

United States Highway Number Seven at one time was the primary south–north route, all the way from Norwalk to Montreal. For this purpose it has been supplanted by New York's Interstate 87, and its gift shops and motels are not frequented, as they once were. For much of its length in northern Connecticut and southern Massachusetts, it follows the Housatonic River, now on the left bank, now on the right;

and it keeps to the trace of original dirt highway of the nineteenth century and before. It passes through some very pretty hill country, deeply wooded, above Candlewood Lake. Artists live around here; so do writers, and critics, and poets and dancers.

Above New Milford, drops splashed randomly on the Porsche's windshield, beaded, and raced off. Soon Diana had to switch on the wipers. It was the beginning of what was to be one of the heaviest rains of the year, nearly three inches before the day was done, but at that moment it looked to Diana like a passing local shower and she hoped they would soon be through and out of it.

Around three o'clock, that afternoon, in a driving downpour, they saw a road sign: "Cornwall, Town Of. Inc. 1740" and shortly thereafter came into the small crossroads community of Cornwall Bridge. There was not a soul in sight; the rain had driven man and beast to shelter.

There is one general store in Cornwall Bridge, Monroe's AG General Store with a Mobil gas pump, but Diana discovered it was closed on Sundays. She turned eastward from Cornwall Bridge, onto State Highway 4, and drove slowly for a while, looking for any sign pointing to Dudleytown. A mile out, she turned around and came slowly back. "See anything familiar?" she asked Day.

He shook his head. "I've never been here before."

She liked that. *He* had never been there before. She wondered if it would help to put him into a trance again, but, apart from her reluctance to chance something that had already given her a few bad moments, she knew that he couldn't see anything with his eyes closed anyway.

There is one service station in Cornwall Bridge, the Berkshire Garage, an Esso station, and she pulled into it, but discovered that it too was closed on Sundays. She stopped there anyway, turning off the motor and saying, "Well. Now what?"

He asked, "Don't you even know which direction it is?"

"You said east," she told him. "*He* said east." She pointed "That's east." Apart from the State Highway 4, which they had just tried, there was nothing to the east but a high forested hill.

He offered, "I could just go and knock on somebody's door and ask them."

"You'll get wet," she pointed out. "Let's wait a while."

They waited a while, more than a while, fifteen, then twenty minutes, half an hour, but the hard rain did not slacken. If anything it became harder, curtaining all the windows of the car so thickly they could not see out. Diana wanted to smoke a cigarette, but in the stuffy atmosphere of the closed car she did not want to bother Day, who, she had discovered, did not smoke. Then, more than needing a cigarette, she realized she needed to find a toilet. She wondered if the Berkshire Garage's restrooms were locked. She waited another ten minutes for the rain to let up. It did not. She waited until she could wait no longer, then said, "I'll be right back," and opened her door and made a dash around the side of the building, looking for a doorway marked "Ladies." She found none. She looked all around her, and ran behind the building and into a clump of bushes. The damp branches scratched her and wetted her. She crawled on her knees as deeply into the bushes as she could get, then squatted and tugged her jeans down to her ankles.

When she returned to the car, her hair and clothing were soaked, and the knees of her jeans were covered with mud.

Day looked at her for a moment, then he said, "If you can get wet, so can I." He got out of the car, and she wondered if he needed to go to the bushes too, but she watched as he ran swiftly across the highway to the nearest house and leapt onto the porch and began knocking at the door. Through the curtain of rain she could not clearly see what response he was getting.

When he returned, he was wetter than she. His shirt clung to him, his hair clung in matted bangs over his forehead, his ears and nose dripped raindrops. He said, "*They* never heard of it."

She sighed.

"Are you sure," he asked, "that this is the right place?"

"It was you," she protested. "You said Cornwall Bridge. This is Cornwall Bridge." Then she suggested, "Let's just drive around some more."

She started the car and drove slowly back down U.S. 7, watching the left of the road carefully for any side road. There was nothing but a few driveways. The village trickled out; she turned around and drove slowly back once again, and then again turned east toward State Highway 4, determined to follow it farther this time.

She had driven only a short distance when Day said, "Hey, look!" and pointed. She slowed the car. There, to the right of the highway, was a small asphalt road that did not seem to be a driveway. It had a signpost on it, an ordinary urban street sign, saying "Dark Entry Road." She turned into it.

But only a short distance up this road the asphalt pavement stopped, or rather it curved into the driveway and garage of a large new ranch-style house with an immaculately kept lawn. There was, however, a continuation of the road at the curve: it became suddenly a rough, rutted trail of dirt turned by the rain into mud. Beside it had been erected a small hand-lettered sign, apparently by the owners of the ranch-style: "No parking within 15 feet."

Diana eased the car into the crude trail, and kept going. All along the woods to the left were new signs nailed to trees, printed on yellow metal:

NO HUNTING
NO TRESPASSING
Under Penalty of the Law
—*R. Wendell*

The trail was steep, and the Porsche's rear wheels began spinning in the mud; Diana realized the car would go no farther. Slowly she backed down the trail, steering with one hand and craning her neck to see through the rear window. She backed all the way to the broad asphalt driveway of the ranch-style, and there turned around.

Day gestured at the house and said, "I'll go ask them if that goes to Dudleytown."

Diana observed, "If the Wendells live there, obviously they don't want anybody using their road anyway."

There was one other house farther on down the road, near the highway, an old colonial saltbox nicely restored. "I'll try that," Day said, and got out of the car and ran off through the rain. This time she saw that the door of the house was opened to him, and he went in, and did not reappear for many long minutes.

He was smiling triumphantly when he returned to the car. "This is it, all right," he declared. "I talked to a nice old lady. She even offered to have me dry my clothes. She says this is the original Dark Entry Road which goes on up the hill to Dudleytown. But listen, there's nothing up there." He paused to let this sink in, then he said, "That's what she says, there's nothing at all up there, and anyway you can't drive a car up there, and she says you can't even go on foot because a rain like this washes the trail out."

"Well, darn it," Diana commented in disappointment.

"But wait a minute," Day hastened to add. "She told me something else...."

Ten

At Length Dudleytown Is Located and Partially Explored

"I told him there was a better way to get into Dudleytown," Miss Mary Elizabeth Evans related to me, that bleary afternoon in March of the following year. She served tea. I showed her the two photographs. "Yes, that was him," she said, pointing at one of the photographs. "He told me he was a Boy Scout from New Jersey. But I didn't see *her*. Perhaps she was the other one in the car. He just told me that he and a friend had heard about Dudleytown and wanted to explore it. I said, 'Young man, what kind of exploring can you do in a rain like this?' but he said they weren't in any hurry for the rain to stop. Well, anyway, I told him the best way to get into Dudleytown was to go back down

Route 7, the way they'd come, for about a mile until they came to
Route 45 on the left, and take that for about another mile until they
came to the first road on the left. That's the real Dudleytown Road,
you see. I knew they wouldn't get very far along it, either, not in that
low-slung sports car they were driving, but at least the going on foot's
a lot easier from that side. More tea?"

I shook my head, and she went on, "Much later in the summer
I heard that somebody was camping out up there, but I never thought
to make any connection with them. I thought this Boy Scout just
wanted to spend a couple of hours poking around amongst the old
cellar holes, you know, and I thought a rain like that would probably drive them away. He seemed such a young man to be going into
Dudleytown, even with a companion, so I told him, not just out of
perversity but because I was concerned about him, he was a *nice*
young man, I told him Dudleytown is haunted. That's the truth, it
is. I said, 'Wait, young man, and let me tell you about the "Curse of
Dudleytown."' But he just said, 'Thank you, lady, but I'd rather find
it out for myself.' And he walked right out that door."

The turnoff into Dudleytown was easy to find, and neatly asphalted,
with a white center line at the intersection. Diana mashed the gas
pedal to the floor and started up it; they passed several houses, first an
old brown-shingled colonial, then a rustic brown-clapboard chalet of
the general Swiss-modern type, then an even more modern house of
gray shingles. People of means lived in these; *this* end of Dudleytown,
at least, was well inhabited.

The asphalt road continued climbing, becoming wider and
newer, all the way up to the top of the hill, where it ended in a broad
turnaround. Although no houses were visible from here, it had all the
earmarks of a housing development street. Beyond the turnaround,
Diana noticed, the old road continued, a crude trail through the
woods similar to the beginning of Dark Entry Road. She drove into
it, the car hit a hole and bounced, and the undercarriage scraped a
rock or something with a jarring rasp. She slowed to a crawl, and
continued. The road here was level but then it began to descend.

At least there were no "No Trespassing" signs here; no signs of any kind. As the descent became steeper, and the car's wheels began sliding, Diana braked to a halt and stretched her head forward to peer down into the declivity. She was not at all convinced the Porsche could manage such a road, and she told Day so; then she backed—or tried to back—out. After several minutes of spinning the rear wheels in the mud, she managed to back the car next to a level glade beside the left of the road, and to back the car into this glade, off the road, with a minimum of scrapes on the undercarriage. The rain had slackened some, but was still coming steadily down. They would walk from here; they were both so wet already, it didn't matter.

Diana got one of her suitcases from the rear of the car, and opened it, not to remove her raincoat—because she did not want to wear a raincoat if Day had none—but to get a pair of hiking shoes to replace her sandals. After lacing them up, she closed and locked the car, and they continued down the rugged trail on foot.

The woods on both sides of them made a tunnel over the trail and sheltered them from the full brunt of the rain. Diana tuned all her senses to take in the experience; the first sense was of smell: the rich woodsy fragrance of the forest, enhanced by the wetness of the rain.

The downslope of the trail was abrupt and, because of the mud, slippery. Several times Diana stumbled but Day caught her arm. He seemed to be watching out for her. Now, at least, she was dependent on him.

Except for a great stone wall bordering the road in the woods to their right, there was no sign at all of anything left by man. The forest was all second growth—but a second growth which had begun growing seventy years or more before. The hardwoods were large in girth, and dense hemlocks and spruces filled the spaces between the hardwoods.

The ground cover, the carpet of the forest, was what she liked most. She asked Day if he knew what it consisted of, and he readily named the names for it, rattling them off his tongue almost mechanically: seven different kinds of fern, moosewood or striped maple seedlings with big green leaves the size of a baby elephant's ear, and everywhere the low light-green diadems of the ground pine. She bent down and picked one of these and held it to her nose.

The stone wall was massive, a work of great effort and determination; large sections of it had been toppled by frosts and winds, animals and earth tremors—whatever there is that doesn't love a wall.

They came to a broad gap in the wall which obviously was not a toppled section but an opening that had once been a gate. They walked through it, and looked for signs of a house but found none, and so came back to the main road and continued down it.

The rain fell without any thunder or lightning; if it had been an electrical storm, Day, a good Scout, would not have wanted to be out.

Vapors hung like low clouds among the trees.

The forest was dark; Diana realized she was still wearing her sunglasses and pushed them up on top of her hair; still the forest was dark.

An old road diverged into the woods at the right, in an avenue between the massive stone walls. They did not take it.

On the trail ahead of them they caught a swift glimpse of a small animal scurrying across the road. Diana asked Day what it was but he said he hadn't seen all of it, just its tail. A fox, maybe.

At five o'clock they came to the first cellar hole.

Diana had never seen a cellar hole before, and did not know what it was. Day, pointing it out, told her. A large clump of white birch grew up out of it. They brushed their way through weeds and bushes to reach the edge of it, and stood on the edge looking down. In the dank hole Diana could see rubble: fallen stones, bits of rotted wood, pieces of thoroughly rusted iron, shards of old crockery. Diana wanted to ask him who had lived there. To get an answer, she would have to put him into a trance. It did not seem to be an important cellar hole. She would wait until they came to something else. They went on.

They passed the exact center of Dudleytown, some time later, without knowing it: the junction of Dudleytown Road with Dark Entry Road. They did not even notice, to their left, in the brush beside a giant maple, the dark exit of Dark Entry. They walked on past a turning of the trail before coming to another cellar hole. This one was larger than the first, but just as barren; a clump of gray-green poplars nearly filled it.

They hiked another quarter-mile without finding anything of significance, except another cellar hole. Diana did not know if they had reached Dudleytown yet; she did not know that they had passed it; but she was becoming a little tired of hiking. Her jeans were soaked and chafed her thighs. She felt like taking off her shirt and wringing it out.

There was no shelter. No roof remained in Dudleytown; no rock ledge to get under out of the rain. The nearest ceiling she knew of was that of her car—a mile? or more behind them. But then the rain ceased, for a while.

"You're trembling," Day told her. "I'll make a little fire, and we'll rest."

She laughed. "With what? What will you make a fire with?"

"Do you have a match?" he asked.

From the pocket of her jeans she drew out a limp book of matches, showed him how wet they were, laughed, and threw them away.

He picked them up and gave them back to her. "Don't litter," he said. Then he fished in his own pocket and brought out a jackknife. It was a regulation Boy Scout pocketknife, even with the official crest on it. "I always carry this," he said.

"I suppose it has a built-in Ronson lighter," she said.

"Wait here a minute," he said, and left her beside the cellar hole while he plunged off into the woods.

He was gone more than a minute, closer to ten minutes. When he came back out of the woods, he was holding something in each hand: in one hand what appeared to be some sticks, in the other hand a small mass of some fluffy-looking stuff and a rock.

"You're just going to rub a couple of sticks together, I suppose, and presto!" she said doubtfully. "Where did you find dry sticks?"

"They're not dry," he said. He squatted beside a large flat rock and began whittling the pieces of wood into a pile on the rock. "I found them on a burnt white pine," he explained. "It's got so much pitch it'll ignite in a downpour."

"Ignite with what?" she asked.

"Just you watch," he said. After making a small pile of the slivers of pine, he dumped the pile onto the small mass of fluff he had found. It seemed to be thoroughly dry.

"Where did you find anything so dry?" she asked.

"In a hollow log," he said, and added, "of course"—somewhat smugly, she thought.

He placed the rock ("flint, of course," he explained) besides the little pile of fluff and began striking it with glancing blows from the back of his pocketknife. Then he quickly knelt and began puffing at the pile. Soon she saw a tiny wisp of smoke curl upward from it, and, as he continued blowing, the shavings of pine suddenly ignited with a billow of thick black smoke. "Now," he said, getting up, "anything you put on that will burn, wet or not." He picked up several twigs and sticks from the ground and piled them on.

Within a few minutes, he had a crackling blaze going, and while she stood drying herself beside it he roamed the woods for more fuel.

After he returned, with an armload of sticks, she told him, "You are a perfect genius."

He held up three fingers in the Boy Scout sign and said, "My good deed for today." He put more wood on the fire, then rolled a small boulder close to the fire and patted it with his hand, saying, "Have a seat." She sat on the boulder, and felt the heat already drying the denim on her legs and knees. "Comfy, now?" he asked. She nodded vigorously and smiled. "Welcome to Dudleytown!" he said.

She laughed. "Where is it?" she asked.

He swept his arms in a wide arc. "All around, I guess."

"But how do you know this is the right place?" she asked. "Unless…does this seem at all familiar to you?"

"Very vaguely," he said. "Not the sight of it, but just the…the spirit of the place."

"Do you like it?" she wondered.

"It's not bad," he said. He squatted close to the fire and raised his arms, pinching the sides of his shirt to tug it away from his skin.

Soon it was no longer stuck to him. "It's very peaceful up here," he remarked. Then he asked, "Do you hear anything?"

She listened keenly, a bit alarmed at his question, but heard nothing, except the dripping of drops from trees, and a distant bird call. "No. Why?" she asked. "What do you hear?"

"I…it just sounded like…" he said, and seeing her tensed expression, "it's nothing. Do you know Beethoven's Sixth? The *Pastoral*? The part toward the end, after the storm, when the storm has passed…?"

"Yes?"

"It just sounds like that," he said.

"Oh," she said. She stood up. She raised both arms above her head. She lifted high one leg. He stared. Slowly she wound into a grapevine, then, bent, broke at the waist, double, hearing the oboe form a rainbow, then, to the rustic yodeling of the clarinets and horns, she began to move, spinning, drifting, caracoling around the old cellar hole and around the fire. He could light fires in rain. What could she do but dance? Her one talent, in exchange for his: that is what you can do, see what I can do. She interpreted the post-tempest allegretto of the *Pastoral*: she wove a country jig and hornpipe of well-being: *Hirtengesang, Frohe and dankbare Gefule nach dem Sturm.* A saltatory shepherdess.

He watched, entranced, but then he rose and slapped her, smartly, his palm clapping the side of her neck.

Abruptly she ceased her dance.

He showed her his palm, the tiny smear of her blood around the crushed wings. "You had a mosquito," he said.

She rubbed the spot it had bit. The magic of the moment was shot, her dance squashed like a bug. She smacked him on his ear, then showed him her hand, saying, "So did you," but the bug she killed on him, at least, had not yet gorged itself; she'd killed it clean. Did Beethoven's shepherds, gladsome and thankful after the storm, swat mosquitoes while they sang?

They laughed and walked on, a ways, waving their arms around their heads to keep the bugs away. The rain began again, to snuff their fire.

"You dance good," he said, offhand, ungrammatical.

"You make fires good," she returned.

They found a byroad, dropping off to their left and disappearing into the woods. They thought, mistakenly, that this was Dark Entry, and turned into it. It went down to a small swampy brook, one of the many narrow forks of Bonny Brook, its indigo water sloughing through bracken and wild blue iris. They stepped over it, the road ascended and they followed it up the hill to its end, in a glade.

Diana gasped. All around, all over this glade on the hillside, sprawling in rise after rise, were thousands of snowy white blossoms, large multi-floreted clumps stretching up from their dark green shrubs and raising their cups to the raindrops. Inhaling, Diana caught a smother of the sweet fragrance that pervaded the air. Exhaling, she sang a small "Oh!" in enchanted awe. She had never seen so many blossoms in one place, so white, so teeming, so sweet. She plunged among them, crying, "Look, look, oh *look*!"

"Mountain laurel," said Day matter-of-factly, and then, as if to belittle their magic, "state flower of Connecticut. Pennsylvania too."

"But so *many* of them…" she said. "Everywhere. All over. Didn't anybody plant them, once?"

"I doubt it," he said. "They grow wild."

Diana swung around, a pirouette through the mountain laurel shrubs. "Wouldn't this be a great place for a house?" she said. This rise of ground was open, a glade free of tall trees; uphill the forest of hemlocks became dark and deep again, but *here*, if the sun were shining, they would be in the light, and the dazzling white blossoms would be in the light too.

"Maybe there was a house," Day said. "The road came here." He began looking around for a cellar hole. She joined him, and they tramped back and forth all over the glade, but found no remains of any dwelling.

They wandered farther and farther away from the glade of the mountain laurel. Diana realized they had been strolling through the woods for some time, keeping to no road or trail or path, for there was none. She was surprised at how easy it was to drift at random through the woods, without obstacle or impediment—no briars or thorns to snatch at them, no quicksand to step into, not even very many fallen trees to climb under or over. But then she wondered why they were doing this, and asked him, "Where are we going?"

"I don't know," he replied with a shrug. "Where *are* we going?"

"We could get lost, this way," she said.

"I've never been lost," he said.

"Is that *you* speaking?" she asked. "Or grandpa?"

"Just me," he said.

What they needed to find, she decided, was a cemetery, the Dudleytown cemetery, wherever it was, and what she needed to find was a headstone or two engraved MONTROSS, his parents or relatives. But a cemetery out in the middle of a dark and haunted forest would have unsettled her, would, in fact, have terrified her. She didn't need a cemetery.

Nor did she need the next thing they found: a trail. A clearly marked trail winding around through the woods with the trees on either side of it blazed with small painted white triangles.

"Aha," said Day.

"Aha what?" she said. "What is this?"

"This," he said, pointing at one of the painted white triangles on a tree, "is the blaze mark of the Appalachian Trail."

"Oh, drat!" she said. The Appalachian Trail! The main thoroughfare for hikers, all the way from Maine to Georgia, running right through the middle of *their* Dudleytown! She looked both ways up and down the trail, expecting to see a safari of back-packing Alpine-clad hikers come trudging cheerily along.

"Well, let's follow it a little way," Day suggested. "Probably it rejoins one of the Dudleytown roads."

The Appalachian Trail *does* rejoin the Dark Entry Road at one point, but not in the direction they turned. Thus they walked on up the trail for a considerable distance without finding a road, while in the upper atmosphere high above their heads new winds blew new combinations of air and cloud into a mass that was statically charged. They did not see the first flash of lightning, beyond the hilltop, but they heard the distant rumble of thunder.

"Uh-oh!" Day said. "Now we're in for it." He began to trot.

"Wait for me!" she cried, trying to keep up with him.

The trail began to descend, and Diana hoped that by some wondrous luck it might suddenly come out onto the Dudleytown Road right beside the safety of her car. She did not know that they were running in the opposite direction.

The woods were for an instant illuminated by a nearer flash of lightning, and the following report of thunder sounded like cannon fire.

"Well, there's an old saying," panted Day over his shoulder at her, trying to sound flippant, "'If you heard the thunder, the lightning did not strike you. If you saw the lightning it missed you. If it did strike you, you would not have known it.'"

"You cheer me up enormously," she said.

As the trail mounted the crest of a small knoll, Day suddenly stopped and pointed. "Look!" he said.

A huge boulder, large as a grounded yacht, seemed to be perched upon a group of smaller boulders at one end of the knoll. Dark crevices showed on its underside: a tiny cave, a shelter. Day took her arm and ran toward it.

The niche, the snug den, was just large enough for the two of them to sit side by side, half-reclining. Diana did not feel completely secure, thinking of the tremendous weight of the boulder balanced overhead.

Day read her thoughts. "It would take more than lightning to crack this rock," he said and gave it an appreciative rap with his knuckles.

They were, then, safe. Except for having to swat at mosquitoes now and then, they were cozy. Evening was coming on, and Diana did not want to stay there after dark. But it was a nice temporary refuge from the storm.

Cloudburst, thunderclap, downpour, were so noisy as to make conversation difficult, had they not been placed, by the confines of the den, so close beside one another, mouth to ear. They talked.

Diana conjectured that such a large boulder, rare for the area, must have been there a long time. She knew little about geology, but as she told Day, she knew the boulder must have fallen off a bluff, yet there were no bluffs in sight. The point was, she said, that the boulder must have been there when Daniel Lyam Montross was young, and, if so, he would probably recognize it as a landmark.

She asked his permission to find out. A formality.

He readily consented, but reminded her that with his eyes closed he could not see the boulder, and asked her to open his eyes. It could be done, easily, he said. He told her of a time he had watched Mr. Sedgely open a girl's eyes so she could see an eighteenth-century chamberpot he had found and correctly identify it for what it was. A test.

"Well then," Diana said. "Go to sleep, Day."

He did, and she moved him back to the fifteenth year of her grandfather, and told him he was in Dudleytown, Connecticut, reclining beneath an enormous boulder in the woods. Then she told him to open his eyes and see the boulder above him.

Eleven

Under a Rock in the Rain, an Exchange Is Had with Young "Daniel"

Do you know where you are?
————Sure. Looks to be ole Landlocked Whale.
Is that what you call it?
What I call it. Some jist call it The Rock.
How far is your house from here?
As near as no matter.
How near is that?
Two whoops 'n a holler.
You're looking at me. Can you see me?

Naw, I'm blind a one eye, 'n caint see out th'other.
Really?
'Course I can see you, nimsky! Who are ye, anyhow?
You don't know me?
You aint Violate, less ye blanched yer hair.
Violate? Violate what?
T'aint what but who.
Violate who, then?
Violate Parmenter.
Is that a name?
Naw, it's a gull! Hoo.
Who is she?
Eph Parmenter's gull. Who are you?
I'm just...a friend.
Friend a whose?
Yours.
Do say? Are you a Thornback?
No. Who are they?
T'aint they but them. It's a what.
What's a thornback?
Maiden gull. Aint you past marrying age?
Well...maybe by your standards I am.
What in tunkit are ye doing here in the belly of the Land-locked Whale?
Waiting for the rain to stop. And I'm lost.
Lost from where?
Dudleytown.
Huh? It's not but right down the hill, yender. How'd ye get lost?
I just...went the wrong way...in the woods.
Do ye want I should show ye the way?
Please, thank you.
Soon's the rain quits. Which house ye going to?
Well...I guess the Montross house.
Huh? That's my house. What're ye going there fer?
I...I'd just like to meet your father.

Why? Are ye some kin a his?

Yes...distantly...on my mother's side.

My father's dead. Didn't ye know that?

No. I'm sorry. I'm sorry to hear that. When did he die?

Few months back. Fell in one a the charcoal pits. 'Least that's what people think. I shouldn't wonder but what he uz pushed.

Who do you think pushed him?

Ferrenzo Allyn, that skunk.

Why would he have pushed him?

Pure spite. Dad bested him, once.

Do you just live with your mother, then?

Yep. Just me and her.

No brothers or sisters?

They've all flew the roost.

Where'd they go?

Ohio. Illinois. Nick's all the way out to Montana, last we heerd a him.

Why did you stay here?

Huh? Somebody's got to look after Ma, don't they?

Is she not well?

Not so's she can manage on her own. She has spells frequent. Able to set up 'n eat a few porridges, though. Say, you wouldn't be looking fer a place, would ye?

A place?

A position. Hire on fer your keep. Only wondered, happen but what ye was, Ma'd be glad to take ye in, and...I could go off some'ers and look fer me a good job a work. But naw, I cal'late you're too pindling fer chopping wood and such, aint ye?

Do you want to leave home?

Who wouldn't, on half a chance? Dudleytown's all pegged out, dead to your navel. Weren't fer Ma 'n Violate, I'd a been back a beyond long since.

Is Violate your girlfriend?

Some has been known to say so.

Do you plan to marry her when you grow up?

Grow up? Dear me suz! Aint I growed enough yet fer ye?

Naw, prolly Eph Parmenter won't 'low it. 'Sides, Renz Allyn's done staked her out.

The same one who pushed your father...?

Yep, 'n Satan git'im.

Is he bigger than you?

Naw, but a good sight older.

The rain is slacking. Could we go now?

Yep, let's hyper out! Come on, it's not far, 'n Maw'd be proud to meet ye if you're some kin a Dad's. Jist a piece down the path, yender....

———

What's the matter?

That tree. Don't reckerlect it being there. And somebody's been pushing stuns off Jenner's stun wall. He won't like that.

———

Now what's wrong?

Right peculiar. I could swear this here's our gate, but look at all the weeds! I just mowed the durn thing last week.

———

Great keezer's ghost! Would ye take a gander at that! If I aint slipped a cog, the mountain laurel bushes has eaten up our house, be jiggers!

Are you sure that's where your house is?

Sure? Why, sure as God made little green apples! Them laurel bushes has swallered up the house! And where's Ma? Ma!

All right, Daniel, close your eyes. You are coming back, you are moving on back to the present, and on the count of three you will be back in the present time. One...two...

Twelve

An Awkward Situation Is Encountered, Also a Disappointing Revelation

"I thought we were under a big rock," Day said. "How did we get back *here*?"

"You led me back here," she said. "Or *he* did. He claims this is where his house was."

It was strange, more than strange, Diana thought, that he had led her back to the same glade of mountain laurel where previously she had exclaimed, Wouldn't this be a great place for a house? Could it be that in his subconscious (or even his conscious, if he were only feigning his trances) he knew that she liked it and would consider it an ideal site for a house? The skeptic in Diana was stirred. A beautiful and seemingly authentic conversation she had had with "Daniel," but she could not quite dismiss the possibility that it was only the product of Day's imaginative mind.

"It's getting awfully late," Day observed. "Shouldn't we...don't you think we ought to be getting out of here?"

"I just wonder where that cellar hole is," Diana said, looking around.

"Maybe all the houses didn't have cellars," he said.

"That's a fortuitous explanation," she said. "And gratuitous too."

"It's too dark to search any more now," he said. Then, as if in consolation, he added, "We could come back...."

"When?" she wanted to know.

"Well..." he scratched a mosquito bite on the back of his neck "...whenever you want to, I guess."

She turned her back to him for a last glance at the lovely mountain laurel. Without facing him, she asked, "Did you want to go back to New Jersey tonight?" She might have been alone, asking the question of the woods.

"Well…" he stumbled, clearly uncomfortable, "I…I didn't know what you had in mind. I guess so, yes. I thought we were just coming up here for the day, and now the day's almost over. I…"

She turned. "Let's go find something to eat, and then we can talk about it. I'm famished."

Full dark settled on the woods before they reached her car. Hiking back up the Dudleytown Road in the dark was difficult; she tripped on rocks and stepped in mudholes up to her ankles. From a tree overhead an owl hooted like a horn out of hell and momentarily petrified her. Day, too, jumped, but then he laughed and told her what it was.

The dark bulk of the car loomed in its glade like a welcome oasis. She was so glad to be back to it that after getting in she just sat for a moment relishing the comfort of the soft bucket seat and letting the cool evening air dry the sweat on her brow. She found a pack of cigarettes in the glove compartment and lighted one, and never had a cigarette tasted so good. If only she had a drink. She decided to find one as soon as possible. She started the car and drove quickly out of Dudleytown.

In the village of Cornwall Bridge, everything was dark and closed; the Bonny Brook Motel did not seem to have any restaurant attached. She wondered where the nearest eatery was. If she had crossed the bridge, she would have found on the opposite bank of the Housatonic the "Elms Restaurant," a small Coca-Cola-type roadside cafe where they could have had, if not drinks, a decent supper, but she did not know that, and would have to find some other place. She pulled up alongside an outdoor phone booth next to Monroe's General Store, and consulted the yellow pages, looking under "Inns." The first entry was "McDonough Motor Lodge, Cornwall Bridge." Where was it? Had they passed it on Route 7, coming into the village? She believed they had, and drove out that way.

It was a mile back down Route 7. She pulled into it and parked. The inn was a pretty, almost lavish place, converted from a colonial house, freshly painted red, and having the general appearance of an expensive country restaurant.

"We can't go in a place like that looking like this," Day said.

"Oh, why not? It's Sunday night and nobody dresses up," she said.

"They'll throw us out," Day said. "Did you ever read about what happened to Justice Douglas of the Supreme Court and his friends when they tried to stop at that inn in Maryland after hiking in the rain?"

"I don't care, darn it," she said. "I'm hungry and thirsty. I doubt if they have curb service, but maybe they could put up something to take out. Look, you just wait here and I'll go see what I can see."

Diana got out of the car. She noticed that the motel units of the inn were in a separate row of red buildings topped with cupolas to look as if they had been converted from a carriage barn or stables. She went into the inn and found one room marked "Dining Room," another marked "Bar"; she took the latter. There were only a few customers in the room, which was opulently decorated in colonial motifs with a militaristic aspect: guns and drums and wall decorations of soldiers and Indians. She caught sight of herself in a mirror: her stringy wet hair: she looked like a drowned Angora kitten. A man sitting at the bar began to stare at her. The bartender, or proprietor, or innkeeper, was nowhere in sight. She waited, as inconspicuously as possible, at one end of the bar. While she waited, she thought.

Hunger and thirst often inspire one with desperate and even uncharacteristic stratagems. When a man finally appeared whom she took to be in charge, she asked him if they had any rooms.

"Yes, we do," he said pleasantly, looking her not in the eye but at the top of her wet hair. "Single or double?"

She kept the ringless fingers of her left hand in her pocket to keep them out of sight and said, "Double." For an instant she had wanted to say, "Two singles" but that would have seemed rather unusual.

The man produced a card for her to fill out and sign. On impulse, she wrote "Mr. and Mrs. D.L. Montross." She hoped that there weren't any relatives or Montrosses still living in the neighborhood.

"That your Porsche out there?" the man asked.

"Yes it is," she said.

"Nice," he said. "Very pretty."

"Is it possible," she asked, "to have dinner in the rooms?" When the man looked up at her, she said, "You see, my husband and I have been out picking mountain laurel, and we got caught in the rain, and my husband twisted his ankle, and—"

"Oh, certainly. Certainly," the man said, and he handed her a key, and said, "that will be Unit 5. Just across the way there."

"Thank you," she said and turned to go.

The man stopped her. "Here's a menu," he said. "Just phone in whenever you like."

"Thank you," she said again and returned to her car. She got in and backed it out of its parking place.

"No curb service, huh?" Day said.

"No," she said and turned the car around to drive it close to Unit 5 of the motel wing on the other side of the lot.

"Well, there's bound to be a truck stop or something on down the highway," Day said.

"I'd rather eat here," she said, pulling to a stop outside the doorway of Number 5, and hoping she wouldn't have to do any explaining to Day, and hoping even more that he wouldn't have any objections, or put up any argument, or have any scruples or whatever. If he got difficult, she told herself with a smile, she could always just put him to sleep with a few magic words.

"What's this?" Day said, as the car stopped, and she got out.

"Our private dining room," she said. "Come on. And just in case anybody's looking, you're supposed to have a twisted ankle, so limp, will you?"

Day obligingly limped. She put the key into the lock and opened the door. It did not, unfortunately, look very much like a private dining room. It looked like a bedroom. There were twin beds, at least, amply separated. On the whole, the room was a very pleasant one; it was spacious and looked both comfortable and expensive, both of which it was.

"Well well," said Day, looking around. "Money will do anything, won't it?"

"That's a boorish remark, sir," she said. Then she sat on one of the beds and reached for the telephone. "The first thing I'm going to do," she told him, "is have a drink. Do you want one?"

"Sure," he said. "I'm so thirsty I could drink a barrel."

"Of what?" she said.

"Pepsi Cola?" he said.

"I'm going to have a big, double, frosty gin and tonic," she said. "Wouldn't you like one?"

"Pepsi Cola is okay with me, if they have any," he said.

She picked up the phone and ordered one gin and tonic and one Pepsi Cola.

Then there was the problem of dry clothes. Would it be fair of her to change, if he could not? Did she have anything he could wear? He was at least five inches taller than she, and, though thin, at least fifteen or twenty pounds heavier. Would anything fit him? Her raincoat, at least?

"Would you bring in my luggage?" she asked. "No, I'm sorry, I forgot about your poor ankle, dear. I'll get them."

"I'll get them," he said. "What's supposed to be wrong with my poor ankle dear?"

"You twisted it on our hike in the rain," she said. "That's why we have to eat in our room instead of the dining room."

"Oh, ow!" he said, rubbing his ankle. Then he took off his belt and began wrapping it carefully around the ankle in what seemed to be an official Boy Scout sprain-brace.

She laughed. "That's the wrong foot."

"Huh?" he said. "Did you have to specify which foot?" He laughed too, and wrapped the belt around the other ankle. "There," he said. "That will hold it until you can get me to a doctor." Then without levity he asked, "Did you tell them...did you have to say that I'm...you know, pretend that we're...that..."

"Mr. and Mrs. Montross," she said. "Mountain laurel pickers."

There was a knock at the door, and a blonde waitress brought in a tray with their drinks. Day turned away from her and limped toward the bathroom. Diana searched her purse for change to tip the waitress, but decided to wait and put it on the larger tip for dinner.

The waitress put the tray down and took out her order book. "Are you ready to order dinner?" she asked.

"We just got here," Diana said. "I'll phone it in."

"Certainly," the waitress said, and went away.

Diana sipped her gin and tonic, lighted a cigarette, and studied the menu. She heard the toilet flush in the bathroom, and in another minute Day came out, and, still limping, went out the front door. He returned carrying both of her suitcases. "You want all that other junk brought in, too?" he asked.

"What other junk?" she asked.

"There's a box of books, and some pictures and stuff…"

"Oh, that's just from cleaning out my room at the college," she said. "Never mind that."

Day sat down across from her, on the other bed, and while she studied the menu he seemed to study the back side of the menu. Suddenly he said, "Well damn."

She looked up from the menu, astonished to hear his first cuss word. "Damn what?"

He jerked the menu out of her hands and turned it over, showing her the reverse side. "Look," he said. "Just look."

On the back of the menu was a map, a black and white spider web of roads and trails and streams. Upon the map was printed: "Dudleytown, 1747–1920." Beneath that in large letters was:

LEGEND OF DUDLEYTOWN

followed by four paragraphs of text, with faulty punctuation and syntax:

Supposedly doomed from its beginning, Dudleytown, located in Cornwall today consists of cellar foundations barely seen through forest growth. In its time Dudleytown supplied charcoal for the Salisbury Iron works a booming industry in the early 1800's. The settlers were hard-bitter Puritan people who toiled ceaselessly at their charcoal pits. With the coming of improved Iron making techniques, Dudleytown days were numbered, but, it has been said that for more than economic factors were responsible for the death of the town.

The Dudleys were a family of no little importance in England. The beginning of the 16th century, they had recurring periods of bad luck in which English Monarchs beheaded them. For the next 125 years misfortune plagued the inhabitants of the doomed town. The last American Dudley went mad and disease and famine depleted the population. When Horace Greely failed to win the Presidency the cause was rumored to be his Dudleytown bride.

In 1901 the town was deserted and the area was called Owlsburg by the people of Cornwall because of it's haunting sounds. The road leading to it is called Dark Entry.

Today houses fringe its borders and hikers report nothing menacing inside it. If the Dudley curse is finally dead, or if it ever existed at all is a matter of question— some people disclaim talks of ghosts and the Dudleys doom, but the fact is that as yet nobody has tested it. Some surprises might be in store for the man who lives on the ground Abiel Dudley trod before him.

"Makes it look like the local tourist attraction, doesn't it?" Day remarked.

Diana nodded. It was a shock, and a revelation for her, to see that the town which they had "discovered" after so much trouble was already discovered and exposed to anybody looking at the menu of a local inn. It dampened her enthusiasm. She could take the dampness of the rain but not this. Day as well seemed disappointed, and she found herself apologizing, "But we didn't see any tourists or hikers."

"Of course not," he said. "Because of the rain. But on clear days, you probably have to stand in line and buy a ticket."

"Oh, I doubt it," she said. "We didn't see any footprints or any sign of anybody having been there."

"The rain too," he said, "would have washed any footprints away."

"Well," she said, feeling somewhat exasperated, "shall we just forget the whole thing?" It was a rhetorical question and he did not make any reply. She reopened the menu and handed it to him. "Here," she said, "we might as well salvage something out of this. What do you want to eat?"

As he studied the menu, his eyebrows raised, probably at the prices. At length, he said, "I believe I'll have the roast beef."

"You had roast beef for lunch," she reminded him.

"You're right, I did, didn't I?' he said. "Well, hmmm. I guess I'll take the veal scallopini."

"I will too, then," she said. "Shall we have a wine? Or do you prefer Pepsi Cola?"

"Iced tea," he said.

She phoned in the order. For herself she ordered a half-bottle of Antinori Classico, a Chianti.

Then she opened one of her suitcases. She announced, "I'm going to shower and change into something dry."

She took a quick shower and put on one of her better summer dresses. For such a fancy dinner, even in your room, you ought to dress. Especially if your dinner companion is a poor teetotaling Boy Scout who has nothing to dress in. When she came out of the bathroom, she plugged in her hair dryer and put the net over her head. Then she reached over and took her London Fog raincoat out of the suitcase and tossed it to him. "Here," she said. "See if this fits. You ought to get out of those wet clothes."

Thirteen

A Rapport of Sorts Is Reached

It was an excellent dinner, if a peculiar one. Day would not come out of the bathroom until the waitress and her cart were gone. Then, when he did appear, Diana tried hard not to laugh. Several inches of wrist protruded out of the sleeves of the raincoat, and he had to hold his breath to keep the front buttons from popping. Then he had to be careful how he sat, because he had nothing on underneath.

They ate leisurely, but did not talk much. Diana remarked that her wine was a superb one, and wouldn't he like to sample just a sip of it? He did, but did not seem to appreciate it very highly.

At one point, he confessed, "I drank a beer, once."

"A whole bottle?" Diana said in pretended awe. "Did you pass out?"

He frowned at her. "My parents drink," he said. "But in New Jersey, you know, the legal age is twenty-one."

"I see," she said. Boy Scouts take a pledge to be honest and trustworthy and all that. And Methodists take The Pledge, period. Probably Daniel Lyam Montross had been a drunkard, and was paying the price for it in his present incarnation.

"I took some speed once, too," he boasted.

"Really?" she said. "Well, that's something I've never tried."

"I didn't like it, though," he said.

"I hear it's sometimes quite unpleasant," she said.

"Yes. I'll bet you've smoked pot, haven't you?"

"On occasion."

"Is that much fun?"

"I'm not sure 'fun' is the word. I didn't particularly like it, but on the other hand it didn't seem to do much for me."

"I was offered some, once," he admitted, "but I don't smoke."

"I doubt you missed anything," she said.

So went the tenor of their table talk. When they were finished eating—or rather, after Day finished his dessert, strawberry shortcake, which she did not have—she asked if he would care to find out if there was anything interesting on television. He turned the set on, and they watched the last twenty minutes of a variety show—acrobats, a talking dog, a weightlifter and two singers—then the eleven o'clock news and weather report. Clearing tomorrow.

A late movie came on, but Diana turned the set off. "Let's just talk," she said. The gin and wine she'd had were making her feel very sociable.

"Okay," he said. "What about?"

She sat on her bed, her back propped against the pillows and headboard. She lighted a cigarette, and after blowing out the match she looked at him and asked him, "Who are you?"

"Me?" he said. "I'm Day Whittacker. Who are you?"

"Diana Stoving," she said. "I just graduated from Sarah Lawrence and I don't know what to do. And I'm nearly twenty-two."

"I just graduated from East Passaic High School," he said, "and I don't know what to do either, although there're lots of things I could be doing and should be doing but won't because I can't. I'm nearly nineteen."

"How do you do?"

"Fine, thank you, so far, I guess. And you?"

"When I was a little girl," she said, "just three years old, my grandfather, whom I had never met before, abducted me." Diana realized that the gin and the wine had made her just a little giddy. "He never harmed me," she said, and realized that her eyes were wet, "but they had to kill him to get me back."

Day did not say anything, although his face was full of compassion. Diana knew that the only way she could keep the tears from leaving her eyes and rolling down her cheeks was to laugh, so she laughed, as hard as she could, and then said, still laughing, "So now I've abducted *him*. Isn't that priceless?"

Day did not seem to find anything funny about it. He stared at her with a puzzled expression, and then hesitantly he asked, "You mean…you aren't going to take me home?"

"Oh sure," she said. "I'll take you home right now, if you want me to." He did not say anything.

"Well?" she said. "Shall we go?"

"It's up to you," he said.

"No," she said. "No, it isn't. Because, you see, since you're concerned about legality and you're a good Boy Scout and all that, you're still a minor. I'm not. I don't know what the laws are, but—"

"We aren't doing anything wrong," he protested.

"No," she agreed, "we aren't."

"Okay," he said. "If you want to know the truth, I don't really want to go home."

"Fine," she said. "And if you want to know the truth, I don't really believe in reincarnation, not for one minute, and I don't believe in hypnosis either, and I certainly don't believe you're my grandfather, and I don't believe his house was in that grove of mountain laurel up there. I don't believe any of it. But—" she qualified what she was saying "—I would like to believe. I would like to find out. Wouldn't that be marvelous, to be able to believe?"

"I guess it would," he said.

"The trouble with me is," she said, "I don't believe in anything. I would like to find something to believe in."

"Me too," he said. "I sort of feel like that, myself."

"Are you with me, then?"

"I'm with you," he said. "All the way."

Fourteen

They Become Somewhat Better Acquainted with One Another

Diana Stoving and Day Whittacker did not have sexual relations in their motel room that night. Undoubtedly the possibility must have crossed their minds, but they slept chastely in their separate beds. Diana, for her part, was certainly not unmindful of the fact that he was a male and she female and that they were spending the night together. All questions of incest aside, and rightly so, for the time being at least, Diana presumed that a clean-living Boy Scout who neither smoked nor drank and was, although not at all bad-looking, a somewhat timid and reserved young man, was in all likelihood a virgin, and thus, even if she had felt like it, which she did not, it might have created awkward moments for both of them if she had introduced a romantic note, or even a nonromantic sexual note, into their relationship at this point.

They did, however, before putting out the lights and going to sleep, talk for well over an hour, getting acquainted. Here, more or less, is what they learned about one another:

Diana Ruth Stoving was born twenty-one years ago in St. Vincent's Hospital, Little Rock, to B.A. (Burton Arthur) Stoving and Annette M. Stoving. She was their only child. A Libra, she took a short-lived interest in astrology while in college after reading that *Harper's Bazaar's* horoscopist had correctly predicted that she as a Libra would have "unlimited quantities of money to spend as you please," but after being told later in the same "Eye on the Sky" column that she should spend her money for "idealistic causes" she was unable to think of one, and unable to sustain her interest in astrology. Her other qualities, as a Libra, according to the horoscopes, were a "great imaginative capacity" and "an inclination to take the lead in any endeavor."

Her father had met her mother while on army maneuvers as a
captain, in the Ozarks. Her mother had been a country girl; Diana's
father, after his discharge from the army following the war, had spent
some time trying to find her again, and, succeeding, had eloped with
her. She was twenty when he married her in a lavish church wedding in Little Rock, befitting the social background of the Stovings
but scaring the wits out of a poor country girl of obscure origins.
Anne Stoving apparently adjusted to her new life without difficulty,
however; Diana did not learn that her mother had been a country
girl until she, Diana, was almost ready to go away to college and her
mother, after several drinks, confessed her rural origins. It helped
Diana understand, for the first time, why her mother had been in
the habit of using certain quaint words and expressions, but apart
from that it meant little to her.

The episode involving her grandfather was a vague memory;
she had to reconstruct it with the aid of a newspaper clipping which
she had discovered in (and stolen from) a shoebox in her mother's
closet. This was during a Christmas vacation when Diana was home
from her final year in prep school. She had never been told that the
man who abducted her was her grandfather. To her, at the age of
three, he had been simply, as her mother put it, "that bad old man
who came and got you but now he won't bother you any more." The
newspaper clipping told her that the bad man had wounded three
sheriff's deputies and two state troopers; apparently the rifle wounds
had been inflicted with uncanny accuracy meant to disable rather than
to kill, but the lawmen had come to believe that the only way they
could conquer the bad man was to kill rather than to disable.

Diana could remember the sound of gunfire, and the sight
of the bad man falling; it had disturbed her, because she had been
thinking of him not as the bad man but as The Good Man.

Although Diana's earliest memory was of the week she had
lived with him at his yellow house in the Ozark woods, at the age
of three, she did not recall much of her childhood before the age of
eight, when she was transferred from Forest Park Elementary School
(public) to St. Andrew's Day School (private, parochial, Episcopal).
She remembered this transfer because she had had to give up several

friends who were classmates at the public school. The remainder of her schooling was in private schools. For the ninth through twelfth grades, she was sent away to Margaret Hall, an exclusive Episcopal girls' school in Versailles, Kentucky. She graduated third in a class of forty-two, and was accepted at Sarah Lawrence not so much on the basis of her grades and college boards as on the recommendations of her teachers, all of whom agreed that Diana was "highly original and creative, and lends contrast and color to any group."

During the years of her preparatory schooling, her father, B.A. Stoving, advanced rapidly to his present position, chairman of the board and president of National Community Life Insurance Company, headquartered in Little Rock, with branches throughout the south and mid-west. He also serves on the boards of two banks, six industries, three colleges and an airline. Diana's mother is active in social, cultural and charitable work.

Mr. and Mrs. Stoving were spending the current summer in Europe; their flight for Paris had departed the day after they attended Diana's graduation from Sarah Lawrence. It was to be both a grand tour and a second honeymoon for the Stovings; consequently they had not wanted to invite Diana to accompany them. As a substitute or consolation, Mr. Stoving had offered to send her on her choice of several other tours of Europe, and, when she rejected this offer, even to send her on an unguided tour alone or in the company of whichever friends she might like to invite along. When she rejected this too, he gave her as a graduation present the automobile of her choice and an exorbitantly large sum of money in traveler's checks. She chose the Porsche on the recommendation of some of her college friends. "Keep in touch," her father had said in parting, and had provided her with their itinerary, a list of famous hotels in all the major European cities.

When Diana had entered Sarah Lawrence, she had entertained a general notion of becoming some sort of writer. During her sophomore and early junior years she had studied under Kynan Harris, that imp of black humor, who was also her don (advisor) and also, very briefly, her lover (she did not tell Day this; "We were close" is the way she put it), who, however, gave her his frank opinion of her writing, which was that it was much too conventional. "Pedestrian" was his word, and the word stuck in her mind; a pedestrian literally is one going on foot, and she decided that since she was going on foot she would not walk but dance, and spent the rest of her junior year and all of her senior year studying with Bessie Schönberg, the dancer. An unusually large number of Sarah Lawrence students seemed to be taking dance during her senior year, and the competition was severe. While she was assured, by Miss Schönberg, as well as by Mr. Redlich and Mrs. Finch, the other dance teachers, that she could dance professionally after graduation (they encouraged her to try out with Merce Cunningham), she was not confident that she was all that good.

These are Diana's interests:

Martha Graham, of course, particularly her *Appalachian Spring*. She danced the principal role in the Sarah Lawrence production of this work.

José Limon, Betty Jones, Doris Humphrey, and Ruth Currier, particularly the latter's *Search for an Answer,* which she also danced, to acclaim, at Sarah Lawrence.

She does not like classical ballet very much, although the movie of the Fonteyn-Nureyev *Romeo and Juliet* made her cry.

In music: among the moderns, nobody later than Tschaikovsky except possibly Aaron Copland and Charles Ives. Among the ancients, Telemann and the anonymous composers of English Country and Morris Dancing as recorded by John Playford during 1651–1728. As her senior project, she choreographed a modern adaptation of eight Playford dances.

In art: the early Venetian school and Giorgione, particularly his "Tempest." Among the moderns, only Kokoschka.

In literature: she enjoyed reading the Greek tragedies as a requirement, but would not have read them on her own. Among the moderns, she has read most of the novels of what she calls her "five Johns": Updike, Barth, Cheever, Fowles and Hawkes; as well as Kynan Harris, Donald Harington and her special favorite, Nabokov.

Other miscellaneous interests: the films of Stanley Donan. Although she does not particularly care for rock music, being overexposed to it by her roommates' phonographs, she does not object to it. In sports, she has played some tennis, which she likes, and some lacrosse, which she doesn't. She has watched a few football games on television. Politics holds no interest for her at all. Nor does religion; although raised an Episcopalian, she has attended church only a few times since leaving prep school.

If she were forced to choose a career, she would probably—but she would never be *forced* to choose a career.

Charles Day Whittacker was born nearly nineteen years ago in San Diego, California, where his father, Charles J. "Chuck" Whittacker, was stationed before being sent to Korea. After the Korean War, Chuck Whittacker returned with his wife, Jane Billings Whittacker, and their infant son, to his home town, Rutherford, New Jersey, where he found employment as a salesman for Lang Manufacturing Company, makers of asphalt roofing and siding. Young Day, who from birth was called by his middle name to distinguish him from his father, attended Antonio F. Calicchio Elementary School until the third grade, when his parents moved to Wood Ridge, New Jersey, after Chuck Whittacker took a position as salesman for Hendrie Products, distributors of sulfur and mineral pitch. Day finished elementary school in Wood Ridge and attended Hackensack Avenue Junior High School for two years until his father moved to East Passaic after becoming a sales engineer for Rohn Refining Corporation, makers of a diversified line of solvents. Day finished junior high school there, and attended East Passaic High School, graduating twenty-sixth in a class of 456.

One of the very few things Day Whittacker had in common with Diana Stoving was that he was an only child. His mother had had ovarian cysts requiring surgical removal.

While attending elementary school in Wood Ridge, Day joined Cub Scout Pack 16. He became a Tenderfoot Scout in Beaver Troop 22, advancing rapidly to Second Class, then First Class Scout, then Heart, then Life, and finally Eagle during his sophomore year in high school. In the process, he earned merit badges in archery, astronomy, beekeeping, bird study, bookbinding, botany, camping, canoeing, citizenship, cooking, first aid, fishing, forestry, gardening, geology, hiking, Indian lore, insect life, lifesaving, nature, personal fitness, pioneering, radio, reptile study, safety, scholarship, signaling, swimming, weather, woodwork and zoology. One of the very few merit badges he failed to earn, after two trials, was that for public speaking.

For three summers past, he served as a cabin counselor at Camp Whanpoo-tahk-kee near Lake Hopatacong in northwestern New Jersey. He also attended the Valley Forge Camporee and the International Scout Camporee in Nova Scotia.

After lengthy consultation with his vocational counselor in high school, Day decided that he wanted to become, first choice, a forester, and, second choice, a national park ranger. Neither of these choices, however, matched the aspirations Mr. and Mrs. Whittacker had for him. Mr. Whittacker hoped the boy would enter a premed or predental course in college, while Mrs. Whittacker clung to a long-cherished wish that he prepare for the ministry, even after she learned of his second failure to pass the public-speaking merit badge examination. Dutifully, Day applied for admission to Rutgers, Monmouth, Newark State and nearby Farleigh Dickinson; the last three all accepted him but he had taken no further steps to enroll. None of the three offered programs in forestry.

Apart from disputes over the matter of college attendance, Day's relations with his parents were, if not ideal, harmonious and unstormy. He strove to be a good son. Perhaps because he was an only son, their yardstick for his measurement was a bit warped. Mr. Whittacker, particularly, exhibited great disappointment at anything less than excellence, and his strict discipline had caused Day, at the age of only five, to run away from home (the police found him within eight hours). Curiously, at the same time that Mr. Whittacker demanded excellence, he was resentful of Day's intelligence. Mr. Whittacker himself was not terribly bright, but he prided himself in having "horse sense," which, he often reminded Day, his son did not have. In other ways, too, there was little resemblance between father and son. Day was taller than his father but nowhere near as muscular. His father liked to "go out with the boys"; Day did not, except for Scouting activities. His father had a mechanical bent and could repair anything from a washing machine to an automobile; Day had little mechanical aptitude.

Other than his Scouting accomplishments, Day had not produced a strong extracurricular record. In his sophomore year, at his father's urging, he had tried out with the track team and was very good in the short dashes and hurdles, but what the coach needed was a distance man.

P.D. Sedgely was Day's English teacher in both the eleventh and the twelfth grades, and Day attended several discussion meetings of the Psychic Research Club, as Sedgely's small group of after-hours students called themselves. He himself did not volunteer to become a subject until the spring of his senior year. He had been thoroughly suspicious of the proceedings, but the first time he listened to a playback of his voice under hypnosis and age regression, he knew that he had identified the source of the voice that had been "bothering" him for years.

His parents were not unaware of his relations with Sedgely and the Psychic Research Club. He never kept anything from his parents. His mother arranged for him to have a chat about it with their minister. He did. It turned out to be not so much a chat as a sermon. The minister, Rev. Eugene B. Dobler of the East Passaic Church, talked to him about Christ's promise of a second coming and a last judgement, but pointed out that there is nothing anywhere in the Bible about reincarnation.

But Day read all he could find on the subject. Still, he was never ready to dismiss the possibility that Daniel Lyam Montross was only the invention of his own imagination, or the imagination of his subconscious.

Then he met Diana, who said she was the granddaughter of Daniel Lyam Montross. He believed her, and knew then that such a man had actually existed.

These are Day's interests:

Scouting and camping, of course, but he likes back-packing on long hikes more than fixed camping.

Wood. He likes everything about wood and its uses. He knows the scientific names as well as the familiar names of every American tree; he knows their ecology, habits, growth rate, life span, and economic value. He knows how well or how poorly each wood burns, when green as well as when seasoned. Although he has no great civic pride in New Jersey, he is proud that Joyce Kilmer was a New Jerseyan.

He does not think that "Trees" is a great poem, but he likes it. Actually, his taste in poetry runs to W.H. Auden and e.e. cummings. He can quote three or four of the latter's poems from memory.

He has not read much fiction. An aunt gave him a complete set of Jack London for his sixteenth birthday, but he read only part of one volume and did not like it. In high school, he was required to read *Lord of the Flies* and *The Catcher in the Rye*; the boys in the former were too young for him to identify with, while the boy in the latter was too smart-ass (he did not say this to Diana; "too Huck-Finnish" is the way he put it, although he had never read Huck Finn). His candidate for the Nobel Prize in Literature is Walt Kelly; he has read all the Pogo books, and reread them several times.

He had a course in art appreciation in high school, but very little of it remains with him. He remembers liking Hobbema's "The Avenue of the Middelharnis" and Rembrandt's etching "The Three Trees." In modern art, he likes Van Gogh's cypresses and Rousseau's jungles, but thinks Picasso is a joke.

Despite the closeness of his region of New Jersey to Manhattan, he has never seen a stage play, much less a dance performance. He has visited Manhattan only a few times, once for an extended tour of the Museum of Natural History, once to attend a Scout Council meeting, and once to see a movie on West Forty-second Street. The movie was a "skin flick," which he found both stimulating and tasteless.

He has had few dates, of a formal nature, with girls. He took his minister's daughter, Lila, to a high school football game. He escorted another girl from the church to a hayride sponsored by the Methodist Youth Organization, but after the haywagon (actually just a flatbed truck) was already out in the moonlight he discovered that she was several years older than he. He took a fellow member of Sedgely's Psychic Research Club, who had been an Eygptian slave girl in a previous life, to the junior picnic. For the senior picnic he chose a girl who lived on his own block, and who was a Girl Scout, but he learned that most of her merit badges, as well as her interests, were not in the outdoors but in homemaking, nursing and child care.

One of his favorite subjects in high school was American history, and he has visited almost all the historic sites and battlefields in New Jersey.

In contemporary music he likes the folk singers but not rock. His taste for classical music, particularly Mozart and Beethoven, is the result of listening to WQXR for several years on a homemade FM set which he awkwardly but painstakingly constructed as part of the requirements for his merit badge in radio.

All in all, he considers himself a reasonably average and normal young man. There are only two abnormalities he is aware of: one, of course, is this reincarnation business; the other is that, for as long as he can remember, he has had a feeling of being lonely, more so, he thought, than most average, normal people.

Fifteen

Diana Goes Shopping, Suffers Some Bad Moments, but Prevails

Diana did not sleep well. Several times, waving on the outer strand of slumber, she came awake to wonder: what am I doing here? Each time, to go back under, she had to explain it patiently to herself, but with a different explanation every time. Never could she answer to her satisfaction who it was bothered her most, herself or him. Nor could she interpret the tatters of certain dreams that clung to her stubbornly when she surfaced from sleep, yet these seemed somehow more real than the reality of trying to sleep in a motel in Cornwall,

Connecticut, in the same room with the reembodied remains of her grandfather. In time she could not distinguish: did she wake to sleep? or sleep to wake?

Did she rise up when dawn came? Or was this just one more dream? It seemed she rose, and was sitting on the edge of her bed. It seemed some light seeped through their window, the aquamarine light of early dawn. The hills were too high to let the sun up yet. It seemed she sat awhile, and was looking at him. He slept deeply, it seemed, his mouth open, his upper lip swollen, his arms akimbo, one leg nearly off the bed, as he lay face down covered by a sheet only, only to his waist; sometime in the night he must have removed the tight raincoat of hers he was wearing. It seemed he seemed very young, a child, his sleeping face empty of any guilt or care or even experience. He seemed to have no soul, neither his own nor another's.

It seemed she sat a long time, absently looking at him and waiting, waiting not for him to wake but for herself to. Did she wake? He would not, for several hours yet; but did she? In this dream that seemed awake, or this wakefulness that seemed dreaming, she rose up and dressed, realizing she could sleep no more...nor stay awake longer. She would have to go out. It seemed she began hunting for something to write with, to leave him a message. Did she find a pencil or a ballpoint? No, it seemed she searched through her lipsticks. They were all too pale, but it seemed she found one which was a redder pink than the others. Would she write with it upon a piece of the motel's stationery, or use the mirror in the bathroom? It seemed she chose the mirror, and it seemed she wrote: "Going out. Going shopping. Order breakfast. Back soon. Diana."

Then it seemed she was in her car and on the highway, and she decided, *If this is a dream, I've never had one quite like it, before.* She drove into Cornwall Bridge and stopped beside the same telephone booth whose yellow pages she had used to locate their inn the evening before. This time she looked under "Camping Equipment," but the first entry there was a store in New Britain, which, she discovered after consulting her roadmap, was a long way off. The second and only other entry was for Llewellyn's Sporting Goods of 521 Elm Street, Torrington. She located Torrington on the map. It wasn't very near, either, but it was much closer than New Britain, and the day, of course, was young.

When she reached Torrington, after a thirty-mile drive through nearly unpopulated countryside, she found that it was still much too early for the stores to open, but she located a Dunkin' Donuts shop on South Main which had just opened for the day, and she had a breakfast of orange juice, French crullers and coffee. Then she had another cup of coffee, and smoked a cigarette. After the second cup of coffee, she became reasonably certain that she was not asleep and dreaming.

"Getting an early start?" remarked the manager of the sporting goods store as he unlocked the door and let her in. Then he said, "what can we do for you?"

"I need two of everything," she said.

"Sure," he said. "Two shirts, two pairs of jeans, two belts...."

She saw then that most of the stuff in the store was clothing. "I was interested in camping equipment," she said.

"That's downstairs," he said, and switched on a light and led her to the basement.

It was fun. She picked out a pair of sleeping bags with bonded Dacron filling, a pair of air mattresses of tufted rubber, a pair of Coleman gas lanterns, a pair of battery lanterns, a pair of aluminum mess kits, and a pair of folding camp chairs. She selected a large umbrella tent, with aluminum poles and suspension, which had a floor space of twelve feet by twelve feet. "What else do I need?" she asked herself aloud.

"A camp stove?" suggested the merchant, and she picked out a Bernzomatic propane stove with double burner.

"An ice chest?" he said, and she chose a Cronstrom with a capacity of ninety pounds of ice.

"How about a portable john?" he said, and showed her several models. She picked one that used chemicals.

"You'll want a good first aid kit," he suggested, and she took one.

"A hand pump for the air mattresses?" he said. "A rope hammock? Extra propane cartridges? Skewers for kebabs? Salt and pepper shakers? Spray insect repellent? Clothes hooks?"

She added these items to her equipage, and said, "Well, I guess that does it."

"An inflatable boat?" suggested the merchant. "A folding picnic table? Charcoal brix? Paper plates? Snakebite kit?"

"No, thank you," she said. "I believe I've got enough."

"A fly swatter?" he said. "Binoculars? A telescope? A compass?"

"I believe I've got all I can carry," she said.

"Carry?" he said. "That your car out there? You'll never get all of this into it."

"Well…" she said.

"What you need is a roof rack," he said.

"Where could I get one of those?" she asked.

"Well, we have the small aluminum carrier, the deluxe two-tone luggage rack, and also the suction-cup bar carrier which you don't want because the suction cups will leave rings on the finish."

She selected a carrier for her roof, and the manager offered to put it on for her and adjust it. While he was doing this, with some difficulty because of the slope of the Porsche's roof, she realized she ought to pick out some clothes for Day. But she didn't know his sizes. That could wait.

She asked the merchant if he would accept traveler's checks. He did, gladly. He helped her load all of the equipment into the back of the car and onto the roof rack. "Come again," he said, and stood on the curb waving as she drove away.

It was nine-thirty when she got back to the motel room, and she could hardly wait to see Day's face when she showed him all this stuff. But Day, she discovered, was gone.

A maid was cleaning their room. "Did you see my husband?" Diana asked her. The maid, after giving her a strange look, shook her head. Diana walked to the dining room of the inn, but he was not there. She wondered if he had seen the message she had left on the bathroom mirror. She returned to her room and looked at the mirror, but there was no message on it. "Did you erase my message?" she called to the maid, but there was no answer. She stepped out of the bathroom. "Did you—" But the maid was gone.

Had Day ever been there? The bed was made, his clothes were gone, there was no trace of him behind. Had she dreamt that too?

She got into her car again and drove down the highway, south down Route 7. Monday morning traffic had commenced; there were cars ahead and behind. She had not driven far when she spotted him, up ahead, standing beside the highway with his thumb in the air. But before she could reach him, a car ahead of her stopped for him, and he got in. Whether he had seen her or not she could not tell. She followed. The car ahead accelerated, and she had to drive fast to keep up with it. She followed for more than a mile before coming to a straight stretch of road where she could swing out into the other lane and pull abreast of the other car. She rolled down the window on that side; the driver of the other car was a young man about Day's own age; Day was sitting beside him. "Day!" she yelled, and both boys turned to look at her. She started to ask him if he wanted to go home, but a car coming from the other direction forced her to slam on the brakes and get back into the proper lane. The car in which Day was riding pulled off onto the shoulder of the road and stopped, and she stopped behind it. Day got out, but the car did not leave. He came toward her car. She got out and went to meet him. "Day," she said. "Are you going home?"

His eyes were still puffed from sleep; apparently he had not been awake very long. "I thought you had already left," he said.

"You didn't see my message?" she said.

"No."

"But my luggage is still in the room. Didn't you notice?"

"No."

"You didn't think I would go off without you, did you?"

"I didn't know."

"Well, I didn't. I wouldn't."

"I just saw the car gone, and you gone, and I thought—"

"Well, I'm here."

Day turned and walked away. For a moment she thought he was going to get back into the other car, but he only stuck his head in the other car's window and said, "Thanks a lot anyway. That's who

I was looking for. Thanks a lot. Sorry to bother you." Then he waved at the driver and came back and got into Diana's car.

She made a U-turn and drove back toward the inn. Day asked, "Where did you go?"

"Shopping," she said, and pointed toward the roof of the car. Day said, "What's all that stuff up there?"

"Just wait'll you see," she said. "I've got everything."

She parked beside their motel room. She asked him if he had had breakfast yet. He said no. She suggested the inn's dining room, but when he seemed hesitant, she said they could order something delivered to their room.

Then she showed him her purchases. Of course she didn't unfold the tent, but she lifted a corner so he could see the strong stitching and the mosquito netting and the sturdy aluminum poles. She opened the propane stove and removed the lid from the ice chest. She showed him everything.

He did not say anything.

"Well, what do you think?" she asked.

Still he did not say anything. He seemed to be half-asleep. Perhaps he thought that he was dreaming. Or maybe he was disappointed because she had not asked for his advice in selecting the things. She wished she knew what was going through his mind.

"Don't you like it?" she asked.

"It's okay," he said. "Pretty good outfit. First class, in fact." "Well —?" she said.

He asked a shy question: "Is it for us?"

"Of course," she said. "Who'd you think?"

"Let's go, then," he said. "Let's get away from here. Breakfast can wait, can't it?"

"Sure," she said. "I've already had mine, anyway."

"I'd rather have mine," he said, "with wood smoke in it."

Sixteen

A Pleasant Day Is Had in Dudleytown, and a Pleasant Evening

Day had his breakfast with wood smoke in it. Eschewing her Bern-zomatic propane double-burner camp stove, he constructed, with rocks and sticks and a small excavation of earth in the glade of the mountain laurel, an Official All-purpose Boy Scout Campfire, and proceeded to fry bacon and eggs, bake biscuits and make coffee. She watched him. It looked so good her appetite came again, and she had a second breakfast.

They had stocked up on groceries at the general store in Cornwall Bridge, enough for several days at least, with Day doing the picking, so that even if he really did feel piqued because she had selected the equipment without his advice, this must have helped make up for it a little. On the first portage from the place where they had to leave the car, the same as the day before, to the site in the glade of mountain laurel, they had carried only the cooking and eating utensils and part of the groceries.

After breakfast they began a series of portages to carry the rest of the gear from the car to the glade, a distance of perhaps a mile. They each together made two additional trips to the car and back before they were finished; so it was that their morning hike covered a total distance of about five miles. By noon Diana was fatigued, and, after a light lunch, she inflated one of the air mattresses and took a nap. While she napped, Day finished the setting up of their camp, and when she woke around three o'clock she found he had cleared a large area of brush, weeds and ferns and erected the tent with its awning on poles and a drainage trench dug around the perimeter on the uphill side; the camp chairs were unfolded and set up on either side of the fire, the utensils hung in a neat row on a rack of sticks. Everything, despite its newness, seemed to have been settled there for a long time. Diana laughed in surprise when she saw that Day had added a few "decorations": apparently he had made one more trip to the car and brought back the stack of framed pictures which had been in her room at Sarah Lawrence, and these he had hung from tree branches on the perimeter of the camp: her reproductions of Kokoschka's "Bride of the Wind" and of Giorgione's "Tempest"; photographs of Martha Graham in *Appalachian Spring* and herself in *Search for an Answer*; and even the "Make-Love-Not-WAR" poster which had been Susan Trombley's, not hers.

"No place like home, huh?" Diana said.

"Yeah, but I don't like that tent," Day said.

"What's wrong with it?"

"It looks like it belongs in 'Shady Acres Kozy Kampground' inhabited by a fat butcher and his fat family on their first trip out of the city. I would rather make a lean-to out of sticks and brush."

"And let the mosquitoes bite us," Diana said. "And let the rain trickle down our necks. No thanks."

"You might at least have got a green one. Or even a gray one. But a *yellow* one, for gosh sakes! The tourists will think we're a concession booth and want to buy something. What can we sell them?"

"Bouquets of mountain laurel," Diana suggested. Then she said, "What tourists? I still haven't seen anybody in these woods."

"Just you wait."

Diana rose up from her air mattress, and had a good stretch. The air mattress had been surprisingly comfortable, but it had left a few kinks which she had to stretch off. While she was stretching, she looked around her, unable to find something which she realized she needed at once.

"Where did you put the john?" she asked him.

"The what?"

"The john. Our portable privy. The chemical comfort station."

"Oh, that." He pointed. "It's right over there."

"Where? I don't see it."

"*There.*"

She looked. She looked again. Then she realized why she had

not seen it: it was nearly covered with a profusion of wildflowers that had been arranged into an artful bouquet springing out of its hole. "Lovely," she said. "But I need to use your flower vase for something else."

"Use the woods," he said. It was not a suggestion but a command, and in the same peremptory voice he added, "Lady, I can live with all this other superfluous junk of yours, but I refuse to desecrate God's earth with an unnatural chemical contraption. Use the woods."

She used the woods. Or, rather, the bushes, threading her way through the dense mountain laurel shrubs until she was well out of sight. Then, when she was finished, she realized she had forgotten something. "Day!" she called out. "Did we get any tissue paper?"

After a moment his voice came back to her. "Are you wrapping presents?"

"Day?" she called. "Didn't we bring any toilet paper?"

She waited. His shout finally came: "I can't find any."

"Any Kleenex?" she called.

"No."

"Well," she called out, "do you have two fives for a ten?"

After his laughter, Day's voice bellowed, "God didn't make leaves just for photosynthesis!" His sibilant esses ricocheted through the woods and echoed back, like snakes rustling through dry leaves.

When she returned to camp, Diana gave Day a little look, a *moue*, and said, "I wish you'd leave God out of this. I don't need Him around as head counselor."

"All right," he said. "*I* will be head counselor."

"Yes sir," she said, and saluted, not with the three-finger Scout salute but with one finger, the middle one. "Sir, what shall we do this afternoon? Have you planned the afternoon's activities, sir? Knot tying? Basket weaving? Calisthenics? Or a séance?"

"Do you want to see if we can find Dark Entry Road?"

They spent the rest of the afternoon exploring Dark Entry Road. It was not hard to find. She had torn off the little map from the back of the Cornwall Inn's menu, and they used that as a guide. They followed the branch of Bonny Brook that ran below their mountain laurel glade, and it crossed under Dark Entry Road right alongside the cellar hole of what had been the Dudley house itself. The stream did not merely cross under the road any longer but *through* it, having long since washed away the small bridge; and it tumbled on down a narrow, winding cataract in its wild urge to meet and join the main course of Bonny Brook, which ran parallel to Dark Entry at this point. They followed Dark Entry, which was indeed dark, sheltered everywhere from the sun by a canopy of trees, down its length, past the foundation of the old mill, to the dam. The dam was an impressive work of dry masonry, its center section washed out by the brook but the two ends still standing in neat courses of huge slabs of stone: the most monumental structure remaining in Dudleytown.

A short distance below the dam they found the falls, identified on the map as Marcella Falls, named perhaps for some settler's daughter or wife, a spectacular cascade of water rushing off a ledge and dropping eight or ten feet into a foaming vortex. Rainwater from the day before had filled the brook and increased the rush of the falls. It was the prettiest spot Diana had seen yet in Dudleytown, even prettier than the glade of mountain laurel; in fact it was the prettiest spot, the *freshest* spot, she could ever recall having seen.

It would make a fine natural showerbath. Diana, perspiring freely after the hike through the warm woods, wanted to walk right down into the falls, clothes and all if need be, but preferably without. She wished she'd brought one of her bathing suits along on the hike. She stood so long staring at the falls with longing that Day began to fidget; he tossed pebbles into the pool of the falls; then he looked at her and, seeming to read her thoughts, said, "I'm going to go on down the road and look for the place where the charcoal pits were. You could come along later…after…when…if you want to, you know, if you want to take a skinny dip or something, you know, I'll go on down the road and you could catch up later."

"How did you know what I was thinking?" she asked.

"Well, I just thought…" he began. "I mean, after all, *anybody* would, wouldn't they? It's a nice watering place."

For a moment there she was about to attempt to persuade him to join her, but even if his modesty would crumble she wasn't positive her own would. "Thanks, Gramps," she said. "I believe I will." Day turned and continued walking down Dark Entry—or what remained of it, a steeply descending trail spilling over ledges and boulders that not even a jeep could take. She waited until he was out of sight beyond a turning in the road, then she climbed down the bank to the edge of the pool. Waist-high in ferns, she took off her clothes. She tested the water with one toe. It was icy cold. Hugging herself, she waded into the pool, to the depth of her calves, and began shivering. She didn't think she would be able to brave stepping under the falls. Even its spray, flicking her, chilled her to the bone. She cupped her hands into the pool and raised a few handfuls to spread upon her arms and ribs, and that was all she could stand. She splashed some on her face, then waded out of the pool and stood in a spot of sunshine and breeze for a few moments to dry.

Had the women and girls of Dudleytown ever come here to bathe? Probably not, if Dark Entry had been a public highway then, exposing any bathers to view. No hard-bitten Puritan would have been seen indecent, but only a hard-bitten Puritan could have endured the sting of the icy water.

Diana suddenly had an intuition that she was being watched. She scanned the woods all around for a glimpse of eyes, but saw none. "Who's there?" she asked, but received no reply. Quickly she dressed, then climbed the bank to the road and went off in search of Day.

It took her a while to find him. He had said he was going to search for the charcoal pits, but she passed these without seeing them, and he was not there. She went on, following Dark Entry almost to the edge of the forest where it begins to rejoin civilization, before she heard a "Hey!" behind her and turned to see him following her.

Catching up, he asked, "Where are you going?"

"Just looking for you," she said.

"You didn't stay in the water very long," he said.

"How do you know I didn't?"

"Well, I mean, you're *here*, aren't you? You wouldn't be all the way to *here* if you were still in the water."

"Where were you?" she asked.

"I was…just off in the woods…looking at things."

"See anything that interested you?"

"Just some more cellar holes."

"Let's go back to the camp," she said. "I'm not used to all this walking." They hiked back up Dark Entry toward home. As they passed Marcella Falls again, Day asked, "How was the water?"

"Cold," she said. "You must try it some time."

"I will," he said.

Back in camp, as the cool of the late afternoon came on, the mosquitoes began biting. They took turns spraying each other with the aerosol can of insect repellent. It smelled like decaying lemons. But it was effective; the mosquitoes hovered over them for a while, then went away. Day began preparing supper. He built a fire, then scooped out a small hole in the ground and put two large potatoes into the hole, then shoveled hot coals on top of the potatoes. "Can I help?" Diana asked. He told her to make the salad if she wanted to. She wanted to. She opened the ice chest and got out the lettuce, tomatoes, pepper and cucumber. While she had the ice chest open she got a can of beer. "Want one?" she asked, and held the can up when he turned to look. He shook his head. Then he turned and walked off into the woods.

She sighed, thinking, Well golly gee I didn't mean to offend you just by offering you one. She popped the top off the can and took a sip. The poor guy didn't know what he was missing, a frosty cold beer on a summer afternoon in the woods. Still, she wished she had picked up some Schweppes and a bottle of gin.

Day came back out of the woods with his fists full of weeds. She wondered if he had been out tearing up weeds in his rage or shame or anger or whatever adolescent emotion he was having. He thrust the weeds at her. "Here," he said. "Put these into the salad. And I changed my mind. I will drink some beer." He dumped the weeds into her hands and then got himself a can of beer out of the ice chest.

She held the pile of weeds as if it were bug-infested, and made a face and said, "What's this?"

"Watercress," he said. "And purslane and wood sorrel and

chickweed and a sprig of wild garlic. How do you open these damn things?"

"Just put your finger through the ring and pull," she said.

He broke the ring off. "Now what?"

"Try another one," she suggested.

"Hell," he said, and took his pocketknife out and gouged the rest of the top off. Then he raised his can toward her and said, "Here's!" then drew the can to his mouth and took a large swallow. He smacked his lips, said, "Good stuff," then coughed for a while. Then he said, "I saw a lot of mushrooms. Do you like mushrooms?"

"If they're not poisonous," she said.

"These aren't," he said. "I know."

"Boy Scout honor?"

"Boy Scout honor." He raised three fingers.

So they had a supper of potatoes baked in coals, a half-wild salad, and a grilled London broil steak smothered with sautéed mushrooms. It needed a good Burgundy, but they had beer instead. She would remember to pick up a few wines on the next shopping trip.

"This is nice," she commented, after the first few bites. His mouth full, he only nodded.

After supper they just sat in satiety. "That was awfully nice," she said.

Birds sang. Frogs croaked in the marsh. A jet airliner passed over, reminding her that there were other people in the world. But the first day had passed without anyone coming into their woods.

They sat, still and quiet. Evening fell. Eventually Day spoke. "Are you bored?" he asked.

"No," she answered. "Are you?"

"Not at all," he said. "I just wondered if maybe you were."

"I haven't been so *un*bored in a long time."

"That's good. There's nothing to do."

"No place to go."

"Nothing happening. This is where it isn't at."

She laughed. "I like the way you put that. 'This is where it isn't at.'"

Then after a while she said, "But you're wrong, you know. This is where it *is* at."

"Yes," he said. "It surely is."

"Go to sleep, Day."

First Movement

Landscape with Two Figures

For there is hope of a tree, if it be cut down, that it will sprout again, and that the tender branch thereof will not cease. Though the root thereof wax old in the earth, and the stock thereof die in the ground; yet through the scent of water it will bud, and bring forth boughs like a plant. But man dieth, and wasteth away: yea, man giveth up the ghost, and where is he?

Job 14:7–10

�֍ 1 ✖

This is where it is at. Where I am born. That I am born, beslimed and puling, onto the straw tick of life, is not a come-off for joy in the faces of those watching. Black looks from my audience are my first sight in this new world. I am to blame. The withy blob of me's the harvest of my sire's last fumbling. His hands boggle out what his perkin boggled in. He should learn. But I'm his last. I slither from his grasp, like a fish, like an eel, and bounce on the straw tick, a bouncing babe, clumsily caught on the rebound, upended, clumsily spanked, his hands all thumbs. I squall: whose fault? whose fault?

If I were a dog I would bite him. The woman is crying, but not from any sorry upon my plight. "As much pity," says the man, "to see a woman weep as a goose go barefoot," then he fumbles me into her arms. Her catch is good. But her breath is bad, and her vision worse. Every mother thinks her duckling a swan. My mother has not seen a swan. She thinks her duckling a hoary bat. Her first word at me: "Bleach." My first word at her: *WHY?*

Before I am put to breast, my nakedness is hid in a white dimity dress. Then I am named. My first for the prophet, he of the den of lions, my second for my mother's father Lyme. Born in poverty the last of a rowen crop of children, last and unneeded, all I have is this dimity dress and this knit link of my name, the three sounds bonded at two junctions of end and beginning: Daniel-Lyam-Montross. God bless Daddy-pa and Mother for some small jot of mother wit.

Before I am put to breast, the older children are herded in, to peer at baby brother. Ethan, the eldest, stands at the foot of the bed with his hands folded solemn and his face folded solemn as if he were viewing the remains in a coffin. Nathan and Nicholas prod and poke each other, to force the other to look first. Emmeline the older girl has been studying in school a lip exercise for young ladies: to look proper upon entering a room first recite "Papa, prunes and prisms." Emmeline has been saying over and over to herself, "Papa, prunes and prisms," and her lips look as if she has been eating prunes. Charity, the younger girl, the baby but for me, does not know any lip exercises; her mouth hangs open. To all of them I cry: *why? why?*

Before I am put to breast, my father leads us all in prayer. God is thanked that I am whole. We are obliged to Him that my delivery had no hitches. He is enjoined to keep it that way. He is asked to look after me. He is requested to see to it that I do my share of the work. He is called upon to make me strong and lend me a long life. He is told that my personal happiness matters naught, that my life is to do His bidding, and if His bidding be to chasten me, Praise His Name. We are all grateful, amen. *Why?* I wail.

Before I am put to breast, my father says to the older girl, "Now then, Em, say your pome." Emmeline opens her schoolbook, whispers to herself, "Papa, prunes and prisms," then with those pursed lips she recites:

> *Our birth is but a sleep and a forgetting;*
> *The soul that rises with us, our life's star,*
> *Hath had elsewhere its setting*
> *And cometh from afar:*
> *Not in entire forgetfulness*
> *And not in utter nakedness*
> *But trailing clouds of glory do we come*
> *From God, who is our home:*
> *Heaven lies about us in our infancy!*

My sister reads on and on and on, until my father says, "Shouldn't wonder but what that's enough, now, Em," and she closes her book and prunes and prisms her mouth once more before she leaves the room. It is, in truth, enough. My sister has told me why. But I am not still. I cry, not so much from hunger of the guts as hunger of the soul. *Cheer!* I cry for. *Ease! Peace! Eats! Feed!*

Before I am put to breast, my mother sends the other children from the room, and sends my father too, first stopping him to make him promise that he will never lie with her again. He complains, "Wal, where in Halifax will I lie, then?" "You know what I mean," she says. My parents have a lengthy tow-row, before I'm put to breast.

My father leaves. Now I am given a brown teat, one pap for the other. There is no milk. I am too tired to care.

I am the dead spit of my father. This too comes between the woman and me. It does, for all that she does not know it. She does not know why she does not dote on me, except that I am too many...and perhaps I seem not a swan but a hoary bat. Her name is Hopestill, no fault of her own, a good virtue name her mother gave her. But she does not know what she should still be hoping for. Not me, for sure.

But though I'm the spit of him, the dead spit of him, my father too does not dote on me. He knows more than she, though. He knows why. His name is Clen, is how he's known by all, a clip nicked off of Clendenin. His grandfather was he who emigrated from England, Glendenning "Mountain Horse" Montross who fought with General Heman Swift at Valley Forge in the War of Independence. Clen Montross has seen no battles but for those of bed and board. Nature herself does not do battle with him. He makes a living from the wood of the woods. He has lived all his life in Dudleytown, as did his father before him. His grandfather was the first. And I am the last.

An itinerant parson, a pedlar of the Word, named Asenath Prenner, came upon Dudleytown by happenstance one day in 1819, having lost the road between Litchfield and Sharon. Mountain Horse told this to his son Murdock who told it to his son Clendenin who will tell it to his son me. Asenath Prenner lodged the night with Eliphalet Rogers and, hearing from his host the chronicle of Dudleytown's misfortunes and the legendary curse that purported to be upon the village, decided to bide a while, for the town's pleasure if not its redemption. As well as hawking the Word, Asenath Prenner also hawked books and miscellaneous appurtenances for the home and farm. Also he gave demonstrations of ventriloquism and legerdemain. Also he exhibited the first kaleidoscope seen by any man in these parts, which, he claimed, could reveal the future.

Asenath Prenner played Dudleytown for one week, departing with considerable of the town's pin money, and leaving behind several newly spiritual-minded folk, a wagonload of books and trifles, and a whole schedule of divers prognostications. One of these, bought by Mountain Horse's wife Sophronica in a ninepence session with the kaleidoscope, was that if any Montross ever had as many as seven children, the seventh child would be the last. The last Montross of Dudleytown.

Mountain Horse himself did not swallow this, but Sophronica believed it, and stopped at six. Of those, only two, Murdock and Jared, were boys. Jared begat only three children, while Murdock begat five, all sons, three killed during the war against the rebels, two surviving, Uriel, a bachelor, and Clendenin.

Clendenin is not of a superstitious turn, but the old prophecy of Asenath Prenner has survived in the family such a long time that he has respected it enough to keep it in his own confidence. Hopestill has not heard it; for aught she knows, she might not care a straw about it.

The third child of Clendenin and Hopestill, Patience, a girl, died in infancy of thrush. Had she survived, there would be seven of us. I the seventh.

My mark will I learn, this stigma. A babe is the innocent butt of all stigmas, the ready mark of all marks. Mother, your milk is the decoction of all thy bitter draughts, boiled in the fire of thine ire.

Colicky are my wakings, fidgety my sleep. I need each dream to clear up all these puzzles. Gnawing of the bowels, knowing of their scowls. My study is of their faces. In dreams I try to read their meanings. A mean mien in a dream is both scrutable and monstrous. Always I wake crying.

Of those so near around me, my kin, whose face is soft? Aptly she's named, sweet Charity. She can't be twenty months my senior, but they let her hold me. They would make her hold me, but she volunteers. Emmeline will hold me too, but briefly, her face no longer soft as Charity's, her face pruned and prismed. Spittle flecks from her lips and splatters me when she practices her prunes and prisms.

Charity thinks I'm her dollbaby. There is her one flaw. Charity is feebleminded. Mother and father do not know this, yet, she is too young. I read it writ large as milestones in her eyes. But love needs no mind, nay, wants none.

She admires a live coal in the fire like a jewel and plucks this ruby from the fire to gift me and adorn me. Lover and loved alike are burned, from playing with what charms the heart but needs a mind. Mother banishes her from me. Her bandaged fingers no more will cradle my blistered head.

I did not cry. But I cry when she comes close, comes close, and cannot hold me. She fears me more than the fire.

Alone, I learn to play alone. My ten fingers, lords and ladies, frolic, antic, bow and curtsey, trip and curvet. Things fall into my cradle I clutch: a trinket, playpretties, the arm off a doll, a flower, spray of mountain laurel, moonbeams and stardust and dust motes. All I can touch I can suck.

Or I learn to lie quietly, watching the plaster fall, learning gravity and the weight of me, my body a stuff, a chunk of flesh, this clod: my head bigger than my trunk, my rays four bent spokes with saps surging noisily through, I hear these humors, and the throb of their pump, my brain is bathed, and keen to all these coursings and hummings, these thrummings and ripples, these burbles and dronings, these stirrings and settlings, these quivers and driftings. This tone and tune and time: I live, I draw the breath of life.

I mire my dydees, and wait a long time to be changed. I've learned it doesn't help to cry.

My father, once, holds me to a mirror in the hall. I know I live; I do not need this proof. But I like the eyes. The outlook from my eyes is more solemn than any of theirs. Solemn and silent. Speech is all I lack. But who will look into my eyes?

When weather's warm, I'm taken out to sun. The laurel

burgeons in the yard. I gaze into the sun, and clamp my eyes. I'm blind to swarming gnats and bright green flies. My swisher's gone up to the well to get a drink. Wings and feelers flick my touchy skin. I am pinked. Aeolus wafts a gust to drive my pests away. The elements care for me. I've found my true kindred. I sleep my first true sleep.

This is all I know of my first year unto heaven.

✦ 2 ✦

Nor did Diana and Day do it that night either. In a tent twelve by twelve, it is possible to position the air mattresses and sleeping bags so that there is a space of at least six feet separating them, and this, because a tent is a condensation of a house, enables you to feel almost as if you have your own room. You could share such a tent without discomposure with your mother-in-law. Or even your grandfather. Diana waited until the gas lantern was extinguished before putting on her pajamas and getting into her sleeping bag. She zipped the bag up snugly, for the night was cool.

From his side of the tent, Day's voice said, "I'm sorry about what I said about the tent. It's a nice tent."

It was. The canvas still smelled too new, but already the smell of it was becoming submerged beneath the smell of the woods and the night air and the mountain laurel.

His voice said, "Tomorrow let's do some archaeology, and see if we can't excavate some remains of the Montross house."

"That would be fun," she said.

"Well, good night, Diana," he said. It was the first time he had called her by name.

"Good night, Day," she answered.

They would sleep a good night for eight hours. Except for a

time, at midnight, when Diana would be awakened by some strange noises outside the tent, they would sleep a good sleep.

And while they slept those eight hours in their tent in Dudleytown, Connecticut, that night of June 21, elsewhere in the country: 3,823 babies were born; 632 old people died, of natural causes; 721 died of heart disease, 310 of cancer, 202 of stroke, 52 in motor vehicle accidents, 27 of cirrhosis of the liver, 21 of suicide; of the latter 11 were by firearms, 5 by poisoning, 3 by hanging, 2 by sleeping pills; firearms also accounted for 17 homicides and 3 accidental deaths.

A family of seven died in a fire in their sleep in Nebraska.

Two carsful of teenagers met head-on on a desert highway in Arizona, killing nine.

In Manhattan, two, in the Bronx, three, in Brooklyn, one, and in Queens, three young drug addicts died of overdoses, infected needles, or other related causes.

In San Francisco, two persons, one male, one female, died as a result of injuries sustained in multiple rapes by multiple persons.

In Beverly Hills, a movie idol died of lung cancer. Elsewhere, sixty-one others died of the same injury.

A father of six, in a Chicago slum, took a last look at the luxury apartments rising across the park, then put away each member of his family by strangulation, himself by hanging.

The inventor of the contrate wheel died in Sandusky, Ohio.

Near Harlan, Kentucky, a G.I. on furlough shot and killed his fiancée and her father, mother and sister.

Nationwide, eighty-nine infants died in childbirth, twenty-two taking their mothers with them.

Twelve babies were born to heroin-addicted mothers; one of them mercifully died at birth; the other eleven babies began immediate painful withdrawal.

A woman in Texas gave birth to quadruplets.

As contrasts, a son was born to a fifty-eight-year-old woman in Pendleton, Oregon, while in Beaufort, South Carolina, a girl was born to an eleven-year-old woman.

There is only one way to come into this world; there are too many ways to leave it.

After breakfast, cooked and eaten amid wood smoke and morning mist and a heavy fallen dew, they began a meticulous search of the mountain laurel glade, hunting for any relics of the Montross house, any vestige of a former abode. All morning they tracked the ground and beat the bushes, without finding anything, until Day declared that he would have to have some sort of shovel.

She invited him to accompany her on the shopping trip, but Day declined, saying that since he had retreated from civilization he had no wish to return to it again so soon. Diana wondered if his real reason was that he was uncomfortable being seen with her in public. She told him she wanted to get him some clothes, and didn't he want to pick them out? No, he did not care what they looked like. With a shrug, she got him to give her his sizes.

He did walk with her the mile to the car, as though she needed an escort in broad daylight. Before she left, he said, "While you're at it, we could use a good axe. A short-handled tomahawk axe will do. And if they have it, see if you can get the kind of folding shovel that also has a pick and mattock on it."

"All right," she said. "Would you like for me to pick up a tape recorder so I can play back for you what *he* says?"

"Where would we plug it in?"

"There are battery models."

"No," he said. "It would seem out of place. Besides, I'll take your word for it, what *he* says."

She drove to Torrington in good time and was able to do her shopping and return to Dudleytown within the space of a couple of hours. The man at Llewellyn's Sporting Goods had been delighted to see her again, and he had asked if everything was going okay in her camp. Then he had asked her where she was camping, but she had answered only, "The woods."

When she returned to camp, her arms laden with packages, Day was not there. She called for him, and waited, then called again, louder. She thought she heard some answer, but it was only a distant echo of her own call. She collapsed into a camp chair and rested for a while, then opened a beer and drank it and waited. She wondered if Day's adolescent instability had gotten the better of him again.

But he came at last. She heard him whistling before she saw him. He came, whistling some snatch from a Beethoven quartet, into the glade, naked to the waist, his shirt swinging from his hand. When he saw her he stopped and began putting his shirt back on.

"Wait," she said. She opened one of her packages and took out a shirt, a bright cotton plaid of yellow and lime green and azure blue. "Here," she said, and gave it to him. He tried to unfold it but it was stuck with pins. He fumbled with the pins, but could not find the right ones to pull out, and the shirt started to twist up. His mother must have opened all his new shirts for him. "Let me," Diana said, and took the shirt back.

When he had his new shirt on, she opened the other packages and showed him what else she had bought for him: four more shirts, two sweaters, two pairs of blue jeans, a pair of dress slacks, a pair of hiking boots, a pair of sandals, a pair of slippers, a bathrobe, bathing trunks, and shorts, undershirts, socks, belts, handkerchiefs. "Gosh," he said. "Merry Christmas."

She gave him the new camp shovel, which, true to his request, had a combination pick and mattock built into it, and he put it right to work, excavating around a pile of rocks enclosed by the mountain laurel shrubs.

He spent the rest of the day digging. She did not know what she could do to help, and as he seemed to be finding nothing she grew tired of watching him, and went to lie in the hammock and read a paperback book she had found on a drugstore rack in Torrington, *Reincarnation for the Millions*, by Susy Smith.

Late in the afternoon he called to her, "Hey, come and look."

She found him up to his knees in a hole he had dug, and around his feet a litter of objects, rusted metal pieces. He held up something which she recognized as the bit from a horse's bridle. The rest of the stuff she did not know.

"Well, it proves there was something here," he said. "Maybe the barn."

"What are all those things?" she asked.

"I don't know," he said, and picked up a large metal object that looked like the sort of semicircular bucket filled with water that garage mechanics use to roll tires in, to hunt for air leaks. "We could find out, though," Day said. "I'll bet *he* would know."

"We'll see," she said, and she put him to sleep and moved him back to one of Daniel Lyam Montross's years in Dudleytown, then told him to open his eyes. Then she asked, "What are you holding in your hands?"

He looked down. "This?" he said. "It's an oil trough, it is."

She asked, "What is an oil trough for?"

He said, "This'un's fer nothing. Too weather-wasted and rust-cankered."

"What would a good new one be for?" she asked.

"Fer greasin' wheels, a course," he said.

"Wagon wheels?" she said. "How do you use it?"

"Jist prop the thimble skein on something and lower the wheel so the felloe's covered, then you roll her slow through."

She thought he said "fellow," and she thought it quaint to refer to a fellow as "her." She asked him about this.

"Felloe," he said. "The felloe's the wood rim a the wheel. Not her nor him but it."

"I see," she said. She pointed at something by the toe of his shoe. "What's that?" she asked.

He picked it up and examined it. "A clevis," he said.

"What's a clevis for?"

"You sure don't know chalk from cheese about wagons, do ye? A clevis is fer hookin' the harness to the whiffletree."

"Whiffletree," she said. "That's a lovely word."

"It is," he agreed, smiling. "Whiffletree's what the wagon says when it's moseying through the grass of the meadow."

"That's nice," she said, and thought to make a game of it. "What else does the wagon say? What are the other parts of the wagon?"

"Wal now," he said, warming to her game, "there's the king bolt. That's what the wagon says when it hits a bump, 'less the bump's a real thank-ye-ma'rm, then the wagon says HAWN! 'Course there's front hawns and there's hind hawns. Hind hawn is what the wagon says if it's a buggy. If the wagon's a sled, it don't hit the bump, but just says *rave!*"

"What's a rave?"

"**Part a the runner on a sled.**"

"Do you have a sled?"

"**You bet ye. A good 'un.**"

"Where is it?" she asked, and realized, too late, it was a perverse question.

He was turning around, searching. "Uh…" he said. "Aw… it's…" He was looking bewildered and hurt. "Aw, jeepers…"

"Never mind," she said. "What is your horse's name?"

"**Got two of 'um. There's Boneyard, and there's Mistress, she's the off horse.**"

"What's an off horse?"

"**Huh? Where do ye hail from, anyhow? Don't ye know the first thing 'bout horses? The off horse's the right one in a span.**"

"Oh. Your horses make a team, is that it? They're not riding horses?"

"**Mistress leaves me ride her, if I want. Boneyard's too spiney. Craunches my witnesses.**"

"Your witnesses? Who are they?"

"**Aw, now, dang, ma'rm…**" He was blushing. "**You and your fool questions.**"

"Oh," she said. Then she asked, "You don't use a saddle?"

"**Can't spare the price a one. Lief as not hitch the wagon, anyhow.**"

"You know all about wagons, do you?"

"**Like a book,**" he said. "**Backwards and forwards, and right down to the ground. The wagon's not been made that will flummox me.**"

"I believe you," she told him. Then she told him to close his eyes and she brought him back to the present and woke him. "What's a whiffletree?" she asked.

"A whiffle-what?" Day said.

"A whiffletree. Think very hard, and tell me what a whiffletree is."

He pondered. "Some kind of hatrack, maybe?" he said.

"Day," she said. "Look me in the eye and swear on your Boy Scout honor that you don't know what a whiffletree is."

"I've heard the name, somewhere," he said. "I just don't remember what it is. I know it's not any kind of tree. Not a *tree* tree, anyway. Maybe something like a shoe tree."

"Have you ever ridden in a wagon?" she asked.

"Well, I went on this hay ride, one time…."

"You told me."

"But it wasn't actually a wagon, just the back of a truck."

She reached for his hand and pulled him out of his hole. "Come here," she said. "I want to read you something." She led him over to the hammock where she had left her paperback book, and she opened it and read him this paragraph:

> One of the things known for sure about hypnosis
> is that some entranced subjects will make every attempt
> to please the hypnotist, and often carry out what is
> expected of them. The hypnotist's own beliefs about
> what he is doing, the tone of his voice, his manner, and
> his mode or procedure cause the subject to enact faith-
> fully the role thereby handed to him. This is then taken
> by the hypnotist as evidence confirming the correctness
> of his original belief. Because this is true, age regression
> is complicated, and past life regression is problematical,
> to say the least.

Day took the book from her and looked at its cover with disdain. "Where did you get this?" he asked.

"I found it in a drugstore in Torrington," she said.

"'*Reincarnation for the Millions*,'" he quoted its title with a slur. "An appropriate title. For amateurs. And look at this picture on the cover. Like a flying saucer."

"I just thought I'd like to read something on the subject," Diana protested.

"I could give you a bibliography of more respectable volumes," he said. "But what you just read is, in fact, the truth. It's the major defect in hypnosis. The hypnotized person—not *all* of them, mind you, but a lot—will say what he thinks the hypnotist *wants* him to say. Like a Pavlovian dog. If the hypnotist thinks his subject is the reincarnation of George Washington, the subject is going to do his best to please the hypnotist and sustain him in that belief."

"But how can you *lie* under hypnosis?"

"It isn't exactly lying. Have you ever seen a stage hypnotist performing? If you hypnotize me and tell me I'm the world's greatest violinist, even if both my arms are gone, I am going to stand up and do a virtuoso pantomime of a violinist."

"But you couldn't do something you didn't know how to do. If I gave you a real violin and told you to play it, you wouldn't sound like the world's greatest."

"Probably not. Or not to you. But to myself I would. *I* am the one who is deluded."

"But I still don't understand how you could know something you didn't know. I mean, like just now when you were hypnotized, you mentioned all these words—whiffletree and clevis and hawn and I forget what all   parts of wagons—so how would you know these words if you didn't know anything about wagons?"

Day shrugged. "I could have been reading your mind," he suggested.

"But I don't know these words myself!"

"Well, have you ever heard of what they call 'genetic memory'?" he asked. "Maybe there's something in each of us that knows everything."

She frowned. "You sound like you're trying to eliminate Daniel Lyam Montross."

He laughed. "If he *can* be eliminated, then he doesn't exist. If he exists, then he *can't* be eliminated. You know something? I *would* eliminate him if I could. Sure I would. Sometimes I've wanted to kill him. But I don't think I can...short of killing myself, of course."

Oh, I am, I am. If I were not, who then would I be? Would I were another, would I were even you, but there is not a pin to choose. I am what I be, and I be what I am. Who else would be me?

Who else would choose Castroline, four spoons daily after feeding? Emulsion of Norwegian cod liver oil? Who else would choose worm syrup, would choose my worms? Even if once she fooled me with worm cake instead, saying it was candy. Paregoric? Laudanum? And that sham of shams, Lactopreparata? Who would choose spirits of nitre? These bitter draughts she doses me with, in the stead of milk.

I drool chemicals when I drool. At one I'm weaned, the way they do it: suddenly and completely, to "cry it out." Notwithstanding she has broken five and one-half infants before me in this way, my mother twinges at the size of my crying. All these draughts I take dope not my guts but her guilt. My worm medicine is for her wormy heart.

Early I learn to walk, as if to get away. Soon I learn to run, as if to get away sooner. The white dimity dress of my first year has been changed for one of pale blue chambray, the easier to clean, and for me the easier to run in and fall in.

It's queer about the twigs and pebbles of the ground: if I walk slowly on them my bare feet hurt like time, but if I run, scorning them, pounding upon them as with the pads of a rabbit, they never hurt at all. I run, I run.

My fears are small. The dark does not scare me, nor the woods. Animals do not frighten, except those I imagine, which are not, which I create only to frighten me because there is a need of it. Why is this need? All that's to fear is fate, which is not seen. Fate takes seen form in the things I imagine: I denizen the skirts of Dudleytown with tigers and lions, leopards and crocodiles. They never get me but I know they're there. Fate waits, luck lurks, destiny rests in ambush.

One thing I fear that's real: one day unseen I follow my

father to work at the sawmill. I have heard this screaming before, but imagined it the death throes of those fate-beasts being slain by others. I find it is the screaming of the tree, the tree screaming as the great sawblade whirls whirring through it. Before, I did not know that trees could feel. In pity I wail my heart out. My father sees me now, and yells something at the other men, and they stop the saw. They look at me and laugh. My father sends me home. They do not wait until I'm gone before they start the saw again. On the road home I stop to hug a tree. *Oh, tree!*

Tonight I dream bad dreams. My father wakes me. His great heavy hand on my hair: "Scairt, little feller? Wha'sa matter 'ith ye, lad?"

"Saw cut me open."

"Saw don't never cut folks. Jist timber."

"Hurts. Timber hurts."

"Thunder no, boy. Timber don't feel nothing."

"Heard it scream."

"That wa'nt the timber. That were the saw. Nothing but the metal a the sawblade, made that. Why, if timber could try and talk, it'd jist say how happy 'tis, being squared inter nice lumber."

"How come? Then it's *dead*."

Scratches his hair. Scratches mine. "Not at all, son. Jist changes fer the better. Tree standing in the woods, it aint good fer but shade and birdroost. Don't live very long, even if it aint hit by wind or lightning. But you take a tree and make good charcoal outen it, and that charcoal helps 'em make iron in the furnace, and *iron*, boy, it lives forever."

"Don't like iron."

"Well, never ye mind, jist now. You get to sleep and hush your tossin' and turnin'. Your poor mother's got dyspepsy, and neuralgy on top of it, and you're keepin' her awake. Now shut them eyes and drop off the deep end."

His great heavy hand presses my head into the pillow and holds it down a while, then lifts, I am lightened, and he is gone.

But the trees redeem, they redeem! Day unto week I watch them do it. By their own law, nature's unwritten writ of replevin, they take back what was theirs. Even if their numbers are sacrificed to the making of iron, they will outlast all iron. My father is wrong. The trees deceive him. They will outwait and outwit their users. Already the alders are reclaiming half of Parmenter's meadow; though he curses them and cuts them, soon they will have it all. Alders breed faster than rabbits. I see a litter which wasn't there yesterday.

I hear the men talk, I listen to their idle grousings. The news is that the Mount Riga ironworks in Salisbury, closed since '47 may never reopen, and the Sharon works may soon shut down. This is the beautiful irony of iron: that the furnace of Mount Riga helped make the iron horse, and the iron horse made Mount Riga extinct. Dudleytown's own furnace, down at The Bridge, where the railroad runs, may soon go. The men talk of selling their charcoal for common stove fuel, a disgrace.

The men talk about "this biggity Britisher, Bessemer," who has found a way to make steel out of pig iron, and to use cheaper ore, at that. The men have a favorite thing they say, each of them, every day: What is the world coming to?

The world comes, for me, to these lairs and aeries that are my range: my lodges in bushes and beneath the house, my nests in certain trees that let me climb them. These are my diggings, my restings and roostings: my theatres and gymnasia: my courts and pleasances: I will do what I like here. Or I will do nothing at all.

Or I will do nothing at all: I will just sit here in the half-dark and stillness. And when they call to me, if I do not wish to I will make no answer. And when they come close and speak to me I will make like I am not here. If any or all of them tell me that dinner is ready I will not be hungry. I will say they cannot if they say they can see me.

I will just sit here in the half-dark and stillness. When they say it is time for my naptime, I will make like I am napping. I will say nothing. I will say they are wrong if they say I am sickening. If they bring spoons and bottles I will clamp my lips tight. If they force my lips open, I will not swallow but spit later. Because I am me and no one else will be me, I will be what I wish, for I have to. I will not eat my turnips, neither my greens. If they say this will make me spindly and pindling, then I will wither and waste to nothing and become a wisp, drifting on air too high and far for them to reach.

If I choose, I will just do nothing. In the half-dark and stillness I will just sit here.

My father yawps: "You shinny down outen that tree 'fore I let loose on ye, you little dickens!"

I climb to a higher limb.

"I'll give ye a dose a strap oil!" he bellows. "Light down outen there, you devil!"

I climb to a higher limb.

"Get your little tail back down here!" he yells. "I'll clobber ye silly, you brat!"

I climb to a higher limb.

"Want I should come up arter ye?" he shouts. "Don't think I won't! If I have to climb up there, I'll truly thrash the sauce outen ye!"

I climb as high as I can go. It is an old chestnut, high as time, and I'm near the top. He can't even see me, though I can see him: he leaps for the lowest limb and grabs hold but cannot pull himself up. He twists and dangles and says terrible bad words. He yells: "How'd ye get up there, anyhow?" He drops back to the ground and goes toward the barn. I think he has given up, and I start to climb down, but then he comes back, bringing a ladder. "Wal now," he says, "jist let me get my hands on you." He climbs and climbs.

Can I fly? Oh, I've had dreams of flying! I dream full many a time of taking the air! The air is easy to take: you just take it into your arms and climb over it, kicking your feet. Slow it is, and thick, but lighter than a leaf, down, lighter than a fluff of seed puff, up. Up.

He's climbed as high as he can go. His hand gropes up for my limb and my ankle.

I take the air.

Oh, I soar! Oh lovely I mount the air and drift there one lovely instant, hovering free. But then I fall. The air denies me. Down, down I plunge, through branches, the hard earth waiting.

I ask the tree to save me. And she does. Her lowest arm she puts beneath me, and when I hit it it bends gently with me and stops me, and I hold it. It lowers me slowly to the ground.

I stand a moment, getting back my wits, and then I run, leaving my father in the tree. He is yelling, "Wal I'll be hanged!"

$$\text{✝ 4 ✝}$$

Her third day in Dudleytown, Diana began to keep a diary, of sorts. More a journal in some respects, more an annals in others, it was casual; she did not intend to keep it faithfully and regularly. It was something to do, when she felt like it. It was something, she realized, with long foresight, which she could read again in her old age, when there are no longer any adventures.

These are her first entries:

June 23

Today we found that chestnut tree, the one he supposedly climbed and jumped out of. It was dead, it had been dead a long time (Day says a "blight" killed every chestnut in the country back in the early part of the century) but it was still standing.

It looks like it will stand a long time. Its limbs are mostly gone, the limb that caught him is gone, but the sturdy trunk endures.

Dead a long time but still *here*.

I had to explain the significance of the tree to Day. He choked up. There is something curiously similar between his love of trees and *his* love of trees. Suspicious too. They aren't *supposed* to be alike.

Big question: is Day projecting into the "other" parts of himself, or, if this is for real, is the "other" somehow shaping Day?

We had an imu for supper. He began preparing the imu early in the afternoon and condescended to explain it to me: he dug a hole and lined it with rocks, then built a fire in the hole and let it burn down to hot coals, then shoveled the coals out, and took a whole chicken and some potatoes and carrots and wrapped them in wet leaves and put them on the bed of hot rocks in the pit, shoveling the coals back in on top, and covering the pit with dirt.

He left it, his imu, like that for 3 or 4 hours, while we went off exploring. Then at suppertime he just dug it up and we ate it. I've never tasted better chicken.

I'm going to learn to do these things myself. He does so much, I ought to do the cooking.

Oh, and I nearly forgot, the eggs at breakfast, the way he did them, poached them or coddled them or whatever: after we had eaten our oranges, in halves, he broke an egg into each half-orange shell and laid them directly onto the fire coals for about 10 minutes. Delicious! and just faintly tasting of orange.

I wonder how much of all this he learned from his Scout handbooks, and how much he learned from Daniel.

Daniel, at the age of 4 or 5, ran away from home, after getting out of that chestnut tree, and was lost for nearly 24 hours. Of course, when they found him, they gave him a severe beating.

June 24

Our temperatures are about the same. Which is to say that both of us are more on the cool side. I don't have much energy, and here in the woods with this idleness I would seem indolent to anyone but Day, whose temperature is as slow and cool as mine.

Daniel, on the other hand, seems to have the highest temperature possible. Today I felt his pulse, and timed it, and then afterwards when he was just Day again I felt Day's pulse and timed it. Results Daniel, 110; Day, 75. But maybe it's only because Daniel is still only a child and children have higher pulses.

Yet everything he says has a higher pulse. Day's words just trickle out. Daniel's *erupt*. It makes me understand that old-fashioned word referring to speech, "ejaculate." I used to be confused or embarrassed, in reading old novels, to come across "He ejaculated," or, worse, "*She* ejaculated."

Today we found the location of Bardwell's store on Dark Entry Road. Every Sunday afternoon Daniel got a penny from his father; his older sisters each got two pennies; his brothers, three. They went to Bardwell's store, the only store in Dudleytown, and bought candy. It is one of Daniel's favorite places. He is sorry about all the things in the store which he can never afford to buy, but he has so much fun standing in front of the glass showcase and trying to decide which candy he will spend his penny on.

There is no trace of the store now except its stone steps, leading up into air.

Wild greens for supper, and a kabob on a spit pit: the spit a long green stick strung with lamb chunks, onions, peppers, tomatoes and mushrooms, turned slowly over a pit of coals. It took Day two beers to finish his share of it. He was almost a little tipsy.

June 25

Occasionally, but not terribly often, I have to justify all this for myself. The past couple of days I've found myself wondering, Am I doing my own thing? But it doesn't bother me. The answer is always yes. I might be lazy, but I am never incurious or indifferent.

Daniel fascinates me. I want to learn as much about him as I can. Over Day's mild protests, I bought a tape recorder, and I'm recording on tape everything he says, his whole life from beginning to…how long will this take? At this rate, months, maybe. But it is a fascinating life, at least the way he tells it. It is a life I could never imagine, and sometimes I find it nearly impossible to believe that Day could imagine it either.

But there is always that suspicion. Last night I did some gazing at the stars. Exposed to them, on a clear night, to the zillions of them, I just gazed at them for a long time, until bedtime. I felt the way I always do, gazing at the night sky: the sense of personal insignificance. Stars die. Even stars. When a thing on puny earth dies, it is dead. For good. Isn't reincarnation a preposterously vain and arrogant dream, a selfish foolish delusion?

Well, isn't it?

Today we found the site of the schoolhouse, south up Dudleytown Road, very near the place where I've been parking the car. Nothing there, of course, although Day excavated a funny little tin contraption, like a telescope, which Daniel later identified as a collapsible drinking cup. Why collapsible? So it would fit into the child's lunchbox.

The teacher's name is Abigal Fife. Now *that* certainly sounds like a made-up name. I pretended I was Miss Fife, and followed Daniel through his daily school routines. Apparently he is the only child in his grade. Whether he was the last child born in Dudleytown is not known; at any rate he was apparently the only child born that year, and the only one in the first grade.

For supper, four small poached trout, which Day claims he caught in Bonny Brook with grubs baited on a hook fashioned from chicken bones. I didn't see him do it but I believe him because how else could he have got them? (I ribbed him about not having a Connecticut fishing license.)

Hot rocks have it all over Teflon as a cooking surface. We honored the fish with a domestic white wine, a Pinot Chardonnay from California. I explained to Day the niceties about white wine with white meat and red with red. I believe he is beginning to appreciate wine.

June 26

Intruders today! I heard them while Daniel was talking and had to bring Day back. We listened. Voices from the woods in the distance. They did not come any closer, and we didn't go to investigate; whoever it was has as much right to be here as we do, I suppose, but I couldn't help resenting them. There was laughter from time to time. Later, after a few hours, the voices went away. We went and found their encampment or picnic spot or whatever you could call it: near the Caleb Jones cellar hole they had built a small clumsy fire and roasted hot dogs and marshmallows, leaving behind their considerable litter of napkins, and paper plates with imitation walnut grain printed on one side. Day demonstrated that he actually knows some strong curse words.

But it is Saturday, and this was the first time anyone has been here but us, and we did not see them nor they us.

I asked Daniel to tell me what he looks like, at the age of seven, but it was hard for him to do. I pretended I was Miss Fife again and his "assignment" was to describe himself without looking in a mirror. He has long dark bushy hair (Day's is short and light brown), that's about all of interest I could determine. And he wears short pants.

I asked him to locate the church or meeting house but apparently there isn't one and never has been. That seems strange, because it had been a town of religious people, Puritans in the beginning, later Congregationalists. Daniel doesn't go to church. But every night at bedtime he says the "Now I lay me" prayer, ending with, "And God bless Papa and Mama and Charity and Emmeline" and all his brothers and relations and friends. "Friends." That's funny. He has none. None his own age.

The menu this evening: just plain old ordinary prime porterhouse steaks! Grilled on charcoal which he made himself. Steaks black on the outside, bright pink inside. With a bottle of Chateauneuf-du-Pape. For dessert: wild strawberries. It took us nearly two hours this morning to find and pick less than a quart of them, but it was worth it.

June 27

More visitors. Seen this time, as well as heard. Dudleytown was uncomfortably overpopulated today. Sunday traffic. A man and his wife, middle-aged, with back-packs, who had apparently been hiking on the Appalachian Trail, detoured through our glade this morning and paused to ogle us. The man scowled as if in disapproval of our obvious sinning, and started to say or ask something, but his wife tugged him on. This afternoon two boys in a jeep came driving up, stopped, backed, and over the roar of the jeep's motor they tried to make conversation, but I couldn't hear them. They were Day's age, I guess. They smirked and leered at me, and nudged one another, then drove away laughing. Day gave evidence that at some time in his life he must have overheard some sailors swearing. Or maybe Daniel taught him those words.

Still later this afternoon another group of Appalachian Trail hikers, five altogether, of various ages but wearing identical red-white-and-blue nylon back-packs, came through our glade. One of them stopped to ask me if I didn't know that this was a haunted ghost town we were camping in. I said I knew it was a ghost town but we have been here nearly a week without being haunted. "Nervy," was all he said before moving on.

I was beginning to feel paranoiac, with all these people coming into our glade, so we went for a walk, just to get away. But on the Dudleytown Road we met a whole family on an outing. First we saw the boys, throwing rocks at something in the woods and generally raising hell, fat little brats. Then the fat father, who looked like a plumber or a cook or something, carrying a fat baby, and the very very fat mother, puffing. Politely we said "Hello" as they passed, but they only stared at us, as if we were strange specimens of wildlife and this their first trip to the woods.

For supper tonight he agreed to let me do the cooking. I did the one thing I've had some experience with: spaghetti. I did it nicely, too, but somehow the meal seemed out of place, not a woods thing.

Guess what, dear diary. Romance! Tonight he held my hand.

✝ 5 ✝

Girl. Why's a girl? I have seen Charity and Emmeline. Why the bare groin? Both are blank there. A congenital defect? But Reuben Temple says they all of them are. Rube's a year older than me, but I tore it out of him when he tried to tell me how I was born. Laced his jacket, I did, and sent him bawling home. Nobody can say things like that about my mother and father.

Still I studied it, afterwards, and I bethought me: maybe he was right. I have never seen a stork. I have watched, and once I saw a bird, but it was some kind of crane, not a stork. We come from God, but how? I don't believe in angels either.

I guess I thrashed poor Reuben because he told a truth I didn't want to hear. As if you know, because of the thunderheads, that a storm is coming, but still you stay out, and when the storm hits you it seems a surprise.

They tease me in school, that I do not have a girl. All the others, olders, have a girl. Felicia is Jonathan's girl. Alvina is Hector's girl. Violate is Renz's girl. My own sister Charity is Seth's girl, even if she doesn't know it because she doesn't know anything. What do you do to have a girl?

> *Danny, Danny, little manny*
> *Pink ears and purple fanny*
> *Never had a girl but Granny*
> *Never can he, never, can he?*

is what the boys chant, ringing round me but keeping their distance because if they come near I will clobber them. I am not little, my ears and rear are neither pink nor purple, and both my grandmothers returned to dust 'ere I was born. All taunts are false and unfair.

And I would have a girl if there was one. But all are older, and taken.

Yet now there is one who, though taken, and though older, seems to decide to become mine. It is all in sport, of course, or seems to be, the way this afternoon when school is over she comes and sits upon my desk, the others around her, behind her, and she rumples my hair with her hand and smiles, and says to the others, "I'm going to be Danny's girl."

The others titter and giggle; this makes me think she is just joshing, but she says to them, "I mean it. I am."

She must be two or more years older than me, though she's not any bigger. Her name is Hattie Rose Pearl Bardwell, least daughter of Storekeeper Bardwell. Nobody calls her just Hattie, because Miss Fife doesn't. Miss Fife always calls her Hattie Rose Pearl.

"Hattie Rose Pearl," I say, "you leave me be." She is too old to be my girl, past eleven at least. But she's a pretty one, I have to say.

"Oh, Danny," she says, and rumples my hair some more, then she sits beside me at my desk and puts one arm around me. "I want to share your desk," she says. Nobody shares my desk; all the other desks are shared, two and two; not mine. I've never had a deskmate.

"You're Zadock's girl," I remind her.

"No more, I'm not," she says. The others are still tittering. "Miss Fife won't let you share my desk," I say.

"She will if I ask her pretty-like."

Close as she is, her girl-scent is a new thing to me, and rife, and sweet, even her hair, like mowings.

Girl. Why's a girl? Her arm around me tightens, hugs.

My face is hot as time, my tongue frozen.

When the others keep tittering, she says, "Scat!" to them and hugs me even tighter as if to protect. "Danny's my boy. Have off!" They leave us. The schoolhouse is empty but for us. It's even harder to be alone with her. I fidget.

"Put your arm around me," she says, "and I'll be your girl."

"I have to go and do my chores."

"Not yet you don't."

"I do."

"I'll walk you home."

Outside in the schoolyard the others are still waiting, even Zadock, whose girl she is, who makes a lip. He's big enough to eat me up. He doesn't join the others, who join hands and ring round us, singing

> *Danny, manny, little squirrel*
> *Got himself a pretty girl*
> *Hattie's Danny's rose and pearl*
> *Dance her, Danny, with a whirl.*

I do not dance her but run. One thing at least, I'm the fastest runner in the school. I outrun them all. Except her. She hangs on my heels, until all the others have dropped back. I'm nearly home. Still I run, until I've reached the marsh path to my yard. Here I stop for breath, and here she catches up with me and, panting, asks, "Don't you like me?"

I, panting, accuse her, "You are only trying to make Zadock jealous."

"No," she says. "I truly want to be your girl."

"Why?" I ask. "Why me?"

"Because you don't have one."

"Then Zadock won't have one."

"Yes he will. He's after Felicia."

"I don't know as what I need a girl."

"If I'm your girl, I can snitch you some candy from Papa's store."

Now this sounds to be the square thing. A toothy lure. But what's my end of the deal? What does having a girl require? Why's a girl? I've never had one. I'm only nine.

My breath is back, I'm not panting but just unsteady: "Well, if you want to."

My chores can wait. We walk together to her father's store. She asks me what's my favorite? Jujubes, I tell her. She has me wait outside while she goes in. She returns, later, empty-handed. I am disappointed. We walk on back toward my house. But where the road goes into the woods, she draws me into the woods, behind a screen of cedars. She lifts the hem of her dress high, I see the length of her pantaletted legs. From beneath her dress she takes out a whole paper bag of jujubes. We laugh and share them, one by one.

She walks me on home. Our swinging arms brush, our hands touch, then hold. Shivers shive me. The holding of hands's a thing of wonder. Trees hold hands. I've never, except in play. A hand's a nice thing. Animals don't have them. All the pads of her palm cup and suck the pads of mine. A hand is for holding.

I have a girl.

✢ 6 ✢

Then there were certain matters which she did not record in her diary.

Diana slept well every night. With the exception of a few occasions, early on, when she was not accustomed to the normal woods noises of the night and had awakened in fear at the strange sounds (once, investigating with the flashlight, she discovered it was merely a raccoon trying to break into their food chest), she generally slept better than she ever had. The combination of the fresh and fragrant night air, the comfort of the air mattress and sleeping bag, in short, the sheer *relaxation* of the whole situation, made her nights deeply restful.

But Day, on the other hand, was a fitful sleeper, every night flouncing around on his air mattress, groaning in his sleep and occasionally even grinding his teeth. She supposed it was because he was "possessed." Once, after a particularly rough night, when he appeared haggard and sleepless at breakfast, she asked him about it. He told her that he had just been through "a double-feature nightmare." She asked him if the dream involved Daniel Lyam Montross. No, Day said, it had nothing to do with him. Well, she had asked, who was in it, then? His mother? His father? Anybody he recognized? "Just you," he said.

For all her intelligence, Diana was embarrassingly slow in coming to grasp or guess the possible source of Day's affliction.

One night, after she had easily dropped off to sleep, she came awake again—or rather her eyes snapped open, not to any sound or audible disturbance—she wondered later what in fact had actually wakened her—her own dream? or a telepathic summons or something?—her eyes came open and saw, in the dim light that a crescent moon cast through one of the mesh windows of the tent, Day lying face down upon his bag and mattress, seeming to embrace them, his pajamas removed, his pelvis writhing. He made no sound but he was violent. She nearly spoke, but didn't. Finally he stopped, sighed, then seemed to go to sleep. She was not even certain that he had been awake. The next day, while he was away fishing, out of curiosity she investigated his sleeping bag, and found starched places on it.

It was the evening of that day that he had held her hand. It had been spontaneous, apparently; they were sitting with their chairs side by side before the campfire, in the early dark, some time after she had been listening to Daniel telling of his first "girl," Hattie Rose Pearl. Day's arm and Diana's arm were close, on the arms of their chairs, and their hands suddenly touched then clasped; she wasn't certain which of them had instigated it; perhaps it was simultaneous; she had been thinking about it.

They merely sat for a long while, in silence, holding hands. Several times she came extremely close to blurting out, "Day, would you like to make love?" She even considered being more matter-of-fact or even blunt about it, and saying, "You can screw me if you want to." But she just couldn't. And even if she could, could he?

She tried to rationalize her way into it by thinking, *It's bound to happen sooner or later.* But was it?

We aren't here on a date, she reminded herself. We are explorers, not lovers. And besides, after all, he was three years younger, more like a kid brother.

And then of course the biggest hitch of all: he could be her grandfather. That would be incest, wouldn't it?

But these were all excuses, she realized. Then what was her real reason?

If he asked me, I would. Or if he even made the first move. There. That was it. There was only one man she had been to bed with, and she had practically asked him; that is, she had pursued him, played upon his vanity as teacher and writer, made herself available, schemed and plotted, and then, when it finally happened, she didn't think it was particularly enjoyable. At least not very satisfying. Not the kind of thing the books made it out to be. She was nagged by the suspicion that it would have been better if she had not been aggressive, if she had waited and let the man court her.

Would Day ever ask her? Or make the right move? She hoped, when they held hands, that it would lead to something. But it didn't. Later, when they were getting into their sleeping bags, she nearly forgot her resolve again and decided to go ahead and make the first move, to get into his bag with him. But she didn't. She couldn't.

Now here comes the one incident she would never, could never, record in her diary: the next day, in the afternoon, once when he went off to "use the woods," she impishly and stealthily followed him, to spy on him. Out of simple curiosity? Or out of some unformulated suspicion? He sometimes seemed to take an inordinately long time when he went to use the woods. At a distance she hid behind the mountain laurel and spied. She almost gave herself away stifling a giggle at the sight of him peeing. He spouted a thick stream; that must be the beer he had for lunch. She thought she was going to choke trying to swallow her giggle when he was finished and was shaking it. Then he began doing something that made her cover her eyes with both hands. But then she had to peek through her fingers. She could not help herself. She had to watch. Once she had tried to imagine how boys did it, but couldn't quite. So this was it: the fist, the fist as surrogate.

Now this is what she would never be able to put into her diary: this is the strange thing: for a while, watching him through the fingers of her hands that covered her face, she was partly fascinated but mostly just embarrassed and ashamed of herself for watching. But then suddenly she realized that she was becoming very much aroused. She was breathing very hard. *I'm no voyeur, damn it!* she tried to tell herself, trying to fight it. But there it was: this passion coming on her in sight of his passion.

"Save that for me!" she almost called out, but didn't. If he saw her he would die. If he saw her she would die. Sharply she inhaled and the waistband of her jeans slackened; she thrust her hand down inside, and did what he was doing, not his way but hers. If he sees me I will die.

His eyes were closed; was he thinking of her? She closed her eyes and thought of him. But then she had to open her eyes and look at him again.

This would have been pretty, if she could have brought herself to record this in her diary: "We had simultaneous orgasms."

Then she ran away, and kept running. She felt terrible. She

had never had any problems before, but *this*.... When she was twelve she read in a book that everybody does it, so it never bothered her. But *this*.... She was both ashamed to face Day again and angry with him. Damn him, why did he waste it on himself? Why couldn't he get up his nerve and ask her? Maybe he didn't even like her. Maybe he wasn't attracted to her. Now she felt rejected, as well as ashamed, and she kept running.

She ran all the way to her car. Possibly, when she started the motor and backed out into the road, she fully intended to get out for good and keep going, and certainly the way she scraped hell out of the car's underside driving over the rough road would have indicated this haste and determination, but after she was out of Dudleytown and on the highway she had cooled down a bit and realized that she only wanted to restock their supplies. The food was nearly gone, they had had the last of the beer with lunch, the ice had long since melted.

But still, when she returned to Dudleytown again, she couldn't face Day. All by herself she portaged all of the new groceries from the car to camp, without trying to find him and ask him to help. She even lugged two fifty-pound blocks of ice, one by one, the long distance into camp. She worked up a good sweat doing it, and took a long bath in the pool at the falls. This time the icy waters didn't bother her in the slightest.

When she finally saw Day again, at suppertime, she couldn't look at him. She busied herself with preparing supper and didn't look at him. They ate supper without looking at each other.

Finally he asked, "Is something wrong?"

She looked up and looked into his eyes for the first time, but then looked away again.

He kept looking at her, and she thought she might have detected in his eyes some glint of...of something. It couldn't be possible that he had known she was watching him.

She couldn't look at him. And she didn't want his eyes on her. "Go to sleep, Day," she said.

⚕ 7 ⚕

Violate's her name. Without disregard. Is what her people called her. Prettier, in sound, than Violet. No transgression nor harm meant in it. We're some kin, her ma a cousin of my ma, and I've known her since I was old enough to know. But it is late in my eleventh year now before I come to know her well.

The older boys tattle about her. This summer they have let me into their club. It's called "The Oatsowers," they haven't told me why. They will. I had to do some things to be let in. Then with pokeberry ink they dyed my perkin reddish purple and it still hasn't come off and I wonder when it will. Then I was told I would have to collect a lock of hair from Hattie Rose Pearl, and I did, but they told me that wasn't the hair that was meant, and told me what was meant, and Zadock who's in the club too told me he would kill me if I did, and I didn't know what to do. But I wanted to be let in the club, so once I asked her if she had hair there, and she said not much but some, and I asked could I have a lock and she slapped me, but later she said she'd misunderstood me and thought I'd asked to have a look instead of a lock and she'd been thinking about it and decided I could have a look and a lock both if I'd do the same for her, but I didn't want to because I was dyed with the pokeberry ink.

What would she think? But I wanted in the club. So I did. And I got a snip of a curl of a lock of her hair there, but when she saw mine covered with the reddish purple pokeberry ink she shrieked and ran, and isn't my girl any longer, and then when I took the snip to the club I got in a fight with Zadock and he nearly killed me but I got in a few mean licks on him too and he decided to let me live. Then the last thing I had to do was drop my trousers and stand and keep the stand hard without touching it for one half of an hour while Seth timed it on his pocketwatch.

Now I am in the club. The club is for secrets and mysteries, and for finding out things. For watching bulls and stallions do it, and even roosters. For showing off and measuring. Renz has the longest, twice at least the size of mine. But I'm bigger than Reuben and Seth, and twice at least the size of Jonathan, though I'm the youngest.

We have to tattle on our girls. Since Hattie Rose Pearl is Zadock's girl again he has to tattle on her, but we don't believe him, the things he's claimed to've done with her. She told me once she knows that babies come through the navel. Since I have no girl now I have to tattle on my sisters. I have seen Charity embrace a tree.

It is Renz who tattles on Violate. He brags they were but seven the first time he drove his perkin through her vale. The others have large eyes and open mouths when they listen to him tell this, and they believe him. At seven, he says. And then at eight, several times. At nine, often. All these were dry. The first wet funicle was at ten, and, he says, it gave him a turn, struck him all of a heap, he thought he'd bursted a vein or thew.

What is this wet? Dearly I would I knew. Once I thought it was only tinkle, and some others did too, Reuben's brag is of a peefunicle with his girl. But we are wrong.

Wetness is each and every. The maple tapped in March seeps its sap. The pine oozes resin. The earth itself pours out its water through its springs. The spider spews a sticky strand. Grab a grasshopper and he'll burb a bubble of tobacco juice. The dew at night is the weeping of the stars. My eyes weep. My nose runs. My sisters have their monthly courses. Cows milk. Snow melts. The fish milts, or roes, in spawning. All is burble and surge, and spurtle and spume, and steep and jet, and dissolving and flowing.

My witnesses are a pair of pools, and heavy, I fathom that. Round reservoirs. Wetness in my witness. But how draught them off? I'll ask at the club.

My chance comes. "Renz," I say, "what is it that makes the wet? I mean, when you're he-ing and she-ing, like you told, how come it comes out? Do you have to grunt and bear down or what?"

Renz twinkles at the eye. He pops my shoulder and says, "Why, aint you ever drew water up a pump? Same principle. Just work the pump handle up and down. Like so." He makes a grab, as if at a pump handle, and raises it and lowers it.

As soon as I'm alone, I try it. It's awkward, pumping the handle of yourself, you have to turn your hand around or else your elbow's in the way. I pump and wait, anxioused up, wondering what it will be like when the wet comes. But nothing comes. I pump a bit harder. It's stiff and hard to bend down; on the downstroke it pains me some. But I keep on. For nigh on to an hour before I quit.

At the next meeting of the club, I say, "Renz, you tole one. It don't work. You were just pulling one over me."

He laughs, and says, "Why, did you try it on yourself?"

"I did," I say, "and not a thing come of it."

Some of the others are laughing too, and this makes me think that Renz is making a fool of me.

"Don't you know," says Renz, "that a pump won't draw before it's been primed? You aint been primed yet."

"How do you get primed?" I ask.

"That's what a girl's for," he says.

This is how I come to get in over my head with Violate.

I think they've put her up to it. But I can't be all too sure. How did she know I was in the corn? I am in the corn, high of midsummer, just lying on my back and watching the clouds break up into white wisps on the blue. But lately pretty nearly everything I see makes me think of he-ing and she-ing, and the way pieces of corners of clouds break and tear away is like the wet in my witnesses wanting to pull loose and get out. And above my head the corn has tasseled, and I am tasseled, and the tassels spill their pollen on the waiting silky silks. I stroke a silk and it reminds me of the lock from Hattie Rose Pearl.

The corn is high and I am deep into it; I don't know how she finds me, even if she was looking for me. It might be an accident. "Oh, hello, Danny!" she says, nearly tripping over me. "Dear me suz, what are you doing here?"

"It's Pa's cornpatch," I say. "Can't I set in it if I've a mind to? What are you doing here?"

"Oh, I'm just gadding about," she says. "Such a fine afternoon," she says. Then she kneels and says, "I'll just set with you, I will."

She does. I don't gainsay her. She's my cousin, and she's two, maybe three, years older. But she's a girl.

She is looking me up and down and all over, as if she's never seen me before. Maybe she hasn't, in a way. "My, you're getting to be withy and big," she says, as if she's not noticed before. "And you're not even twelve yet, are you?"

"Will be soon," I declare.

"I hear you're in the club now," she says.

"Yup," I say, not trying to sound too self-proud.

"We have a club too," she declares.

"I know it," I say, and I do. The girls call themselves the SS, which I think stands for Secret Society. A pink hair ribbon is the badge, and Violate is wearing hers.

"And," she says, with a kind of a leer, "Hattie Rose Pearl told what you did."'

"I was bounden," I tell her. "The club obliged me to do it."

"Also," she says, "Hattie Rose Pearl told that your perkin is purple as a plum."

God rot that Hattie Rose Pearl! Now my face must be purple as a plum. "That...that's the club's doing, too," I say. "They did it. It's not but pokeberry stain, is all it is."

She smiles. She says, low and quiet, "Let me see."

Damn me if I will. I've already frightened one girl off, showing it, I'm not going to scare another. "It's not fit to be seen," I say.

She pouts. "You're just afraid to show me."

"No, I'm not, neither. I'd show you if the stain was off."

"I'll wager it's bonny and sightly, even with the stain."

I shake my head.

"I'm not squeamish like Hattie Rose Pearl," she says. She puts her hand on my leg, up on the upper part. I have never had a girl's hand on my leg. Hattie Rose Pearl never did that. It is as if she is showing me that she's not like Hattie Rose Pearl. Now she says something else, too: "I'll do anything you want me to, if you'll show me."

Will you prime my pump for me? I nearly ask, but she might think that's too forward. Instead I say, "Fair enough." Then I show her. I watch her face closely. She does not blanch. Her eyes glitter and her mouth beams. "See?" I say. "All over it's purple."

"No," she says. "Violet. Like my name." She laughs. "They've made it violet for Violate!" She gives me a hug. My violet starts rising. She looks at it again. "It won't come off?" she says. She wipes her fingertips across her mouth and dabs at my violet, as if to rub it off. It won't rub off, but the stroke of her fingers gives me a quick stiff stand. "Good heavens!" she says, and leaps back a little, as if from a snake. Then she asks, "Is that for me too?" And then she asks, "Danny, have you ever been primed?"

Now this is when I begin to smell a dinge in the stovewood; this is when I hunch that maybe they've put her up to something. But the trouble is, I don't care. I'm too excited. I shake my head.

"Do you want I should prime you?" she says.

I nod, I nod.

"All right," she says. "Just lie back down." I lie back down 'twixt the corn rows, and she kneels between my legs. She takes hold of the pump handle and starts lowering it and raising it. She giggles and covers the giggle with her other hand. The giggle is suspicious too, but I make one myself, it is all kind of silly, this girl pumping the pump handle of me. She pumps the handle up and down, the downstroke is even more painful than when I tried it myself, I'm afraid it will break off. She raises and lowers, and lowers and raises. But nothing happens. My skin is crawling and my heart is thumping like a runaway wagon and I am sweating. But all her pumping brings nothing out of me.

After a long time she stops and says, "Well well, I guess you're just not man enough yet." The way she says this is like she has rehearsed it, as if someone has told her to say it. I am bilked and cast down.

But she is not grinning. She is staring at my perkin, which stands as before. Her face is empty and absent, save for a twitch at one corner of her mouth.

Suddenly she is falling on me, hiking her dress hem, whispering in my ear, "Danny, will you promise never never to tell in the club what we did?" I nod, I nod.

And then down below I feel the hair silks of her vale brushing down on me, and I know then why it's a vale, a valley, a dell down riding, up through the vale riding, my perkin, my violet perking perkin caught and taken, up through the vale riding.

I knew it, I tell myself I knew it all along, that this was the way it was really supposed to go.

"If you tell Renz, he'll kill me," she says. "He'll kill you too."

"I won't, I won't," I say, "I won't tell a soul."

And on me she rides, and I riding with her, and she panting, and saying, "I wasn't supposed to do this," and saying, "But I am," and saying, "I had to," and asking, "Do you like it?" and me panting, and saying back, "Pretty fine," and then both of us not saying anything more because we can't talk.

And there in the corn with the breeze dancing the corn leaves over us, in tune to the dance of our thrashing, I begin to become a man, knowing the wet is going to surge and break out, feeling her vale milking me, waiting, working and waiting for it.

But then she does a strange thing: she stops. Of a sudden she stops thrashing and lies hard upon me, squeezing me, hugging all heck out of me, as if she is trying to mash me right into the earth. I cannot move beneath her. For a while her vale itself alone goes on milking and stripping, but then it too is stilled and tight, in the long still squeeze that goes on until I cry for breath.

At last, when I cry for breath, she eases up and rolls off me, and lies there beside me smiling and looking dreamy-eyed, so I know she hasn't really been hurt. I am relieved, for I thought I'd broken something in her, but she isn't hurt at all.

I pant my question: "Why did you stop?"

"Why—" she pants back at me, giving me an odd look, "why, I finished. Didn't you?"

"Finished?" I say.

She looks down at my perkin. It stands taut as ever. It is wet all over, but I think it's hers, not mine. I'm pleased to see that some of the poke stain has been scrubbed away. "Lordy goodness," she says. "I thought you'd fetched. Didn't you fetch?"

"Fetch what?" I wonder.

She looks closer. "Well, I 'spose I didn't prime you, after all, did I? Fetch is when you're done and your quid spurts out. Maybe you don't have any."

"I do too," I protest. "I bet I do. It was on the way, you just didn't give it time enough."

She is doing some thinking, and I am hoping that she is thinking about trying again. But then she seems to get nervous, and says, "I wasn't supposed to do this. And now if you tell on me I'm going to be in for it."

"I told you I won't ever tell."

"You'll forget, and brag."

"Cross my heart," I cross my heart.

But she stands up, and smoothes down her dress. "You had better not," she says, and she turns to leave me, but turns back to say one more thing: "They wouldn't believe you if you did."

Then she disappears through the corn.

I try to follow her, but my witnesses are so sore I can't walk. I sit down in the corn again, and wonder if she's done some everlasting harm to them. Maybe I am too young. I'm afraid to touch them for fear they will fall off. But I sit and study their stinging, and at last it comes to me that this is not pain of overwork but ache of unfinishment, as when you swing an axe at a sapling and miss it and your arms and shoulders twinge and suffer with the empty missing. I have missed. I'd like to catch Violate and throw her down, I'm big as she. I need a vale. I funicle the air, and imagine, but it's no good.

Now I discover again my hands. I line one hand with cornsilks. It is a poor and sorry make-believe, but it is all I have. I am furious and impatient. I close my eyes to see Violate.

I fetch alone, and when at last I do, and have become a man, it hits me on the chin. I wipe it off and study it. She'd called it quid, but it isn't anything at all like a quid. Like the milk in a kernel of corn if you pierce it with your thumbnail. My man-slick. I'm proud. More, I'm lightened and eased, happy as an earworm in a cornpatch.

At the next meeting of the club, Renz pops me on the shoulder and says, "Well, have you got yourself primed yet?" "No," I say. "I guess I aint man enough."

✝ 8 ✝

A single entry in Diana's diary, that for June 31, is somewhat longer than those before it:

I have been rereading what I've written here so far, and it strikes me that I've placed undue emphasis on what we've been eating, as if all of this is only one big glorious picnic and my chief interest is in the menu. Well, it is true that sometimes I'm having such fun at mealtime that I forget what we're here for. And I've put on a little weight. And Day, who needs it more, has also. But I don't want to leave the impression that food matters all that much. (Occasionally I've wondered if perhaps the food is a replacement—or displacement—for sex.)

If I were required to list formally my (I should say our) concerns or interests or involvements, food wouldn't be very high up the list. I suppose the list would look something like this

1. The life of Daniel Lyam Montross.
2. The death of Dudleytown, Conn.
3. The possibility of the actuality of reincarnation.
4. Nature—the woods and everything in it.
5. Amateur "archaeology"—exploring what is left.
6. Day Whittacker as a person (he grows on me).
7. Fresh air and sunshine, and stillness and peace.
8. Sex (some of Daniel's exploits titillate me).
9. Food (oh be honest, Diana, it comes before #8).   [No it doesn't]

But take Number Four for example. I've never before had much interest in "nature study." Before, I could identify birch trees

124

because they're white, but that's about all. Now I'm getting a new education…from Day, who seems to know everything. He's always pointing out things and explaining things.

Like this morning he showed me some cocoons, and gave me a little lecture. Of course I knew that moths and butterflies go through a caterpillar stage, but what I didn't know is that the larva itself goes through several successive changes—sheddings of its skin—before becoming a caterpillar. Day injected a little allusion to the idea of reincarnation, or *karma*, the idea that the person goes through successive incarnations on the route to perfection, to the butterfly stage. The Greeks, he says, identified the butterfly with the goddess Psyche. I remember pictures and sculptures of her, she is beautiful. I'd like to be a butterfly.

Much of Day's nature teaching seems filled with subtle and not-so-subtle allusions. An example of the latter: I was admiring a green carpet of lichen the other day, and Day explained to me that lichens aren't one plant but *two*: the "symbiotic" union of two completely different plants, alga and fungus. They (or it) couldn't exist without each other: the fungus furnishes the support and the water, and the alga provides the food. In a sense, they're parasites on each other.

I caught the allusion quickly (or thought I did), and in jest I've nick named him "Fungus" and he's nicknamed me "Alga."

"Fungus," I will say, "the water bucket's empty. Haul some more."

Or he will say, "On your next trip to the store, Alga, pick us up another bag of flour."

But it's not just water and food, not just sustenance. He's giving me an education (and of course he's "giving" me Daniel, too), and I'm giving him…well, I'm giving him companionship. And I bought him a radio. Or, I should say, I bought *us* a radio. But it was his idea. A four-battery portable, which, at night, will pick up WQXR. Our woods are full of music now.

Now I will tell about our first kiss. (Apparently all courtships go through three stages: first, holding hands, second, kissing, and third, sex—and it seems strange that Daniel missed the second stage; whether or not we *ever* get to the third stage remains to be seen, and

I've promised myself that if he doesn't make an overture before long I'm going to have to start something myself.) Well, tonight after supper, with the radio turned up full blast to a baroque recorder ensemble (with no neighbors to disturb, it's better than stereo, it's like being in a concert hall), Day asked me to dance for him. So I got out my black leotard and changed into it (I didn't go into the tent to change, and I didn't care whether he was watching me or not), and then, while the radio was playing something by Telemann, I improvised a dance, our mountain laurel glade for a stage, our Coleman lanterns for footlights, throwing my shadow against the trees. The dance of that shadow was like nothing seen before, and it inspired me. It awed Day, too.

Afterwards he modestly asked me to explain what I had done, to interpret it for him. So it was my turn to lecture him, and I laid on a glib elucidation about how Telemann's music, to me, seems to have something important to do with the body-mind relationship, and how, in my dance, I was trying to evoke both the conflict and the accord between mind and body. Day thought it over for a while, and seemed to understand.

The baroque ensemble had finished, and the announcer said the next selection after the station break would be Ralph Vaughan Williams' *Pastoral Symphony*—I half-expected to hear him add: "at the request of Miss Diana Stoving and Mr. Day Whittacker," it was so right, so perfect. "Come and dance with me," I said to Day.

"I can't dance," he said. "I never tried to learn."

"Forget that," I said. "Come on." I took his hand and pulled him out into the open space of the glade. He stood awkwardly with his hands in his pockets. "Now," I said, with a large smile, "we are going to perform 'The Symbiotic Affiliation of One Alga and One Fungus in a Pastoral Setting Furnished by Vaughan Williams.'" He laughed.

As the languid first movement began, *molto moderato*, I began to drift and sway, my arms floating. "I am air," I said to Day. "I have air, I exist in air." I danced a while through air. "You," I said, "by just standing there like a bump on a log, symbolize support…roots…inertia." He shifted his weight from one foot to another. "Just stand," I said, "while I do my dance. The first movement is mine." I danced.

"In the air is food and sunshine," I said and kept my mouth open as if to infuse the food and sunshine from the air. "Wherever I go I can effortlessly find it. Nature provides. The country is mine. But I am lonely." My dance was of searching, of a drifting search. "What do I yearn for? I am thirsty and need water. And I am loose and need roots." I executed a series of leaps. "I relish my freedom!" But the leaps took me nowhere. "But I yearn for a toehold, for a home place." I finished my dance. "I am air, and food, and yearning."

The first movement ended, and the second began, sluggish but lithe, *lento moderato*. "Now all of this movement is yours," I said to him. "You are water. You are fluid but listless." He began making a slow swimming breaststroke with his arms. "Oh, no, Day!" I said. "Too literal!" He stopped and stuck his hands into his pockets again, and glowered at me. He was too self-conscious. "Turn around," I said. He did. "Look at your shadow up there on the trees." He looked up at his giant shadow projected by the Coleman lanterns against the trees. "Now just listen to the music," I said, "and watch what that shadow becomes."

He just stood there for a while, his back to me, just listening to the music—which was all right, for he also symbolized support and roots. But then he began to move. And it was beautiful. Truly beautiful. I was astounded. He was watching his shadow, and at first it was as if he were only moving his body to project a shadow dance, but that shadow dance was the essence of water, flowing and coursing. After a while I said, "But you are yearning too. Though you have roots and water, though your water is lovely and pastoral, you are starving. For air and food." And believe me, diary, that *water starved for air and food*! It was an abstraction, of course, nothing whatever literal about it—Day moving with studied aimlessness and searching, around the glade and around, his long body just as lithe as the music, and in nearly perfect time to the music.

In the third movement, *moderato pesante*, we danced together. This was the happy meeting of water and air, of roots and food, of—oh, I can't describe it. (The nice thing about the dance is that, like music, it is so nonverbal—is that why I switched, at college, from writing to dancing?) I didn't have to give Day very many instructions. "Don't touch me yet." "You're a little too slow there." "Now, pick me up!" "Am I too heavy?" I was not, and he held me aloft with his hands on my waist, and I continued my dance up there, really in the air now, the alga attached to the fungus, the fungus anchored to the earth and holding, and sending up "water," and the alga breathing the air and its food.

We never finished. That strange vocal descant in the fourth movement was just too glorious. That wordless song, like an echo heard from a distant hillside, it was the love song of the air, of the alga, the air singing through the alga, singing its love for the fungus. I don't see how Day held me up there so long, his arms straight up over his head, unless the sheer beauty of that song was giving him some uncustomary strength. He held me up there while I finished my dance, which ended as he lowered me slowly down to him and kissed me—or did I kiss him?—his face was waiting there, and his mouth was in the way of my mouth, which met it, and for the last minute or so of that spine-tingling vocal descant the only movement we were making was of our mouths together, the alga and the fungus completely wedded at last.

Then he lowered me on to the ground, and we just stood there for a while looking at each other. He put his hands back into his pockets. "I guess," I said, awkwardly, "that I don't know how to do the rest of it. But there's just a minute or so left until the end."

"You were beautiful," he said, "while it lasted."

"So were you," I returned.

"We'll have to make up some more dances, sometime," he said.

"You're good," I said. "You make a perfect partner."

"Are any of your books about dance?"

So now, while I am writing this, he is reading my copy of Havelock Ellis' *The Dance of Life*. That won't tell him anything about the modern dance, but it's a good beginning on dance in general. I hope he notices my notes and underlinings (I've a long habit of "talking back" to my books) and I hope he notices those places where Ellis discusses the relationship between dance and sex.

Yesterday he consented to listen to a playback of several of

Daniel's tapes. Before, he had been resistant, had said he didn't want to. I don't think it was because he wasn't interested in Daniel. I'm not sure just what it was. Perhaps he was afraid of finding that Daniel's life had been so exciting in contrast to his. Anyway, he listened with full attention, and I watched him with full attention. Day's blushes are a sight to behold. If, as I am never completely able to discount, Daniel is only the creation of Day's imagination, or of his subconscious, then he is a beautiful dreamer. But I can't conceive how he could fabricate some of that language. For instance, those sex words—"perkin" and "vale" and "funicle" and all that. I've read a lot of historical fiction, and I've read some of the so-called pornographic stuff too, *Fanny Hill* and *My Secret Life* and the *Life and Loves of Frank Harris* and all that, but I've never seen any of those words before. I wish I could find some scholarly study of Connecticut Yankee colloquialisms and try to check out some of his expressions.

"Got an early start, didn't he?" was Day's only comment about the tapes.

"Early start, late finish, they always say," I said.

I'm sure he envies Daniel, there's no question of that. On reflection, this might reinforce the idea that Daniel is the creation of Day's fancy. Maybe Daniel in some ways is what Day would have liked to be.

I see I've neglected to mention what we had for supper tonight. Well, just for the record, it was....

I have to stop now, Diary. It's past bedtime. Just now Day turned in. Before he went into the tent he stood a moment behind my chair with his hands on my shoulders, and to my back he said in a low and funny voice, somewhat hoarsely, "Diana, do you know what I want to do?"

I nodded.

"All right?" he asked.

"All right."

☩ 9 ☩

She turned off the Coleman lanterns. Then she went into the tent. She **She blows out her hurricane lamp. Now she comes into the barn.** could not see in the dark, whether he was on his mattress or hers. She **She cannot find me in the dark; she whispers "Danny, where are** knelt at her own mattress and gently touched it; he was not in it. She did **you?" "Over here," I say, and she gropes her way through the hay** not like it that he expected her to come to him, but it didn't matter. Slowly **to me. She says, "I didn't know as how you'd really be here, as how** she removed her leotard. Then she knelt at the other mattress and put out **you'd dare." Now she lifts her dress up over her head. "Are all your** her hand; it touched his chest, which was bare, and trembling as if chilled, **folks fast asleep?" she asks me. "Long since,"** I say. Now she drops though it was hot. She stretched out alongside him, crowding him over so **down and lies beside me in the hay. We wrap our arms about one** that she could lie upon the air mattress too, then she embraced him, but **another. She is trembling. "Are you cold?" I ask her. "No, just a bit** his shivering increased. "Are you cold?" she asked him. He shook his head **skeert, sneakin' off from home of a dark night like that," she says.** but went on shaking. "Then what's the matter?" she asked. His answer **"Nothing to be skeert of," I say, bold and brave though scared some** was a choked whisper, "Just sort of nervous, is all, I guess." "Relax," she **myself. Now it occurs to me she might be scared of what she's getting** said. But he didn't, and her gentle stroking of his back only seemed to make **into, or what's going to get into her. "Didn't you and Zadock** it worse. "Haven't you ever done this before?" she asked. "Oh sure," he **never do it?" I ask her.** "He never tried to," she says. "He never said, but he didn't sound convincing. She asked, "Then why have you **asked me." I wonder why that is, but Zadock's a kind of hidebound** waited so long to ask me?" He replied "I thought you might be offended. **fellow. "Do you know what we're supposed to do?" I ask her. "Do** I mean, I didn't want to spoil a good thing by making the wrong move." **you know how it's done?" She says, "All the girls in the club know** His talking seemed

130

to slow his trembling. "I wondered if perhaps Daniel **that. Violate told us. She told us it hurts the first time, a little, so** was holding you back," she said, and impishly added, "Do you think he **I'm a bit uneasy about that, I guess."** would approve of this?"

Oh, certainly I approve. Let's get on with it. All this gab takes the fun out of funicle.

"Funny you should mention *him*," Day said. "I was just wondering how you were taking the idea of going to bed with your grandfather." "Don't say that!" she said. "Are you trying to make me nervous too? After all, it's not his body. It's *your* body." And as if to reinforce these words, she put her hand on his penis. It was not, she discovered with some surprise, in sufficient condition, and her touch seemed to start him shivering again.

Now in my hand, the hand that first held hands with hers, I cup her warm vale, and fondle it. Violate's is much larger, I think. The touch of my hand makes her shiver. I am eager and ready, near to bursting with impatience. I pull her up onto me where Violate had been.

"Well," she sighed, "you don't seem to be very much in the mood." She found his mouth and tried kissing him. She held him tightly to her and mashed her mouth all over his, and wiggled against him. She thrust her tongue between his teeth. I hate myself for doing all the work, she said to herself. But he was beginning to respond. He crawled over her, on top.

Now that's a notion, it is. To be on top. More likely to get somewhere. Odd I never thought of it. Violate's way seemed natural. I ease her off, and down, and now I mount her. The neb of my perkin prowls her vale in search of the flume. But finds none. I'd like to strike a light and have a look, I can't find it. My fingers are better for feeling and I grope in the dark. Is this it? No, too far back. Then this? Is this the right place?

She had, finally, to guide him with her hand. She was convinced now that he'd never done it before, he had no idea where to put it. She guided him home. He was still shaking, and once he was inside at last his shaking grew worse than ever. She reflected wryly that it was a novel sensation, being laid by a vibrator.

She moans, and trembles. "Am I hurting?" I ask. "Some," she says. I try to be gentle, but gentleness doesn't get me in. Now I must shove, but when I do, she shrieks. "Shhh," I say. I hope she's not roused the whole house. Now she is crying, and I still haven't made a dent in her vale. "Stop," she tells me. "I changed my mind. I don't want to."

Then it was all over. He didn't even need to begin moving. The tremors of his convulsion merged with those of his nervous shaking, but she could separate them, and knew that he was having his. She sighed, and salvaged some small pleasure from the pressure of his throbbings inside her.

"Aw, Hattie Rose Pearl," I say, "is it all that bad?" "I want to go home," she says. "Aw," I protest, "if you could jist stand it a little bit longer...." She is shoving against my shoulders. "Get offen me," she whines. "I'll tattle," I say. "I'll tell Violate and she'll tell the others in the club that you couldn't do it." "I don't keer," she says, "you're killing me this way."

But he went on shaking. Wouldn't anything calm him? "Now what's the matter?" she asked. He didn't answer, at first. Then he said, "I'm scared." "Of what?" she asked. "You might get pregnant," he said. "Oh, don't worry about that," she told him. But he kept on babbling. "You could, you know," he said. "Do you want to?" "No, it's all right, don't you worry about it."

"Are you scairt you'll have a baby?" I ask her. "No," she says, "that don't bother me. Violate says you have to wait until the right time a month, and it's that time, but I never dremp it was going to hurt so. Please get off me."

He seemed to quit worrying about *that*, but he went on worrying. He lay beside her, still shivering (maybe, she thought, it was the air mattress that magnified his vibrations), and went on babbling. "Oh, hush," she said. "No," he said, "I lied to you. I've never done it before." "All right," she said, "forget it." "I guess you didn't enjoy it much, did you?" he asked. "Hush," she said. "Let's just lie still and relax." "But I don't want you to get the impression that—" "*Oh, go to sleep, Day!*" she said, and "Oops!" she said, but he was already under. She started to bring him back, but suddenly she was struck with a wild idea. Perhaps, if she had not been still so heated up and left with her unfinished desire, she would not have done this, she would not have brought Daniel into it. Perhaps it was some tantalizing curiosity, more than simple desire, which made her do it. At any rate, she made him into Daniel, and with her hands she reincarnated his perkin.

Well, how come you're cosseting it so, if you don't want it?

What? Why do you think I don't want it?

You just said ye didn't, you nonny!

I did?

Hattie Rose Pearl, are you befooling me again?

I'm Hattie Rose Pearl? Oh. I thought perhaps I was Violate.

Huh? What's got inte ye, girl?

Nothing, yet.

Ha! Aren't you the sauce, though! Did Violate put you up to trifling with me? Have you jist been holding out, of a purpose?

Am I holding out? Here I am, Danny.

Now you're talking. Well, here goes. I wish you hadn't frittered away till now. How's that? Hurt still?

No. Go on.

Well I'll be blest! You sure loosened up awful fast.

You talk too much, Danny.

I aint going to be able to say a word, in the twinklin of a bedpost.

Then don't. Hurry.

And she, this suddenly willing fickle funicler, enfolds me, arms and vale alike enfold me, I'm held round and swallowed, the shaft of my back in the clench of her arms and legs alike, the shaft of my shaft in the clench of the strong valves of her vale, and we are balmed and bathed in the wets of our sweating and the damps of our clamping, the dew of her slew and the drip of my tip, we slip and we skid in the sluice of our juices and I'm happy as a frog in his bog or a hog in her wallow, a fish in its swishes, a snake in a lake, or a planetree in the rain. I want to ask her how she feels, but she's told me not to talk, and I needn't ask, the way she moans and moves.

She was not thinking about grandfathers, at all. As a mere point of logic, Danny could not be her grandfather, at least not at this time, because he did not exist, and not at *that* time either, for she was not born then. What then was she thinking? Oh, that was just it, that she was *not* thinking, of anything at all. That was what was so nice about it, to have such pleasure without any interference from the mind. If any thought ever crossed her mind, in the minutes and minutes following, it was only a brief bemused reflection that a thirty-year-old well-known writer was being put to shame by a twelve-year-old Connecticut farm boy.

She's far better than Violate, she is, is Hattie Rose Pearl, she is, oh. And I know she's going to be my girl again, oh. With a hey in the hay and a hey nonny no, oh. Her throes don't startle me as Violate's did, for I know what they are. "You're fetching," I tell her, **whisper in her ear. "It's called fetching."**

Oh hush, and fetch yourself. **She says, in her long sigh.**

I try. Oh, I try to, and I'm fast as a jackrabbit in a forest fire, fast as the foam-flakes drift on the river, fast as music from a trumpet, fast as a thunderbolt, as a hawk, as a shadow, as a thought, as a falling star. I'm fast as time.

It's taking him, she reflected. But that could be simply a matter of body chemistry. It *was*, after all, Day's body, and she knew from her brief affair with her don that the second time takes longer. But good Lord! how he was going on! Now she was ascending again. She tried to hold back, out of fear he would get there before she did, and leave her. But he didn't get there.

It's news to me, girls can fetch twice. And nice. Nay, more than nice. And yea, more than twice. But she says I'm going to make her sore. Soon, soon, I say. Yea, more than twice: thrice, and thricest is nicest, her throes so mighty they tear my fetch right out of me at last. I think I'll die. I'll die right out of myself. Nice to die, knowing you can come again.

In his arms she drifted off to sleep, forgetting to retrieve Day.

Now I find she's gone to sleep on me, and I didn't even get to ask her if she'll be my girl again. But I think she will. I would

wake her, but I'm terrible sleepy myself, and her head's on my chest. It's still a long way to dawn.

✛ 10 ✛

Hypnotized subjects, if left in their trances, will eventually fall into deep sleep, and eventually awaken, themselves again. But Diana did not know this. Thus, when sunrise woke her, and she saw that she was beside Day, and began slowly remembering, she wondered if he, in deep sleep still, was still Daniel, and, if so, what he would do when he woke up and saw that she was not Hattie Rose Pearl. She woke and wondered this idle wonder in a state of warm and dreamy euphoria. She felt good and happy and cozy, and she snuggled closer against him. In doing this, her bottom wiggled, and the dull ache there told her that she was going to be sore all day, but she didn't care.

She fell back into sleep, and came out of sleep, several times, one time thinking or realizing, *I am in love with Daniel.*

Then she was finished with sleeping. She lay there and looked at him. He was sleeping on his back. Day always slept on his stomach. His penis—his perkin was not limp; it canted in a long tough curve; if she could bear it she could have it again. But she was too sore. She could only hold it, and did.

It even had his pulse in it, which the tip of her forefinger could feel and take in the dimple of the ogival arch on the underside of the crown's rim. She tried to time it, without a watch. It seemed to be slow, not the pulse of Daniel, but then of course a pulse is slower in sleep. It was quickening, though, beneath her touch.

Then he woke. She didn't see him wake, because her head was on his stomach and her eyes on his perkin, which she was giving her full contemplation. In the light, in the daylight, she had not seen one so close before. *Nature study,* she said to herself. *Part of my education.*

But she'd not seen anything in nature with quite the resemblance. Not red like rhubarb, nor green like asparagus or okra, nor gray like a stallion's, nor pink like a cat's, nor vermillion like a dog's. The closest resemblance was to a certain mushroom she'd seen recently while exploring the woods with Day. "What's that?" she had asked, pointing, and then, joking, "Did you drop something?" He had blushed scarlet. "*Mutinus,*" he'd said. "Just a worthless mushroom." "That means it's a fungus, doesn't it, Fungus?" she'd twitted him. Oh, she oughtn't to tease him so. Besides, the mutinus had a rather sharp-pointed tip, whose flesh color made it all the more formidable and suggestive. *His* tip wasn't sharp at all, just pleasantly pointed, enough for entrance. It looked like a soldier's helmet, no, a fireman's hat, with a dent in the top. It was cute as a popsicle, cute as a—

"I'll make you a present of it. It's yours."

Her head snapped back so suddenly she bopped him on the chin. She said, "Oh, I'm sorry," and stroked him lightly on the chin and looked sympathetically into his eyes. But he wasn't hurt; he was smiling. She "replayed" his words in her head, and tried to decide if they were Day's or Daniel's. She couldn't tell. The expression on his face wouldn't help her; he just looked dreamy and a little lascivious, a little bedroom-eyed.

She couldn't very well ask, straight out, "Who are you?" so she just tried to make conversation. "Did you sleep well?"

"Like a log," he said. But Daniel could have said that.

"What would you like to do today?" she asked.

His eyes got bedroomier, and he put his arms around her. "Funicle," he said.

So then he was Daniel! She was both delighted and a little nervous. But he could see her plainly; wasn't he able to see that she was neither Violate nor Hattie Rose Pearl?

Now he was pressing her down and clambering upon her. She resisted. "No," she said. "Really. I can't. I'm much too sore. You really used me up last night."

He looked at her strangely. "You're being sarcastic," he said.

Was this actually Daniel, after all? Well, maybe he was Day. Or a little of both? "If you're not used to it," she said, "if you haven't done it in a long time, then you have to get used to it." She added, by way of consolation, "I'll get used to it. But not now."

He fell off of her and lay beside her, a pout on his mouth like an eleven-year-old boy's. "But look what you did," he said, pointing at his still stiff perkin. "I saw you playing with it."

"It was already up," she said. "I didn't make it do that."

"Well, you can't go off and leave it looking like that."

She knew he was Day, and somehow, because he was Day, his perkin lost its handsomeness. It was not a perkin but just a penis. She wished he'd cover himself.

She crawled over him, getting up from the air mattress and looking for her panties.

"Where are you going?" he asked.

"It's time to start breakfast, Fungus," she said.

"Please," he said. "Don't go."

"What do you want me to do?" She tried to sound patient, but her words came out irritably. She found her panties and stepped into them, as if to close off what he could not have.

"You could…you could come and…and play with it some more."

She hesitated, half-willing, half-repelled. Then she unzipped the mosquito netting in the tent door and stepped out. She turned and said through the tent door, "Play with it yourself."

Then she began preparing breakfast. Bent over the cooking fire, brushing smoke and her hair out of her face, she wondered: *Was I unkind?* And decided: *Yes.* And then wondered: *Why?* and tried to ponder this ambivalence: that it was the same body, that it was Day's body, but that the person she had fallen in love with was not Day but was in a sense imprisoned in Day's body. And thinking of bodies, she abruptly realized, with some surprise, that she was going about the business of getting breakfast ready, still clad only in her panties, nothing else. It was a warm morning, and the air felt wonderful on her body, and the sunshine. She felt a kind of freedom, a liberation, but then a twinge of self-consciousness. Was Day staring at her from the tent? Well, let him.

She had finished the bacon and was cracking eggs into the

frying pan, when his voice came from the tent, mock-ominous, almost light, "If you don't put some clothes on, I'm going to come out there and rape you."

She laughed. Then she said, "You couldn't."

"Wanna bet?"

"I'm busy. You won't get any breakfast if you rape me."

"I'd rather have you than breakfast."

"Then come and see what happens!" she challenged him.

He emerged from the tent, his silly penis leading the way. He formed his hands into claws, and warned, "You'd better run."

She stood her ground. He came on toward her, and grabbed her shoulders. "Go to sleep, Day," she said.

But as soon as he did, she brought him back, and said, "See? You're helpless against my weapon."

"That's not fair!" he protested.

"My one defense," she said. "What's a poor girl going to do to protect herself out in the woods alone with a lecher like you?" She turned back to her cooking.

"You're mean," he said. "You're heartless. And I know why."

She looked at him. "Why?"

"You don't want to make love with me again because I disappointed you last night."

Now *that* might be true. But she shook her head, and said, "No, I don't want to make love with you because I'm still sore and you'll just have to wait until it's not sore."

"How long?"

"I don't know."

"An hour? A day? A week?"

She sighed. "Maybe tonight."

"Promise?"

She thought about it. It was…oh, it was like being unfaithful to Daniel. But she decided that was silly, because Daniel didn't know it was her. What was sillier was that she felt jealous of Violate and Hattie Rose Pearl. The relationship was not an ordinary "triangle." It had begun as a simple dyad, Day and herself, and then become a triangle, and then a quadrangle, a quintangle, a sexangle, a—

"Why are you counting on your fingers?" Day asked. "Are you figuring how long I will have to wait, or enumerating your lovers?"

"I was just trying to count our *dramatis personae*," she said. "It's getting complicated."

"Oh," Day said. "You're thinking of *him*." He said this with jealousy, as if he were referring to her other lover. Come to think of it, he was.

"Let's eat our breakfast," she said, "and then get on with the story."

✢ 11 ✢

The birch lashes down into the bed I sit on, SNOCK! Missed me by a foot. "THIS'LL LEARN YOU, YOU SCUM!" my father shouts. Again he raises the birch. Again he misses me. On purpose he misses? In a quiet voice, behind his hand, he says, "I told your Ma I'd chastise ye. Holler, why don't ye?" I holler. "WENCHING IN THE SIGHT A GOD!" he yells at me and smacks the bedclothes with the birch again. "Ow! Stop! Don't!" I holler. In his low voice he says, "Din't ye have sense enough to git her outen the barn afore cockcrow?" and then yells, "GITTIN TOO BIG FER YUR BOOTS, YOU VILLYUN!" and whops the bed with his birch. "Quit! Help! Leave off!" I holler. "How'd ye like it?" he asks. "Is that Bardwell gull a fair funicle?" "Oh, fair enough," I allow. "I'LL LEARN YE TO PESTLE AROUND AT YOUR AGE, YOU BLACK SHEEP!" and whops the bed. "No! Ouch! Let up! I'll never do it again!" He says, quietly, "I'll wager ye made a woman of her. Was it heavy sleddin'?" "No, I had a right soft time of it," I tell him. "FER SHAME! YOU SINFUL DEVIL! FIE UPON YE!" He whops the bed several times, SNOCK! WHUMP! THRICK! "Now mark me, Dan'l," he says, low, "you want to be tendin' to what you're about. You could git a gull with a come-by-chance, don't ye know? You wouldn't have no use fer siring a come-by-chance at your age." I tell him, "She said it twa'nt the time a month fer that." "NOW HOW'S YER HIDE FEEL, HUH? THAT'LL MIND YE TO MEND YER WAYS!" He gives the bed a few more blows. "Well, good," he says. "That's a careful lad. But another thing. You don't want to let ole Bardwell git wind a this. He might could cut off our credit, ye know." My father laughs, and winks. Then he says, "Now dab some spit around yer eyes, to make 'em look wet, and go out a here holdin' yer bottom."

Passing my mother in the buttery, I whimper and complain, "He whomped the whey outen me."

"Sarves ye fair!" she cries, and clutches herself for support. "My soul and body! Don't ye ever let me catch ye at *that* again!"

I go on out. She has said it. I will never let her catch me, I will never be caught, again. If what I do is wrong, I will never be caught at it.

But soon it is known, to all in the Oatsowers and the SS alike; Hattie Rose Pearl has bragged there to the other girls, I have bragged here to the other boys.

Zadock doesn't seem to mind.

Renz taunts him, "You going to jist stand there and let Danny git away with it?"

"I don't care," Zadock says.

"You don't care," Renz says. "Haw. How come ye don't care? Aint ye able to do it to her yourself?"

Zadock blushes, but says, "Don't matter anyhow. I'm leaving. Pa says we're leaving bright and soon tomorrow morning."

"Huh?" says Renz. "How come ye're leaving? Where you going?"

Zadock shrugs. "I guess out westwards where it's flatter. Pa says fifty acres could stand a family in the flatlands but not up here in these hills."

"What's the world coming to?" Renz says.

"I won't see Hattie Rose Pearl ever more," Zadock says. He begins to cry. "So I don't care what she does." I have never seen a big fourteen-year-old boy cry before. "She can funicle all day and night for what I care."

"What's the world coming to?" Renz says.

One of my first jobs of paid work is taking apart Zadock's house. Nobody else's gonna move in, I guess, my father says, might as well salvage the lumber and nails. All day, for weeks, I remove nails from boards, and straighten the nails and save them. I am paid eight cents the hour. My hands become too raw to hold Hattie Rose Pearl.

"Did you hear Zadock's gone?" I ask her.

"I heard."

"What's the world coming to?" I say.

My work takes weeks, and when it's done there are four cellar holes in the village now. I made one of them. It seems like making a grave. Zadock's ghost lies there, but is not buried; the grave will not be filled. We miss him, for all that he was my rival. I'd give up Hattie Rose Pearl to get him back.

She misses him too, and once when my perkin longs for her vale she denies me, saying she can't help believing that Zadock left on account of what we did. Aw, I protest, it was Zadock's dad who did the leaving, not him.

Still she denies me. And it doesn't matter, long, for soon, in the waning of summer, she is the next to go. Bardwell closes his store. There is no business, he says. Bardwell is a cousin of Mary Cheney, who left Dudleytown and married Horace Greeley, who said, they say, Go West. Bardwell is thinking about that.

Bardwell goes west, taking Hattie Rose Pearl.

She says she will write, and I say I will follow. But she doesn't, and I don't.

There is no store now in the village. We have to walk or ride to The Bridge if we want something.

Violate says to me, "I guess I'm all you've got in the way of a girl now."

I study her face to tell if she's joshing. "You're still Renz's girl," I say.

"He can't last as long as you," she says.

"Is he leaving too?" I ask.

"That's not what I mean," she says.

What she means, I find, in a field atop Dudleytown Hill one fine brisk Indian summer afternoon, in a dell of the field out of sight of all but autumn birds, for beyond an hour and then beyond another hour, is the way it takes me, the way I stay, and the way I can recur.

Dear me, she says, dear her.

Wake up, she says into my ear, in the fading light. You're not tired, are you?

No, just resting. Her eyes are green; I had thought they were brown. She rumples my hair and puts my hand upon her breast, inside her dress; the hard nipple is like a perkin funicling the vale of my fingers.

She pulls me onto her again. How many, she says, so far? Three, I say, You? Five, she says.

But I must have lost it all, there seems to be none left, she's taken all the quid there was. Six, she says. I keep on, but can't get there.

My hips ache from their constant speed. I slow, but when I do she hurries.

Seven, she says, and then: Do you like to kiss?

I never have.

Then kiss me.

I do, and the feel of her soft wet mouth against my mouth gives me my fourth, along with her eighth, and that's more than enough for today.

She says, I'd like to have a baby. I'd like to have a hundred.

You'd better not, I say.

Then someday can we? she says. Pretty the way she puts that, then someday can we? Sure, I say. A hundred? she says. All you want, I say.

Now school days are upon us again, although Miss Fife is not. She has gone too, there're not enough pupils to keep her here. First day of school we stand and sing the school song, "Happy School, Ah, From Thee Never Shall Our Hearts Long Time Be Turning," beautiful, but it is not Miss Fife who leads us. It is a mother. The mothers are taking turns doing the school.

The schedule is the same, with two quarter-hour recesses, one at ten-thirty and one at two-forty-five. Violate and I go to the woods each recess, although fifteen minutes is scant and hurried.

But one recess, Renz follows us and catches us at it.

"I'm going to kill you, Dan," he says.

"You'll have to catch me first," I say.

And he can't. I can outrun them all.

✦ 12 ✦

One afternoon in July, driving home from a trip to the liquor store in Cornwall Bridge, Diana passed an old man, walking along the highway. She stopped and backed up, and asked him, "Can I give you a lift?"

He raised his craggy wrinkled face and stared at her for a moment, then said, "Just up the road." Did he mean that she could give him a ride just up the road, or that it was not necessary because he lived only a short distance away? He was a very old man, perhaps in his late eighties or early nineties.

"Get in," she offered, "and I'll take you." She opened the door.

"Thank you," he said, and got in. "Right hot day, aint it?"

"It is," she agreed. She drove on. Then she asked, "Have you lived around here very long?"

"Long enough," he said. "I cal'late nigh onto ninety years."

"You were born around here?"

"Right up in Calhoun Corner," he said.

"Where is that?"

"Just up the road, way you're heading."

"Oh. Where Route 45 branches off?"

"That's it."

"I didn't know it had a name."

143

"'Taint much of a place, is it? Never was. But it's Calhoun Corner, and here we be." He pointed. "Second house on the left, yender."

She pulled off the road beside his house and turned off the motor. "Have you ever been to Dudleytown?" she asked him.

"Sure I been there. Not lately, though. Aint a tormented thing left of that place."

"When you were young," she asked, "did you know any of the people who lived there?"

"A few."

"Did you know anybody named Montross?" she asked.

"Montross, ye say?" He scratched his head, and wrinkled his brow in concentration for a long moment. "Might've," he said. "I've knowed so many people in my life their names have fled my mind."

"Daniel Montross would have been about your age, maybe a few years older," she said.

"Daniel Montross," he said, and became silent again for a while before continuing, "now, that *does* seem to kinder ring a bell, but I jist couldn't say."

She tried out other names she knew: "Ferrenzo Allyn? Violate Parmenter? Hattie Rose Pearl Bardwell? Zadock Savage? Reuben Temple?"

"Where'd you hear all them names?" he asked.

"I'm doing genealogical research," she said.

"Well, I was only a kid when that town died out, and that was a mighty long time ago. But Bardwell, now...wasn't he—?"

"The storekeeper?" she suggested.

"Yeah, now, mebbe you're right. I seem to reckerlect there was a store there, run by a man named...well, yeah, I guess it could've been Bardwell."

"Do you remember any definite names?" she asked.

"Well, I knew the Jenners," he declared.

"The Jenners?" she said, and tried to recall if "Daniel" had ever mentioned the name, but could not.

"That was one of the biggest families still there when I was a kid."

She made a mental note of the name, and then she tried a different tack, "Do you know what a whiffletree is?"

"Whiffletree?" He looked at her. "You wouldn't be meaning *whipple*tree, would ye?"

"Like on a wagon," she said.

"Sure, that's a whippletree, 'cause it whips back and forth. It don't whiffle."

"Nobody around here ever called it a whiffletree?" she asked.

"Wal, mebbe them east Connecticut folks might call it that, but I've never heard that anywheres about here."

She tried another word, bravely: "What is a perkin?"

Did she detect a hesitancy, a slight look of embarrassment? "Oh, there's lots of Perkinses between here and Litchfield."

"No, not a family name, a common name. You don't know what a perkin is?"

"No, I do not, I'm sorry," he said, and seemed tired. Was she annoying him?

She tried one more, one last: "What does funicle mean?" and watched him closely for any suggestion of a blush.

But he was only annoyed. "Herod all handsaws!" he exclaimed. "Is this some kinder quiz contest? Thunder, no, I never heard of no funicle."

She had heard that "Thunder, no," from Daniel, but she had not heard the other. "What does 'Herod all handsaws' mean?" she asked.

"It just means you're pestering me no end," he said.

"I'm sorry," she said. "I didn't mean to. I'm just interested in Dudleytown and trying to find out some things."

"You ever been up there?" he asked.

"I just came from there," she told him.

"Huh?" he said. "You *did*?" He began shaking his head back and forth. "A young thing like you, all by yourself? Crimus, don't you know there's a powerful curse on that place? Don't you know it's haunted?"

"I've read something about that," she admitted, "but it didn't scare me."

"Well let me tell you—" he began, and he told her all he knew about modern manifestations of the Curse of Dudleytown. At one time early in this century there was only a single resident remaining, a Pole, living by himself at the old Colonel Rogers place, but even though he was a strong man, sturdy and stolid, not easily frightened by anything, his constant subjection to the weird noises of the forest broke him down and forced him to seek out human company in some other place. He was followed by an Irish laborer, who with his wife and two sons took title to one of the abandoned farms on Dark Entry Road because he liked solitude, and because, being Irish, he was no stranger to fairyfolk or little people or whoever habited and haunted the place. He pastured sheep on the hillsides, and kept losing lambs without finding out to what or to whom. His sons became outlaws and were chased out of the country by the local constabulary. His wife took over the sons' work, and overworked herself and died of consumption. He himself stubbornly clung to the place, like the lonely Pole before him, fortified by his pride and the courage of his race that could not be daunted by the dreadful hooting of banshee owls. Patrick, as he was called (but not by the villagers of Cornwall, who gave him wide berth when he occasionally came into the village, in his rags), lived from one year's end to the next without seeing a living person in Dudleytown other than his own reflection in the millpond. To get him out, the fairyfolk—or fiends or whoever—had to burn down his ramshackle house, on a wild night in August. He tried to save the house, or at least save his clothes and meager possessions, but he was denied even this. No one knows where he went.

Nor was he the last. There were two more (before the two of Diana and Day); these were city people, a professor of medicine from New York, Dr. William C. Clarke, and his wife, who knew nothing of the Curse and were attracted by the wild woodland. With his own hands the professor chopped a home site out of the forest, then chopped hemlocks and hewed them to make a cabin. He wondered why he was unable to hire any people from the village nearby to help him. When the owls hooted at him he knew what they were and was not frightened. The Curse must have been dormant, for it permitted the professor and his wife to come every summer for several years and live happily until autumn. But one summer he was called suddenly to New York on business and had to leave his wife overnight, and when he returned he found his wife had gone mad; soon she took her life, and he moved to some other place.

"Consarn it, you couldn't pay me cash money to get me to go into that tormented place," the old man concluded.

Diana wanted to tell him that she had been living in Dudleytown for several weeks without any trouble, but she decided it wouldn't do to have the local people knowing that she and Day were camping up there. So she merely remarked, "It's a very pretty place."

"Yeah, pretty as the fire of Hades," he said.

Diana drove slowly home, thinking about the old man and what he had said. She wasn't certain that his irritated response to her questions about such words as perkin and funicle wasn't simply an unwillingness to discuss the subject with a female.

As soon as she got back to camp, she found Day and turned him into Daniel, and asked him, "Who are the Jenners?"

The Jenners?

Yes, the Jenners. Who are the Jenners?

———**Oh, that's just some of these folks.**

Which folks?

———**Well, there's Enos Jenner and his wife Arvilla, and his brothers Theron and Belding, and Belding's wife Cate and their sons Girshom and Gurdon.**

You've never mentioned him to me before.

Don't know 'em too mighty well. The Jenners is quality folks, you might call 'em upper crust. They never have the time a day for us Montrosses.

Where do they live?

Big house right this side of the brook, on Dudleytown Road.

I thought you said that was the Jones place.

Well, it used to be. The Jenners bought it from 'em.

Let me ask you something else, Danny. Why do you call a whippletree a whiffletree? Everybody else calls it whippletree.

Yeah, I know. I guess 'cause Grandpa Montross called it that,

'cause his folks called it that. Old "Mountain Horse" Montross was a downstater, you know, and they talk different. And anyhow, whiffle means suffle, you know, the whiffletree sort of suffles and plays, that's how it got the name.

All right, she said, and woke him up.

Then she said, "I met an old man." Then she told Day everything the old man had said.

When she finished, Day said, "Well, as for the Curse of Dudleytown, I would be more inclined to believe in something as fantastic as reincarnation before I could make myself believe that these woods are haunted by fairyfolk or ghosts. As for the old man's ignorance of such words as perkin and funicle, well, possibly, of course, the fact that you are a girl…."

"But he couldn't remember any of the people Daniel has been mentioning, except the Jenners, whom Daniel never mentioned, until just now I asked him—I asked you—and you seemed to take a long time to remember them, almost as if…as if you were making them up."

Day nodded, then hung his head. "I've been thinking about this," he said. "A lot." He looked sad. "What if," he said, hesitantly, "what if all of it is nothing but my imagination?"

"That's what I'm dying to find out," she said. "What are we going to do if we can prove that Daniel Lyam Montross never lived in Dudleytown?"

"Even so," he said, "even if we should ever be able to prove that, I want you to remember this: I still love you."

☩ 13 ☩

Oh, he loves you, he does. In my stead. For I cannot. Though I would if I could, incest be damned. You are the spit image of your fair grandmother, whom I loved more than any other woman in my life, who gave birth to your fair mother, without whom you would not be. But I can't talk to you, now, of love, for you don't yet know what it means, and you can't say to him what he said to you, that you love him. I'm not sure he knows what love means either, though perhaps he knows it better than you. But I intend for the two of you to find out what it means, just as I had to find out, painfully if need be. This is my gift for you, in the stead of the love I cannot give you.

Sometimes Day sang to her. It made her terribly self-conscious, at first, and she found it difficult to look at his eyes when he was singing to her. But he had an excellent tenor voice, which resounded through the woods, and he held his high notes well, and the high notes tolled and tinkled off the trees. He sang to her love songs, things like Beethoven's "Ich Liebe Dich" and in time she overcame her embarrassment and was flattered by his singing. She wanted to sing something for him too, but the only love song she knew all the words to was "Danny Boy," and when she sang this for him, meaning it for him, he wouldn't believe that she didn't mean it for Daniel, and his feelings were hurt.

I could never sing a note. Except for that old school song, "Happy School, Ah, From Thee Never Shall Our Hearts Long Time Be Turning" just squawking it more than singing it. So I envy that boy, I do, and I wish he knew it; it might make up for all his confounded envy of me. No, I couldn't sing. But eventually I learned to play a real decent fiddle. And he will too. In time, after your travels to some other place, you will buy him a fiddle, and I'll play it for him, or teach him to play it himself.

Also he knew by heart all the love poems of e.e. cummings, which he must have been saving up for the time when he would meet his first true love and get a chance to use them. He recited all of them, to her, several times. His particular favorite was "Somewhere i have never travelled, gladly beyond," and after reciting it to her, he even explicated the poem, showing her how well it fit her, and him, and how well it fit this situation that they were in, almost as if cummings had written it for her, for them, just as Vaughan Williams had written the *Pastoral Symphony* for their fungus and alga. Diana was very moved, but at the same time she felt extremely guilty, because she could not feel such depths of emotion toward him. It bothered her greatly that he loved her so much. But although she couldn't give him her love in return, as a substitute she choreographed a dance to cummings' poem, a dance of traveling somewhere gladly beyond, and of silent eyes, of frail gestures, of unclosings and openings, of death and forever with each breathing, and she danced this dance with him and their shadows projected against the trees, and it was almost as good as being in love.

Why are your pretty dancings, your pretty singings and poetry-recitings, and your pretty funiclings, never disturbed by the ghosts of Dudleytown? Why does the Curse never curse you? I wish I could boast that it is because I, over here on the Other Side, have the power to keep them from it, to make them let you love and play in peace. But that would be a vainglorious contention, because I haven't the slightest power over them. Perhaps you are amusing them, or entertaining them, and they are waiting until your dance is over before driving you away.

Diana realized that she and Day were getting to be "old friends" when they reached the point at which they no longer felt the need of "using the woods" in order to use the woods; that is, eventually they were able to "use the woods" in each other's presence, without much modesty or embarrassment, although sometimes, when she watched Day peeing, the fact that she was watching him gave him an erection, which wouldn't go away, and sometimes made peeing difficult, and always made an immediate funicle mandatory. They funicled a lot. Sometimes in the morning, in the afternoon, in the evening, in the middle of the night. They bathed together in the pool below Marcella Falls and enjoyed some interesting underwater funiclings.

Unfortunately, he nearly always fetched before she did, and sometimes she couldn't fetch at all. But only on rare occasions did she find herself left feeling so keyed up that she had to turn him into Daniel again.

Diana discovered that Day was a better lover after several drinks, and so was she. Perhaps they did drink more than was necessary, and Day made a rather sloppy "Daniel" when he had been drinking. But Daniel himself, Diana found, took up drinking at a relatively early age, homemade beer and, less frequently, rum and hard cider.

There was one period, in late July, when the weather seemed to turn against them: a spell of damp, humid days when everything seemed to be wet and wouldn't dry out, and the mosquitoes became worse. It was times like that when she needed a lot of beer, wine and gin just to bear the atmosphere.

Toward the end of that month, Day wrote a postcard to his parents, which Diana mailed from a box in Torrington. It said: "Dear Mom and Dad—I'm all right, so don't worry about me. In fact, I'm fine, and having the best time of my life. But I'm not coming home. And don't try to find me, because you can't. Day." Diana considered, briefly, writing to her own parents at Rome, but decided against it.

They never bought a newspaper. They had no desire to. But they could not help hearing occasional news broadcasts between the music on their radio, so they were not ignorant of that summer's lunar expedition by the astronauts.

The moon itself, Day explained to her, is an ancient symbol of reincarnation—its appearance, increase, wane, disappearance, followed by reappearance after three nights of darkness.

One day he came to her, all excited, and said, "Come and see what I've found out!" and took her hand and led her toward their campsite. She thought maybe he had finally found part of the foundation of the Montross house, but what he had found, she discovered with a laugh, was that their two sleeping bags could be completely unzipped and then zipped together to form one double sleeping bag. In celebration of this momentous discovery they had a bottle of champagne before trying out their new bed.

That night they lay together and listened to a radio broadcast about the progress of the moon exploration.

"Think about it," Day said, hugging her closer. "Just the two of them alone up there on the moon. Just the two of us alone down here on the earth."

"Nice," she said, but then she corrected him. "No, there are three. Three of them up there. Don't forget the guy in the command module, orbiting around them."

⚜ 14 ⚜

All my brothers are gone. And one of my sisters too. Ethan has written once from Cincinnati, Ohio, where he works in a factory and has taken a bride. Nathan is in Illinois, where he clerks in a store. We do not know yet where Nicholas is; Nathan has said that Nicholas was intending to go farther west, out to the high mountain country. Emmeline has followed Nathan to Illinois, but not the same town, she is near the big city, Chicago, and says she is going to marry the man she works for, in a dry goods store. She wants us to come out for the wedding, and my mother dearly wants to go, but my father says How? We have no money for such a long way.

I think he's afraid that if he went he'd never come back. And he keeps telling me, Dudleytown is our home.

What town? There is no town here now.

Charity's the only one left but for me. And she will never leave. She stayed in the first grade for three years, before they knew she couldn't do school. She can milk the cow, is all, and that slowly. The pity's she's so pretty, now that she's full grown. Any man would want her if she had a mind. She was Seth's girl a year or two, in a way, because Seth was none too bright himself. But even he is gone now.

For some time now, my mother has tied Charity's hands behind her back, with a handkerchief.

Why? I asked.

So she can't harm herself, my mother said.

My mother unties her hands five times each day, three times for meals, twice for milking the cow.

Charity cannot talk, but she can make noises, as she does in her bed at night with her hands tied. A wonder she can sleep that way. My room is too close to hers.

I think a lot: can she think? Do any thoughts invade her mind, or is she all feeling only? Can you have emotions without a mind? And if you can, are your emotions stronger than smart people's? I wonder a lot: is Charity better off than us?

Once I try to reason with my mother: But you can't go on tying her all her life, and all your life too.

I will if I have to, she says.

But what if she outlives you?

Daniel, what a thing to say! she rebukes me.

Long time now I have not been with Violate. Renz told her dad on us, and old Eph birched her within an inch of her life and said he'd take the other inch if she ever came near me again. Eph Parmenter's a mean and terrible case.

There are no clubs now, neither SS nor Oatsowers, nor need of any; there's nobody here who doesn't know all the facts of life and more. Except Charity, who knows nothing.

Who knows nothing except that her vale burns her and that the hands which cooled it are bound in a handkerchief behind her back. This much I calculate.

I've tried to get to her, to ask if she knows why her hands are tied, but her speech is only noises, for all that she's a full-breasted woman of sixteen. I wonder a lot: is she maybe really smarter than all of us, but has no time for talk, or doesn't care to talk in the kind of noises that we make?

Mother never leaves her go from sight, except at milkings, and then she times her so she's not gone for long. I hide in the cowstall and talk to her for ten minutes at morning and evening milking.

How much can you say in ten minutes? The weather's nice today. Your hair is done up pretty. Bossie seems good and full this morning, don't she? Your eyes are larger than all time. Have you heard there's only four of us left at school? Renz quit out last week.

I'd give my arm to give you a mind. Both arms. Hear Bossie loo-ing. Do you reckon she'd like a calf? If anything could physic you, I'd buy it with a mountain in my arms. 'Pears Dad broke another wagon neap. If you could but speak and say that having no mind keeps you from ever thinking that you're lonely, then I'd wish I had no mind too. Sometimes I get so lonesome. I wish we'd go to Ohio or Illinois or some other place where a lot of people are. Dunno's I know we ever will. Me and you are gonna rot away together on the vine. You're all I know.

Once, one evening in the cowstall, I say first thing: Do you want I should milk the cow for you? I'll milk her for you if you want. But she doesn't understand. I take the pail from her and sit on her stool so she can't sit on it and I commence to milk. She just stands there watching. She doesn't know what to do with her hands.

But then she does know.

That's right, I say, trying not to watch. Go ahead. Mother may think it's wrong, but I don't. Everybody does it, I guess, except Mother. If you weren't my sister, we wouldn't have to use our hands.

Often now I milk for her. In her bed at night she doesn't make her noises so much any more.

Often now I think and ponder and wonder: why would it be wrong? Cattle and dogs don't care if they're blood kin. Bulls and boars and billies funicle their sisters without giving it a thought. Because they don't have thoughts to give. And neither does Charity. Does she even know that I'm her brother?

In the Oatsowers club they used to say that if your sister had your baby it would be feebleminded. But funicling's not just for having babies; funicling's for fun, and for not making noises in your sleep at night.

But I'd never have a chance, anyway, except at milking, and even if we both milked together we'd never get it done in time.

Yet now one bright and fair Saturday morning, early, my father hitches the wagon and says he and Mother are driving into Cornwall to see some of Mother's kin. My mother says to me: Now listen, as soon as she's done with the milking, you get that rag tied back on her hands right away. You hear me?

I nod.

Promise? she says.

I promise. They are gone.

Charity comes back from the barn with her pail of milk. She leaves the pail in the buttery. I hold the handkerchief in my hands. She puts both hands behind her back, crossing her wrists there; she's done this so often she doesn't think. She doesn't think anyway. I hold the handkerchief. But I did promise. So I tie her. She doesn't bat an eye.

Come, I say, and lead her to her room. I'll do it for you. Lie down. She does, on her side, because her hands are behind her back. I do with my hands what I've seen her do with hers. She closes her eyes, there is almost a smile on her mouth.

This is something new for her, somebody else's hands, better than her own. Her fetch is wild.

Now she's had hers, I want her to give me mine. But she can't understand, because she can't understand. And her hands are tied behind her back. I won't break promises. I lie behind her and lay my perkin on her near palm. She grasps, those hands that can so milk a cow. But the milking stroke is downward; I need an upward too. After a time, I turn: my feet where my head was: now her stroke is upward. I wrap my arms around her thighs.

Too late, as my quid begins its rise, I know I'm going to blotch her bedcovers or her dress. I look around for something else. There is nothing but the handkerchief on her wrists. I get it off just in time.

She doesn't need it anyway, I'm going to watch her all day. As good as a promise. That I will stay with her all day and watch her and see to it that she never touches herself. I will touch her *for* her.

But hands are not enough, there's the hitch. Near noon, whilst she milks me yet another time, as we lie facing side by side, she seems to show a first real thought, she seems to think: now maybe this was meant to be inside me, and she draws nigh, urging her vale nearer, and yet nearer, and higher, until her hands cannot move for being in the way, and she removes them.

I think: if I hadn't lost Violate I wouldn't do this.

But I do it. And oh! great Caesar's ghost how she carries on, as if this was all she were ever meant for, as if all her life she had waited for this, as if all her mind could do was make her ready and ripe, as if, since she had to live, she lived for this.

Near the end I ask her if it's the right time of month, and somehow I even expect an answer, so I'm a bit put out when she won't or can't. I'll take no chance. When she's seized by her fetch, and the valves of her vale commence milking mine out of me, I pull away and use her handkerchief once more.

Then there is the afternoon, after we have eaten, and the bed again.

When our mother and father return at supper, they do not seem to notice that it is a different hankerchief she is tied with.

Tonight, late, I learn I am wrong to have hoped that I could have done enough to hold her for a while.

She falls into my bed, her hands still tied. I whisper: if we get caught. Will she have to be tied to her bed? Our folks are fast asleep, but the straw tick of my bed rustles and crackles with our flouncing.

You can't sleep with me, I tell her afterwards. Go back to your charmber. But she won't. I have to lead her. I tuck her in. Now you go to sleep and don't get up again. I kiss her goodnight, on her mouth.

I love Charity. Once I was her dollbaby, now I am her love. I understand this first fact about love, that there must be some part of pity in it, that love is not just passion but compassion. I love her because I weep for her, and I weep for her because I'm all she has for love.

I dream and scheme of taking her away.

Especially must I dream and scheme when her belly begins swelling. I'd thought I was always out in time; there must have been some left over one time.

All day my mother screams at her: Who was it?

I think my father guesses but he doesn't say, and my mother would never think such a thing.

Night after night my mother conjectures: Ferrenzo Allyn? Reuben Temple? Maybe Seth came back in the middle of the night? A passing stranger? The Jenners' hired man? And she keeps raging at Charity: Oh I wish you could talk! Who in Sam Hill was it did it?

Charity's kept in her room all the time. I do the milking now, and while I milk I think: I will just take her and we will go far away, where we can't be found, and nobody knows us, we will just escape to some other place where we can live and be happy evermore, and if the baby is an idiot....

If the baby is an idiot I would have to let it die.

In the middle of the night I will saddle the mare Mistress and snitch some victuals from the larder, and Charity and I will ride away and be in Massachusetts before morning.

But I sleep through the night, exhausted by my thoughts and held by my dreams, dreams of flight, of flying. Only the sun wakes me and then it is late. There is nobody in the house but me. I wait. Soon the wagon comes back, my father alone on the buckboard. "Had yer breakfust yet?" he asks me. "I guess you'll have to fix yer own. Me and you'll have to fend fer ourselfs a while."

"Where's Ma and Charity?"

"I jist put 'em on the train, down to The Bridge. They're goin' clear out to Illinoy, to stay with Emmeline a spell. Took ever blasted cent I had to my name to pay fer the fare. Guess me and you'll have to look fer some job a work, or eat nought but beans."

The sawmill has been closed for some time, the charcoal pits have been cold a long time, there isn't much work. Trees for charcoal have to be at least twenty-five years old, and most of those are gone.

My father humbles himself to ask Enos Jenner if he's got any work for us to do. Jenner at first says no, but then he bargains with my father and gets a good price for a new shingle roof. I'm taken out of school to help. There's only three in the school now, and the school closes, the three left have to walk more than a mile to the school down at The Bridge. One of them is Violate, and I wish I were still going to school so I could walk her there and back.

Once, on Jenner's roof, while we're working, out of nowhere my father spits out his mouthful of nails and says to me, "You know, if ye wa'nt near 'bout big as me, I'd beat yer hide off."

But that's all he ever said about what I did to Charity. Living alone together, the two of us, hauls us closer together. We are good friends. I'm all he's got left. I've always felt closer to my father than to anybody else, except Charity, we're so alike. As he says, I'm near about big as him, and he is big.

He talks to me many a time and oft, he who is not a talking man, as if in this solitude without a carping wife to check his tongue he must say all that he has left unsaid. Although the charcoal pits have long been cold, sometimes he goes and lights one, and makes a small bit of charcoal because this was all he'd ever known to do and doesn't know how to quit for good. Sometimes I go with him, and listen to him, and he says, once, "I'd train ye how to keep a good charcoal pit, jist as my dad trained me, but what good? Better ye learned a more timely trade."

When he says he doubts that I will stay in Dudleytown, I protest that I'll stay as long as he. Now he tells me of the ancient prognostication of Asenath Prenner, that the seventh child in a Montross family will be the last. But there were only six of us? I say. No, you had another sister who died young. But I don't believe those superstitious things, I say. Well look, he says, *already you're the last.*

Already I'm the last. I learn from him of this town and its past and its Curse. His grandfather, old Mountain Horse Montross, talked to him in his dotage of seeing and knowing, at the end of the last century, Abial Dudley, the last of the Dudleys. "Old Bial" in his nineties considered myself to be "Mayor of Dudleytown"; the dignity of this office helped him obscure the fact that he was penniless, that the town kept him alive by farming him out, each year, to the lowest bidder at the pauper auction. Some said, later, that it was Old Bial who brought down the Curse upon the town for this indignity. But the Curse had been there from the beginning, when Old Bial's father and uncle had founded the town, in 1747. No, the Curse had come with them, from England, through generations of ill-fated Dudleys going all the way back, in some medieval time, to the very first, whose name was given him "from the dodder lea." A lea is a meadow. A dodder is a parasitic vegetable. Old Bial was a parasitic vegetable in his last days, pretending he was a mayor guiding the town to greatness, for which the town owed him his existence.

The better sons of Dudleytown always left, and some found their way to prominence elsewhere, as soldiers, statesmen, judges, professors. Why don't I leave? Because I'm not a better. Those who stayed were those who can work the land. Like my father. Like me. Oh, I have thoughts of being a soldier, I would like to be a statesman or a judge, I might even be a professor. No, I'm not in school more. I can't even finish school. What would I like to be? I'd like to be mayor of Dudleytown and keep it from dying.

But its illness is already fatal. Two epidemics hit the town, in 1774 and again in 1813, and killed off large sections of the people. A town must grow to live, and this town has not grown since it was born. A blight has fallen on the land itself: the hardwoods have reclaimed these former pineries. The little pine still remaining is too little, and the hardwoods take its sun and water.

I brood on dodder lea: that dodder lea, that Dudley, that Dudleytown itself has been a parasite on this land, and this land has rejected it, with violence. We are not wanted here. It bothers me that my father goes so often to brood over the cold charcoal pits and to light small fires in them, out of memory.

The few of us who're left ought best cleave together in our isolation and infirmity. But we do not. Shipwreck survivors on a sinking raft sing songs and hold hands. But we do not. We are all strangers here. These few families live on their islands and speak to no one, or speak sharply. Once, my father says, the men used to work together at cider making in the fall, and beer making in the spring. For the great beer making, one man would raise hops, another wintergreen, another would gather sassafras root and twigs, another prince's pine, another birch and spicebush, and in the spring they would bring all this together and make their wonderful beer and have their great beer spree. I sampled it more than once myself. But now the men brew their own, each his own, a second-rate suds, and drink it all alone.

And they drink it faster than they can make it. There's not a sober man around. That means my father too. That means me as well, more often than not. The gas in the beer highs the head and holds off the horrors of this life.

My father comes home with a nosebleed and drinks a pint to stanch the flow. I ask him how he got it. Ferrenzo Allyn, he says.

"*Renz?*" I say. "Renz hit you? Where is he? I'll even the score for you, with more than just a nosebleed!"

"He's down at the corners," my father says. "But you'll have ter wake him fust. He's clobbered cold. Nothin' wrong with me, I jist tripped in the way of a lucky punch."

"What'd he hit you for?"

"Aw, I hit 'im fust. Him and his mouth, scallionin' me. Cal'late mebbe he's miffed on account a that gull Violate a his is still holdin' a torch fer *you*, son. Mighty snide he says to me, 'It 'pears yer family keeps gettin' smaller, Mister Montross,' says he. And says he, 'Why'nt you'n Dan git out and make it smaller yet?' So I says, 'Whut're ye so het up on the subjick fer? Whut business a yours is it?' And then he says, 'I hanker to see ye both gone. Dan aint good fer but mischief, and you aint good fer but nothing nowadays.' 'I aint, huh?' says I. 'Wal, mebbe I'm still good enough to learn the likes of Ferrenzo Allyn a mite of respeck fer his betters!' And he snorts and says, 'Haw. 'Twant fer ye bein' sech a old codger, I'd make ye eat them wuds!' So I says, 'I aint so old as ye figure.' And I hit him. Knocked 'im clean off his feet. He got up quick, and swung a few at me, but he missed ever time. So I knocked him off his feet again."

My father pours himself another pint. I tingle at his telling, proud of him. His nose has stopped bleeding; he touches it lightly and says, "He'd a never got in that one good lick 'cept I tripped. Sort of fell into his fist. Made me mad as hops, then. So I really laid him out. Guess he's still laying there, havin' bad dreams." My father laughs, a short one, an ironic one. "One thing about this town bein' so small," he says, "aint much traffic on the roads more. Guess he'll lay there a good while before anybody stumbles on 'im to pick 'im up."

"I'd like," I say, "to go down there and wait till he wakes, then put him out again."

"Naw," my father says. "Guess the poor bastard's had enough fer today. Have some beer."

But I should have. Oh, I should have. I should have beaten him meek and unmanned that very day. I should have pounded him into the next county. Renz Allyn is a big bully who will come to no good, who will become the town's rowdy, who will torture small animals, who will afflict old men, who will anguish old women, who will beat his wife, who will be Violate. He will beat her to death and be sent to jail, and then Dudleytown will be empty. But that is some years ahead yet. It is not what I know but what I dream.

Yet I dream this too: my father burning. How did I dream it? The terror of the dream wakes me. I wake, and rise, and search the house. I light a lantern. The Eli clock reads half past twelve. My father's bed is empty. This is no dream now. But there is nothing burning. I call him. Perhaps he's only out to the privy. I go there, and it is not burning, but he is not there. I call him loudly, I call him east and west. Only an owl answers. In the black night I see no smoke nor fire nor burning. My dream said, there are stones all around. Said my dream, the brook is near. My dream had it, a pit, a pit with coals. I run, the moon abreast and mocking me that I cannot outrun it. Down to the branch, and leaping, the lantern flying in my thrashing hand, across the branch, cloth ripping and I knowing I'm still in my nightshirt and not caring, up to the road, and down the road to the corner, and there into the mill road, the pit road, and down it, the soles of my feet scorning the sharp pebbles. Ahead in the road, out of reach of my lantern, a figure. "Pappa!" I call to the figure, but the figure scurries into the brush, and out of sight. Maybe only a deer. But on two legs? I run on, on my two legs, leaping. Past the Bardwell store, dark and boarded up. Past the

Bardwell house, falling. Past the place where Zadock's house stood until I took the nails out of it. The road levels, then drops again, steeply. Past the sawmill, its big blade broken and propped against a tree. Then I smell the smoke. The smoke which is not just smoke, not coals alone smouldering. Burning cloth, and hair, and something other, so foul I slow and pause and nearly stop, and nearly turn to run the other way. But I go on. To the pit. Leaving the road and crashing down to it through brush. There is no light, no light from it. Just smoke. I raise my lantern high. The smoke pours and rolls from a long loglump lying on the coals. A loglump with arms and legs. I set the lantern down. There is no way to climb down into the pit. Beside the pit is an oak bucket, old, which the pitkeepers drank from. Empty. I fill it in the brook. I pour it into the pit. I fill it again and pour it again. Steam hisses and sizzles and the smoke billows more. I fill the bucket again and pour it into the pit. I fill it again and pour it into the pit. Until the coals are out. Steam still rises from the figure, but the coals are out, out enough for me to walk on them with my bare feet, though still they burn. I grab the figure and roll it over. It is black as pitch but the very shape of it I can recognize, in my own image. Owls say Who. I answer them in screams. I hear laughter. Owls do not laugh. I rage against the dark. These stones have been here too long. Yell at the dark: I'll get you for this. Owls say Who. Drag the figure out of the coals, into the cool grass, listen for a heartbeat, ear to hot scorched breast. Hear heartbeat, but is my own. The heat of the body chills me. I'm cold. I'm cold and all alone.

Where are you? Come out and show yourself and let me kill you. But only laughter. I run. I'll race him home. I'll beat him home, and then I'll beat him. I can outrun anybody. I can outrun them all. His house is high up toward Dudleytown Hill, but I can run faster uphill than most can run down. But I am out of breath when I reach it. I pound on the door until his old mother comes with her lantern, but I can only pant at her. She stares at me and says my name and asks why I'm out of breath. I can only pant at her.

At last I grab my heaving chest with both hands and get enough air to say, but weakly, "Where's Renz?"

"Fast asleep like every decent soul at such an hour," she says.

"I don't believe it," I pant at her. "He's not here."

"What do ye want with him at this time a night, and you in your nightshirt at this time a year?"

"I want to see him. I don't believe he's here. He's not here."

"You tell me whut ye want 'im fer, and I'll fetch him," she says.

"I just want to see if he's here," I pant at her.

"Then come," she says, "and see." She with her lantern and I with mine go into the house and through the parlor to a chamber. There is a bed in the chamber, and someone beneath the covers. I pull back the covers. It is Renz. His eyes are closed, he seems fast asleep. But his brow is damp. Is that sweat on his brow? And isn't his breathing hard? "See?" says Mrs. Allyn. "Now d'ye want to wake him?"

I stare a while longer. Is that sweat on his brow? Is he breathing hard? A bad dream? He could have run around the back of the house and come through the back door quietly while I was panting at his mother on the front stoop.

"Well?" says Mrs. Allyn. "Do ye want to wake him, or no?"

"No," I say. "I'll see him later."

I go home. I despise myself. But there's nothing I can do until the first light. The empty house haunts me. Father, why did you go to the pits so much? And did he club you over the head before he pushed you in? You did not trip and fall, did you? Or have a stroke? Or faint? You felt hands pushing you in, or you felt a stick breaking over the back of your head. I hope the stick blacked you out so that you did not feel the burning. I hope you did not feel the burning.

I talk to him until the first light. Then I hitch the wagon and drive to the pit for him. I back the horses and the wagon to where he lies in the early light, blackened and cold. I lift him, I lift my father up, up from the ground, and into the wagon. I take him home.

Then I search the house for any money. I have not a cent. In the burnt pocket of his jacket I find a burnt purse with a few pennies in it. Not enough. I search their chamber, the drawers of my mother's bureau. Nothing. I could ask the Jenners for a loan, but I don't. I unhitch the wagon and put the bridle on the mare Mistress and ride her at a trot, back down the road past the pits, on down the mountain to The Bridge. At the railway station, I say to the telegraph man, "My father's died, and I must send for my mother in Illinois, but I have no money except this." I show him the pennies. "No other kin?" he asks. They are all gone too, I tell him. But my mother will pay you when she comes. "I'm not allowed to give credit," he says. "Government law." He looks at my pennies. "You've got enough there for postage, haven't ye?" he says. I frown at him. "Wal, tell ye whut," he says. "You could work it off. Sweep out the station, and dust everything. All right? Now what do ye want to say in the message?"

> FATHER WAS BURNED IN THE CHARCOAL PITS LAST
> NIGHT AND DIED. DANIEL.

The morning I spend in sweeping the station until every bit of dirt and dust is up. Then with an oilrag I began dusting the benches and counters. The telegraph man stops me before noon. "That's enough," he says. "You can go." Then he asks me, "Can you read?" I nod, and he hands me the slip of yellow paper. "Just came in," he says.

> BODY WONT KEEP TILL I GET THERE. SEE HE IS
> BURIED PROPER. MOTHER.

I go home. Father, do you want a box? You felled trees, Father, and you cut them up, and you burned them to make charcoal to make iron, and the charcoal burned you. Do you want a box of wood? The box will rot, and you will too. You don't need a box of wood, do you, Father? I bury him on the hill behind our house, in a hole as deep as I can dig. Before I fill in the dirt, I fetch the family Bible from his chamber. On the family page, where it says Clendenin Murdock Montross, Born April 24, 1843, I write: Died March 30, 1895, and then I carry the Bible up to the grave on the hill, and open it, and try to find something in it that will do. I don't know the Bible well.

Most of the things I read in it make me feel like laughing. It takes me a long time to find something appropriate. But there is no hurry. I keep reading, until I find this, which is what Job said:

For there is hope of a tree, if it be cut down, that it will sprout again, and that the tender branch thereof will not cease. Though the root thereof wax old in the earth, and the stock thereof die in the ground; yet through the scent of water it will bud, and bring forth boughs like a plant. But man dieth, and wasteth away: yea, man giveth up the ghost, and where is he? As the waters fail from the sea, and the flood decayeth and drieth up: so man lieth down, and riseth not: till the heavens be no more, they shall not awake, nor be raised out of their sleep. O that thou wouldest hide me in the grave, that thou wouldest keep me secret, until thy wrath be past, that thou wouldest appoint me a set time, and remember me! If a man die, shall he live again? All the days of my appointed time I wait, till my change come.

I speak these words over him, then scatter some pieces of his charcoal over him, then fill his grave with the dirt. I make his marker of wood, of pine, he who lived by wood and died by it. With my pocketknife I carve his name and his dates, and this: "The last Montross of Dudleytown, but one."

Now I go looking for Renz. But he is scarce. His old mother says he has gone to work for a man in the next town, Goshen. What man? She does not know his name. How long will he be gone? Who knows? she says. When he comes back, I say, tell him I am waiting for him.

Should I see the constable of Cornwall? Would it do any good? Could he find any evidence, or force a confession? No witnesses. An impoverished middle-aged man, drunk on beer, falls into a charcoal pit and burns. Who would care?

My mother takes five days to come. A boy from The Bridge brings me a message: your mother has arrived on the train but is not able to make it home. Come for her. I hitch the wagon again and drive to the railway station. She is lying on a bench, her eyes closed. She has not brought Charity back with her. I put my hand on her face and feel her fever. She opens her eyes. "I'm ill, Daniel," she says. "Take me home to die."

The train men help me get her into the wagon.

✝ 15 ✝

One afternoon in August with already a hint of autumn in the air, Diana took Daniel up the hill in search of his father's grave. She did not expect to find a headstone—the marker had been made of wood, which would have rotted long ago—but if she could only find a mound of earth that looked like a grave in the right place, it would be *something* to believe in.

But even a mound of earth settles and sinks after so many years, and the woods gave no bearings to Daniel in his search for the site of the grave. They could not find anything. Diana heard laughter, and for a moment she was certain it was Ferrenzo Allyn laughing at them, and she quickly brought Day out of his trance. Day listened too, and heard laughter. "Just another intruder," he said.

The laughter was coming from the direction of their camp. They went back downhill, away from the unfound grave, to see who was laughing in their camp.

They found their camp occupied, by a group of seven persons. These persons at first glance were indistinguishable as to sex, for the males among them had shoulder-length hair. All of them were young; no older than Diana, no younger than Day; a few years earlier they would have been called hippies. It was the older of the males, also bearded, who was doing most of the laughing, and when he caught sight of Diana and Day he laughed again and said, "For joy. Thou art children, and blessed. Glorious sight."

One of the others said, "Behold, thy dwelling place is fair."

One of the females said to another, "For I am persuaded of

166

good chimes here, Rebekah. Dost thou hear good chimes?" and the one addressed as Rebekah said, "Glorious."

The laughing one, the original speaker, turned to Day. "What is thy pilgrimage, brother?" he asked Day. When Day did not immediately reply, he continued, "Art thou settled? Or abidest thou here only for the eventide?"

Day exchanged looks with Diana, and she declared, "it isn't exactly a pilgrimage."

"All men pilgrimage," he said. "What is thine?"

"Nature study," Diana said.

"Glorious!" said several of them at once.

"But," said the laughing one, "what dost thou study nature *with*?"

Diana gave him a puzzled expression and shrugged her shoulders.

"Acid?" he said.

She knew that word. She shook her head.

"Thou are not a head, then," he said. "So how dost thou swing with nature? What is thy potion? Grass?"

"No," she said.

"Bennies?" he said. "Crystal?"

"No," she said.

"Art thou shooting smack?" he asked

She shook her head.

The boy who seemed closest to the laughing one, always keeping near him and occasionally grasping his elbow as if to hang on, said to him, "This brother and sister walk the straight path, Zeph. They are pharisees."

"Verily," said the laughing one.

One of the girls said, "Let's crash here, anyway. I get good chimes in this place."

"Verily," the laughing one said. He asked Diana, "Couldst thou nurture these thy brethren with any morsel from thy table?" There was no trace of beggary in his voice; he sounded as if he were offering to do her a favor.

"Sure," she said, and walked over to the ice chest and opened it. "Let's see what we've got."

Diana found a package of ground beef, but not enough to go around. Enough, at least, for spaghetti sauce. "How about spaghetti?" she suggested to the laughing one.

"Glorious," he said, and the others echoed him.

Day filled their largest pot with water and built a fire to boil it. Then he went off into the woods to gather greens and mushrooms for the salad. He did not seem terribly pleased at the prospect of dinner guests, especially these.

There were not enough plates to go around, nor enough forks, but this did not hinder the guests, who shared plates and who, fork-less, ate with fingers. Diana passed around a large bottle of Chianti, and the guests drank from the bottle. They seemed to be extremely hungry and thirsty, and all of them had second helpings; some had thirds. The bottle was soon empty, and Diana, lacking another, opened a domestic Burgundy and passed it around.

The guests were appreciative. They frequently said "Glorious" during the meal, and after the meal they lay on the ground holding their stomachs and chanting "Glorious" and "Rejoice" and "Exceed-ingly Glad."

The laughing one decided to introduce himself and his friends. He was Zephaniah, he said. Had they ever heard of Zephaniah, formerly called Mu, formerly of the rock group called The Grape Group? No? Well, here beside him was Esaias, also formerly of The Grape Group, formerly called The Flake. The other brother over there, he hadn't belonged to The Grape Group, they picked him up in Massachusetts. His name was Barnabas. The four "sisters" were: the larger blonde, Bathsheba; the lesser and lighter blonde, Zeresh; the brunette, Vashti; and the auburn-haired, Rebekah.

Rebekah and Vashti were dressed in shirts and jeans; the two blondes wore daishikis; all, like the men, except for the one called Barnabas, were barefoot, and all had scarred and scabbed soles.

Diana asked Zephaniah how they had happened to stumble upon this camp. He explained that until recently they had been com-munards in The Fellowship of The Vital Flesh, up in Massachusetts, where they had discovered their saviour Jesus and his wonderful teachings, but the fellowship had become too crowded and they had been evicted for holding heterodox interpretations of the Divine Message. Since then they had been wandering, and just last week had discovered the Appalachian Trail and decided to follow it.

"And behold, it brought us here," he said. "So how long hast *thou* dwelt here?"

"About nine weeks," she answered.

"Wondrous!" Zephaniah exclaimed. "Nine weeks! Glorious! But why?"

"It's a long story," she said.

"So?" he said. "Time is long."

Diana had already been asking herself if she should reveal to these people the true nature of their "pilgrimage." It might impress them, especially the part about reincarnation. But she didn't know how Day would feel about it; he would probably be reluctant to demonstrate for them. He wasn't comfortable with these people, she could see that. As for herself, she respected flower children or Jesus freaks or whatever they were, even if she could never be one, and she welcomed company after such a long time alone with Day. At least she thought she did. She told herself she did. But their "pilgrimage," hers and Day's, was a private thing and she didn't want to tell them all about it. So she merely answered, "There used to be a town here, and we're exploring it."

Zephaniah looked around him. The others looked around. "Where?" several of them said. "Yes, where?" said Zephaniah.

"Out of sight," Diana said.

Zephaniah laughed, but then he gave her a look that questioned if she were mocking. "Verily," he said. "*Verily.*"

"You didn't notice any of the cellar holes?" she asked.

"What is a cellar hole?" Zephaniah asked.

"Come on," she said. "I'll show you."

Slowly they all got up off the ground and followed her in single file down the trail toward the center of Dudleytown. Zephaniah caught up with her and walked beside her. Day brought up the distant rear. She gave these people a guided tour of Dudleytown, pointing out the cellar holes of the houses of Parmenter, Jones-Jenner, Dudley, Bardwell and Temple, the yards around still growing long-ago planted clumps of locust, lilac, rose and tansy.

"Verily, a forsaken place," Zephaniah said. "A forsaken place. Why did they leave?"

"Various reasons," Diana said, and gave the group a short history of Dudleytown and its decline.

"Man, they just lucked out!" said the one called Barnabas, and got a frown from Zephaniah.

The girl called Bathsheba held her arms out as far as they would reach from her sides and exclaimed, "Hey! Wouldn't this be the right place for a commune!"

The one called Rebekah agreed. "Yeah! Let's start a commune. I really get good chimes in this place."

Several others said, "Glorious! A commune! Verily! Let's start our commune here!"

Day gave Diana a most pained look.

Zephaniah cocked his ear and said, "Hark. Is it the sound of water mine ears heareth?"

Diana pointed. "There's a waterfall right down the road there."

"Glorious! Let us go there!" Zephaniah suggested and began to trot down the road toward Marcella Falls. The others trotted after him.

Day and Diana followed together. Day said to her, "It looks like we're stuck with permanent guests."

"No," she said. "They'll move on if we ask them to."

"And what if they won't?" Day said.

"They will. One thing about these people, they're considerate for the feelings of others. It's part of their code."

As soon as the group reached Marcella Falls and saw the pool below it, all of them began undressing. "Let us exalt the flesh," Zephaniah declared. "Let ablutions in this glorious water cleanse our vital bodies and refresh our spirits." Several others said "Amen." Soon they were all naked and jumped into the pool with whoops of "Glorious" and a few screeches from the girls because of the cold water.

"Come join us and be cleansed, brother and sister!" Zephaniah called to Day and Diana.

Diana hesitated.

Day asked her, "Do you want to?"

"Yes and no," she said. "I will if you will."

"I don't see the point," he said. "We just had our bath here a few hours ago."

"On the other hand," she said, "they'll think we're awful squares if we don't join them. Come on. It's a very innocent thing. And when I'm an old lady I can tell my grandchildren about the one time in my life when I went for a communal skinny dip."

Day laughed, but with some discomfort. "Go on, then," he said, "but I'll tell our grandchildren that Grandpa was a chicken and just sat on the bank and watched while Grandma had her fun."

"Oh, *Day*," she said, disappointment mingled with delight at his picture of them talking to their grandchildren. She quickly kissed him. "Come on," she said. "Let's don't be prudes with these people."

The others seemed to be thoroughly enjoying themselves. They were having water fights and playing tag and in general romping and flouncing around in the water without any trace of self-consciousness or modesty. The girl called Vashti had very large breasts which bounced a lot. The blonde called Zeresh was definitely not a blonde in her pubic hair, as Diana was. Barnabas and Esaias were circumcised, she noticed, but Zephaniah was not. Esaias had an erection, but was not self-conscious about it, and none of the others seemed to notice. *Well*, Diana thought, *at least I can tell my grandchildren that I watched a communal skinny dip.*

"Go on, if you want to," Day said. "I don't care."

"Are you sure?" she challenged him.

"Sure," he said. "I'll probably get a kick out of watching you."

"Voyeur!" she said. But she discovered that her fingers were unbuttoning her shirt.

"If it weren't for us voyeurs," he said, "you exhibitionists wouldn't have any fun."

She continued undressing. "I'll tell our grandchildren you said that!" she said, laughing, and then, fully naked, turned her back to him and climbed down the bank to join the others.

"Welcome, sister!" Zephaniah exclaimed. "Thou hast a freedom unknown to thy fainthearted friend." And he took her hands and waltzed her out into the water. The other boys were giving her admiring looks, while the girls were giving her green looks. She knew that her figure was as good as any of theirs.

She joined their play, and splashed back at them when they splashed her, and participated in their game of water tag. But the sport, she noticed, was becoming not-so-innocent. The one called Esaias, who had an erection, had apparently decided to use it. He grabbed the one called Rebekah and dragged her down into the water and got himself between her legs. Rebekah squealed with pleasure and said "Glorious!" Diana felt suddenly embarrassed and realized she was blushing; she quickly sat down in the water, covering herself to her neck.

Zephaniah came and sat down beside her. Indicating with a nod of his head what Esaias and Rebekah were doing, he asked her, "Art thou aghast? Dost thou not know that our saviour commands it?"

She felt his hand, under water, on her thigh. She brushed it off. "Your saviour," she said. "Not mine." She glanced over her shoulder to see if Day was watching. He wasn't. He was in conversation with a stranger, a middle-aged man in khakis.

"Thou must not close thy mind to the message," Zephaniah said, and put his hand on her thigh again.

"We've got company," she said, and pointed toward the stranger. Zephaniah squinted at the man talking to Day on the bank. "Pig?" he said.

"Maybe a game warden or something," Diana said.

The girl called Bathsheba came over and seized Zephaniah's erect penis and said, "Hey, this is mine, not thine," and gave Diana a look both defiant and catty. Then she sat down into Zephaniah's lap.

"Cool it," Zephaniah said to the girl. "The Man is watching. If he's not a pig, he could be a narc."

But the man, after a few more words with Day, turned and

walked off. Bathsheba began bouncing up and down in Zephaniah's lap, and Zephaniah wrapped his arms around her and groaned, "Oh, glorious!"

Diana got out of the water and climbed the bank. She asked Day, "What did he want?"

"He's just some local landowner," Day said. "He asked me what we were doing here, and why I wasn't in the water too and how come I didn't have long hair like the others, and then he said, 'Why, it looks to me like those two kids are fucking,' and I said, 'Yes, that's what it looks like to me too,' and then he said, 'Well, I don't own *this* land but if I did I would put a stop to this fucking,' and he asked me again what I was doing, and I said I was just watching, and he said, 'You like to watch that fucking?' and then he asked, 'Why aren't you out there fucking too?' and I said, 'I like to do my fucking in private,' and he said, 'Me too,' but then he just gave me an odd look and walked on off. Diana, what if we just went on back to the tent? Do you think they would follow us?"

"Maybe not," Diana said and quickly dressed. She took Day's hand and they walked up the road toward home. "Maybe," she said, "they will get the hint."

Back at the tent, Day asked her, "Do you find that Zephaniah character very attractive?"

"Well," Diana said, and pondered the question. "There's something sort of instinctual about him which probably draws girls to him. Sort of an animal magnetism. But no, he's not my type."

"Am I your type?" Day asked.

She gave him a playful kiss. "No, but I like you a lot better."

As dusk fell, it began to rain. They took their radio into the tent and turned it on to WQXR. Diana and Day searched the camp for anything else that should not be left out in the rain, and discovered two guitars and seven assorted packs, satchels, and blanket rolls belonging to Zephaniah and his friends. She asked Day to help her move this stuff into the tent and out of the rain. Day said, "They're bound to come back for these things."

"Yes," Diana said with a sigh, "and they're bound to seek shelter from the rain, and we're bound to give it to them."

These words were scarcely out of her mouth before she saw them coming, laughing and leaping in the rain. Zephaniah thanked her profusely for having the foresight to move his guitar and bag in out of the rain, and to show his thanks he tuned his guitar and played a rousing rock-spiritual number for her, first turning off the Sibelius that was coming from WQXR.

The nine of them sat in a tight circle inside the tent, and Esaias opened his bag and took out a pipe and filled it with marijuana and lighted it and passed it around. Diana knew that she was more or less immune to the stuff, so when her turn came she took the pipe and inhaled. To her surprise, Day did not pass up his turn, but he had a bad coughing attack on the first round. The second round he was more careful.

Esaias joined Zephaniah with his guitar, and the two of them played their repertoire of rock-spirituals. The marijuana pipe was refilled and recirculated. For a while the group attempted to continue speaking in their biblical language, but eventually most of them, especially the girls, lapsed back into obsolete hiplingua: "Right on." "Do a number." "Far out." "Spaced." "Turn his head around."

All of them except Diana herself seemed to be high on the marijuana. Day was glassy-eyed but restless. Zephaniah and Esaias stopped pounding on their guitars. The conversation trickled out, but the pipe continued on its rounds.

Day stood up. He spread his arms wide. He announced, "I am a tree."

"Go to sleep, Day," Diana said.

⊹ 16 ⊹

Fush to Bungtown! Day unto day, my mother lies abed but she is not dying. All her talk is of what a pretty place Emmeline has in Illinois. Once, irked, I blurted, "Why didn't you stay there?" And she wept. And a little harder I had to harden my heart. The tree of me grows around a stone in its bosom.

I haven't told her it was Renz. I haven't told a soul. But I wait for him. Before the April rains came, I went back to the charcoal pits and searched all the ground around; in the mud were my own bootprints and at least two of my father's bootprints, but one bootprint which was different. I mixed a plaster and poured it in and let it harden, and now I have this cast of it, this print, and I am waiting, and if it matches his boot I warrant me I will kill him.

It's time to plant peas, my mother says. If I could just get up long enough, she says. If you won't tend the garden, she says, we'll sure to starve. I've never done a garden, but she tells me how, and watches from her window. But something tells me that we won't be here to harvest it.

I beg the Jenners for a job of work, but though they have plenty of work they say they have nothing to pay me. It comes, in time, to my begging to do their work for the pay of five pounds of flour and ten pounds of dry beans. Old Eph Parmenter pays me a pound of salt pork to shovel the dressing from his cow stalls and spread it on his fields; it takes me two days, and twice I have a glimpse of Violate but I calculate old Eph has given her to know that she can't even come out of the house and speak to me.

I can cook a fair bait of beans, but Mother gets tired of it, and so do I. She tells me to use Dad's gun. Three days in the wood bring home a partridge, a gray squirrel, a red squirrel, and two pigeons, and I've used up all the shells but one. One. One to save.

Most days I can find no work. Sometimes I fish in Bonny Brook or go beyond the mountain to the river, the Housatonic, which means in the Indian tongue "beyond the mountains." Mostly, though, I just walk the woods and roads, waiting for Renz to show again. I plan a lot about how I will knock him down and take off his boot and take the boot home to see if it matches the cast. Once while I'm walking in the woods it comes on to rain and I get myself under the old big boulder in Parmenter's back pasture, and there is this girl there, this stranger, prettier than Violate, with light hair, but older than Violate; I guess she is just hiding from the rain too, and right off she asks me if I know where I am.

Sure, I say. Looks to be old Landlocked Whale.

She asks me, Is that what you call it?

What I call it, I say. Some jist call it The Rock.

Very talky she is, and asks, How far is your house from here?

As near as no matter, I say, fooling with her.

She keeps on. How near is that? she asks.

Two whoops an' a holler, I say.

Then she says something so peculiar I begin to wonder if she is touched. You're looking at me, she says. Can you see me?

So I say, Naw, I'm blind a one eye, 'n can't see out th'other.

Really? says she.

'Course I can see you, nimsky! Who are ye, anyhow?

Then she says, You don't know me? as if I should.

Well, I say to her, You aint Violate, less ye blanched your hair. Violate? she says. Violate what?

T'aint what but who, I tell her.

Violate who, then? she says.

Violate Parmenter.

I know then she must be a stranger from way off, because she asks, Is that a name?

Naw, it's a gull! I say and laugh.

Who is she?

Eph Parmenter's gull, I tell her and then I ask, Who are you?

But she won't tell me her name. We keep on talking, and I ask her how she happened to be here in the belly of the Landlocked Whale and she says she's waiting for the rain to stop and she's lost. I ask her where she's lost from and she says Dudleytown and I tell her it's not but right down the hill and I offer to show her how to get there, if she'll tell me which house she wants, and then she says it's my house she's looking for, and I wonder what she's going there for, and she says she wants to meet my father, she's some distant relation of his.

My father's dead, I say. Didn't you know that?

No, she says. I'm sorry to know that. When did he die?

Few months back. Fell in one a the charcoal pits. 'Least that's what people think. I shouldn't wonder but what he 'uz pushed.

She asks me now, Who do you think pushed him?

I haven't told a soul this, but for some reason this girl makes me tell her, so I say, Ferrenzo Allyn, that skunk.

"Stop, Daniel. Are you really under that rock with that girl?"

Stop, Daniel, she says. Are you really under that rock with that girl. My head feels peculiar.

"Open your eyes, Daniel. Now look at me. Am I that girl?"

Open your eyes, Daniel, she says. I didn't know they were closed. Now look at me, she says. Am I that girl? she asks me.

Yes, you are that girl. You make my head hurt.

"Tell me what I'm wearing."

Tell me what I'm wearing, she says. I wish I had never met you Now you're making my body hurt too. You are wearing some man's denim trousers and a lady's waist with the sleeves cut off.

"Do other women in Dudleytown dress like this?"

Do other women in Dudleytown dress like this? she asks me. Not generally, no.

"Then how can I be in Dudleytown, in this year of 1895 or 1896? Are you sure that you met me under the rock? Are you really remembering me?"

You make my head hurt so, with your questions.

"Who are these other people here?"

Who are these other people here? she asks me. I don't know, I've never seen them before, except those two, that one's Jared Story, and that one's Renz Allyn and I'm going to kill the sonofabitch.

Him? He's Renz Allyn? Are you sure? Does Renz Allyn have a beard and long hair?"

He could easily of growed it while he's been gone to Goshen these three months, to try and disguise hisself so's I wouldn't be able to know him when he comes sneaking back to Dudleytown.

"Daniel, look at me. Are you absolutely certain that you met me under the rock called the Landlocked Whale when you were fifteen years old?"

I aint absolutely certain of nothing any more.

"Go on, then. Forget me. You didn't meet me under the rock. It was something you dreamed, maybe. Go on, until it is later, until you meet Renz Allyn again. Did he come back to Dudleytown? Did you meet him again?"

I do meet him again, yes, though he has disguised himself with a beard and long hair.

"No, Daniel. This isn't Renz Allyn. Close your eyes and quit looking at him. This isn't Renz Allyn but somebody you don't know, whose name is Zephaniah."

He is too Renz Allyn or my name aint Dan Montross. That disguise of his don't fool me a bit.

"Close your eyes, Daniel. Now, tell what happens. What happens when you meet Renz? Where do you meet him?"

Where do you meet him? she asks me. I see him here in the belly of the Landlocked Whale.

"No, you're confused. You didn't see him under that rock, did you?"

No, you're confused, she tells me. Yes, I am confused, but I know I see him in the belly of the Landlocked Whale because he has come here to lie and wait for Violate to sneak out and meet him, probably, but probably Eph Parmenter won't let her out of the house, and so Renz has fallen asleep while he's waiting for her, and I know it's him even though he has let his hair and beard to grow, so I tear off for home as fast as I can run, and I haven't even run that fast the time I tried to beat him home but I'm not running out of fear of him, no, but to get my cast of the plaster I poured into the bootprint and to get my father's old gun with the one shell left in it, and then I run back as fast as I can tear toward the Landlocked Whale but when I get there Violate has come up and joined him and the two of them have already begun funicling as fast as they can funicle, as if old Eph has just let her leave the house for two minutes to go to the privy or something and she has to get it over with and get right back, so I know that I can't kill him there while she's around because I can't have any witnesses, but at least I can sneak up and try matching the print with his boot, him funicling her without even taking off his boots or even dropping his trousers but just poking his perkin through his fly and into her, the two of them so busy funicling with groans and grunts and gasps they don't even notice me sneak up and match the plaster with the sole of his boot, which matches like a key fits a lock, no mistake whatever, and I nearly went ahead and put the bullet through both of them but I still loved Violate some who was the only thing even like a girlfriend or a girl or a female I had in all the world, so I waited for her to leave and go back to the house but when she did go back to the house Renz got up and went with her, at least as far as the pasture gate and by then he was too far for me to get a good shot at him and too close to the house anyway so I cut off through the woods to meet him on the road and hope that he would come and get a good look at me and know who it was that was going to put a bullet between his eyes or into his wretched heart and maybe even listen to him beg for mercy before I shoot him down like a dog, but when he comes, around a bend in the road, I see he's not alone but walking with his old chum Jared Story and rubbing himself in his crotch and bragging to Jared, Boy oh boy I funicled that gull so hard she was fartin holes in the ground, and Jared laughing fit to be tied, until the two of them catch sight of me and stop, and just look at me standing there holding the rifle, until Jared says, What are you huntin, Dan? and I should say something like partridge or squirrel not to give myself away, but I can't help it, I say, murderers.

And Renz still hasn't said anything; maybe he's hoping I still don't recognize him in that beard and long hair but I'm looking him right in the eye and pretty soon he knows I know who he is, and he says, You wouldn't be callin ole Renz Allyn a murderer, would ye? And I say, I would call him a lot worse than just that. I would call him a lowdown shit-eating chicken-hearted killer. I have lost my temper something terrible and forgotten I've only got one bullet and not enough to kill Jared too, but I will kill with the bullet whichever one makes the first move and kill the other one with my bare hands. Now Renz blusters, Well, if you aim to kill me, you'd best do it right now. And he takes out a segar and strikes a sulphur match to it and stands there just smoking his segar cool as Christmas.

But Jared Story is nervous and kind of walking backwards waiting for the right moment to turn and run. You Jared! I yell at him, just hold on. I don't want him running off and being a witness that I shot Renz. But I can't kill him too and he seems to know it. I aint murdered a soul, he says, What do you want to shoot me fer? And he keeps edging backwards. I up the rifle at him. He's near the bend of the road. Stop, Jared, I say. But he bolts and ducks and runs. I fire. He falls. But hits the dirt and springs up and runs on. Renz still smoking his segar, hasn't moved, says cool, You've missed him and lost him. Better load again, he says. Then he starts walking toward me. I don't have anything to load with even if I had time. He grabs the rifle by the barrel and yanks it out of my hands and throws it into the road. Then he draws back his fist. But before he can swing I pop a jab into his jaw, another into his gut. He bends, staggers, straightens, lashes out and gets me on the ear. Then on the nose. I punch his body and his face, not aiming for any place, just slugging him wherever I can land. He blocks my fists and slugs back at me. I block some too and get in a good one on his face, a better one on his shoulder which spins him back. For a dirty killer no clean fight: I slam my knee into his crotch and grab him by his long hair and throw him into the road. Jared! he hollers, Come back and help me! I jump on him and stomp him, my feet and then my knees pounding into him.

"Hey, dig the cat zapping that baddie!"

"Shhh, don't hassle him, man."

Now I...now I lay...now I lay me down on him and wrap my fingers around his neck and squeeze for all I'm worth. Oh, he purples and will choke and die. No struggle. My fingernails pierce his skin. Father, here he comes.

Eph Parmenter raises my chin with his rifle barrel and says, Whoa, Dan, let up now, and Jared says, See, I told you he was killing him.

Up, Dan, says Eph, or I'll fire.

"Down. Oh man, what a bummer!"

☩ 17 ☩

From Diana's diary

August 24

Oh, I wish, I wish that when he had asked "Couldst thou nurture these thy brethren with any morsel from thy table?" I had answered in a lie, "I'm sorry but we barely have enough for ourselves," or even given him some money and told him how to find the Cornwall Bridge general store. I want them here but I don't want them here. I wish they would go away but I wish they would stay. I have asked them to leave, twice today I have asked them, but they haven't, and maybe won't. I can't blame them for liking this place so much, but if they *really* intend to start a commune here then Day and I will have to leave or else we'll have to revise our life styles to match theirs, and I don't think Day could do that. I'm not even sure I could do it.

They aren't as dumb as they seem on the surface. The girls are, for the most part, mindless, giddy sex machines, although the one called Bathsheba is a Vassar drop-out, and the boy called Barnabas had a scholarship to M.I.T. and Zephaniah himself (I almost capitalized "Himself") keeps bragging about having an I.Q. of 155. Most of them didn't realize what Day was doing when I hypnotized him; I guess they thought that he was simply "freaking out" on all the pot he'd smoked. I didn't say anything to them about reincarnation. I just told them that Day "believes" that he used to live here in Dudleytown back in the 1890's under the name of Daniel Lyam Montross, and I filled them in on a little of Dan's history. Some of them were too high on pot to really care or seem interested, but a few of them, including Zephaniah and Esaias (oh, I *hate* their phony names!) paid close attention.

After I brought Day back from his trance, the girl called Vashti began to take a new interest in him. I guess she was impressed by his "freak-out" or felt that he needed to be comforted or guided through his bad "downer" or whatever. Anyway, she got pretty affectionate with him, and sometime during the middle of the night she crawled into his sleeping bag with him, and it looked to me as if he made love to her.

The reason I know this is that I was awake at the time. Yes, all nine of us, after all the pot smoking, slept together, "together," in our tent. It was still raining, after all; I couldn't very well make them leave, even if I had wanted to. I guess I'm more susceptible to marijuana than I thought I was. I was surprised our tent was big enough for all nine of us. But it was rather crowded. "Crowded."

Day hasn't confessed anything to me about what he did with Vashti (maybe he was too stoned to know what he was doing), but in a way I hope it's true because then I wouldn't feel so guilty myself. Because when Zephaniah crawled into my sleeping bag, I was past caring what he did. Maybe it was just the effect of the pot, but he was a terrific lovemaker, and I could understand why all these girls have attached themselves to him, although there was something rather dispassionate, even mechanical, about the way he did it.

But now I'd like for them to leave, and it's more complicated because Zephaniah knows that I enjoyed that. He said that they didn't want to freeload and would just find some nuts and berries to eat, but I drove into Cornwall Bridge and loaded up on food and the other girls helped me cook supper. Tonight, though, since it has cleared up, I'm going to insist that they can't sleep in the tent with us.

And I won't make Day demonstrate Daniel for them again. In retrospect, I was just doing it to show off, to entertain them, and perhaps out of curiosity to see what effect the marijuana would have on "Daniel." It was a disturbing experience for Day, I think. That business about "Daniel" remembering a conversation he had had with me, which couldn't possibly have happened to the real Daniel, reawakened my suspicions about this whole matter of reincarnation and Day's imagination. The fact that he "thought" that Zeph and Esaias were Ferrenzo Allyn and Jared Story, which was an obvious projection of his hostility toward the two boys, was all the more grounds for suspicion. I want to play that section back and have Day listen to it and confront him with these ideas, but he refuses. He seems to have been avoiding me all day, maybe because of his guilt. Would it make him feel better if I told him that he isn't the only one who is guilty?

Now he and Zephaniah are arguing because Day wants to listen to WQXR on the radio but Zeph wants to pick up a rock station. I will have to stop here and intervene.

August 25

They're still here. Five pounds of pork chops for supper. You've got the money, Diana. But kid, you don't want to marry them forever. I even had a little chat in private with Zeph this afternoon, trying to explain to him that Day's and my "trip" (or "pilgrimage" to him) is a private thing and I wished they would at least go off and pitch their camp in one of the cellar holes or some other place, but Zeph just gave me a "sermon" about "the beatitude of togetherness" and how "glorious" we all are together; then he used the occasion of our being alone together to try to seduce me and I had to tell him that I didn't want to get involved with him, but he just said "So who's getting involved?" and tried all the harder to seduce me, and I gave in, because this morning Day and Vashti went off into the woods together; he said he wanted to show her how to identify edible mushrooms, but I'm sure that's not all they were interested in. I think he has gotten over his aversions to these people even quicker than I did, but he absolutely loathes Zeph, and the feeling is mutual. Zeph keeps saying to him, "Get thee behind me, pharisee."

Late this afternoon we had brief but very unpleasant visitors. Four men in a jeep painted with the sign "Bill's Wrecker Service" came driving into our camp, and tried to get their kicks out of harassing us. They were urging us to let them "see some fucking," and when we refused they seemed on the verge of getting violent, but even though they were brawny roughneck types I guess they sensed that we outnumbered them by nine to four, so after calling us every foul name in the book they drove away.

Tonight I'm insisting that the tent belongs to Day and me alone. Unless it rains or something. The nights are getting very cool, I hate to make them sleep out on the ground, but you have to stop somewhere.

August 26

It didn't rain, but after the pot pipe had been circulated long enough it didn't matter so we all slept in the tent. I think I slept with all of them. Once I felt his head to see if I could tell who it was that was on me and he was short-haired. Day. Vashti must have been showing him some tricks.

I confess that I'm jealous of her. She is closer to Day's own age, and she's a very pretty brunette. I'm half expecting to hear Day announce that she is the reincarnation of Violate, and then the two of them will live happily ever after.

Today I've been trying to get these people interested in doing some group dances that I've choreographed, but without much success. As Zeph says, "Why ball the air?"

They have discovered the only remaining standing building in Dudleytown, west of here, the remains of what was probably the modest shanty or cabin of that couple who were the last residents, the doctor and his wife who went mad. It is not so much standing as leaning at a precarious angle. All of the roof and doors and windows are gone, but Bathsheba has persuaded the boys to straighten it up and fix it up and use it as the first building for their commune. They haven't started work on it, but I think they're serious.

August 27

Zephaniah is gone. For a while at least. Last night we used up the last of their supply of marijuana. Today they asked me if I knew where we could get some more, and I said I'm afraid that I didn't know anything about sources of supply. Zeph said he knew a guy up in Stockbridge, Mass., who had a lot of it. He asked to borrow my car. He assured me that he was a good driver and that he would just be gone overnight and back in the morning. Although a couple of girls wanted to go with him, he insisted that they stay here as "hostages" in security for the car. He intended to go by himself, and take no one. It all looked completely aboveboard, but I still made a "deal" out of it: I told Zeph that he could borrow my car on condition that he and his friends leave as soon as he got back. I said that they could fix up the old shanty if they wanted to, since it's at least a mile away from our tent, but that in any case they were to leave our tent for good and leave us alone. If that's the way you feel about it, he said. Promise, I said. Okay, he said, I promise.

So now he's gone, overnight, in my car. The others seem completely listless and disoriented with him gone. They're just sitting around, as if they're in a waiting room waiting for him to get back. I'm thinking of taking a little walk with Day some other place so we can have another session in private, to find out what happened between Daniel and Renz Allyn. I doubt I could get him away from Vashti, though, darn it.

Oh-oh. Here comes that jeep and those men again. I'll have to stop. No, *two* jeeps! *Three*! God help

☩ 18 ☩

Seven months later, in March, I located and interviewed Felix G. Spofford of West Cornwall, age 39, who gave his occupation as truckdriver for the town of Cornwall and volunteer fireman.

I showed him the two photographs. "Her," said Mr. Spofford, pointing to Diana Stoving's photograph, "I didn't much notice. There were lots more girls than boys, maybe five or six girls but only three boys, that's what made some of the guys mad, you know, the thought of those three boys getting all those girls to themselves, like a, you know, a goddamn harem or something. But him—" Mr. Spofford jabbed at the photograph of Day Whittacker, "I remember distinctly, one, because he didn't have girl's hair like them other two boys, and two, because he put up the worst scrap, I mean, hell, he dislocated poor Billy Evans' shoulder and he knocked several teeth out of Lou Posolski, and poor Jim Burland was in the hospital nearly a week with a goddamn hairline fracture of his goddamn skull, and me, hell, I've still got a scar or two myself."

Here Mr. Spofford unbuttoned his shirt to show me a scar

remaining from a minor chest laceration. "We never did get him, neither. I mean, we couldn't lay him out. Finally, Sam Rompiello got his shotgun out of the jeep and I think he was really gonna use it on that kid, but I stopped him and said that would be murder, you know, and so we just told him—we told all of 'em—to get the hell right out of there and if they were still there the next day we would have state troopers in there and lock 'em all up for public indecency or something, and then we hung around, you know, to make sure they weren't coming back, and they took off in every direction and never did come back. We kept what was worth keeping, ice chest, lanterns, folding chairs. But Lou Posolski had already ripped up that yellow tent with his hunting knife, so we burned what was left of it and threw in the fire some of the other junk they left behind, a pile of books, and them blankets that smelled so strong of cunt and come that you could hardly stand it and smelled even worse when they were burning. Holy Jesus.

"But don't get me wrong. I wasn't part of that bunch of guys that went up there solely for the purpose of making those kids fuck right in front of 'em. No. That was George Zim and his bunch. Sure, we were all together, in three jeeps, but like I say, me and Lou was going up there just to run 'em off for public indecency and not because we had anything dirty in mind like George and his bunch. But when George and his bunch started trying to make the kids fuck right in front of 'em, me and Lou didn't want to interfere, I mean, hell, mister, if they *did* fuck, that would be proof of public indecency, wouldn't it? and if need be then we could testify against them that we saw them do it. And sure enough, when George and his bunch kept putting the pressure on 'em, one of the two long-haired boys asked for a girl to volunteer and one of these big-tit blondes volunteered and took her dress off right there in front of all of us, and laid down on the ground too, but Holy Jesus, that poor boy must've been so scared he couldn't get him a hard-on.

"That girl kept rubbing at it and telling that boy that if they couldn't do it we were going to beat them up or worse, and that maybe we'd leave 'em alone if they did it, but that poor boy could never get it in. So that other long-haired boy tried, but he couldn't

get him a hard-on neither, ha ha! So then old George says well, by
God, those boys are probably fucked out but George says he has a
nice big stiff one himself and, so help me, he yanked it out and nearly
started screwing that girl himself, but that's when the other boy, this
short-haired one here in your picture, he got mad or something and
started fighting. He should of known better, him against twelve of
us. But he was a real devil, and like I say, we never could lay him out,
although we conked the shit outa those other two, the long-haired
ones. Maybe just goes to show that if you keep your hair cut proper
you can still keep your strength and can still put up a fight, but if
you let your hair get long like a girl's you can't fight no better than
a girl, though I got to admit, those girls were putting up a good
scrap themselves, I got a hank or two of my hair pulled out by the
roots, and old George nearly got his dick pulled off. But we laid out
a couple of those girls too. I don't mean, ha ha, *laid* 'em, but laid
em *out*, you know.

"Anyway, that's one bunch of kids that probably thought twice
before they ever went swimming without their clothes again in public.
I bet they went back to New York where they came from. But anyway
they never showed up in Dudleytown again. You know, some folks
say there's a curse on Dudleytown. Far as I'm concerned, those kids
and their immoral ways was the curse, and we wiped it out. But far
as *they* were concerned, ha ha, we were the curse on them. And the
cursed wiped them out. You could go up there today and not find a
trace of 'em. The only thing left behind, and this is funny, was a few
days later me and Lou went up again, just to check to be sure they
hadn't come back, and we saw this fancy red sportscar parked off the
road on the other side of Bonny Brook. At the time we figured it just
belonged to some of these rich artists that live around here, although
it had New York plates. But three days later it was still parked there
in the same place. After a week and it was still there, we got the state
troopers in to check that maybe it belonged to somebody who had
killed himself in the woods. But they searched all over the woods and
never found any bodies. So they checked the registration in New York
and found it belonged to some girl only twenty-one years old, and
that's when I figured it must have been one of those hippie girls, but

if that's so, how come she didn't drive off in it? Unless maybe they were all so scared, and ran the other way. Yes, come to think of it, our jeeps were parked between their tent and that car, but you would think they might have tried to circle back around us to get their car, or maybe come back in the middle of the night or something.

"That was a real expensive type of sportscar. Finally, it was towed off to the town garage, and matter of fact that's where it still is, and after twelve months have passed, if it isn't claimed, the town can auction it off to the highest bidder. Some of the guys are suggesting that the money we get from it ought to be used to have a patrol of citizens to check all of the woods regularly to make sure we don't get any more undesirable hippie-types running around without their clothes and misusing our property. Me, I think that's a good idea myself. God should have blasted those kids out of there with a lightning bolt or something, but God seems too busy elsewhere these days, so us citizens have got to do some of His work for Him.

"Mister, how come you're interested in these two, anyway? Are they more special or important than the others?"

☩ 19 ☩

Diana and Day spent the night holding each other in the niche in the underside of the rock called the Landlocked Whale. They didn't know where the others were. Bathsheba, Zeresh and Rebekah when last seen were dragging the still unconscious Esaias into the woods, in the general direction of the old shanty, although Diana did not know if that was their destination. Barnabas and Vashti had been talking about finding the highway and hitchhiking to Boston. The Landlocked Whale was far enough from their camp so that the men couldn't find them, yet near enough so that they could hear the distant voices and the sound of the jeep motors, and smell the burning of the tent and blankets. Diana and Day had grabbed up all that they could carry before fleeing: their sleeping bags, most of their clothes, a small sack of food, and the only thing that really mattered to Diana other than her purse with her pills and traveler's checks: the tapes and the tape recorder. They didn't have a free hand to carry a lantern, and thus had to find their way in the dark, and, when they reached the tiny cave under the Landlocked Whale, in the dark Diana had to rip up one of her shirts to make bandages to wrap the bleeding knuckles on both of Day's hands. She was still in a state of shock from their ordeal, but also in a state of awe and admiration over the way that Day had done battle with those men. She took a deep breath and said to him, "That must have been Daniel fighting for you."

Day said only, "Yeah. It must've."

"I think you nearly killed two of them," she said.

"If I could get them one at a time, I would kill them all," he said.

Late into the night they could still hear the distant sound of the men's voices, and finally, exhausted, they drifted off to sleep holding each other tightly in their sleeping bag in the den below the rock called the Landlocked Whale.

At dawn Day woke her and said, "I'm going to check around."

"Don't," she said. "What if they left a guard?"

"I'll be careful," he said.

"Come right back," she called after him.

He was gone for only half an hour, and returned to report that all the men were gone but that everything in their camp had been destroyed. "Nothing left," he said. "Not a scrap, nothing." Then he said he was going through the woods to see if the others were at the old shanty.

"Why?" she said. "What if they are?"

"Maybe they need help or something," he said.

"Or maybe you just don't want to lose Vashti or something," she said with a frown.

"I just want to see if they're okay," he insisted.

"Please don't bring them back with you," she said.

"I won't," he said, and went away again. This time he was gone longer, nearly an hour. She was hungry, and looked into the small sack of food they had saved. There was a loaf of bread, and a jar of strawberry jam. There was no cutlery; she used her finger to spread the jam on a slice of bread. While she was eating, she heard the sound of a motor, like a jeep's motor, and hoped that Day would hurry back. What if the men sent a search party all around through the woods to make sure that nobody remained? The motor seemed to stop in the vicinity of their former camp. She rolled up the sleeping bag and stuffed it and their other things and herself into the innermost corner of the den. Day almost didn't see her when he came back. "Hey!" he said. "Are you hiding from me?"

"Shhhh!" she said. "I think there are men around. I heard a motor stop at our camp."

He crawled into the den beside her, and said, "There's nobody at that old shanty. Nobody anywhere. They must have all left Dudleytown completely."

"I don't blame them," she said. "We ought to leave too."

"What is Zephaniah going to think when he gets back and finds everybody gone?" Day said. "He'll see that pile of ashes where the tent was and he'll wonder if we burned ourselves up, or, if he's smart enough, he'll figure it out that we were raided. And then he'll keep your car."

"Or maybe," she said, "Esaias might be lying in wait for him somewhere in the woods on the Dudleytown road, and he'll intercept him and tell him what happened, and then they'll make a getaway."

"In your car," Day said.

"Well, what can we do?" Diana said.

"That's a good question," Day said, and they spent most of the morning huddled together in the den, talking off the tops of their heads about what could be done, about all the various possibilities and eventualities, such as perhaps that Zephaniah would come at the wrong moment and be caught by some of those men. At one point, they had to stop talking, because they could hear voices coming nearer, and they waited in fear for several long minutes before the voices went away. "I guess they're looking for us," Day said.

The morning dragged on.

"Hey, I've got an idea," Day said. "Let's listen carefully, and if we hear a motor that sounds like your car, I'll sneak around through the woods and try to reach Zeph."

But the morning passed, and the afternoon passed, without any sound of the motor of Diana's car, although they listened carefully. It was not a noisy motor anyway; that was one disadvantage of an expensive Porsche. Day conjectured that the place where he would have to park the car was too far away for them to hear it, and suggested that they go find a hiding place nearer the place where he would park the car, but Diana insisted that they wait until dark. So they waited. For supper they had cheese sandwiches, and that was the last of their bread.

Day spent some time after supper brooding. She had learned to detect those moments when he would become distant from her, even though he was right beside her. "What's the matter?" she asked. "Do you miss Vashti?"

"No," he said.

"Really?" she said, trying to draw him out. "Not at all?"

"She didn't mean anything to me," he said.

"Then what are you thinking about?"

"You," he said.

"That's nice," she said. "What are you thinking about me?"

"I'm just wondering," he said. And then he turned his face to hers and said, "Listen. Tell me the truth." And she prepared herself to have to confess her various peccadillos with Zeph and Esaias and yes, Barnabas too. But he said, "Did you really have a grandfather named Daniel Lyam Montross?"

She laughed, partly in relief that it was not the question she was expecting. Then she said, borrowing an expression used by their recent friends, "Oh wow."

"Well, did you?" he persisted.

"Here all along I've been suspicious that you are just inventing him out of your fantastic imagination, and now I learn that you're suspicious that he never existed at all."

"Answer my question, Diana." He had begun to tremble; he was getting very overwrought. "I need to know. Did you or didn't you?"

She could have answered him easily enough, but it disturbed

her that he was so insistent, so lacking in faith. Did he think she was a liar? Worse, did he suspect that she was just some thrill-seeking spoiled rich girl, at loose ends, who had stage-managed this whole summer just for kicks? Worse yet, did he even suspect that she was perhaps in cahoots with Zephaniah and his friends, or even, for that matter, the men who had invaded them? Money will do anything, won't it?

"Go to sleep, Day," she said. He did, and she got out her tape recorder and put a fresh tape into it and switched it on. Then she told him that he was Daniel Lyam Montross and she told him to open his eyes. He did, and she smiled at him and said sweetly, "Hello."

"Howdy, girl," he said, smiling back at her.

"You *do* know who I am, don't you?" she asked.

"I reckon I do."

Say my name.

He said her name.

And what relation am I to you?

My daughter's girl.

And where are you?

Right now? Back in the belly of the Landlocked Whale once again.

But what year is this?

He named the present year.

Really? How can that be if you died nearly twenty years ago?

Nothing ever dies.

Do you know why we're here under this rock?

Sure. You and that foolhardy boy got yourselves into a scrape with the local yokels, and it took me nearly every punch I know to get you out alive.

So you have been watching out for us.

All the time, pretty near.

Can you read the future? Do you know what's going to happen to us now?

What does "future" mean? It's just one of those meaningless words. The future is past.

Can you tell me what Day and I will do now? What will become of us?

Even supposing I can tell you, I won't. It would take all the fun out of finding out for yourselves.

Do you think this is "fun," hiding here in this hole?

If it would make you feel any better, yes, I do. It's exciting and suspenseful. High time, too, that something commenced happening. Things were becoming pretty dull and boring there for a while.

You're funny. If you know so much, can you do anything to prove that you exist?

Holy Jehoshaphat, that's a tall order, young lady! Can you do anything to prove that you exist?

Well, I'm here.

So am I. I'm here as much as you. Maybe more so.

No, you're just Day. You're just a bunch of synapses in Day's fantastic brain.

All right, if you want to believe that. I don't mind being anything but that. To choose between being and nothingness, I'd choose that. Some people are worse off.

I wonder if you could tell me why Day has suddenly started suspecting that I just made you up, that I'm not really your granddaughter?

Well, who's to blame him? For all I know, since you claim that I don't exist anyway, perhaps you did just make me up. It's you, not him, who's all full of doubts.

I guess there's no way at all that I could ever prove that you are real, so I might as well forget it.

Suit yourself, girl. But I would be disappointed if you chose just to "forget it." Haven't I entertained you enough, so far? Hasn't the story of my life in Dudleytown been worth your while, been worth your stay here, been worth, even, this ordeal you've suffered? There's quite a lot more to my story. You've got only fifteen years of it. If you don't want me to exist, then I'll go on being nothing but synapses in Day's brain, but that would make me terribly sad....

Oh, Daniel, I want so much for you to exist!

Good. Then let me.

"Oh, I'll let you! Go on back, then, back where we were, in 1895 or '96. You were telling me about you and Ferrenzo Allyn...."

Yes.

"Did you kill him?"

I haven't yet.

"Where are you now?"

In my house. I am talking to my mother. And I remember my infancy, that heaven was told to lie about me but would not, that she did not want nor need me though she needs me now like a leech. Hopestill is still hoping, else she would die, but perhaps death is all she is still hoping for. On and on she talks of what a pretty place Emmeline has in Illinois, a white cottage, a garden of flowers, bowers and arbors and a fine carriage, an Acme Royal surrey, the latest Acme Queen parlor organ, a Gem graphophone talking machine, and plumbing in the house! Mother, why won't you go back? Emmeline has written and asked you to. There's more than plenty of room, Emmeline says in her letter. Because I intend to be buried beside your father, she says. But mother, you'll live for ages yet. The wagon's hitched, all's to do is for you to pack your trunk, I'll do it for you if you can't stand, and then down to the station we'll go. Daniel, are you trying to get rid of your poor old mother? No, but I want to get shut of poor old Dudleytown, it's carrying me into its grave. The wind creaks the boards in Bardwell's dead store. Moss grows on the rocks of Temple's cellar hole. Mildew blooms on all our cloth. Spring never sprang this year. And I can't leave you behind when I go off to seek my fortune. You could go, she says, to Illinois with me. No, that's too far and Emmeline says it's pretty much all flatland. I don't like the flatland, Ma. My mother thinks, and sees in the glow of her mind the white gleaming earthenware washdown siphontrap closet bowl, with a chain to pull afterwards, instead of the old cold bailed chamber pail I have to dump each day. And she says, Where would we get the money to buy my ticket? You just let me take care of that, I say. And she thinks some more, dreaming of the bowers and arbors, and says Yes, yes, I shouldn't wonder but what that might be best. So I pack her trunk for her and hoist her into the wagon and hoist the trunk and drive her down to the station at The Bridge, and say,

Wait here. Then I drive the wagon and the team to the nearest farm and ask the man, How much for this fine team and wagon? Them horses 'pear mighty old, says the farmer. Boneyard's not but nine and Mistress is just past ten, I tell him. Wal, he says, fifty's the most I could ever hope to give ye and I don't need another team anyways. Sold, I say. The ticket's only thirty-eight, so I'll have twelve left over as a nest egg to get me out of here. Goodbye, Mother. Goodbye, Daniel, you must be sure to come and visit. I'll try. And Mother…I never asked you, but I've just been wondering, whatever become of Charity? We put her away, Daniel. In a state home. The state of Illinois has relieved us of the burden. Well, I guess that's best. Goodbye, Mother. Goodbye, Daniel, and don't forget, when my time comes, I still want to lay my head down beside your father.

Now at the store in The Bridge I buy a box of .38 longs for my rifle, only forty-three cents for a box of fifty, more than I'll need. Then on foot I hike up the mountain toward home. Dusk settles on Dark Entry Road. Who would know this was a town? The charcoal pits are grown up in weeds. In school I learned there are lost cities in Peru, lost kingdoms in the sea, an empire of the Romans fell. Here in the dirt below this lilac tree I once built villages and wiped them out. Through this grove of mountain laurel I built roads and meandering highways and drove my toy wagons through them. And here are the trees I climbed. And there is my father's grave.

Who would have my house? Enos Jenner, will you buy my house? Why, he says, where are you going? I'm leaving. He says, No, I don't think anybody'd want that place. But I'll give you five dollars for the hay in your barn.

I close the house, taking nothing, save the clothes I wear, and my rifle. Now in the dark I lay me down in the woods across from Renz's house. Everybody will know it was me who did it, but they'll never catch me. I know a way through the woods northward that will get me out of the town unseen.

One lamp burns in the house, Renz's old mother sits alone, she bred the devil, I ought to shoot her too. But I'll wait for Renz. He's probably off some other place fooling with Violate. I'd halfway like to ask her to run off with me. I doubt she would.

It is nigh on to midnight when at last he comes, carrying his lantern, so I can see to shoot him.

I fire twice, hit him with both. He falls and dies. I don't wait to see if his old mother wakes and comes to find him. Into the woods I run and turn northward, stumbling in the dark but making steady tracks.

"Daniel, did you really kill him?"

Oh, I killed him deader than a doornail!

"But wait a minute. You said before—Let me see if I can find it, I've been looking for one of my tapes, and I think this is it. Listen to this":

... should have pounded him into the next county. Renz Allyn is a big bully who will come to no good, who will become the town's rowdy, who will torture small animals, who will afflict old men, who will anguish old women, who will beat his wife, who will be Violate. He will beat her to death and be sent to jail and then Dudleytown will be empty. But that is some years ahead yet....

"That was a few months before. Of course, you said it's not what you know but what you dream. Still, it conflicts with—"

Who is that talking? Whose voice is that I hear?

"Yours. Your own. When you were fifteen."

Where did it come from?

"My tape recorder. Don't you know I'm using a tape recorder? And I want to know: did Renz Allyn become the town bully and get jailed for killing his wife? Or did you kill him?"

What difference does it make? I never saw him again.

"You left Dudleytown that night and never came back?"

That's right.

"Where did you go?"

Upcountry. The bigger mountains. Vermont.

☩ 20 ☩

On the first day of September, Diana Stoving and Day Whittacker, hungry and tired and chilled, took leave of Dudleytown, Connecticut, on foot, having given up hope of Zephaniah's returning with the Porsche, and weary of constantly dodging and hiding from the jeep drivers who returned periodically to make sure that they weren't there. They left Dudleytown as they had found it, leaving no trace of themselves except the ashes of their tent. The mountain laurel had long since stopped blooming, but the floor of the woods still wore its carpets of ground pine and fern, though some of the ferns had faded from deep green to yellow and tan. Diana tossed a late-blooming wild rose into a cellar hole as they passed. Silence hung around them, and though they strained to hear they caught no trace of the country jig and hornpipe of the shepherds and shepherdesses. There was no wind, in the early morning; morning mists hovered above the lower trees. The road rose ahead of them in its tunnel of still trees, and they climbed the road to leave the dead town resting in its uneasy slumber. Maybe, said Diana, someday they will cover it with asphalt and make a shopping center there.

Still, said Day, after all was said and done, it had been the best summer he'd ever had.

And now, she asked, what are you going to do?

Maybe it's time, he said, that I ought to be thinking about going off to college.

With an imagination like yours, she said, you ought to study to be a writer.

He laughed. I would need you around to "turn me on," he said. And laughed again. But she saw that his eyes were wet, and then that the wetness was trickling down his cheeks.

Day, she said. Oh, Day.

She took his hand, and held it tightly as they walked.

I hear, she said, that Vermont is truly beautiful in the autumn. I wouldn't know, he said. I've never been there.

Boy Scout honor? she asked.

He raised three fingers, then used them to wipe his cheeks.

Well, would you like to see it? she asked.

Sure, he said. Would you?

There are lots worse things that we could do, she said.

If you don't mind walking, he said.

I don't, she said.

The tunnel of trees opened, and let them out of Dudleytown, toward some other place.

Second Movement
("The Unfinished")

Vanished Life among the Hills

*People aspire to love. Their Its aspire to love.
Few people ever achieve it. To put it crudely,
the two-hole privy is man's aspiration to love.
As few people ever truly use two holes together
as ever really achieve love together.*

— *Henry Fox*

*Why do lovers quarrel? It is the battle of their
Its fighting down to that level from which
they might spring up to loving again.*

— *Henry Fox*

*When I think of what you have meant to me
for all these years, sometimes it's more than
I can stand not to tell you so.*

— *Old Vermont farmer to his wife*

Was Eve bored? Is that why she ate the apple? Once when nothing at all was happening I asked Diana if she were bored and she told me that most women in general are going to be bored throughout their lives anyway and that as far as she was concerned she would rather be bored in *this* way than any other way she could think of. I thought that was a very nice thing to say.

I always wanted to see Vermont, but my parents' idea of a vacation was usually Atlantic City or Cape May. There are trees in Vermont that are really *trees*. And there are a dozen or more little ghost villages and nearly-ghost villages scattered all over the state, tucked away in haunted hollows and lost dells. I guess I picked Five Corners because it was the only one I had actually read something about—in an old issue of *Vermont Life* that I had found once in the library of East Passaic High School. Daniel Lyam Montross *could* have lived in Five Corners, for all I know. For all *I* know, he might have lived anywhere. Anywhere you find the right place, where a village once was and is no longer, there's probably some trace of him he left behind. Anyway, *he told us* that he had lived in Five Corners, for about eight years, from 1896 to 1905. But I didn't tell Diana that I had read something once about the place and the gold mines that were there. I hadn't told her I had been to Dudleytown before either, but I had, during a hike that Scoutmaster Pelton took the guys on, a couple of years before, on the Appalachian Trail; we just happened to pass the place and I just spent half an hour at the most poking around in the cellar holes and wondering about what sort of town it had been. But I swear I never read up on the subject, and I truth-fully did not know how to find it from Cornwall Bridge or from the public highway, because, as I say, we went into it via the Appalachian Trail. I just knew it was there.

What if, after all, Daniel Lyam Montross is just my imagination? But if that is so, how would you account for this: when we were invaded by the "bad element," those Jesus freaks, Zephaniah and his crowd, I thought it would be a good idea to "parallel" the past and present by concocting or fabricating some sort of "invasion" of Dudleytown by undesirable elements during Daniel Lyam Montross's time—perhaps religious evangelists or the nineteenth-century equivalent of Jesus freaks—and I actually *willed* this to happen in his narrative, but for some reason he refused to include it. Most of the time I don't think I have the least bit of control over what he is saying.

Or what if, as far as that goes, Diana just told me that she was Daniel Lyam Montross's granddaughter, just for kicks, or just to "play along" out of curiosity? I can't discount this, but I have seen him clearly in my mind, usually when I'm asleep but sometimes when I'm awake too, and there is a distinct family resemblance between him and Diana. And besides, I don't think that Diana has the talent to be a good liar. *I* know what kind of talent it takes. For one thing, as she said once, you have to have an excellent memory to be a good liar, so you don't get things mixed up.

What if, then, Daniel Lyam Montross not only actually existed—and still does, for that matter—but also that he has such power, because he's from "the Other Side," that he can do things like dig holes in the Garden State Parkway so that Diana's car will hit one of those holes and have to be fixed in a local repair shop so that she will have to wait and while she's waiting she will discover the story about me and Sedgely in the newspaper, and then come and find me, so that Daniel Lyam Montross can regain what he lost eighteen years ago when they had to shoot him to get her back from him? How about that? It's spooky as hell, but I draw the line at just how much you can be expected to believe about "the Other Side."

There's one more "what if," and this what if is the only one which I could believe in, because it's the only one which I can't explain away or prove unfounded or incredulous. And that is: what if I have just imagined Diana too? If I'm crazy enough to think that I'm "inhabited" by the soul or ghost or spirit or essence of a guy named Daniel Lyam Montross, then maybe I'm crazy enough to daydream (or Day-dream) that I have met this really good-looking blonde who's got loads of money and a fancy car (damn, I wish I hadn't dreamed that car away; I wish we still had it), and she's good to me sexually, better than a succubus anyway, and here I am wandering around all alone by myself in these ghost towns that I wanted to explore, and making myself believe that I've got this absolutely first-rate companion and girlfriend. As a matter of fact, she isn't the first girlfriend I've imagined I had. It seems like ever since I can remember, ever since my first wet dream at the age of eleven or twelve, I've been pretending convincingly to myself that I've got one girl after another. And they're always blondes. So what if Diana is just my best "creation" after years of practice?

Sad, in a way, to think that. But what does it matter, so long as I believe it? Whether "Diana" really exists or not (and I've wondered about the little coincidence that my first name, and hers, and Daniel's, all begin with the same letter), I know this much:

"She" went to Vermont with me.

On foot, most of the way, although she could easily have afforded to take a bus, or even hire a taxi, or even, for that matter, buy another car. (Once when she wasn't around, just out of curiosity I counted the traveler's checks in her purse. And she must have God knows how much in a trust fund she inherited when she turned twenty-one—inherited from her paternal grandfather, not from Daniel Lyam Montross, who never saved a cent.) Well, if you're going to invent a girlfriend, you might as well make her a rich one. But anyway, we walked most of the way to Vermont, because I wanted to.

Which doesn't mean we didn't spend any money. We stopped at this sporting goods shop in Great Barrington, Massachusetts, and Diana asked for my advice in picking out two complete outfits of back-packing equipment: knapsacks and pack frames and bedrolls and a light tent and cooking gear and everything—I think she paid more for this stuff than the first time for our Dudleytown gear, and we spent most of the first two weeks of September hiking toward Five Corners, Vermont, pitching our small tent each night in some other place. That's the way I like to travel; you can see a lot more that way, and we passed all kinds of cellar holes and some abandoned houses and stores, and two or three genuine remains of ghost villages. Every so often, Diana would make me into Daniel Lyam Montross in order to find out what route he had taken when he had emigrated from Connecticut to Vermont, and for the most part we kept to his original route. We had to stop for a few days in a ghost village called Glastenbury, Vermont, because Diana had a bad case of foot blisters and needed some time for them to heal. I liked Glastenbury, and considered the possibility of staying there, but apparently it had never been much of a village, just a scattering of houses and a logging camp. So we went on.

The last good-sized town we passed through was Manchester, Vermont, and Diana stopped there and said to me, with this kind of wistful expression that she wears half the time, "You know, this time of year I'm always picking out my back-to-school fall wardrobe, but this is the first year in sixteen years that I'm not going back to school. Still, I think we ought to have a fall wardrobe anyway, don't you?"

So we spent a day going through these shops in Manchester, and she spent I don't know how many dollars on as much stuff as we could stuff into our packs and still have to carry some in the hand—all of it mostly stuff we needed for cool days and nights in the woods: wool things, wool and flannel mostly, plaid shirts and sweaters and new boots and everything. Gee, when I took a couple of twenty-dollar Pendleton shirts I knew I must be dreaming her up.

Vermont is quite a lot different from Connecticut. Most people wouldn't notice too many differences except that Vermont's mountains are bigger, but I noticed all kinds of differences. For one thing, there's a greater range of color, and I don't mean the autumn color, which hadn't really got started yet—a lot of the maples on the higher slopes were already red but nothing like the real riot of color that would come later on—but just the greens, for instance. Somebody (maybe me, eventually) ought to work out a list of the forty-seven different shades and tints of green that you can see in Vermont, whereas they're only about twenty-six in Connecticut. And even the wildest parts of the Housatonic country, like Dudleytown, don't begin to compare with the really *wild* wilds that you can get into here in Vermont. I saw a few stands of trees which I could have sworn are genuine virgin timber, and you hardly ever find any virgin timber in New England.

We had a good time. Late one afternoon around the middle of September we climbed a steep hill and came into one of the prettiest little villages I've ever seen, called Plymouth Notch, which would have certainly become a ghost village except for one thing: it was where a President was born and buried. We found this out when we stopped at the little store there, and they had these leaflets that tell how Calvin Coolidge was born in the house across the road and sworn in as President in that house by his father when Harding died, and where he's buried in the little cemetery back down the road. Diana and I walked back down to the cemetery and looked at his grave, a very simple and modest piece of granite with just his name and the presidential seal and his dates: 1872–1933. He would have been just eight years older than Daniel Lyam Montross, and right away we started wondering if maybe he had known him, because Daniel Lyam Montross had told Diana that Five Corners was in this same township of Plymouth, just a few miles from Plymouth Notch.

Plymouth Notch is a store, a church, maybe three or four houses, a cheese factory, and that's all, all of it painted white and set like a huddled toyland on this high valley, with range after range of green hill and bluegreen mountain and blue peak rising and rising behind it. Something about the place really got to me, especially while I was looking at old Calvin Coolidge's humble grave and reading his words printed in the leaflet about him—he was talking about Plymouth and he said, "It was here I first saw the light of day; here I received my bride; here my dead lie pillowed on the loving breast of the everlasting hills." I know he wasn't a great President, just a good President; still the idea that this was his home, the idea of a homeland, where people lived simply and honestly, and had devotion to work and to duty and had faith in democracy…well, hell, it raised a lump in my throat. And I wished that Plymouth Notch was Five Corners, even if it wasn't quite a ghost village. But I hoped that Five Corners, because it was in the same township, would look just exactly like Plymouth Notch…only be abandoned.

We went back to the store to ask how to get to Five Corners but the store was closed for the day, so we had to knock on a door, and the man told us to take the road that goes up through Calvin Coolidge State Park, but he said we'd never make it on foot before dark and why didn't we just spend the night with him if we cared to, but we were in a hurry and thanked him and went on.

The state park swarms over the crest of a high and steep hill, and consists of a number of platforms for tents, and a number of rustic brown shelters—they call it an Adirondack shelter everywhere except Vermont, and here they call it a Green Mountain lean-to: a windowless log cabin with one side open to the air, the floor just about twelve or fourteen feet square. Nobody was staying in the park, this late in the season, so we just decided we would like to see what it's like to stay in a log lean-to, and since it was late in the day and lightly raining we just picked out one of them, that had a fine view overlooking the mountains. Each of the lean-to's had the name of a native tree, and for no particular reason other than the view, we picked the one called Hornbeam, which is a tree of the genus *Carpinus* with smooth gray bark and hard whitish wood—the tree, not our lean-to. There was a supply of cut wood, so we started a fire right away in the brick grill which fronts the open end of the lean-to. Just as supper was getting hot, a truck came along and this crusty old Yankee said he was the caretaker of the park and the camp was closed for the season and what did we think we were doing camping without permission or without paying the fee, which was four dollars a night. We offered to pay the fee but he just kept saying the park was closed for the season. He was standing there with the rain running down his neck, and we were standing there with the rain running down our necks, and Diana, she began this act, rather convincing I thought, of breaking down and crying. It must have got through to his granite heart, because he finally said we could stay, and took our four dollars, and then said as he was leaving, "You kids aint even married, I bet."

A lean-to in the rain is quite different from a tent in the rain. With a tent, if it's raining pretty hard, you're just plain miserable. You can only sit there and listen to the drops splat on the canvas and know that regardless of how good the tent is, you're still going to get a little wet, and anyway you're all cooped up. But with a lean-to, you can sit there out of the rain and watch the fire roaring like mad and keeping you warm, and still feel that you're out of doors without getting wet at all. It's very nice. So maybe that's when I decided that when we got to Five Corners I would build us a lean-to to live in. It was getting too cold for a tent anyway.

In the cozy lean-to that night, Diana got pretty affectionate. I can tell the difference between when she makes love because she really wants to, and when she makes love only because I want to, and that night was of the former variety. We played and teased and laughed a lot, which is always good for setting the right mood. She ran her fingers through my hair and teased me because my hair was getting nearly as long as a hippie's, which was true; I guess the only thing about those Jesus freaks that rubbed off on me was the idea that long hair is okay on a boy if you want it that way, and besides, when would I have had a chance to see a barber? But I told Diana she could cut it if she wanted to. She said she didn't really want to, even if the long hair made me look so "un-Day." Anything that makes me "un-Day" is just fine with me.

It ought to be plain that she doesn't really love Day, and probably can't, and probably never will. But she likes me, and tolerates me, and occasionally, like that night in the lean-to, she will get very affectionate, and then we will make love and if I try very hard and don't let myself get carried away I can hold out long enough for her; then she will be happy, and for a while afterwards, at least until she goes to sleep, I think she really does love me, for a while.

That night a raccoon got into our knapsacks and ate up all of our food, even the bags of dried and dehydrated stuff, which must have given him a bad case of dry-mouth, unless he took it to some nearby brook.

So the next morning, when we packed up and started off on the last stretch toward Five Corners, I told Diana that we ought to try to live off the land for a while. I know how to do it. We could thrive on berries and nuts, and jerusalem artichokes and arrowhead tubers and acorns and other wild things, and catch fish and small game.

The only thing the raccoon left us was our coffee, which must have been a brand he didn't care for, so we had coffee for breakfast at least, and I found enough wild raspberries to keep our stomachs from growling at us.

The old road to Five Corners leaves the state park and drops and turns and dips and twists...and it branches too, at least three times, and the third time we took the wrong branch and followed the road to its end at a compound of old buildings with a big sign tacked up: "Road's End Lodge." There was an old car parked there, so we knocked on the door to ask for directions, but nobody was home. We poked around the other buildings, including one with a skylight that looked like a studio or something, but it seems that nobody was living there. Off in the distance on a knoll, however, we could see what looked to be the tops of a long row of tombstones, so Diana immediately made me into Daniel Lyam Montross and when I woke up she said that he had told her that, sure enough, that cemetery off in the distance, across a wide meadow and on a knoll, was the Five Corners cemetery. So we started out for it, finding the remains of the road through high grass, two ruts that not even a jeep could take.

The Five Corners cemetery is quite an operation (or I should say set-up or lay-out instead of operation, because it hasn't been "operating" for at least seventy years). This is an interesting contrast with Dudleytown, where we never could find any sign of a cemetery or even a private family plot—I think they must have buried them without stone markers or else they had hauled them off to one of the cemeteries in Cornwall or some other place. The Five Corners cemetery is a big one; I didn't bother to count but at a rough guess I would say there are at least three hundred headstones in the cemetery, and footstones too, because each grave had a small marker at the foot too, I suppose so that you wouldn't chop off somebody's feet when you were digging a grave in the next row. I don't mean to be funny, because the Five Corners cemetery made me very sad. Nobody was taking care of it. Here were all these three hundred people, lying, like Coolidge said, "pillowed on the loving breast of the everlasting hills," but that breast was all covered with brambles and weeds and wild use-less vegetation that I couldn't even identify, and second-growth trees were growing right up out of half of the graves, their roots probably tangled all up in the skeletons, and the thought that this was once a neat breezy lay-out in this picturesque bowl of a knoll nestled in this bowl of a valley and visited by folks at least on Memorial Day with flowers and where once preachers hollered to God to rest the souls of the departed, and now all abandoned and forsaken and uncared for. We just stood there misty-eyed for a while and then we pledged that we would come up here often and try to clean away some of this overgrown brush and straighten up the toppled stones.

But even while I was standing there brooding I had the presence of mind to memorize a lot of the names on the tombstones in case Daniel Lyam Montross needed to have his memory refreshed or something. There were a lot of common names that didn't need to be made up: Johnsons and Butlers and Browns and Adamses and Allens and Smiths, but a lot of names that were a little bit unusual: Headles and Slacks and Earles and Braddocks and Claghorns and Spooners and McLowerys and Rookes, with a lot of unusual first names too: Alpheus and Adelphia, Joel and Melissa, Potie and Kermit, Jeems and Lavinia, and so forth.

The fact that the cemetery was completely run-down and forsaken prepared me in advance to expect that the town itself was probably not taken care of. Since I was halfway hoping that Five Corners would resemble Plymouth Notch, it's a good thing that I was prepared in advance to expect the worst.

Because there's absolutely nothing in Five Corners.

I mean, *nothing*. It's even worse than Dudleytown in this respect. We could have walked right through it without noticing a trace of anything, and we probably would have, too, except that when we reached this old wooden bridge crossing a roaring brook down in a deep hollow completely surrounded and locked in by the hills around it, we happened to stop in this little glade beside the brook where there were the ashes and burnt logs of some camper's or hunter's or fisherman's fire, and there we just barely managed to detect that there was another abandoned road branching off that way, and another branching off *that* way, and still yet the faintest trace of a road branching off up *that* way. Five. Five roads, counting the two of the road that we were coming in and going out on. *Five Corners.*

So Diana immediately put me to sleep again, and when I woke up she told me that this was really the right place, Five Corners. After I got over the disappointment, she took me around and showed me the places that Daniel Lyam Montross had just finished taking her around to and showing her. Here where the five roads converged had been the school, which had been called "Five Corners Academy," where Daniel Lyam Montross had taught for two years. But there was no trace of it, no foundation, no cellar hole, nothing. And here, where the brook was now spanned by a simple bridge of wooden planks, had been a covered bridge, a "king truss" affair that had washed away in a flood toward the end of the time that Daniel Lyam Montross had lived here. And here, beside the covered bridge, was a very large cellar hole, so overgrown with weeds and trees that we would never have found it without the help of Daniel Lyam Montross. This had been Glen House. Glen House had been a hotel. On the second floor of Glen House Hotel had been a ballroom, famous all over because the whole ballroom floor was mounted upon large rubber balls to make it springy for dancing, and over eighty couples could dance there at one time. It staggered my imagination—me, who's supposed to have such a great imagination. And down there was the big sawmill. And here the millpond, which William Hankerson had paid $1000 for the privilege of sluicing and draining in hopes of finding sediment of gold washed down from the hills, a gamble, which paid off, to the tune of $7000. And up there beyond the sawmill was the cider mill. And over there, on the rise, almost in a row, were the four neat white houses of the Earles and Headles and Spooners and McLowerys. Now nothing.

Why had Daniel Lyam Montross settled here? What drew him? To come from one dying town and wind up in another.... But maybe it wasn't dying when he came. We had plenty of time to find out all the answers. First, we had to get settled. I thought it would be appropriate if, as in that glade of laurel in Dudleytown, we made our camp on the location of Daniel Lyam Montross's home in Five Corners. But Diana, after putting me under again and having a long session with him, shifting him back and forth through different months and seasons and years, discovered that he had never had his own house here. He had lived for a time, a brief time at first, in a room at the Glen House Hotel. Then he had a miserable room on the second floor of some kind of handyman's hovel. Then he had a room in a farmhouse high to the south of the village. Then he lived in a kind of shed out back of the McLowery house in the village.

"So finally," Diana said, "I just asked him which of these places he had liked the best, and he said the last one, the shed behind the McLowery house, and he showed me where it was."

She said also that Daniel Lyam Montross was very sad, really terribly sad, to see "what a sorry plight" the village had fallen into. "Yes, all my towns are fallen," he had said, "but none like this."

We began construction of our lean-to on the very ground where the McLowerys' shed had stood, which wasn't a bad spot, at all. It was high, on a slope to the west of the village, with a great view of the village (or what was left of the village, namely, nothing) and far enough back from the road so that if any hunters or forest rangers or anybody came along they probably wouldn't spot us.

But building that lean-to wasn't such an easy task. First of all, I had to hike about six miles north down along what was called the Hale Hollow Road and then along the state highway into Bridgewater, the nearest village where they had a grocery store that carried some hardware, so I could buy a good axe and saw and a hammer and some nails and other things. (And while I was at it some groceries too, because I wasn't doing such a really *complete* job of demonstrating that we could find enough to eat in the woods and stream and fields. So far we'd had only a couple of small bullheads, one scrawny squirrel I caught in a snare, berries and more berries until we were burned out on berries, and large loads of cooked wild greens of all kinds.) Then felling enough trees for the logs, and cutting and trimming the logs, took me about two solid weeks of sunup to sundown labor, and I was always in such a sweat from it that I never needed to go near the fire until late at night when it got cold, and Diana was always criticizing me for neglecting the fire, because she was cold.

The chipmunks. I've nearly forgotten to mention the chipmunks. They were all over the place. Little, nervous, long-tailed furry creatures with white stripes and freckles on their brown and tan backs.

They're worthless to eat, even if you could bring yourself to kill one of the cute little things. But they will eat anything you throw at them, and even come up and eat out of your hand and sit in your lap after they get to know you. They sit up on their hind legs to eat. I guess they were trying to store away enough for hibernation.

I noticed one thing about the chipmunks' movements. *Five Corners.* The pattern of their darting resembles a map of the five roads coming into the village. They will run out into our camp, stop, run a few leaps one way, stop, run a few leaps the other way, stop, and so on, until they've made five runs in different directions. I mention this because I think it's interesting.

Also, there were deer everywhere. After two weeks, they lost their fear of us, and whole families of deer would browse right up to the edge of our camp.

We finished the lean-to at just about the same time that the trees began to change color, and that color…. Diana is wrong in suggesting that I ought to be a writer, because I can't possibly think of any way to describe the autumn color of the foliage in our woods. If you haven't seen it, you just haven't seen it. I remember in the tenth or eleventh grade liking this somewhat cornball poem by Edna St. Vincent Millay, I forget the exact title, but the first line was "O World I cannot hold thee close enough" and there was this other line about "Thy woods, this autumn day, that ache and sag and all but cry with color!" Well, our woods didn't just *cry* with color. They *sang.*

The seeds of the sugar maple ripen in the fall. I pointed out to Diana that the seeds of the sugar maple come in *pairs*, and they are *winged*, and they *ripen in the fall*.

But enough about us. After all, I'm supposed to be telling the story of this part of Daniel Lyam Montross's life, those eight years in Five Corners. I'm not sure I can do it. This "assignment" is a tough one, too tough for me I think, but I might as well try. I've got limitations, and I'm aware of them: for one thing, most of the time I'm more interested in what's happening to me and Diana, even if it's *nothing*, than in what happened to Daniel Lyam Montross; for another thing, I can't even begin to compete with that *voice* of his, and I don't intend to try. Diana was giving her tape recorder a workout just about every day, and we were steadily accumulating another stack of cassettes. One of the things that we had already discovered, back in Dudleytown, is that I'm able, apparently, while under a trance, not only to "play" verbatim everything that Daniel Lyam Montross ever said, with all its idioms or slang or what not, but also I'm able to "play back" anything that anybody ever said to him. So a lot of these cassettes that we were making in Five Corners were not of that fabulous voice of Daniel Lyam Montross but of other people talking to him, and what I would like to do, as "editor" of this story, is to show (or "play") some of those other cassettes, occasionally. If Daniel Lyam Montross thinks that I'm doing this just to get his own fabulous voice off the air, he's probably right.

Well, here goes his story. It was nearly autumn when he first came, too. In 1896. He hadn't meant to come to Five Corners especially. That summer after leaving Dudleytown, after killing Ferrenzo Allyn or anyway *thinking* he had killed Ferrenzo Allyn [what does it matter? Allyn must be dead] he just wandered about from one place to some other place, heading generally northward, pretty much along the same route Diana and I had taken, stopping in one place and chopping wood for somebody to get a free meal, stopping in some other place for a week of work, until finally he wound up in this small industrial town south of here, called Ludlow, and looking for a job, at least a temporary job, he discovered that the post office needed a mail carrier to drive the mail wagon each day on the new Rural Route 6, which went up through Tyson, Plymouth Union, Plymouth Notch, then Five Corners and back through Reading and Cavendish. Well of course Daniel knew how to drive a wagon, but the job had a minimum age of eighteen and he was still short of seventeen. So he had to lie about his age. He at least looked eighteen, or older. They gave him the job, which wouldn't pay a whole lot, but he thought he could get by. The first day, he had to get up at five-thirty in the morning and go to the post office and spend two hours sorting out the mail, and getting it all straight, and then loading the six big leather bags into the wagon, and a couple of paying passengers who wanted to go to Tyson and Plymouth, then he cracked his whip and started off.

When he arrived with his mail wagon at Five Corners he was

surprised to find a big welcome celebration waiting for him, because, as it turned out, this was the first day that Five Corners became a rural delivery route. Although it had been a village for many years, all the way back to the 1830's, people had always had to go to Plymouth Notch or Bridgewater to get their mail but now apparently the post office department thought that the village was important enough to have rural delivery. At any rate, everybody in town had turned out for Daniel Lyam Montross's arrival, and they had even hung red-white-and-blue bunting across the road, and there in front of the Glen House Hotel were tables covered with white damask and pitchers of cider and all kinds of homemade cakes and cookies and what not, and they introduced Daniel Lyam Montross to everybody, and several big men of the town made speeches, and somebody shot off some fireworks, and the village dogs chased their tails, and you never saw anything like it.

Diana has this bug about psychologizing everything. I think she must have taken a course or two in psychology when she was in college. She had a lot of fun making psychological theories about this episode. Daniel Lyam Montross, she says, had been a complete "nobody" back home in Dudleytown. He had been the last child, the unwanted child, in a large impoverished family. His childhood and adolescence, except for a few sexual escapades, had been dull and lonely. Now, suddenly, with the big welcome that was given to him in Five Corners, even if it was really not him but the U.S. Mail that these people were so happy to see, he began to feel that he was "somebody" instead of "nobody." Diana calls this one of the first big turning points in his life. She calls it a "happy trauma."

Anyway, it must have gone to his head, to hear him tell it (or to hear the tape recorder tell what he told me to tell Diana). It took him nearly three hours to get away from the celebration, during which he met several pretty girls, including one, Rachel McLowery, who really turned his head, love at first sight and all that. Rachel was a redhead, the same age as he, although if anybody asked, he said he was eighteen, just to be safe. He told Rachel that as soon as the weekend came and he got off work, he would come and visit her, and she said that he could take her to the contra-dances at the Glen

House where they dance on a floor mounted on rubber balls. And he could hardly wait for the weekend. But when he got back to the Ludlow post office, three hours late, they gave him hell for being so late, and even though he explained that he had been held up by the big celebration in Five Corners, they told him he should have had sense enough not to hang around for three hours for any celebration that interfered with the prompt delivery of the United States Mails, and they fired him on the spot.

And so (or this is what Diana says, psychologizing again), being fired from his new job like that so abruptly, he left Ludlow and went at once, on foot, to Five Corners, gravitating (Diana's word) toward the one place in the world where he had been made to feel welcome, the right place. When he got there (it took him two days to walk the distance) he used his day's pay that the post office had given him to take a room overnight in the Glen House. The people who ran the hotel were sorry that he had lost his job because of the celebration Five Corners had given him, but apart from that, as Daniel Lyam Montross was rather dismayed to discover, now that he wasn't the mail carrier any more he wasn't important to them. He was a nobody again.

Even Rachel McLowery, when she discovered that he wasn't the mail carrier any more, was cool to him, and although she kept her promise and let him take her to the contra-dances on the rubber-ball-mounted floor of the Glen House, she wasn't much fun, especially when she discovered that he couldn't dance well. In fact, he didn't know the first thing about dancing, and tried to pick it up by eye and ear, with very limited success. Rachel said she was busy when he tried to set up another date with her.

Here it was late August, and he was out of a job, and he liked Five Corners very much even if the people no longer thought he was the most important man in the world. He still wanted to stay. So he began asking around about the possibilities of employment, saying he was eighteen and able-bodied and lost his last job through no fault of his own.

Mrs. Peary, who ran the Glen House, asked him if he had finished his schooling, and he lied and said he had. She told him that the Five Corners Academy across the road from the Glen House hadn't found a schoolmaster for this year. He thought he was smart enough to pull it off; even if he hadn't finished school himself, he knew how to read, and he could read the textbooks and keep a lesson ahead of the pupils. Mrs. Peary told him to go see Judge Braddock, who was the chairman of the school district.

He saw Judge Braddock, who hired him on the spot (apparently for lack of other applicants) and then told him to meet him at the school the following Saturday afternoon at two o'clock for an "auction."

Now here's my first example of the cassettes in which it isn't Daniel Lyam Montross doing the talking (in fact, in this case, he never gets a chance to open his mouth) but somebody else talking to him. This is Judge Braddock, talking to him on the day of the "auction":

Shall we stand in the shade of this venerable maple whilst we wait? This tree's got a history as long as my winter underwear, but I won't bother you with it just now, young man; it's too long, and I see the first of the folks coming yonder. There'll be time enough, I suppose. I suppose you'll be seeing more than enough of me, days to come. I don't judge any more—Mrs. Peary was only being polite when she called me that—I did judge once, though, and I hanged a man from this very tree—remind me to tell you about that one. No, I don't judge any more, and I don't even auctioneer but once or twice a year, but I'm *here*. You'll see enough of me, time to time.

Now those two, hitching up by Glen House yonder, that's Jirah and Livia Allen, they hold a two-hundred acre farmplace up Gold Brook, and enough livestock to keep your table brimming. They're not grudging with the meat, either. But the problem there is, they've got a son, a big boy named Marshall, who'll be one of your scholars, and he's the meanest scamp that ever lived, and practically a halfwit, which proves you don't have to be smart to be mean. No, I don't think you'd want to live with them. Seeing him in school each day will be enough for you.

Oh, but isn't it a fair and frisky morning? And see how there's already a spot of red amongst the maple leaves. You have to relish this season, my boy, when the sun's still hot: Three or four weeks, and it gets blithering cold up here in these mountains. Which reminds me, I have to get after Jake Claghorn about stocking up the wood for the schoolhouse. Only part of this job I don't like, being chairman of the school district, is asking Jake Claghorn seven or eight times before he gets around to cutting that wood. Lately he's been agitating to have it made part of the schoolmaster's job, but don't you worry about that. Not as long as I'm still holding the whip.

Now here come the McLowerys, Joel and Melissa. A handsome team and wagon, isn't it? Befits their circumstances, you could say. They've got the biggest herd of sheep in the county. Pure Merinos, a few Cheviots. Can you imagine that absolutely your only problem there would be a surfeit of lamb chops? Ha, ha! But on second thought, they have a daughter, who'll be one of your scholars, and she—well, you *must* remind me sometime to tell you about her.

And right behind them there are the Tindalls, that's Adelphia driving because Aaron fell off the buckboard and broke both wrists. I hate to say it, because they're my own blood relations—he's a third cousin and she's a first—but you don't want them. Cross your fingers. Aaron is able to put away a half gallon of applejack in a single day...and he often does. I fail to see how he gets any work done...and he often don't.

Year before last, they had the schoolmaster, and I'll be switched if he didn't develop an overpowering taste for the stuff himself. I hope you're moderate yourself, young man. Not abstemious, I didn't say. Just moderate. A man can't get through these winters without a little liquid warmth. But mark me, it's my experience that you young fellows can too easily succumb to excess, particularly about the end of February or during March. I take it this is your first position, isn't it? It always is. So just let me say that there's nothing you can do that will surprise me. I'm not going to be watching you every minute, and I don't want you to feel that I am, but if you ever get the urge to do something to surprise me, then put it out of your mind, for nothing will. I guess the only thing that would be sure to surprise me would be to find you standing here beside me at this same time next year.

Look the other way there, coming afoot by the Plymouth fork, that's Matthew and Sophronica Earle. Now *there's* a fine family for you. Townspeople, you might almost call 'em, if you want to call this little hamlet a town. Live in that big old white house up the hill yonder. Matt used to be schoolmaster himself, many a year back, that's how he met Sophronica, who was one of his scholars. He's the only former schoolmaster who ever stayed. Now he's a town selectman. Two of their own children will be your scholars, if you wouldn't mind them underfoot at home. Nice, big, airy room of your own upstairs. I've seen it, and it's got a view. The drawback there is the water isn't any too good. Well's too close to the stable, I think.

Here's Jake Claghorn, dang his bones! YOU, JAKE! WHEN'S THAT WOOD GOING TO BE CUT? HUH? WELL, IT BETTER BE, IT JUST BETTER BE, YOU LAGGARD! Looks to me like he intends to bid too, but you certainly don't want *him*, my boy. He's a bachelor. Lives in a dirty three-room shack down by the blacksmith's. Probably make you cook your own victuals. But you just leave it to me. I've been manipulating these things for years. Some folks have urged me to go professional, and travel the state. But I don't like traveling.

I've heard rumors that some of the towns down in the valley are giving up their auctions. Well, that's nice, but nobody has told me what they are doing for a substitute. Has the legislature passed some new laws that we haven't heard about? We get the county newspaper up here every Thursday, and I read it front to back. I haven't read anything yet about the legislature passing any new laws. I served a term once myself at the state house, and I can't conceive of any good substitute. It's been a tradition in this town all the way back to the day it was founded. Well, maybe not *all* the way back, but Seth and Hiram Earle established the tradition on the very same day the legislature passed the law that school districts have to pay the board of their teachers.

It's picking up, it's picking up. Here come the Johnsons and the Headles, and there come the Spooners, the McIntyres and the Slacks. Good people all. Not a miser in the lot. The Headles especially. Why, they'll even buy you a new pair of shoes! I see Joel McLowery is looking a bit impatient, so I suppose we had best get started.

Now, you being raised on a Connecticut farm, I guess you know that farm prices have a bad habit of what is called fluctuation. Some years are good, some years are bad, so you can't ever tell. This year seems to be rather on the bad side, but you can't ever tell. I just thought I would mention that, because it will probably be reflected in the bidding.

One other thing. I think it would be advisable to let that smile off your mouth. Now hold on! I don't mean you have to scowl, but, you see, it's been my experience that if you are standing up here with a smile on your face while I'm crying you, it somehow don't go over too well with the crowd. I *know* you just mean to look pleasant and personable, they all do, but for some reason, it seems to annoy the crowd. So my advice is, just look properly solemn and serious.

And finally, I might mention that this auction, under the official auspices of a duly elected school board, is completely fair and square. If you know your auctions, you know about "air bids" and "dumb bids" and "straw bids" and all that. Well, we don't tolerate that. We don't have shills or signals or freezes. It's all a straight Dutch auction, fair and square.

Now, sir, if you'll just step up on this little box here, so the folks can have a better look.

ALL RIGHT, FOLKS! WILL YOU COME IN CLOSE? GET OUT OF THE HOT SUNSHINE AND GATHER 'ROUND!

Here he is, folks! Most of you've met him before when he brought the mail. Poor feller lost his mail job on account of that little festivity we threw. But he's young and bright and eager! I've not read his record, folks, but he looks bright as a whistle, don't he? If he's good enough to bring the mail, he's good enough to keep the school. And a big fellow like him, you know he can keep the youngsters in line! And swing a stinging ruler! But big as he is, he don't look like a big eater, now does he? No! I doubt he ever asks for seconds!

So how about it folks and are you all ready? So how about it and let's get to town! So how about it folks and let's go! I'm gonna start at three hundred and how about that folks I'm gonna say three hundred and look for a hand do I see a hand do I see a hand at three hundred what's the matter with you nobody likes the sound of three hundred then how does three-fifty sound to you? Three-fifty three-fifty I'm saying three-fifty and THERE'S A HAND! I've got three-fifty now who says three three three, who says three? Come on and let me see a three! and there's a three! thank you, Joel. Joel's no skinflint, he can do it for three. Who wants to beat him? Who says two seventy-five? Do I hear a two seventy-five? Aaron says two seventy-five and who'll top him? Where's my two fifty? Do I see a two fifty? Come on now, you know you could feed a whole district of schoolteachers on two fifty! *There's* my two fifty, and thank you Jirah and who says two twenty-five, and I feel it coming up, that two twenty-five, and sure enough Joel here says two twenty-five, and who'll top him? Who says two, who says two, two says who, who says who, AND THERE'S MY TWO! Now let's whack it down, folks, we have to whack it down and down and down and who says one seventy-five, and there's my one seventy-five but I'm telling you he's going for one fifty and where do I see that one fifty? Let's see you again, Joel, you've got him for one fifty. Then where's Jirah now? Let's see you at one fifty, Jirah. Come on now, boys, let's see that one fifty. There she is! Headle says one fifty and who'll top him? Let's get on down to that one twenty-five. One twenty-five and you can take him home. One twenty-five and he's all yours. I've got one twenty-five spot cash right here in my pocket to give you if you'll feed him for that, and you know you can, with a little economy. Where's my one twenty-five? For one fifty you could feed him roast lamb every night. Where's that one twenty-five? I don't see it. Are you all done, folks? Knocking down at one fifty? Why, I could feed two of them myself for *that*. Who says one twenty-five? Nobody? Am I obliged to knock it down at one fifty? Are you all done folks? One fifty? All right, one fifty gong twice, going twice one fifty, one fifty going twice...AND NOW I SEE YOU, JOEL, THAT'S A GOOD SPORT! Joel's get him for one twenty-five, folks! Joel's got him unless there's one of you says a hundred....

Anybody want a hundred? One hundred big fat dollars, who wants one hundred even? Well it looks like Joel has got him, then. One twenty-five going once, going once, one twenty-five going twice, and going thrice, and now it's g—

Seventy-five? What idiot said seventy-five? Jake Claghorn! Why, Jake, you don't mean that! Have you been drinking? You don't mean seventy-five, we haven't been down to a hundred yet. Joel here has bid one twenty-five, that's low bid right now, and I'm still looking for a hundred. Somebody with a good farm and a good garden could keep him a year for a hundred, but you Jake, for seventy-five you couldn't buy his flour and salt. So I'm still seeing Joel's bid at one twenty-five and unless there's a *responsible* person who says a hundred....

Now wait a minute, Jake. I *know* a bid's a bid. Yes, and I know the rule says low bidder gets him. But you can't....

Listen to me, folks. Am I right or not? Does any man of you believe that Jake Claghorn could honestly room and board this fine young schoolmaster for the piddling sum of *seventy-five dollars* a year?

Yes, I know I'm supposed to be saving the school district's money, but I've got *principles*, dang it!

Well, a rule's a rule, if that's the way you feel about it.

So all right then, Jake bids seventy-five and who'll top him? Who'll rescue the poor young man? Who says fifty? Do I see a benevolent fifty? Where's your charity? Who says fifty? Nobody? Then sixty, who says sixty? Who'll say seventy, just to keep this young man from starving? Don't I see a seventy anywhere? Seventy, seventy....

You're breaking my heart, folks, but I'm going to have to say seventy-five once, seventy-five going once, and I'm going to have to say seventy-five twice, this is killing me but seventy-five going twice and won't somebody please help...but seventy-five twice and seventy-five thrice, and thrice seventy-five...and this is just plain terrible, folks...but it's seventy-five going thrice...and GONE.

Boarded to Jake Claghorn at seventy-five.

Our diet in Five Corners wasn't nearly as bad as his, but it certainly wasn't anything to brag about. One of our first rough quarrels was on the subject of food. Diana began reminiscing about what a good steak tasted like, trying to make my mouth water too (and it did), and then she tried to reason with me, saying that pioneers and primitive woodsmen must have had steak just every *once* in a while, and couldn't I possibly bring myself to hike into Bridgewater or some other place where there was a butcher? and buy just a teensy pound or two of sirloin? or even some chuck? No, I didn't mind the long hike, it was just the principle of the thing; we *had* to prove that we could live off the land. Well then, she said, why didn't I just go off and find a stray cow or bull and do the job myself? That would be illegal, I said. That's when she lost her cool and started yelling. She called me "impossible" and "stubborn" and "stupid" and "thoughtless" and "mean" and "pigheaded" and a bunch of other things. And when she yelled at me like that, I found myself yelling back at her, calling her "soft" and "spoiled" and "unprincipled" and "indulgent" and "greedy" and "pampered" and everything else I could think of. And we didn't speak or look at each other for the rest of the day. And at bedtime, even though the night was very chilly, she unzipped the combined sleeping bags and separated them and moved hers over into the corner of the lean-to.

Daniel Lyam Montross was lucky to get a sliver of some rancid meat in his beans once a week when he was being fed by that tightfisted Jake Claghorn. So he did pretty much the same thing that I was doing: finding whatever could be eaten from the woods and streams and fields. We had some fine butternut pies. And he learned how to make hard apple cider. And he showed us how.

Alcohol was something else. Of course we didn't keep stocked up on booze the way we had in Dudleytown, and Diana repined about that too, but whenever I hiked into Bridgewater for staples I usually packed in a couple of six-packs of beer on the way back, because, as

I saw it, beer wasn't something you could find flowing out of springs in the woods (later, Daniel Lyam Montross did show us how to make beer too). I guess we were both dependent on a little bit of alcohol just to loosen us up and to relax with at mealtimes, and although that little bit was never enough for Diana, she learned to make do with it. Another thing: without even thinking about it, she gradually gave up cigarettes. It wasn't something she had planned, as a conscious effort to kick the habit. It just happened, spontaneously you might say.

She just said to me, one day, "Funny. Do you realize that nearly a week has gone by since my last cigarette? And I haven't even thought about wanting one."

If you're trying to kick the habit, I guess there are worse things you could do than live off in the woods six miles from the nearest dealer.

Here is Daniel Lyam Montross's "recipe" for making a really wonderful hard apple cider: First you find some wild apples, truly *wild* apples. There were plenty of these around Five Corners in Daniel Lyam Montross's day, and there are still plenty now, but you have to be careful to distinguish between the abandoned orchards, the run-out *tame* apples, and the really wild apples. These wild apples are really hard, and you don't throw away the wormy apples, because a few worms sort of give "body" to the cider. (Diana was just a little squeamish about this, at first.) Then you get your cider pressed at just the right time, right after picking them. Daniel Lyam Montross always took his to the Five Corners cider mill on a cold night when there was a full moon. We used a full moon too, but we had to press the apples by hand with a kind of homemade gizmo that I tacked together myself, and it took all night, until the full moon set. Daniel put his cider into a charred oak cask holding fifty gallons. There aren't many of those around anymore, but I saw a smaller one, a twenty-galloner, sitting on some person's porch in West Bridgewater and he sold it to me for five dollars and I carried it half the way home and rolled it the other half. Daniel kept his cider in the cool cellar of Jake Claghorn's place, a cellar with a dirt floor which is just right for the proper dampness, to age the cider at earth temperature. We didn't have any cellar, just a cellar hole, which proved to be all right if we kept the barrel shaded from the sun. When you get the cider cask into the cellar, you have to let the cider "work off" in the cask, with the bung hole open, until it stops "boiling." Then comes the tricky part. You have to take a small tube—Daniel and I fashioned ones from wood but you can use plastic or rubber—and poke it through a hole into the barrel, making a snug fit and then run the tube over into a bucket of water. And then you bung the barrel. This lets the gas get out of the cider without any fresh air getting in—fresh air would make vinegar out of the cider in no time. When it stops bubbling in the water bucket, you wait about another week—Daniel usually waited a month or more, but we couldn't wait that long—and then it's ready to drink.

You can't buy this stuff in stores anywhere, but it's just about the best alcoholic beverage you ever tasted, and it's much more potent and satisfying than beer.

As soon as our first run of cider was ready to drink, Diana and I had a "cider bust"—one of our really happiest and wildest times. It was sort of like the ancient Bacchanalia, only with apple wine instead of grape wine. It was one of the warmer, sunshiny autumn days, when the autumn color was at its peak, and after drinking a lot of the stuff, we took off all our clothes and ran around in the woods and leaped and danced and chased each other and had a real time. Then we made love in the falling leaves and went back and drank a lot more of the stuff and then ran around in the woods and made love again—it was one of the few times that we did it more than once in the same day. Then we got real chummy and Diana asked if she could read what I've been writing, and I said sure, if she would let me read her diary, and she said sure. And we spent the rest of the day sitting around reading each other's writings and sipping more of the cider, until we were zonked and had to stop reading and go to bed, where we tried once more to make love, but were just too far gone.

The next day, after our hangovers had partly cleared up, we had another quarrel, a real spitting squabble this time, and I guess it was my fault for starting it, this time. Some of the things she had said about me in her diary had put me in an awful sort of self-pity-ing mood, I guess, and I was asking her things like Why the hell did she have to go and get herself laid by all those Jesus freaks? and she came back Well, wasn't I having a great time with Vashti myself? and I yelled Maybe, but that was just one! and she yelled What kinds of things were you doing with Vashti? and I yelled Nothing that you weren't doing with all three of those guys! and she yelled Oh yeah? and I yelled Yeah and I bet you thought all three of them were better fuckers than me! and she yelled What if they were? and I yelled Then why the hell didn't you just go off with them? Yeah! she yelled There's one place you're wrote in what you right! I mean—(she was so mad she couldn't talk straight)—I mean there's one place you're right in what you wrote! And that's where you said you think that I'm just your imagination! Because I am! What else could I be??? What would a nice girl like me be doing in a place like this??? No girl in her right mind would get stuck all alone with you way off in these god-forsaken places!! So you *had* to dream me up! Why don't you undream me??? Why don't you let me go out of your mind???

And she carried on like that for a while, until I was feeling perfectly miserable, but she didn't stop. She accused me of being "devious" with her, by never mentioning the fact that I had been to Dudleytown before. AND WHAT THE HELL DID YOU MEAN BY SAYING THAT YOU "PICKED" FIVE CORNERS???? Oh boy, she was really sore. But the worst was yet to come. After she ran out of things to yell at me about, she started talking about what a lousy writer I am. She said my writing was deliberately stupid, as if I were trying to hide my intelligence. She said that was "devious" too. She said that I was trying to fool the reader into thinking that there was an impossible gap between Daniel Lyam Montross's "sensitivity" and my own "boorish, pedestrian, weak-imitation-HoldenCaulfield style" and I yelled back at her that I never read Holden Caulfield, goddamn it, and she yelled THAT'S ONE MORE OF YOUR SHITTY LIES, BECAUSE YOU TOLD ME YOU DID, DON'T YOU REMEMBER???? And I yelled WELL LISTEN, KID, THE PROSE IN YOUR DIARY ISN'T EXACTLY THE WORLD'S FINEST!!! And she yelled WELL I DIDN'T MEAN FOR ANYBODY TO READ IT AND I MUST HAVE BEEN OUT OF MY FUCK-ING MIND TO LET YOU OF ALL PEOPLE READ IT!!! And I

yelled MAYBE ONE THING YOU FORGOT, SWEETHEART, IS
THAT IT WAS YOUR IDEA THAT WE READ EACH OTHER'S
STUFF, AND ANOTHER THING YOU FORGOT IS THAT
IT WAS YOUR IDEA THAT I OUGHT TO TRY TO WRITE!
PERSONALLY I DON'T GIVE A FUCK FOR WRITING AND
IF YOU'RE GOING TO MAKE CRACKS ABOUT MY WRIT-
ING THEN I

**I don't mean to intercede in a lover's quarrel, no. Or any
other kind of quarrel for that matter. In fact, I think it's good for
you and Diana to "let it all out" once in a while, and I'm sure you
will. But I've got to stop you here, Day, and remind you that you're
using up too much space which I feel is rightfully mine. I don't
care about your prose style; getting the story told is the thing. You
shouldn't think I'm being swell-headed, but I honestly believe that
the story of my experience in Five Corners is more important than
what you and Diana were quarreling about. And at this rate, I'm
afraid, you'll never get it told.**

Well, anyway, she stomped off into the woods going one way
and I stomped off into the woods going the other way and I spent
a lot of time brooding about what she had said, and I decided that
I'd make an attempt to "dress up" the prose a little bit when (and if)
I ever got back to telling more about Daniel Lyam Montross. One
thing Diana accused me of was that the only two adjectives in my
vocabulary are "very" and "really," so I took a vow to watch out for
those.

But my writing is comfortable at least, and reasonably easy,
and I like to think of it as similar to Vermont speech in a way. I
think the native Vermonter deliberately plays down his language, that
he deliberately uses unsophisticated words and grammar which he
knows are not considered "proper," as if to show that he's not of the
aristocracy but just good common folk. Diana was right, in a way,
in thinking that my use of simple writing was maybe a reflection of
my wish to be accepted. If there's one thing I want, terribly, it's to
be accepted.

We patched it up later, of course. We didn't see each other
again until bedtime, and each of us was determined apparently to

wait and let the other be the first to go to bed and go to sleep before the other came in. So we tried to outwait each other, sitting in the woods on opposite sides of the lean-to, shivering in the cold, until after midnight, when her voice called, petulantly, "Aren't you going to bed?" and I answered sternly, "Not before you do," and she said, "Well then, you might be up all night," and I said, "That suits me fine," and she said, "But it's cold, damn it!" and the chattering of her teeth came through her words, so I waited a while longer and then I said, "Let's kiss and make up," and she said something that sounded like "Blecchh!" so I waited and then

Blast you, boy! Go to bed, so you can get on with my story!

First I have to mention that when we finally did patch up and went to bed, Diana snuggled up and got a little bit affectionate, and she did a funny thing: she took my middle finger and put it into her mouth, and sort of rolled her tongue around it. I don't know why she enjoyed doing that, and at first it seemed rather infantile to me, but it was kind of sensuous in a way, and it led me to believe she wanted to make love, but when I tried, she wouldn't let me, and turned over and went to sleep.

Well, Daniel Lyam Montross had a hard time becoming a schoolmaster. It wasn't the lessons that gave him trouble. He could read well, and every night in the beginning he stayed up late reading the next day's lessons, until Jake Claghorn gave him hell for using up kerosene in the lantern, so he used candles, but Jake Claghorn gave him hell for using up candles too, so he had to do all of his reading in the late afternoon before it got dark. But he kept up with the lessons, and knew how to parse a poem pretty well, although he had a little trouble with arithmetic because he didn't know any algebra and some of the more advanced pupils were already well along in algebra. But what really gave him the most trouble, at first, was that he was expected to play the school organ and lead the pupils in song. The school had an old cottage organ, a reed organ that you pump with your feet, which some school committee years before had spent twenty dollars for in a moment of uncharacteristic extravagance.

"I neglected to ask," Judge Braddock said to him on the first day of school, "but I hope you can play this thing." Daniel Lyam Montross said that he'd never seen one before, but he would try to learn. So every day when the pupils were sent outside for morning and afternoon recess, Daniel would sit down on the organ stool and fiddle around with the organ, trying to pick out tunes by ear because of course he had never seen a sheet of sheet music before, much less learned to read one.

Daniel Lyam Montross could never learn the different stops; Diapason and Dulciana sounded just alike to him, and the stop marked "Flute Forte" embarrassed him because its name, and its sound, suggested the breaking of wind. He found one stop, Celeste, which seemed to sound a little bit better than the others, so he concentrated on that, and in time he could pick out a kind of off-key *largo* rendition of "Happy School, Ah, From Thee Never Shall Our Hearts Long Time Be Turning," his old school song.

But after going to the trouble of mastering a fairly competent and presentable version of this song, and attempting to lead his nine pupils in the singing of it, he discovered that they had never heard it before. He asked them if they didn't have a school song, and the eldest pupil, who by the way was that same redheaded Rachel McLowery, volunteered to sing for him, in a self-conscious and whispering soprano, her body swaying from side to side in tune to the slow melody, the "Five Corners Academy Song."

Listen to Rachel singing:

> *Windows are few, and none of them new*
> *And the roof it may leak in a rain*
> *Benches are hard, no grass in the yard*
> *And using the privy's a pain.*

The other pupils joined her for the chorus:

> *Down in a dell is a school we love right well*
> *Where five little roads come together*
> *'Tis not a jewel of a fancy country school*
> *But you'll never find any better.*

And Rachel continued:

> *Stove gets so het up you burn if you set up*
> *Too close, but too far and it freezes.*
> *Sometimes the master gets mean and naster*
> *And gives us each the bejeezus.*

> *Down in a dell, etc.*

> *Lunches are cold, and the water is old*
> *And tastes like somebody's fingers*
> *Air is so fusty, whenever we're musty,*
> *It lingers and lingers and lingers.*

> *Down in a dell, etc.*

> *But this is our schooling, and we say without fooling*
> *Five Corners Academy, we love you!*
> *Our dedication to this eddication*
> *We'll pass on to our children too.*

> *Down in a dell, etc.*

Daniel thanked her, and them, and assured them that he would try his best to learn how to play it on the organ, and then he asked them who had written the song. They said Henry Fox did. He asked them who Henry Fox was, but they just exchanged glances with one another and smirked, as if they knew something he didn't know. Maybe this gave them a feeling of superiority over him, which is a feeling any pupil would like to have toward a teacher. Children aren't as easily fooled as adults, sometimes, and Daniel suspected that his pupils knew that he wasn't all of eighteen years old.

Although he learned to use the organ, he did not learn to use another standard piece of school equipment: the ruler, which was intended not for measurement but for punishment. In a corner of the schoolroom beside his desk, he left untouched the long ruler and the long birch cane indicated for more serious offenses. He never learned how to "ferule" an unruly student; he preferred verbal persuasion to physical force. This uncommon approach led to his first conflict with a parent.

Here, from the tapes, is Jirah Allen, talking to Daniel Lyam Montross one afternoon at the schoolhouse, after school is over, about three weeks after Daniel had begun teaching there. If you listen carefully, you can notice a slight but distinct difference between the speech of rural Vermont and that of rural Connecticut.

Hwarye, schoolmaster? Spare a minute? Suthin's on my mind 'baout my boy Marshall, like t' discourse with ya on it. Fust day a school, Marshall come home with his sis Florianna, and she says, "Guess what! Marsh pulled Agnes Headle's hair, but the new schoolmaster never feruled him!" Secont day a school, they come home and Flori says, "By jimminety! He never birched him today neither, an Marsh was caught peekin in the gull's privy." And thud day a school, they come home and she says, "I don't cal'late he *ever* means to start ferulin' Marsh, and today he bustid a winder and put a toad-frog in teacher's desk!" And later on, she told as how Marshall tortured poor little Ira Spooner, and threw chalk at yer back when ya wa'n't watchin, an pissed in the water bucket, an he put a tack where Agnes Headle'd set on it, and she sot on it, an what with one thing an'other his gen'ril cussedness near 'baout tore up the schoolhouse!

Said to Flori, I did, "By judast! That new schoolmaster orter should've flailed him alive! He must be scairt a him." And Flori says, "No, he aint scairt a him. Dunno as he's scairt a nothing. But he'd jest ruther not use the ruler or the birch." "*Whut?*" says I, "mebbe he jest never seen Marshall do any a them things." Says Flori, "No, he seen him all right." "*Whut?*" says I. "Don't he do a blusted thing to 'im?" "*Wal,*" says she, "he talks at him." "*Talks at him?*" says I.

Yeyyup, says she. Now, sir, you're the schoolmaster, not I, but I kin tell ya it don't do a mite a good fer to *talk* t'that mis'able whelp. His brains is so slow, he don't unnerstand talk anyway, that's the reason he's been in the fust grade fer six years. Only talk he unnerstands is whut the birch says to his backside. A reg'lar dose,

Donald Harington

too. Me, I whup him twice a week, on schedule, whether he's good or bad, jest to keep him in line.

Whut's thet ya say? He's behavin lately, is he? Wal, don't be fooled, don't be fooled. Calm before the storm. Horse pullin the plow and waitin fer a chance t' kick ya.

Mebbe the trouble's yer such a young one, not much more'n a boy yerself. Mebbe yer own backside still remembers too many birchin's. But let me tell ya, there's no way on earth to keep school proper 'thout a birch, so y'orter learn to use one, 'caise if ya don't, yer going agin the childring's upbringin, yer going agin their own folks, an we won't stand fer it.

But Daniel Lyam Montross, it seems, never learned to use the feruler or the birch. It wasn't that he had any modern notions against corporal punishment, nor even that he considered verbal reasoning more effective than physical chastisement, but that he had never administered a flogging, and was afraid to start, was afraid, perhaps, that if he started flogging people he might develop a taste for it. As he told himself, "I don't cal'late to start any new hankering. Got too many now I'm not able to satisfy."

One of these was for hard cider. He discovered, after sampling the first batch from that recipe I mentioned, that he could practice his organ playing with less awkwardness under the influence, and it became his habit for a while to go home after school, pour himself a couple of quick ones, then return to school and spend the balance of the day pounding away at the organ.

One afternoon while he was belaboring the organ for all it was worth, and even accompanying himself vocally—although his voice was terrible—he threw his head back on one particular high note and happened to see, sitting on one of the rear benches, Rachel McLowery, the redhead, his oldest pupil. She was listening and smiling. He stopped playing immediately. He wondered if her smile was amusement over the atrociousness of his singing and the fervor of his playing. He was embarrassed no end, but he managed to ask her how long she had been sitting there listening to him.

Here's Rachel, from the tapes, or rather here's Daniel, or rather here's me saying what Daniel said that Rachel said. Incidentally, these monologues from the tapes, and there are quite a lot of them, might seem to contradict the conventional idea of the taciturn, tight-lipped Vermont Yankee. Judge Braddock, certainly, was not your ordinary laconic Vermonter, nor was Jirah Allen, and certainly not Rachel. Could it have been that these people of Five Corners were exceptions to the rule of silence? Or is the rule a myth? Possibly, part of the truth is that Daniel Lyam Montross was the sort of person who naturally drew people out, the sort of person who makes you want to talk to him. Well, here's Rachel, replying to his question, "How long have you been sitting there?"

Not long. Jest a twink. Your playin gets better'n better, Mister Montross. Honest it does. Few weeks ago you couldn't barely play a note, and now listen to ya.

But I didn't mean to listen in. Not why I came here. I need some help on my lessons. Geography is all right, haven't had a bit of trouble with China or Japan. History too. And arithmetic, you know I kin run circles 'round ya, doing algebrar. But hygiene. Hygiene's suthin else again.

Even if we don't give but fifteen minutes a day on hygiene. Even if we don't but listen while ya read a page or two. Even if we don't have no homework but to mem'rize the bones and muscles and such. I kin do all that.

But I wonder, what's hygiene *for*? Book says tobacco will stunt your growth and alcohol will blind ya, but everybody knows that anyhow. Book says we orter wash reg'lar, and keep clean, but Mum says that anyhow. Book says we ortent spit on our slates, it will spread germs, so we keep little bottles filled with water. That's a lot to know, is it?

But the book's 'sposed to be 'baout takin keer a the *body*, aint it? Aint hygiene 'baout the *body*? Well, then, my lands, why don't the book *tell* 'baout the body, 'sides washin it and keepin germs off it and not givin it any tobacco or alcohol? Book says we got four *systems*, one takes keer a the blood that runs through ya, one takes keer a the nerves that run through ya, one takes keer a the air that runs into ya, and one takes keer a the food that runs through ya. Now is that all? Is suthin wrong with me, or is that all? It aint that you've not got to the right lesson yet, 'caise I've borried that book orf yer desk when ya wa'n't watchin, and read it cover to back.

How come there's not a word to that book 'baout how folks get made and borned? Aint there any *system* fer that? Aint there suthin that runs through the body fer that? Don't ya laugh at me, Agnes Headle's jest as dumb as me on the subjick. She says same way as cows and mares and ewes, and hens and sows and gyps, but I knew this feller, he said them were animals and everybody knows that people are different. That's what he said, everybody knows. But *I* don't know. And that book aint no help.

People, this feller told me, have got souls, and animals aint got souls. How come there's nothing in the book about souls? Don't the soul need any hygiene? No, then why does the soul bleed out of a girl's velvet each and every month? Not a word to the hygiene book 'baout that bleedin. I cal'late that feller must've been right 'baout souls, 'caise I've watched cows and mares and ewes, and hens and sows and gyps, and I've never seen one of them bleed. They don't bleed. No souls.

Well, the book says bleeding's bad, and it tells how to stop bleedin and how to make plasters and bandages and turnicuts. Last time I got to bleedin I tied a turnicut 'round my waist but all it did was give me a stummick ache. Rags won't stop the bleedin but jest soak it up. I know Agnes Headle bleeds too, she told me she did. And why don't the book tell at least why it's each and every month, reg'lar as the moon? Does the moon cause it? Aint a word to the book 'baout the moon.

But what I'd really keer to know is, how come fellows don't bleed too? Don't they have souls like girls? Or do you bleed, but it's not red but that white sirup? But the moon don't cause that. And how come there's not a word to the book about the white sirup? That would tell how you can tell if it's got seeds or not. So you could tell if you'd get a baby or not. When it's in your belly. Or is it always white? His was. Maybe if it'd been red. Maybe red means seeds. He didn't. Book talks about red cells and white cells. Not a

word on white sirup. Is yours? Teacher, what do you know that the book don't say?

If Daniel Lyam Montross had been embarrassed by her eavesdropping on his organ practice, it was as nothing compared with his embarrassment over the subject she had raised. She must have mistaken his nervous laughter as a mocking of her ignorance, but she did not seem to notice that his face was nearly the color of her hair and that his respiratory system was on the fritz. He nearly blurted out, "Wal, heck, I'm not but seventeen myself," which might have cost him, possibly his job, certainly her respect. But in truth those matters which were mysteries to her were largely mysteries to him. He did not know why the human female is the only creature who menstruates. And her questions were terribly pregnant to him, that is, they set him to brooding and pondering about these matters himself. What if, after all, that substance which he had known as "quid" was only blood with white cells instead of red? At length he allowed as how he didn't know anything that wasn't in the book, and if it wasn't in the book it either wasn't important or else it wasn't meant to be learned.

But the nature of this subject had aroused in Daniel Lyam Montross a new interest in Rachel McLowery. At the first opportunity, he sought out Judge Braddock and reminded him that he had told Daniel to remind him to tell him something about Rachel.

Listen to Judge Braddock again:

Ah, yes. Suspect you've been around that red hair long enough to want to see it on the next pillow when you wake up. Schoolmasters and schoolmistresses are just alike, every one of them. They always fall for their oldest scholars. And she's your oldest. And not a bad looker, I might say. We even have an expression. You haven't heard it? You will. "Red as Rachel's hair." Yes. A week ago the maples were nearly "red as Rachel's hair." Aaron Tindall painted his barn this past summer and it was "red's Rachel's hair." Matt Earle gashed his arm on his harrow and it bled "red's Rachel's hair." Sit around the fireplace in Glen House, and you're bound to hear someone remark that the coals are "red's Rachel's hair."

But, my boy, I think you ought to know about her, and I'm surprised you haven't yet. I suppose Jake Claghorn don't talk much, does he? And you'd be the last person the other scholars would tattle on her to. If your heart's running a temperature over her, you'll likely not take me kindly that I'm the one who told you. But if I incur your disfavor, it's better than if you didn't know. What if you were to run away with her and not find out until later?

Because she ran away, that's the story I'm trying to tell you. Couple of years back. She wasn't but fourteen then, yet already bloomed out the way she is now, and those locks like fire around her head. She attracted the attentions of a pedlar, a man from Rutland. I knew the man, at least I'd bandied words with him, I'd taken his measure. A shameless lecher, I'd say.

Now, nobody knows for certain that it was him she ran off with. That's to say, nobody saw them leave together and I doubt that Joel McLowery has been able to beat a confession out of her. But he was here one day, hawking his goods, and he was gone the next day, and so was she. It doesn't take a genius to make the connection.

Well, she was gone near on to three months. We had given her up as gone for good, although there'd been some talk of getting together a delegation of a few of us to go over to Rutland and look for them. Just as well we didn't bother, for when she returned finally, it was learned that it hadn't been Rutland she'd been to, but Springfield. That's all that was learned, though. Joel couldn't beat the story out of her, nor even find out why she had come back.

She just told how it hadn't been what she'd expected, and led us to think she'd come back out of disappointment. Joel got Doctor Beam up from Bridgewater to look at her, and Doctor Beam claimed that her maidenhead seemed to be intact, which got some folks to wondering how she'd preserved it—I'm just mentioning this to you, young man, because some fellows are strict about the condition of their bride's virginity—anyway, that was Doctor Beam's report, and at least it was some comfort to the McLowerys that she wasn't with child.

But the important thing, it seems to me, is that she *did* run off, and was gone three months with the fellow, whether or not his instrument was of sufficient caliber to sever her membrane. He was not, I might mention, a very attractive or even presentable man. He was not rich. He was not intelligent. As far as I can see, he had nothing in his favor except Rachel's lust, which could have been wanderlust but was probably simple heat mixed with curiosity perhaps, which you would think she could have satisfied with any one of the boys here in Five Corners…or even an old gentleman like myself, ha, ha! Pardon my levity, I wouldn't consider such a thing.

Now, if my telling of this little tale hasn't quite stuck in your stomach or turned you away from her, and you have in mind to pursue her, you might possibly, in time, learn the true facts of the matter. If that should come about, I would appreciate it considerably if you'd pass along to me whatever you learn. Not that I'm a busybody, and I'm certainly no scandalmonger, but for my own satisfaction I like to know what's going on in this world, and this business of Rachel is a skeleton in the cupboard that I'd like to see some clothes if not flesh on, you might say. Have you ever heard the old saw, "There's not much happening in this town, but what you hear makes up for it"?

Maybe she would never breathe a word of her past to you. But if she does. If she does. I think it would be worth your while to make me your repository.

Well, how are things at Jake Claghorn's? He feeding you well enough?

No, Jake Claghorn was not feeding Daniel Lyam Montross well enough, but as I have mentioned Daniel was able to keep from starving by foraging for himself whatever could be found in the woods and fields and streams…although now that winter was coming on this became increasingly difficult. Claghorn rarely if ever served meat, although on one occasion some relative of Claghorn's gave him a goose, or rather an elderly gander, and beginning on a Saturday they had meat regularly, on Sunday, cold gander for breakfast, for supper one leg of the gander heated up, on Monday the other leg, and so on, but by the following Saturday, with the gander still holding out, Daniel decided he would just as soon not have meat on the table.

Rachel McLowery noticed at school during lunchtime that Daniel's lunch pail contained only stale bread and apples. Thereafter she began, without asking him, to bring a lunch for him from home, things from the McLowery's comfortable larder, slices of ham, fresh carrots, hard-boiled eggs with some salt wrapped in paper, and a jar of real tea to replace the swamp tea he'd been drinking. Daniel was at first embarrassed by this charity, but then touched by it, and eventually quite grateful for it. Rachel was careful that the other pupils not discover it and learn that she had become the teacher's pet.

She was his pet indeed. Sometimes he played the organ and she sang ballads, alone together in the schoolhouse at the end of day. She made him a present of a nice little mirror she had stolen from home; Jake Claghorn's house had no mirror; Daniel had been in the habit of pausing by the millpond on his way to school in the morning and looking at his reflection in the still water to see if his hair was combed and his face clean.

They talked a lot too, or rather Rachel talked a lot and Daniel was content to listen. She told him who the mysterious Henry Fox was, whose name he had heard mentioned several times. Henry Fox was an assayer from some foreign country—some said Switzerland—who had come to Five Corners way back in the 1860's during the height of the gold rush that had occurred on all the streams between Five Corners and Tyson. Fox bought his way into the Rooks Mining Company, the major operation, and became superintendent, and when the company curtailed its operations he bought it out for a mere $12,500 and still lived, all alone, practically a hermit, in the house at the mine entrance. Rachel offered to take Daniel and show him where it was, but she didn't want to introduce him to Henry Fox. Everybody knew that Henry Fox was crazy as a loon.

It didn't bother Daniel Lyam Montross too terribly much that his pet had a past, that she had run away with a man two years earlier, but he wanted to know about it. He took his time in bringing up the subject, meanwhile talking frankly with her—or listening to her frank talk—about sexual matters. She had not, he discovered, ever heard of such words as "perkin," "vale," and "funicle"—not because of innocence or ignorance but because those were the local idioms of Connecticut or at least of Dudleytown. Here in Five Corners, he learned, the equivalents were "picket," "velvet," and "fuse"—although the latter had a connotation, for her at least, which did not correspond with his notion.

Now the following is a part which I very much dislike transcribing from the tapes, but without it there wouldn't be much understanding of the story, and Daniel Lyam Montross would not respect me if I omitted it. So even though it's distasteful to me, I hold my breath, you might say, and shut my eyes and plunge in. Listen:

Quit callin ya teacher, I will, if ya don't watch out. As lief call ya Dan, Dan. Gettin so's I'm with ya half the time, and the other half I'm thinkin 'baout ya. Papa's started teasin. Says t'me, "Don't ya run off with this one." Says t'me, "You run off with this one, we won't have no schoolmaster."

Oh, shouldn't tell ya, no, shouldn't, shouldn't, but once 'pon a time I absquatulated, I run off from home. Don't ya hold it agin me, neither, I was a fool-headed butterfly lookin t'see th'other side a the mountains, I'd never been as far as to Woodstock. This feller told me he'd show me all the big towns, but he only showed me one and I didn't keer too much fer that one, Springfield, jest lots of big factories and such. Wouldn't've flew off with him t'begin with, 'ceptin he told as how he had this big house in Rutland that I could live in an be a princess, but he didn't tell me till later, when we never got to Rutland but this other town Springfield, that he already had a princess in that house that he was married to. That's when I up and left him quick, and come back home, but by then he'd already done me like a prince does his princess every night. More'n two months, it was.

You won't hold it agin me, will ya, Dan? I was fool-headed an callow, I didn't know the fust thing 'baout all the things I would wonder and wonder 'baout, and he promised to teach me. He did. I'd still not know the fust thing but for whut he taught.

Like he was the one told me how people are different from animals because they have souls. When animals, say like sheep, fuse to make their lambs, the ram has to work his picket into the ewe's velvet, and that way his seed has to pass through all her stuffings before it can reach her belly, and it's all so messy and awkward-like. But when God made people and gave them souls, he fixed it so's the man wouldn't have to use the woman's ugly velvet but could use her pretty mouth instead and that way the seed would go direct to her belly down her gullet.

Thinkin I was his princess, young as I was, I got t'thinkin whut fun t'have a baby, so I let him fuse me like he told. Fust time was terrible hard fer me, but he says fust time allus is. Nearly choked, I did. But it didn't give me a baby. Never swole in the belly the way you're 'sposed ta. Even though he did it every night, and sometimes when he got home from his day's peddlin, he'd jest take out his picket and I'd take it in and swaller.

Ast him why my belly wa'n't swellin the way it orter've, but he jest said some girls naturally can't make babies, which made me awful sad, but he went on tryin anyway. I got to thinkin 'baout it, and once, once I didn't swaller but waited till he'd gone and then I spit it out and looked at it. It was white, and I got to thinkin maybe it orter've been red instead a white, and it was his fault not mine that I couldn't make a baby. But I never said anything 'baout it to him.

What bothered me the most, though, was that he seemed t'get such a hull lot a pleasure out a fusin, I mean, he'd do it so often and allus with lots a jerkin and cooing when the sirup com-menced shootin, it must've been a sight a pleasure fer him. But not fer me. How come, I ast him, if God made people with souls so they could fuse this way 'stead a the nasty way animals do it, how come only the feller gets all the pleasure out a it, and none fer the gull? Wal, that puzzled him some, I tell ya. And he ast me, didn't it give me no pleasure to gobble that nice fat picket and feel that hot sirup pourin down my throat? And I told him, not much it didn't. He said, Wal, some women was that way, that they didn't get no pleasure from anything. That made me feel awful sad too, but try as I could, I couldn't get no pleasure from him, and I begun to think maybe that was his fault too.

I got to thinkin it was on account of he wa'n't very gentle.

Would you be gentle, Dan? He wa'n't, he'd commence by gettin this look on his face, this kind a slit-eyed look with a fleer on his mouth and he'd yank out his picket and say things t'me like, "Come on, gull, I got a hot gift fer ya," or, "Open up, sweet, here comes yer supper!" You wouldn't talk like that, would ya, Dan? And then whilst I would be doin him, he'd sometimes swear at me, and say, like, "Watch yer goddam teeth, kid!" or like, "Faster, you little bitch!" You wouldn't swear at me, would ya, Dan? And he'd get rough, and grab holt the back a my hair and act like he wanted t'poke a hole out through the back a my neck. You wouldn't be rough, would ya, Dan? Would ya?

There's one thing I certainly can't admire very much about Daniel Lyam Montross, and that is that he neglected, right then and there, to straighten that poor girl out of her hideous misconceptions about intercourse. He could so easily have given her the true facts of life, right on the spot, but for a moment he wondered if maybe she were right, if, after all, the correct way for man the "higher animal" to fuse was as she described it, and what is more, her telling of this revolting story, instead of repulsing him as it should have, actually caused him to have an erection, and caused him to want to "fuse" with her in that horribly incorrect fashion.

Diana and I had another quarrel, over this. It seems as if, at times, we were quarreling every day, over anything. She was playing back on her tape recorder this part of the tape, so that I could listen to it, and my shock must have been amusing to her. Then, after Rachel's monologue, came the part of the tape where Daniel Lyam Montross began telling about his first "fusing" with Rachel.

"Turn it off!" I said to Diana. "I'd just as soon not hear it."

"Oh, don't be a prude, Day," she said. I seem to recall that she had called me that a few times or several times before.

"Prude, hell!" I said. "It's not a matter of prudishness. It's a simple matter of good taste and restraint. Daniel could screw his idiot sister all he wanted to, back in Dudleytown, for all I cared, but when it comes to taking advantage of a poor, ignorant—"

"But don't you see?" Diana said. "It wasn't exactly a matter of taking advantage of her. Because he was gentle. *Very* gentle. He was everything that that lecherous pedlar had not been. In fact, she even had an orgasm for the first—"

"Shut up! Shut up!" I yelled at her. And for the rest of that day, I was unable to allow myself to listen to any more of the tapes. I thought: *I'm going to have to kill you, Dan, if you don't watch out.*

The new assortment of epithets which she thought up to toss at me includes: "straitlaced," "intolerant," "narrow" "parochial," "small," and, interestingly enough, "uninteresting."

I called her a few things too.

The next time we were in bed, and she pulled that playful little stunt again, of putting my finger in her mouth, I jerked it out and called her a few more things.

But Daniel Lyam Montross, whatever might be said against him in regard to this episode, was at least kind and considerate enough to lose no time in explaining to Rachel, *afterwards*, what little he knew about the true facts of life, which wasn't much. The poor girl was at first shocked and refused to believe him. Then when he made it sound so logical that she could no longer quite disbelieve him, she cried for a long time.

The odd thing, the terrible thing, is that she *still* thought that natural, *true* intercourse was somehow bestial, dirty and perverted, and even though, eventually, after months of his trying, she let him have her once in the natural way, let him have her natural virginity, you might say, the experience disturbed her so much that she actually vomited and was sick at home in bed with a fever for several days, missing school, which was just as well, as far as Daniel was concerned, for he needed several days to recover from the experience himself. During these days, he made his first trip up the mountain to see the hermit-home of Henry Fox, and even to meet and to talk with the man that everybody said was crazy. This meeting was one of the important things that happened to him in Five Corners. In fact, getting acquainted with Henry Fox was one of the most significant events of his life.

I should have known better, after my previous experience with an overdose of hard cider, which had led to our worst quarrel, but

I liked this beverage more than a lot, and sometimes it was hard to know where to stop. Anyway, the weather was much too chilly, now, for us to take our baths in the brook any more, even on sunshiny days. We usually heated water in pots and kettles on the fire at our lean-to, and instead of soaking we would just use a washcloth, like they do to hospital patients. Diana called this a "spit bath"—an inelegant expression if ever I heard one. Well, sometimes I would scrub her back and she would scrub mine, but this time, because we'd been making inroads on the cider barrel, she didn't stop with just my back. And later, when we were toweled off and drying beside the fire, and drinking more of the cider, I didn't object when she started doing what she did, although it still seemed to me, even in my tipsiness, an infantile if not a perverted thing to do.

Oh, this has been the story of a boy who loves ghost towns, of a lonely boy who goes off into the woods by himself, or with a nice girl if he's lucky, oh, this has been the story of a ghost town where nobody lives anymore, where once there was living, and loving, and singing and laughter, oh, a story of things lost that will never be again, of people who are gone, of buildings built and vanished, of dreams dreamt and faded, oh, this has been the story of man's little pleasures and of his foibles and afflictions, a story of wild places, desert woods, of great trees in breezes, oh, and this has been the story of a boy bathed and naked, dreaming of a pretty girl on her knees.

It wasn't as bad as I thought it would be.

Henry Fox was born in 1849, coincidental with the California gold rush, not in California but in Zurich, Switzerland, to Heimerich Voecks, an Austrian dentist, and Lillibet Holbein, a Swiss beauty. His parents were not married; he never met his father; his mother took him in his infancy to England, where she anglicized his name to Henry Fox and later attempted unsuccessfully to have him enrolled in one of the better public (that is, private) schools. Resenting the exclusive class system of England, she took him to America in search of equality and opportunity. Finding New York too large for her tastes, she lived in, and sent him to public (that is, public) schools in, successively, Bryn Mawr, Pennsylvania, Terre Haute, Indiana, and Eau Claire, Wisconsin.

One thing Henry Fox had in common with Daniel Lyam Montross was a precocious maturity; he ran away from home at the age of fifteen and went to South America to seek his fortune, earning his passage as a steward on a steamship. Three years of hard labor in the gold mines of Argentina taught him all that he knew about gold mining but failed to make him rich, and he returned to America at the age of nineteen nearly penniless, working first as a dishwasher in third-rate Manhattan restaurants, and then as a newshawk on the streets of New York. One day when nobody was buying his newspapers, he sat down on a curb and read one of them and happened upon a small article to the effect that gold had been discovered in Vermont.

He arrived in Five Corners billing himself as a professional "assayer" and offering to make, without charge, an appraisal of any gold that had been found. He quickly surmised two things of importance: one, the gold which had been washing into the streams around Five Corners probably was coming from rich mother lodes in the surrounding hills, possibly even a vein of pure gold quartz; and, two, none of the men engaged in the gold search knew the first thing about mining, other than simple stream panning. One of the men was a local farmer, another a government land agent returned from Indian territory, another a shoe store proprietor from New York. None of these men had ever mined gold before.

Only one of them had capital, the former land agent, Charles Rook, and because of this the company which Henry Fox helped them to organize was called the Rooks Mining Company, although everybody in Five Corners called it the Fox Mining Company because Henry Fox was superintendent.

To add drama or at least showmanship to his work, Henry Fox fashioned a weird contraption out of metal rods, which he called his "divining rod," and set about trying to locate the mother lode. The contraption was worthless, but it fascinated his associates and the crowds of local people who would come each day to watch him hunt. What he was really using was his keen eyesight, trained in Argentina to detect telltale outcroppings indicative of gold deposits. Within a few days of searching, he found a gold-bearing rock on a hill some miles to the south of Five Corners, and after shouting "Eureka!" he claimed that this was the location of a vast mother lode of gold quartz.

The trouble with Henry, perhaps attributable to his youth, was that he stuck to his guns, even if the guns were out of ammunition. Although he had a talent for spotting possible digging sites, he had no talent, indeed, *nobody* had any talent, for determining just how large the vein might be. Ever afterward, Henry Fox would refuse to believe that this spot he picked was not the right place, that the greater part of the gold, if there was any, lay hidden in some other place.

Everybody was so impressed with Henry's discovery that endless capital for the operations began flowing in from eager investors. A boardinghouse was built on the spot, and large crews of men began digging a shaft according to Henry's instructions. When the shaft was finished, construction began on a large compound of buildings: a large mill for the quartz, shaft houses, several dwellings for employees in addition to the boardinghouse, and even a special residence for Superintendent Henry Fox, a two-and-a-half story dwelling which he called "Gold Brook Chateau."

Diana and I made a hike up the mountain to locate the place. The buildings are all gone, except for one fallen wall of "Gold Brook Chateau." The mine entrance has caved in, but rusty iron tracks still lead to it, and mossy timbers jut out of it. I had a kind of strange feeling that if you were to dig into the shaft, you might still find a lot of gold.

But *they* didn't, Henry Fox and his associates. The shaft ran for 365 feet back into the mountain, where it joined a vertical shaft that rose 300 feet to the top of the mountain. Somewhere back in there Henry found some gold. On October 27, 1883, against a backdrop of flaming autumn color, Henry Fox proudly displayed to visitors and newspapermen the first ingot of gold produced by his operation. It was 6 × 1 × ¾ inches and weighed fifty-one ounces and one pennyweight. It was, he declared, $^{97}\!/_{100}$ fine and was worth $1021. News of this was reported as far away as San Francisco, where the newspapers made envious and invidious comparisons between Vermont gold and California gold.

More investments poured in, and a Boston banker bought control of the company, established himself as president, and appointed a board of directors to incorporate the company. The board made plans to quadruple the capacity of the operations, to earn faster profits, and the equipment was dismantled and packed away to prepare for this expansion. Henry Fox had wisely returned all of his own earnings and salary into the company, and now owned several thousand dollars' worth of stock. But the directors, inexplicably, were slow in commencing the expansion, and Henry Fox suspected that this delay was related to a visit by a team of assayers and geologists hired by the directors.

Three years went by without any more action at the mine, and Henry Fox ultimately was forced to sue the directors for his back salary. The court decided in his favor and ordered all of the mine property to be put upon the block at a sheriff's sale in Ludlow. The directors bid $12,000 to get their property back, but Henry Fox raised it by $500 and it was struck off to him.

At the age of thirty-eight in 1887, Henry Fox began his long years as hermit mine owner, panning the brooks for a flake here and there. He was forty-eight when Daniel Lyam Montross first met him ten years later.

How is all of this relevant? Why have I devoted so much introduction to this man who wasn't even a native Vermonter and therefore doesn't have one jot of "local color" to add to our story? Simply because Henry Fox had more influence on Daniel Lyam Montross, for good or for bad, than anybody else he ever met in his whole life. And Daniel Lyam Montross himself, in his old age (if we ever live that long, and get that far), will become a kind of hermit like Henry Fox, in some other place.

Henry Fox looked foreign; he did not look like a Vermonter. He was a thin, sharply boned man with hair already turning yellow-white and a large flowing moustache, also yellow-white. His house was yellow-white and his dog was yellow-white. The dog was the one that Daniel Lyam Montross met first.

The dog was a large, muscular creature, some indeterminate species of mostly hound and partly bulldog, husky, shepherd and fox terrier. The dog had strayed into the yard of Gold Brook Chateau one day a few years previously, and Henry Fox had thrown at it the only hard object handy at the moment, which was a stale biscuit. The dog ate it in one swallow and attached himself for life to Henry Fox. Henry Fox named him "Pooch."

When Daniel Lyam Montross came walking up to Gold Brook Chateau, big Pooch did not snarl nor growl nor bark nor snap like most dogs; instead he "yolloped" (Daniel's word). Daniel's imitation of this sound isn't easy to transcribe from the tapes; the dog sort of opened wide his jaws as if inhaling sharply; on the inhale he said something that sounded like "Yower," on the exhale a louder and more forcible "FROWER." Thus *yowr FROWR!* and again, *yowr FROWR!* The third time that Pooch said *yowr FROWR*, Henry Fox came out the side door of Gold Brook Chateau with a shotgun.

Between the dog's yolloping and Fox's brandishing the shotgun, Daniel got pretty nervous, and when Fox demanded, "What're you here for?" he could not think of anything to say. He couldn't very well say that he had come out of curiosity. Strangely, what he found himself doing was breaking suddenly into song, and singing "The Five Corners Academy Song" about the leaking roof and hot stove and old water and fusty air and all. Singing this song calmed his nerves at the same time it gave him an entry, which was to ask Henry Fox if he had written that song.

"What if I did?" Fox answered. He was quite surly. The dog Pooch said *yowrFROWR!* a few more times.

Daniel explained that he was the new Five Corners schoolmaster and said that he thought the song was the best thing he'd ever heard.

"So?" said Henry Fox, and Pooch said *yowrFROWR!*

Daniel said that he just wanted to tell him how much he liked that song and how much he admired the words, and that he had heard Fox's name mentioned several times by different people, and just thought he'd like to meet Fox and tell him how much he had admired that song and that he had heard his named mentioned by different people several times.

"So?" said Henry Fox, and Pooch said *yowrFROWR!*

Well, Daniel said it had been nice meeting him and he was sorry if he had bothered him or interrupted him or anything and that if Fox ever happened to pass the school he ought to drop in and say hello or something, and anyway he was pleased to have met him.

"I never visit the school," said Fox, "or the village," and Pooch backed him up on this.

Well, said Daniel, that was too bad, and he was sorry to hear that, but that he figured he must have his reasons, and that Daniel didn't want to give the impression of butting in or being nosey or anything and anyway he was pleased to have met him, and goodbye, pleasant day to you, goodbye. Daniel backed off from the dog and then turned and walked off.

Behind his back he heard Pooch say *yowr* and Fox say, "Wait" and Pooch say *FROWR* and Fox say, "Hold it."

Daniel turned.

Fox said, "You didn't tell me your name."

Daniel told him his name.

"How old are you?" Fox asked.

Daniel told him that he was only seventeen, and said he hoped Fox wouldn't tell anybody that, because if he did, it might cost him his job because schoolmasters are supposed to be at least eighteen and besides Daniel hadn't even finished school himself, so he hoped, he said again, that Fox wouldn't tell anybody.

Fox said, "You could pass for considerably more than seventeen," and then he asked, "What was it you said you came all the way up here to see me about?"

Daniel said that he had just heard Fox's name mentioned several times by different people and just thought he'd like to meet Fox and tell him how much he had admired that school song.

"Thank you," Fox said, and permitted himself a small chuckle. "I'm rather proud of that song, myself." Then he said, "Sit," and gestured toward a tree-stump chopping block. Pooch hopped on the block and sat. "Not you, you dorg," Fox said to the dog, and kicked it off.

Daniel sat on the chopping block and Fox squatted on his heels beside him. Fox didn't say anything more, and Daniel tried to think of something to say or to ask him, without seeming nosey. Nearly ten minutes went by, in silence, before Daniel thought up something, which was to ask Fox why he had written that song.

"You should have heard the one they had before," was all Fox said.

Another ten minutes drifted by, Daniel swallowed and asked Fox if he really enjoyed living by himself all alone.

"Well, there's Pooch there," Fox said.

Ten minutes later Daniel asked him if he knew many of the people in Five Corners.

"Know them all," Fox said.

Another ten minutes and Daniel asked him what he thought of Judge Braddock.

"Perfidious," said Henry Fox, and then the interview sort of petered out. Daniel Lyam Montross did not know what "perfidious" meant, but he made a mental note of it, and as soon as he got back to the schoolhouse he looked it up in his dictionary. This was but the first time that Daniel would have to consult his dictionary regarding a word used by Henry Fox; there would be many and many more such occasions; eventually Daniel would even take the dictionary with him when he went to visit Fox. For although Henry Fox's casual speech was sparing of words, and those words usually Vermontish with just a trace of a foreign accent (or an amalgam of several different foreign accents), as Daniel got to know him the man revealed ever greater depths of diction and sententious wisdom. Within six months Daniel's dictionary was worn out, falling loose from its spine. But by that time Daniel knew almost all the words that Fox would use. He knew what "plebeian" meant in relation to Jake Claghorn. He knew why Aaron Tindall was "bibulous" and what connotation "secular" had for Matthew Earle. He understood Fox's coinages: how he could take the name of a Frenchman named de Sade and make it into a word, "sadist," to describe the mean simpleton Marshall Allen, who disrupted the school and pulled wings off of flies. He understood how both Joel McLowery and the weather could be "inclement." And he collected a whole wardrobe of dressy last words for Rachel McLowery: "nubile," "rufescent," "sirenic," "muliebrile," "hoydenish," "artless," "orificial," etc.

Daniel liked to tease Rachel with his newfound locution. He would call her a "gamic gamine" and she would pout and pester him to tell her what that meant, and she would refuse to have anything further to do with him unless he told her what it meant, and finally in the end he would explain that *gamine* is a kind of tomboyish girl with elfin appeal, and *gamic* means sexual, and she would laugh and mock-slap his face and love him all the more because he was so smart and knew such fancy magic words. She knew that he went often to see Henry Fox, in winter on a pair of snowshoes he spent all of his first salary on, but she did not know that Fox was the source of his rhetoric. Nor did she suspect that Fox was the reason that Daniel suddenly seemed to know the answers to all the riddles of life and sex which had eluded him before. He was able to fill in for her the gaps gaping in the hygiene book. She was comforted by his explanation of why human females have their menses. She learned that the manufacture of a baby, although commenced in an instant of abandon, is a nine-month-long toil ending in agony, and she decided it was just as well that that pedlar hadn't given her a child, it was just as well that she was emotionally unable to permit a picket to enter her velvet, it was just as well that, as Daniel assured her, it is impossible for male sirup to reach the womb via the stomach. Henry Fox told him this. With chalk on a piece of slate, Henry Fox diagrammed the female esophagus, stomach and intestines, and demonstrated how they are discrete from the ovaries, oviducts and uterus. Then, to "normalize" or at least define Rachel's misconception about fusing, to clarify such orality, Henry Fox told him a new word derived from the Latin past participle of *fellare*. Daniel didn't like the new word because it rhymed with "ratio," which for some reason (probably related to his distaste for mathematics) he couldn't stand the sound of. So Daniel coined his own substitute, near enough in sound as well as meaning: *felicity*, and Henry Fox agreed that this was a splendid byword for it.

Daniel Lyam Montross was slightly bothered by the fact that, although Rachel would perform felicity on him whenever it suited her whim or his, he was not able to take her to the dances on the rubber-ball-mounted floor of Glen House, because somehow it wouldn't look proper for the young schoolmaster to be seen escorting one of his scholars to the village dance. Rachel went to the dances regularly (as did every single soul in Five Corners…except Henry Fox) but was always required to choose, as her partner in the squares or reels of the contra-dances, a boy other than Daniel, while Daniel had to be content with swinging and sashaying old and middle-aged ladies, the youngest of whom was Rachel's mother, Melissa, a somewhat heavy substitute for the daughter, although Melissa McLowery had the same wondrous It as her daughter ("*It*" being one of Henry Fox's more sophisticated syncopes, *syncope* being one of Henry Fox's more sophisticated cuttingwords, *cuttingword* being one of Henry Fox's more sophisticated synthetic copulations, *synthetic copulation* being one of my own less sophisticated attempts to deal with Fox's terminology, synthetic in the sense of both "hybridizing" and "artificial, man-made," and copulation in the sense of both "linking" and, since Henry had no women to screw, he screwed words, like *cuttingword* derived from the fact that syncope comes from the Latin for "cut," and means, in relation to *It*, that It is a cut or shortened form of a longer word, namely, *Identity*—more about this later). Melissa McLowery had a real yen for Daniel Lyam Montross (Henry Fox explaining that *yen* comes from the Chinese *yin* which means both "addiction" and the moon, shade, femininity, or the passive female cosmic element complementary to *yang*) but Daniel didn't have much of a yang for Melissa; for one thing she was his girl's mother, and for another thing she was a little bit overweight, although the excess fat had accumulated mostly in pleasant female places like her breasts and thighs and mouth. At the dances, and elsewhere, Melissa always seemed to be trying to get Daniel off some other place, or at least making feints in that direction. She was still this side of forty, but her hair was not red like her daughter's, rather more on the auburn side. She loved to dance, and did the contra-dances with great vivacity and flourishes, and taught Daniel all he ever learned about dancing, hopping and skipping on the bouncy floor mounted on rubber balls, he looking over her shoulder to see whose partner Rachel was, and always wishing it was him but knowing it could never be, unless he quit being schoolmaster, which he often contemplated quitting being, especially as harsh, inclement winter dragged on, and his perch at the front of the schoolroom too far from the stove to keep from freezing, and his stomach not lined with enough nourishment to warm him until the noon hour and Rachel's fine lunches, and the education he was getting from Henry Fox making him have a yang for better things than schoolteaching.

What happened was, Melissa McLowery, who had developed such a moony addiction for the sun of Daniel, and who had no inkling that her daughter had been carrying on, after a fashion, with him for quite some time now, espied them at it. Lots of mothers undoubtedly have stumbled by accident upon their daughters petting or even screwing on the living room sofa after a date, or something like that, but how many mothers have gone into a schoolhouse and discovered their daughters squatting in front of the teacher's open fly? Melissa McLowery probably had an urge to flog them both on the spot, but she tiptoed out, unseen, and Daniel didn't know he had been seen until several days later, when he was invited to "call" upon Mrs. McLowery at her house, for "tea and talk." Even so, Daniel figured she just wanted to talk about Rachel's progress in school, or something, and he went to her house equipped with a standard "certificate," his ink on it still wet: "This certifies that *Rachel McLowery* during the past week has been punctual at school, commendable in deportment and perfect in recitations."

Now Melissa, even though she was only a sheepfarmer's wife, fancied herself one of the better bred ladies of Five Corners—as a matter of fact, it was for this very reason that she invited him to tea instead of sending for the town constable or reporting him to Judge Braddock or to her husband. She even served tea in the parlor, that room which Vermonters so seldom use, usually only for funerals or weddings, the room in her case filled with furniture hardly touched, let alone worn, and of, for the most part, the latest mode, bought from mail-order houses: carved and decorated china closet, French marquetry parlor table, dainty golden oak ladies' writing desk, imitation mahogany pier mirror, a deep-tufted Roman divan couch (upon which Melissa sat), a matching Roman reception chair (upon which Daniel sat), the walls hung with colored photographs of rustic scenes and artographs of same, in gilt ornamented frames, the four corners of the room with whatnot shelves and their varied contents, echoing the centerpiece étagère with its four shelves covered with rare, curious bric-a-brac of colored glass, smoked glass, porcelain, and silver. As far as Five Corners went—and Five Corners didn't go very far—it was one of the nicest parlors in town.

Here, if you can take it (Daniel scarcely could), is Melissa:

Sweetening for your tea? Long or short? And try one of these cakes, you'll like it, fresh baked this morning myself, I doubt if Jake Claghorn ever bakes, does he, tee hee. Now here I go making light of what's a tragedy, you getting stuck with Jake and all. Dunno as ya knew it, but I was mad as hops that Joel wouldn't underbid him. Was ya paying mind, you probably noticed that Joel near 'baout got ya, he went all the way down to a hundred and twenty-five, he did, and he'd've gone even lower if I'd had my say, but he wouldn't listen to me, a hundred and twenty-five was the lowest he'd go, even though I begged and pleaded and even told him I'd make up the difference out a my pin money. Joel's so tightfisted, he is. Why, one time Sophronica Earle borrowed a couple dozen eggs from him, and told him she'd return him some eggs soon as her biddies got to layin, but Joel says, "It'll be better t'pay me cash fer 'em. No tellin but the price might go down by the time you come to return 'em." Just goes to show.

But I'll let ya in on a little secret, young man. And that is this: Who do ya think has been fixin those lunches fer ya? Rachel? Oh, 'scuse me, I have to laugh. Soon's school started up, I told Rachel to keep a eye out and see whut ya was eatin fer lunch. Then of a morning I'd get up and when I went to fix Rachel's lunch, I'd fix two a everything, but stuff it all in together so's Joel wouldn't ever notice. Weren't fer me, y'ud be all skin and bones.

Looks like yu've kind a bit the hand that fed ya. Never did I dream that y'ud fall fer Rachel on account a them lunches, or else I'd've gave her instructions to tell you that it was her own mother and not her who fixed 'em. And her not but sixteen. And you the schoolmaster. What've ya got to say fer yourself, young man?

Wal, cough and stammer all ya like, I know whut yu've been up ta. No, Rachel's not let out a peep 'baout it. You think she would? You can't beat the tongue loose from her head. But I found out anyhow. That gull's been in hot water before, and I don't plan to see her in it again. Not with any schoolteacher, anyhow. Oh, how well I do remember when me and Sophronica were school chums, and what a beauty she was and could've married a governor or a senator if she liked, but she fell fer the schoolmaster, who was Mat-thew Earle, and he swept her off her feet, and now look at her. He's worse'n Joel, most ways.

My lands, dunno jest whut I want t'say t'ya, young man. But ya orter know I come to the academy th'other day to invite ya t'call fer tea, and when I opened the door I saw whut my poor eyes can't yet believe, and I closed the door and came home and wet up five or six handkerchiefs 'fore I could stop. Fer all I know, or fer all she'd ever tell me, that sweet little gull's not yet been deflowered, 'less ya want t'count the flower of her rosey lips, tee hee. Aint I awful, laughin this way when I feel like screechin and tearin out my hair.

Wonder. Ofttimes wonder, last couple a days, and many's the time then, wonder whut a picket 'twixt the lips would feel like. If ya dislike my brash words, I don't keer, there's no way else t'say it 'cept for prissy mincing. Yer big thing between her pretty little jaws. Where it don't belong. Aint ya afraid she might could get absentminded and bite it off? tee hee, oh my soul an body listen t'me laughin when I orter squall.

Wouldn't undertake to turn ya in, like ya desarve. Wouldn't undertake to mention it to the Judge. Wouldn't even undertake to let on a word to Joel 'baout it. Wouldn't even undertak t'say to Rachel whut I seen. Jest me'n you's the only ones that know. Jest me'n you. And whut've ya got t'say fer yourself? Nothing. Too shamed t'open yer mouth, I bet.

So whut d'ye think I orter do? Keep Rachel out a school? Lock her up? Try an get her to promise not never to open her mouth again? Ha. Oh, my.

If I had the sense God gave to a chipmunk, I'd up and get Joel's gun and shoot ya. But I aint. So stop yer pantin. I've thought and I've thought. Aint able to get my mind orf it. It's drivin me mental.

Whut I wonder. Whut I wonder is, if you're so hipped on that pertic'lar fancy, if you're so pickin pertic'lar 'baout gettin yer sirup tapped in such a fashion, why'nt ya use a growed woman 'stead of a innocent young gull?

Young man, you've got me to wonderin awful whut a picket 'twixt the lips would feel like. And I mean to find out. And you aint got a ghost of a choice, neither. Yer only choice is fer Judge Braddock to lynch ya, or fer Joel t'thrash ya dead. Or mebbe even fer me t'shoot ya.

Want to pick one a them choices? Then nobody's t'know but you'n me. So latch that door yender, boy, and come here to Melissa.

If Melissa McLowery, in her blackmail-seduction of Daniel Lyam Montross, had only been curious to see what the act of felicity is like, she would not have been disappointed, but as it turned out, she was not willing to stop there; felicity was only, you might say, an entrée. She wanted to do everything, and, as long as she was able to coerce him with the threat of punishment for his moral turpitude with Rachel, he did her bidding. Not long after that occasion when she first felicitated him, she requested, and received, that awful experience which Henry Fox, noting Daniel's failure to nickname it suitably, was to coin *conic licorice*, the first part referring both to the shape and movements of the tongue, the second part to the taste. Henry Fox was the only person Daniel ever told about Melissa McLowery. Henry Fox told Daniel that he had long known of Melissa's yen for sexual adventures (he didn't tell Daniel, then, that he himself had been her lover sixteen years before). Fox's advice was that if Daniel didn't mind it, and did not feel he was being "kept" by her, then *tant mieux*—a French expression meaning, said Fox, don't stare a gift horse in the mouth.

Winter, with its five-foot snows and fifteen-foot drifts, usually isolated the inhabitants of Five Corners, from each other as well as from the outside world. There were people back in the hills who would not be seen again until the first March or April thaw, although their children managed to get to school, on foot or snowshoes or barrel-stave skis. The grown-ups seemed to enter into a kind of hibernation: a minimum of each day devoted to the chores of the barn and house, the rest of the day in a kind of tuned-out lethargy. There were people, especially among the older generations, who could sit in a chair by the stove for ten or twelve hours, fully awake, without doing anything at all except getting up to eat or go to the privy. But not Daniel. In fact, the helpless idleness and isolation of the Five Corners populace made his own activities seem all the more lively. He never stayed indoors at Jake Claghorn's except when he was sleeping, and sometimes he would be invited to spend the night at Henry Fox's Gold Brook Chateau and would arise early to get back in time for school. When he wasn't visiting Henry Fox or exploring the white countryside on his snow-shoes or out setting traps for game, he would be meeting Rachel at the schoolhouse or Melissa in her parlor. There was no need to wait until Joel McLowery went out to tend his flocks of sheep; Joel never under any circumstances entered Melissa's parlor, and besides that he was rather hard of hearing. And only once did Rachel discover Daniel sitting in the parlor, and then he told her that her mother had invited him to discuss Rachel's progress in school. But sometimes Melissa would be restless or impatient, and would go to the schoolhouse after hours. Occasionally Rachel on her way home would meet her mother on the way to the schoolhouse, and her mother would say she was going to visit somebody at Glen House.

Winter would pass and spring would come before Rachel would find out; it was early May before Rachel discovered that her mother was fooling around with her boyfriend. Although Melissa took delight in both felicity and conic licorice, her major pleasure was, unlike her daughter's, ordinary old fusing, and she would perch upon Daniel's desk in the schoolhouse, leaning back on her hands, with her eyes closed and her teeth clenched and her throat saying *yum-yummy yum-yummy* to the rhythm of the punctures of her velvet. Oh, Daniel was quite a stud. *I hate his guts.* And at night in his dreams he would confuse Rachel's red hair with her red monthly blood, and confuse all the orifices, red and pink and auburn and crimson. One of the big questions which he had to have Henry Fox answer convincingly was whether or not such an excess of fusing and felicity might not be injurious, whether or not it might shorten his life or sap his strength or wrinkle his skin or turn him green or something. Henry Fox, womanless these many years, seemed to take vicarious pleasure in listening to Daniel tell of his fusings and felicities. "Get all you can while you're young," was his answer to Daniel's questions, "because when you're my age you might have nothing left but all the recollections." Now to hear Fox tell it, a recollection can be nearly as good as the real article, if you know how to remember—and Fox apparently did, although he never revealed to Daniel the specific amours of his past. It was his theory that, since mankind was the only breed of animal who "fused more often for pleasure than for procreation," God or Mother Nature or The Evolution of The Species had seen fit to insure that fusing could never be injurious or harmful, regardless of how often indulged. This made Daniel feel a good bit better.

There are so many dozens of cassettes of tape with Henry Fox's words on them that it's difficult for me, as "editor," to make a good selection, but one of my early favorites is this one, Fox's reply to Daniel's musings about the particular quality which attracted him to both Rachel McLowery and her mother. Listen to Henry:

It's their *It*, Dan. Eye Tee, It. Everybody's got an It. Look up It in that dictionary of yours, what do you find? It's one of the words with no definition. Can't be defined. All they do is give examples of how it's used. No definition. But It's a word, all right. Short word, syncope. Syncope's from the Greek, *cut off*, a cuttingword, means shortening a word by taking out letters, like sailors say "bos'n" for "boatswain" or "foc'sle" for "forecastle." Sailors have a lot of syncopes, probably because when a boat's in a storm you don't have time to say the whole word. [Fox pronounces "whole" as "hull" like other Vermonters, but I'm not trying to reproduce the inflections of his speech—"Ed."] Well, *It* is a syncope for *Identity*. And what does your dictionary say about Identity? One thing it says is that identity is what you've got that makes me recognize you as an individual. But another thing it says is that identity is what you've got that makes you exactly like all other men. Sounds like a contradiction, don't it? But it's not. Every human creature has an It, which nonhuman creatures don't have, and every human creature's It is just like every other human creature's It, at bottom at least.

But people, because they have Its, keep doing things to their Its. Sounds peculiar, I know, but the It does things to the It. Let me see if I can think up an analogy. Well, take a drinking man, there's an obvious one. I don't mean a fellow like you, Dan, who's just pleasantly pickled on cider half the time. I mean the real serious belch-guts bottle-a-day toper, the inebriate like Aaron Tindall, for instance. Tanking up like that is self-destructive, and he knows it, but that don't stop him. But that's just drunkards. *All* Its are self-destructive, in different ways. It changes and alters Itself, for the worse, from cradle to grave. And the changes It makes on Itself are what gives the It its Itness. It's what makes your It your It alone, unlike my It or any other's It. *It's Its It that It is.* Pardon if I splattered you with spittle.

Now you take women, females. What is the basic ingredient of the female It? Look up woman in your dictionary, look up female. Wo-*man*. Fe-*male*. Woman means "wife of man," means "person," means "It," means "It who is for man." Female, "It who is for a male." Did you know, by the way, that the Latin root of *female* means "she who sucks"? Watch my mouth when I begin to say "female" or when I begin to say "fecund" or "fertile" or your "felicity." My mouth makes a kind of sucking posture, don't it? Well, all of those words come from an old root meaning "suck." So the basic ingredient of the female It is sucking, not necessarily your specific felicity, because the velvet in a sense sucks the picket, does it not? And the female suckles as well as sucks. Why else is a grown man attracted to a woman's bosom? It is all, sucking and suckling alike, the core of a woman's It.

Her It, for some reason, like the drunkard drinking, makes her cover It and keep It covered. Fashion these days dictates that a woman not even permit her garment to demonstrate that she is bimammillate—that is, that she's got two of them. Fashion—which itself is the creation of her It—dictates that she wear a painful corset which squeezes her poor belly—the home of her womb—and squeezes her two breasts into one unbroken bulge with no evidence of the bifurcate cleft dividing them. It has not always been so, but that's what fashion has come to in this day and age.

But while her It requires her to cover It, her It also urges her to symbolize, nay, even to advertise It. The most obvious is the painting of the lips. Always red. Never green or blue or yellow or some other color. Less obvious is the bodily adornments. The necklace hanging in paraboloid curve from her neck forms the shape of that chief entrance into her It. If she wears a bow instead, it will have two strands, slightly parted, like the lips of her velvet. Or her fancy cape will part down the center with another O-shape around the shaft of her neck—and the edges all trimmed with fur, as her opening is trimmed with hair. Why, incidentally, do you think that women, alone of all animal creatures, have longer hair than their males? Think of male lions, think of the peacock. I won't pause to digress on this subject. Why do women top their hair with fancy feathered hats and bonnets, whereas the man's plain cap or bowler resembles the tip of his picket? And when the fe-male loses her male to death, the fancy leghorn hat is replaced with a close-fitting bonnet with a veil that covers and closes the face and the painted lips.

The It of female Itness makes all females female, one velvet like another, all, all alike. So that part is covered, and replaced by the individual It which allows a woman a hat or bonnet of her own choosing, a hair style of her own choosing, a cape or necklace or dress of her own choosing, an It of her own Itness.

I've spoken only of the *sight* of woman and her It. There is touch and smell and taste and sound as well. On one hand, the It sees to it that the Itness parts of a woman, her breasts and lips and velvet, are most pleasant to the touch, but on the other hand, the perverse It is able, when It wishes, to make her velvet the most malodorous place in all creation. Again, the It will douse her with fine colognes and still let her mouth have an effluvia like rotten eggs. Have you had enough experience with women yet to notice that there's some kind of perverse correlation between the intensity of her ardor and the foulness of her breath? Or again, take sound: a woman's voice is dulcet and lovely, but in the throes of fusing her mouth utters raucous yelps and grunts and croaks and gurgles and mewls and brays. And have you ever had the disquieting experience of your girl breaking wind while you fused her?

Strange are the ways of the It. The It knows what It is, and tries to ignore It, or disown It, or subdue It, or hide It, or disguise It. Consequently, most women's Its are imperceptible. Still, there are women like Rachel and her mother. As far as I can detect, there is nothing extraordinary about the sight, or smell, or touch, or sound, of Melissa and Rachel.

Do you suppose, then, that God or Mother Nature or The Evolution of The Species, having endowed woman with such a cantankerous and fickle It, an It capable of self-denial if not self-destruction, saw fit to give the It a sixth quality, an intangible quality, which It could not tamper with? A quality that we cannot see nor taste nor smell nor touch nor hear, but a quality all the same which we can somehow perceive, a quality that shouts, "Here I am, and I'm an It, and I'm all Itness! Come and get It!" a quality that looks, invisibly, like all that man's eyes have coveted, a quality that sounds, inaudibly, like the orgasmic melodies of the master composers, a quality that smells, indetectibly, of the most exotic and alluring fragrances, a quality you can touch, intangibly, like being pressed all over by tingly eiderdown, and a quality that tastes, ingustably, like rich ambrosial flavors, but a quality which, above all, is perceived by that sixth sense not of sight nor sound nor smell nor touch nor taste so much as what I might call the sense of *have*: the wish to have, as one wishes to touch or taste, but a much stronger and more relentless wish.

The sense of *have* objectifies the It. The It is the sole focus of all having. Like the other senses, the sense of *have* could be used metaphorically. As we say, "She looks like a princess," we could say,

"She *has* like a nymph." Or as we say, "She sounds like an angel," we could say, "She *has* like a maenad." We should never say "She *is had*" but always "She has"—the former implies that having her It is taking It, ravishing It. Are you following me?

To have is not merely in the matrimonial liturgic meaning of "to have and to hold." That implies some duration, some permanence. Like the other five senses, the sense of have is temporary, often fleeting, as fragrances fade and sights vanish. But having is all the more sweet for being transitory. Can you imagine how tired you would grow of roast lamb if you had it in your mouth all the time, forever? Your taste buds would atrophy, just as your picket would atrophy if you left it in a velvet for more than an hour or so. Erections are transitory, but also cyclic. Are you still with me?

The It, both the woman's It and the man's It, realizes that It is subject to cyclic, transitory fluctuations. Its wish is to *have* constantly, but it cannot. So what can It do?

It can, and does, perversely it would seem, make Itself deliberately less haveable, make itself *in*haveable, in periodic recurrent intervals between having, or, in the case of those few men and many women destined never to have, constantly, regularly.

Why do lovers quarrel? It is the battle of their Its fighting down to that level from which they might spring up to having again. Do you see that?

The It, then, has two stages, two forms. The right place for the It is in having. But since It cannot constantly have, it must return periodically to some other place, the place of not-having, of, even, anti-having. Only mankind has an It, and must shuttle perpetually between the right place and some other place.

And the trouble with mankind is that, because the right place can be found only in transitory, cyclic moments, mankind is always hunting for, and finding, some other place.

Whew. It's easy to see why Daniel Lyam Montross was sometimes nearly inclined to agree with the people of Five Corners that Henry Fox was crazy. He was never able to grasp fully the fine points of Fox's theories, and anything that he could not understand he suspected was meaningless if not insane. He was just seventeen when he got to know Henry Fox, and he was destined to know Fox, to be Fox's protégé, for nearly eight years.

Diana claimed that Fox's ideas were perfectly clear to her, and that she knew exactly what he meant. In our idleness we would spend a lot of time listening to the "Fox tapes" and discussing his ideas, philosophically you might say, and she would try to explain or interpret them to me, because truthfully a lot of what he said was way over my head.

I have to tell something about Diana. Just as I feel guilty and inadequate for doing such a poor job of *moving* the story of Daniel Lyam Montross through his Five Corners period (I've used up all this space and covered less than a year of his eight years in Five Corners), I also feel guilty for not really showing Diana as a *person*. Often, in these pages, she seems to be just a figure in the landscape, or a blur of a formless female who's always either arguing with me or felicitating me or whatever. Of course, this could lend substance to my gnawing doubt that she really exists and isn't just the product of my imagination. But—and this is rather strange—just at the point where I began believing in her, began, in fact, almost to take her for granted, she herself started having what she called "the It jitters," or an identity crisis.

It was of course that "sermon" of Henry Fox's which started this business. Diana got to brooding about whether or not she really had an It, a female Identity of the kind Fox described, and she kept trying to get me to reassure her. "Do you really think I have an It?" she would ask. "Are you really attracted to my It?" she would ask. "Do you have a sixth sense of *have* which perceives my It and is drawn to it?" she would ask. "You don't really think I have any It at all, do you? You just think that I'm a convenient velvet you dreamed up for your own use. I'm really just a kind of masturbation for you."

This led to another one of our bitter quarrels (I guess maybe there's *some* truth to what Fox said about the de-having or anti-having nature of a quarrel). I told her to stop talking like that. I kept telling her that her It was very real to me and very important to me, and for her to stop brooding about It. "Then why," she asked, "if you really think I have an It and you really are attracted to my It, why is it that you like for me to do you, but you won't do me?" I didn't know what she was talking about, and I told her so. But then she starting hinting around, and making allusions, and roundabout innuendoes, and I didn't have to be a genius to figure out that she was referring to what Fox had called *conic licorice.* "Is that what you mean?" I asked. And she said that she loved that expression; that it put her in stitches. So I came right out and said that as far as I was concerned, there is a world of difference between felicity and conic licorice, I mean, after all, it's not an equal proposition at all, because…well, because the former is at least similar in a way to actual intercourse, and therefore *natural,* whereas the latter is probably rather *unnatural,* not to say unsavory, and in any case it wouldn't make her very feminine to me, it wouldn't attract me to her It, not *that* It. I was very logical about this, but she got angry, and off we went on another storm of insults and taunts and complaints, and the worst thing she said was that if I admired and envied Daniel Lyam Montross so much, why then was I unable to do something that he not only did but also liked to do? To which I replied that I was beginning to admire and envy him less and less, that I was beginning, in fact, to resent and despise him.

But one thing, at least, I had in common with Daniel Lyam Montross during those days in Five Corners, is that he was never able to get Fox's ideas out of his head, and neither was I. He would be leading the pupils in a recitation of "Barbara Frietchie" or "Curfew Shall Not Ring Tonight" when suddenly he would be aware that he wasn't listening to the pupils but puzzling over something that Fox had tried to explain to him. And I would be reading a book or something—I had made a trip on foot into Woodstock once, nearly twelve miles, just to stock up on a pile of paperbacks, mostly murder mysteries and other light entertainment—I would be reading some gripping thriller when suddenly I would lose interest in the plot because my mind was pondering over something that Fox had said to Daniel Lyam Montross.

Even in sex. Before, sex for Daniel Lyam Montross had been a purely emotional experience, but now, right in the middle of fusing with Melissa or felicity from Rachel, he would sort of stop and intellectualize the experience according to Fox's theories. Needless to say, this took part of the fun out of it. *I* know, because the same thing happened to me. It was getting to where Diana and I weren't making love very much any more, because every time I tried, I would start thinking about Henry Fox's theories, and then I couldn't last more than a few seconds.

One afternoon, after waking up from one of my "sessions" with the tape recorder, I found a piece of paper in my lap. "What's this?" I asked Diana. "Read it," she said. It was titled, "Knowing":

> *I knew a man, who taught me all I know.*
> *My mind is like a kingdom of the sun.*
> *What use is knowing, if the heart's in tow?*
>
> *Our prize is wisdom. But with what a show!*
> *I watch my wits cavort in unison.*
> *I knew a man, who taught me all I know.*
>
> *Of all his teachings I could not outgrow*
> *The best and worst are now reduced to one:*
> *What use is knowledge, if the heart's in tow?*
>
> *Mind saps the heart; I think of this with woe:*
> *His life had left off where his wits begun,*
> *This man I knew who taught me all I know.*
>
> *Good living is a simple row to hoe*
> *Until that question comes and kills the fun:*
> *Of what use knowing, when the heart's in tow?*
>
> *This madness like a boil is touch-and-go*
> *Until it festers. A phenomenon.*
> *I knew a man, who taught me all I know:*
> *What use is knowing, if the heart's in tow?*

"Well," said Diana, "what do you think of it?"

"I recognize the form," I said. "It's a strict classic French form, called a 'vanillelle' or 'vallinelle'...."

"*Villanelle*," she corrected me. "Never mind the form. What do you think of the *content*?"

"Where did you get it?" I asked.

"I wrote it," she said.

"Obviously," I said, because the sheet of paper was clearly in her handwriting. "But what did you copy it out of?"

"I 'copied' it," she said, "out of Daniel Lyam Montross's head. Daniel is the author of this poem."

I puzzled over this. To be perfectly frank, I didn't believe it. Whether or not the idea that Daniel Lyam Montross is only the creation of my imagination, or even of my unconscious, is acceptable, I know this much: *I* didn't write that poem. I wasn't *equipped* to write it. I can conceive that all other aspects of the "persona" of Daniel Lyam Montross might possibly have come up out of my unknown inner resources, but I know that isn't where that poem came from. I began to suspect something very disturbing to me: Diana herself was the author (or authoress) of this poem, even though I wouldn't have given her credit for that much talent. She had been brooding about her identity, and perhaps had decided to assert her It or identity by writing poems which she "attributed" to Daniel Lyam Montross. This suspicion was reinforced when she went on to tell me something which she claimed that "Daniel Lyam Montross" had told her during the recent "session": that he was disappointed in the way that I was telling his story, and that if I didn't do a better job of it, he was going to "take over" and do the job himself. And in *verse*, yet! This made me feel terrible, even if I didn't believe it. It was as if Diana, in order to assert and prove her own It, first had to destroy my It. Can't two people have equal Its which can get along together in harmony and cooperation? Goddamn you, Henry Fox, *there's* a question for you!

October 18 was Diana's birthday, her twenty-second, and I decided that if she was having such an identity crisis, it might help or even cure her "It jitters" if I made her birthday into a really special occasion. So I used our reflector oven to bake a big cake for her, with twenty-two irregular candles that I had hand-dipped with string in tallow. Also I killed a fat partridge with my slingshot, so our main course for the dinner was a delicious partridge roasted in an imu pit in the ground. Also, I had spent several days making for her a handsome, colorful necklace, which I fashioned laboriously from bright-colored pebbles found around the brook, each pebble drilled slowly with a hole by heating a nail red hot; it took a long time, and I did it in secret, hiding long hours off in the woods by myself, and the finished product was something to be proud of.

But after supper, after she made her wish and blew out the candles on the cake, although she said "Oh, thank you!" when I presented the necklace to her in a box lined with dark green moss to set off the colors of the pebbles, she didn't seem awfully happy with it specifically or her birthday party in general. I wondered if she had expected me to take some of her own money and go to Woodstock and buy her something fancy and expensive, but I couldn't ask her if this is what she had been expecting, and even if she had, I couldn't have done it, I mean, I couldn't have spent her own money on her. I thought it was more appropriate to give her something I had made myself, like the roast partridge, and the cake, and the necklace. Anyway, I asked her why she was brooding. Was she still having "It jitters"? Did the fact of becoming a year older, and having a birthday, aggravate her identity crisis? Not exactly, she said. Well then, I said I wondered if it was because all of our chipmunks had gone into hibernation. There had been six of these chipmunks that had practically lived at our place, they had eaten out of our hands and had even jumped into our laps, and we'd even given individual names to each of them, although they were kind of hard to tell apart, but now they had disappeared, almost as if they were waiting for Diana's birthday to go into hibernation. Yes, Diana said, she was sad about that, but that wasn't what was on her mind. Well, what was, then? I persisted and pestered. Finally she said it was the wish she'd made when she blew out the candles. What was the wish? I asked. She said she couldn't tell, that you aren't supposed to tell what your wish is, because then you're sure not to get it. Well, I said, sort of playing around as with Twenty Questions, did it have anything to do with me? Yes, she said. Well, I said, did it involve something between me and her? Yes, she said. Well, I said, was it perhaps in some way related to our previous argument? Yes, she said. Well, I said, was she really so preoccupied with it as to make it the object of her birthday wish? Yes, she said. Well forget it, I said.

And that ruined the rest of her birthday, I guess. But I was annoyed, even if birthday wishes and all that are a lot of kid stuff, that all she could think of for a birthday wish, after I'd gone to such trouble to make that necklace and bake the cake and find that partridge and hit it with my slingshot and pick its feathers and clean it and cook it all day in the imu pit, was some trifling unnatural itch of hers.

When I woke up, it must have been after midnight, the fire was still blazing bright and hot, I was sitting in one of our Adirondack chairs and she was sitting in the other. She had a kind of ironic but satisfied smile on her face. I assumed that she had been having another regular session with Daniel Lyam Montross, and that now she would play back the tape for me if I cared to hear it. But I felt very strange, and it took me a moment to identify the source of my uneasiness. The particular perfume that she wears sometimes, *Réplique* I think it's called, was very strong in my nostrils...and in my mouth, along with it, under it or over it or both, that singular exciting piquance which is the carnal tang of her sex, not really like licorice but with the same acridity. I sat there for a while staring at her smile or smirk or whatever it was, and ruminating upon these twin odors in my nose and mouth, and then I said,

"Damn you."

"It wasn't you," she said. "It was *him*. And he made me feel for a while that I might really have an It, after all."

"It's *my* mouth, damn you," I said. And I got up and drank at least a pint of cider, trying to forget. And then I said, "I think your It is positively disgusting and loathsome," and then I went off to bed. And tried to sleep. But my dreams were bad and wild.

Three days later we had our first snow. It was not a hard snow, nothing like the ones to come later, but it was our first snow. It began in the late afternoon, when the heavy sky flaked and dusted our woods with white feathers slow-falling and silent as time. We moved the Adirondack chairs into the lean-to, and sat in them for a

long time wrapped in our blankets and watching the snow fall, and
saying to each other things like "Oh isn't that lovely!" and "Have
you ever seen anything so beautiful?" and "How wonderful!" and
all kinds of gushing stuff like this. And the way it fell, so gently but
deliberately, as if it had a job to do and was going to take its time and
see that the job got done properly. Within an hour, all the ground
was white, all the trees were covered, and some of the trees still had a
few clusters remaining of their scarlet leaves, now like blood on snow,
like Rachel's hair on her pillow. "Let's dance in it," Diana suddenly
suggested, and we threw off our blankets and threw off our clothes
and spontaneously choreographed a Snow-Welcome Pas De Deux,
to the music of her humming and my whistling, all very slow and
white and drifting. Once before we had been air and water, alga and
fungus, in a thing she rigged up to a piece by Vaughan Williams.
Now to our own impromptu music we were earth and snow, she
the snow, I the earth, and this was symbiotic too, the one needing
the other. In the happiness of this time we forgot our little grudges
and prejudices, we transcended ourselves, I guess you could say, or
I guess Henry Fox would've said that our Its found the right place
and abandoned some other place that was anti-having or de-having
because what we finally did was not, to me then at least, unnatural,
but part of our dance, the end of our dance, the snow stopped, and
resting upon the earth, the snowfall ended, the earth covered, the
white blanket resting, and although the feel of the snow was icy and
nipping on our naked skins, it did not seem long, it seemed fleeting
and transitory, that new right place, but it did seem *right*, I swear it
did, that the snow lay with the earth, the snow's soft head upon the
earth's groin, the earth's head buried beneath the crotch of the snow,
all soft touchings and strokings.

Oh, this is a story of a lost place in a snowfall, of a boy and
girl symbiotic and devoted and lost together, oh, this is a story about
a wise philosopher who sought gold and lost it but found wisdom
and shared it, oh, this is the story of his sharing, of his sharing his
wisdom with a young schoolteacher with an empty head ready to be
crammed (oh, how'm I doing, Daniel? is this any better? Could your
poetry beat it?), oh, this is a story of a boy who looked for the right

place where people had lived simply and honestly and had devotion to work and to duty, but found instead some other place of unnatural behaviour, a story of some other place that became for me the right place because there are Its and I have one and so does she, even if she doesn't think so, and so do you.

Oh, It is.

One of the few pictures in Henry Fox's Gold Brook Chateau was a painting, or rather a good copy of a painting which had been painted not by a master but by a nearly unknown late-nineteenth-century academician named Adolphe William Bourguereau. The good copy, which possibly surpassed the original in its pristine clarity and naturalism, was signed only by the initials D.H. The copy of the painting was quite large, over eight feet tall and nearly six feet wide. During the Five Corners gold rush, when there was a saloon among the buildings in the compound at the mine entrance, this large painting had hung over the bar of the saloon, where drinkers could admire it and receive stimulation or at least amusement from it. When the mine operations folded, Henry Fox removed the painting and hung it in his sitting room at Gold Brook Chateau, to serve, as he explained to Daniel Lyam Montross, as a "mnemonic device" to help him in recalling and reliving the lost, passionate Its of his youth, although Daniel doubted that the particular experience depicted in the painting had ever happened to Henry Fox. The title of the painting, Fox told him, was simply "Nymphs With A Satyr," and Fox explained to him what a nymph is and what a satyr is. Daniel thought the painting should have been called "The Reluctant Satyr," for that was the essence of its subject: a muscular, tanned satyr, with a goat's legs and ears, in the lush woods, trying to put up a great resistance as he is being pulled, tugged and pushed by a quartet of extremely luscious and contemporary looking nude nymphs, who with great abandon are determined to get him to go off some other place with them and serve their fancies. Two things about the painting impressed Daniel Lyam Montross, apart from the sheer lushness of the woods and sunlight and dappled voluptuous bodies: the face of the satyr, except for the goat's ears of course, was remarkably like his own face; and the idea that four women, *together,* would so hungrily *pursue* this obstinate fellow. It was a complete reversal of the usual role in which man is the pursuer and woman the pursued. This made it both comic and flattering to the male ego. Henry Fox, expatiating about this painting to Daniel, conjectured that it was an ancient prophecy, as translated by a contemporary man in 1873, of what the world might be like in that distant twentieth or twenty-first century when the lots of man and woman became equal, *having* was equalized, and man became pursued as well as pursuer, and therefore ended all his wars and other aggressions. The importance of this vision, so central to Fox's thought, was somewhat lost upon Daniel, however, because Daniel already enjoyed that rare privilege denied to most men: being pursued by women, by more than one. Looking at the painting, sometimes, Daniel could see not only his own countenance in the face of the satyr, but also a good likeness of Rachel in the nymph who tugged his left arm and neck, and a good likeness of Melissa in the broad-hipped nymph who was pulling his right arm.

Daniel was happy, complacent, and a bit smugly self-satisfied with his life, so that even though Henry Fox warned him prophetically that he would have to learn eventually to live upon the memories of this life Daniel saw no reason why it should ever end. His success as a schoolmaster, due in no small measure to the crash course in brain expanding that Henry Fox was giving him, made him something of a figure in the community. Judge Braddock personally congratulated him, expressing surprise that he was doing so well, and offered him a small raise to continue for another year. The parents who had opposed him for his failure to flog his unruly charges were eventually won over by his success in making the unruly charges ruly without use of the ruler. The pupils loved him almost as much, but not in the same way, as his eldest pupil Rachel loved him. He had become a proficient organ player, and he was able, because of his friendship with Henry Fox, to give his pupils instruction in worldly matters not covered in their textbooks. The only bad time in the whole year happened to occur in early May when Rachel found her mother and her schoolmaster/lover celebrating spring together out in the woods. Rachel hated him for weeks, even months (or years?) afterwards, and hated her mother even more. Daniel reasoned with her and argued with her, to no avail, for the female It, as Henry Fox could have told him, is totally immune to reason or logic. Daniel's primary argument was that since Rachel was constitutionally or emotionally unable to fuse with him in the "normal" way, that he was required to do this with Melissa, and that besides, there was more than enough to go around, wasn't there? No, Rachel believed. It defiled him and it defiled her mother to do that dirty thing like animals do it. And what bothered her most was that the more of himself he shared with her mother the less of himself did he have to share with her. She would no longer bring lunches for Daniel. She seemed to become unhinged. She began to act peculiar in school, and embarrassed the teacher and the other pupils by noisily sucking her thumb a lot. At the end of the term, in June, she failed all of her examinations, so miserably that, even though Daniel wanted to pass her anyway, his conscience as schoolmaster would not allow him to overlook such a poor performance, so she was destined to have to repeat the school year, to be his scholar one more year if he chose to accept Judge Braddock's offer.

Daniel was glad when summer came and school was over and out. He got a job, in return for room, board and a tiny wage, as a farmhand for Jirah Allen. The only disadvantage of this arrangement was that he had to share a room with the boy Marshall Allen, the same simple but evil-minded hooligan who had disrupted the school all year long. As roommates, they lost no love on each other. Marshall had only a little more mentality than Daniel's poor sister Charity had possessed; he could communicate, at least, but usually only by replying "Yeyyup" or "No-hup" to direct questions. As his roommate, Daniel had to suffer being witness to the boy's sadistic nature, his fondness for pulling the wings off of insects and watching their helpless struggles, his subtle torturing of the Allen family's dogs, cats, and livestock, his gross habit of tying up his sister Floriana and fusing with her in her velvet, navel, armpit, mouth, and ear. Daniel considered reporting this behavior to the father, Jirah, but the father already was in the habit of flogging the boy every day, and Daniel saw no point in increasing the lashes. Instead, he got away, as often as he could.

The large Allen farm was several miles south of Five Corners, which put him much closer to Henry Fox's place, an easy couple of miles, in fact, so that even though the working hours on the Allen farm were long and hard, sunup to sundown, he was able, in the evenings, to see more and hear more of Henry Fox than he had during the school year. And he found a favorite spot, halfway into the village, a glade surrounded by thick spruces, where he often met Melissa for a few minutes of pleasure. He didn't see Rachel all summer long. Melissa never mentioned her, and he never inquired of her to Melissa. Personally I think he was being a complete bastard for dropping Rachel like that.

In late August, Daniel went into Five Corners village for the first time that summer, not to visit Rachel but to see two other people: Judge Braddock and Jake Claghorn. He told Judge Braddock that he was agreeable to serving a second year as schoolmaster. Then he found Jake Claghorn and told him that if Jake placed a bid in this year's auction Daniel would kill him with his bare hands.

At the auction, conducted once again by Judge Braddock (for what was to be the last time; a Plymouth town ordinance would abolish the practice the following year), after the bidding had reached an unprecedented low of fifty dollars, which was the Allens' rock-bottom offer, Daniel Lyam Montross was struck off for forty-five dollars to a terribly scowling Joel and a terribly jubilant Melissa McLowery. Joel even lost a little face among his neighbors for such a rash offer, and the neighbors began to gossip that Melissa had forced him to it, not, however, they thought, out of a wish to have him for herself but out of a wish to "line him up" for her daughter Rachel, whom everybody assumed (and hoped) that the handsome young schoolmaster would eventually marry, because the poor girl seemed more and more to need "straightening out" by a strong, firm and smart young man. Rumors of her conduct during the past summer had circulated among the villagers, and her few younger playmates or girlfriends had stopped seeing her. Someone said he thought he had seen Rachel, under a full moon, running naked down the road and through the covered bridge. Someone else claimed that Rachel was often seen to go into the schoolhouse at four o'clock in the afternoon and not reappear until suppertime. But since Daniel Lyam Montross had never been seen in the village during the summer, none of these rumors connected him with her.

When Daniel was taken home by the McLowerys, he found that his quarters were not to be in the rather modest McLowery house but instead one of the outbuildings, a roomy shed which Melissa had decorated (with the grudging help of Rachel) tastefully into a homey, cozy bedroom with its own stove and a good large mirror and a washstand with stoneware pitcher and basin. This was to be his home for most of the next six or seven years…and the site of our home, as I've mentioned previously our lean-to was erected on the same spot, in nearly the same exterior dimensions, as Daniel's shed. From the opening of the lean-to, we could look down the hill to the spot where the McLowery house had stood, with tangled clumps of lilac still around its foundation, and now in November the dead stalks of perennial peonies that Melissa must have planted some long time ago. A few of the immense stone slabs of the barn's foundation are the only other evidence left behind, although there is a spot, the other side of our lean-to, where the gate to the pasture stood, where the ground is still worn in a trail by the hooves of Joel McLowery's sheep. I often thought I could hear sheep *baa-ing* somewhere up the hill behind us, and Diana swore that she could hear them too, but we tamped all over the hill without finding any sheep, so it must have been only the wind. They were Cheviots and Merinos, a wrinkled type with more surface of wool, the meat secondary, and a stronger flocking instinct than most sheep. Joel had several hundred of them, and Daniel's help was needed at shearing time. Although Joel would sell surplus lambs in the spring, the McLowery's income was almost exclusively from the sale of the abundant wool, bought by the textile mills at Bridgewater.

Except for the big stone slabs, which were part of the barn's foundation, the only other trace remaining of the McLowery homestead is a slight depression, a trench about five feet long and a foot deep, in a clump of sumac saplings about fifty feet to the northwest of our lean-to. Although I dislike mentioning such mundane matters as routine body functions, Diana and I had already been using this trench as our latrine before we discovered that it was in fact the foundation of what had been the McLowery privy. I mention it now only because that privy played an important part in the subsequent story of Daniel and Rachel. The trench then was a good bit deeper than it is now, and over it was a small building of pine planks, containing a knee-high shelf or bench cut with two holes large enough but not too large to accommodate the adult buttocks. Furnishings and decor were few: a chromolithographed picture of a small girl rolling a hoop with a stick, a recent calendar (as if the privy user were inclined to stay more than a day!), a bucket of wood ashes in one corner for the purpose of covering the waste, in the other corner a board with its smaller hole to be placed over the larger holes by a child—this not used since Rachel was five years old.

Just why this privy, like most others of the time, was what was known as a "two-holer" is a mystery to me. Perhaps in an emergency, if the privy was occupied, there was a "spare" hole for the impatient, but this must have been very rare. Most users of the privy eventually developed a natural inclination toward one hole or the other, and never alternated between them. And without any spoken rule or principle to the effect, one hole was customarily used by males, the other by females. In the present instance, the north hole was used by Rachel and Melissa, the south by Joel Mc-Lowery, Daniel Lyam Montross, and the McLowerys' hired man.

Now, Daniel Lyam Montross had been living in the McLowerys' shed for several weeks and had never seen Rachel except at school, where she always sat quietly with lowered eyes and hardly ever responded if he called on her to recite, which he soon stopped doing. The window in Daniel's shed commanded a view of the path between the house and the privy, but he had never seen her on the path and supposed that perhaps she used instead a "thunder mug" inside the house. But one evening in late October, after supper, Daniel Lyam

Montross was attending a call of nature at the privy, meditating at length upon some theory or other he had recently picked up from Henry Fox, when the privy's door (it had no latch) slowly opened and Rachel slipped in and closed the door behind her. She did not look him in the eye, and he wondered if, in the half-light of early evening, she could even see him. But when she lifted her ankle-length dress and lowered her calf-length ribbed cotton drawers and sat down on the other hole beside him, her arm brushing his arm, he knew that if she didn't know he was there beside her it was because she was in a trance or something. He didn't know what to say. He didn't exactly *mind*, I mean he didn't have any great modesty, and his embarrassment was no greater than his surprise. In fact, one of his idle musings or fantasies while sitting on one hole of a two-holer had been to wonder what it would be like if two people, preferably of opposite sexes, sat side beside together there—a contingency which never occurred, as far as he knew. He was afraid that if he spoke, if he even said quietly, "Hwarye, Rachel?" she might disappear into thin air. So he jut sat, not looking at her. He heard the faint tinkling of her water. Then the two of them just sat there meditating for a while before she finally spoke.

And this is Rachel, in the outhouse. Listen to her:

Rachel's bad, she is, Rachel's bad, bad, she is, she is, oh, is she? she is yup. Rachel's tryin t'be a creeter, she is, she's wantin t'be a creeter, she's tryin t'be a varmint, she is, 'caise her Dan wants her t'be, he does, he does, so they could run thu the woods and be creeters and do like creeters, breathin a the air a the woods that no human creeter e'er breathe-it, the air a dead leaves and spruce boughs and rotten wood, and the air a skunk even, yes, skunk's not bad from afar, smells of the woods, and mink too, all musky, and weasel and fox, all musky, musky, the woods's perfum'ry, wild creeter's perfum'ry, smells a the wild, of woodsy wild waftins and the wind a-sythin thu putty Rachel's hair, her a weekit, weekit, wild and weekit creater rompin in the musky perfum'ry a-waftin from her Dan-creeter, him a creeter-smellin creeter musky and weekit too with his creeter-pink picket poking out twixt his legs whiffy and salty and sharp t'make putty Rachel's head dizzy and heady, seem's 'ough she'd flung wide her arms and spun round and round in a circle to make her head stagger her and drop her but wild creeters can't stand and spin julluk dizzy putty gulls so she'd need the smell of his creetermusk t'spin her and drop her, inter the dead leaves and spruce boughs and rotten wood, where she'd turn and wiggle waitin, twist and squirm and give off her wild creeter perfum'ry, till he spun and dropped too inter dead leaves and spruce boughs and rotten wood and wiggled with her while the musk a-wafted round 'em, and she would be bad and weekit julluk he allus wanted, and take him inter her weekit velvet julluk he allus wanted 'stead of her putty mouth. But now I will only hold it, I will, like so, in Rachel's putty fingers, and hang on a little, jest t'touch and hold a little, so's when nightfall coops up putty Rachel in her lost bed far from the musky woods wild waftin's she kin lay her weekit head dizzydown on these same fingers and have dreams a woods and creeters if ever sleep takes her and if it don't then in wakey rest she'll lie breathin of her fingers and thinkin still of her Dan-creeter and his woods whiffings. I thank you kindly, sir.

She fled then, and though he called after her he did not pursue her. She did not pause nor turn when he called but ran down the path into her house, leaving him there transfixed by her words and wearing a bothersome erection from the brief grip of her fingers. He was convinced almost beyond doubt that she was not "right in the head" (his words; I'm not making a pun) but he desperately wanted a wiser opinion, so even though it was evening and he had to teach school the next day he took his lantern and hiked all the way up to Gold Brook Chateau to tell Henry Fox what Rachel had done and what she had said. Henry Fox, who rarely laughed, laughed. But then he told Daniel that the incident perhaps signified that Rachel, who considered normal fusing animalistic, was trying to become an animal in order to become "normal." And also that she was trying to show him, by sharing the intimacy of the privy with him, that she wished to share the privy places of her It with him.

"Too bad," said Diana to me, after another of her psychologizings, "that this Austrian Henry Fox, with all his insight, did not have the techniques which his fellow Austrian was developing at the same time for treating mental and emotional disorders." I told her to take Freud and shove him.

The girl needed help obviously (Rachel I mean, not Diana, although come to think of it…), but the only help Daniel could give her was to be as nice as he possibly could and to try to understand the weird turnings of her wandering mind. If she really wanted to pretend to be an animal, he was more than ready to join her in the play-like. But she didn't really; she just wanted to fantasize about it. The uninvited and unexpected call which she paid upon Daniel in the rest room was not her last. She began regularly visiting there, as if she watched from the house to see when he went in, then quickly joined him. He did not mind, although he did not consider the atmosphere particularly "salubrious," and her talk bothered him, and even her presence beside him, even if she did not touch him, was enough to give him such erections as made difficult the business he was there for. All she ever did was talk and touch him; she was not interested in having him nor allowing him to have her. Day after day, she sat silently in school with her head bowed; evening after evening, she sat beside him in the two-holer, talking her wild head off. Once Joel McLowery in obvious need of quick relief barged in on them, but just as quickly backed out, muttering "'Scuse it," and never bothered them any more. Sometimes she would fantasize aloud that they were king and queen, sitting on their throne together. When the weather grew cold in November, they would wrap an arm about one another while they sat. It is a picture, if a crazy picture, and I will leave the picture hanging in this gallery for a time, while I tell what happened to *us*.

One thing I'll have to say for Diana, she did not begin insisting that we use the latrine together. Not then, anyway. Perhaps that would have been going too far. But all along she had kept wanting to "try out" or "act out" or "play" the various things that had happened to Daniel Lyam Montross, so I was a bit surprised that she didn't start joining me at our facility, which, however, was quite primitive in contrast to the McLowery outhouse.

By the first of November all of the leaves had fallen from the trees, and only the carpet of the woods still had some color to it. For nearly a week in early November we had a lot of rain; it was a very drippy time. But whoever said that November is an ugly month didn't know what he was talking about or had not seen Five Corners at that time. Though the trees were bare, their bareness revealed the intricate etching filigree of their branches. November is thought of as a gray month, but not much of it in Five Corners was gray; there was a play of colors: black trees, blacker in the rain that soaked them, white trees—the birches—set off against them, and whiter because of the rain that soaked them, green trees, deep green trees, the thick evergreens, and the rich warm browns of the leaves still clinging to some trees. November is a more mature vision than other months, and more mellow, but no less beautiful than the color riot of October.

And yet, despite the beauty I found so easily in November, I was becoming very much aware that I did not like Five Corners, that I would rather be in some other place. Why was this? I asked myself. Had I grown tired of the place? Was I dismayed by Daniel's behavior? I wasn't sure what it was. One afternoon, I was just leaning on a low tree limb, gazing at the rain-washed beauty of deep blacks and high whites and greens and browns in the woods, and trying to figure out why I wanted to leave, when behind my ear Diana's voice said, "I suppose that sensitive gaze of yours means you think you're more aware of the beauty of these woods than I am." I turned and looked to see if she was just ribbing me, but I think she meant it. Anyway, it led to another one of our quarrels, this time I arguing that I didn't consider myself the least bit more sensitive than she was, and she arguing that it was terribly condescending of me to say that, and soon there we were again flinging epithets at each other, which ended up with my saying that if she really wanted to know what I had been thinking at that moment she accused me of looking so "sensitive," it was that I thought the woods were lovely, dark, and deep, and all that, but that I had miles to go before I sleep, and all that, in other words, I was thinking that we had been here too long and that this place, even more than Dudleytown, seemed to have some kind of curse on it, and that if we continued staying here something bad was going to happen to both of us. And all this quarreling and bickering, I said. I said I wondered if she was maybe getting sick and tired of seeing so much of me and only me, and that maybe she needed to go away to some other place for a while or even forever.

She lay her hand on my brow for a few moments and said, "I think you're running a temperature. And you've been blowing your nose a lot lately. I was just about to say that we've got some unfinished work to take care of here. For instance, we were going to clear brush out of the cemetery. Remember?" She bundled me up in blankets in an Adirondack chair beside the fire, and made for me a hot toddy of cider, and then gave me my notebook and ballpoint, and a huge stack of cassettes for the tape recorder, for me to listen to, and told me to see how much of Daniel Lyam Montross's story I could write down as quickly as possible without worrying about any "felicities of style." Then she took my axe and said she would go up to the cemetery by herself and start chopping the brush out of it. She seemed more cheerful to be "taking command." I sat here and listened to the tapes and tried to write a few more pages about what happened to Daniel and Rachel, but I would read a page after I had written it and then tear it out of my notebook and crumple it up and throw it into the fire. I don't know if my trouble was that I was ill, or that I had some kind of "Writer's Block," or that I just wasn't able to face the "reality" of what happened to Daniel and Rachel. Probably the latter; for example, I tried unsuccessfully five or six times to write the description of a scene where that sadistic idiot Marshall Allen meets Rachel McLowery out in the woods. This is recorded in Rachel's crazy words on the tapes, and I just couldn't straighten out all the details. It seems that Marshall Allen, with his warped half-brain, had been watching farm animals mate, and had developed the fixation that the bull or ram or stallion always comes up *behind* the cow or ewe or mare and grabs her from behind and enters her velvet from behind. There were some rumors and jokes circulating around Five Corners about what had happened to dumb Marshall when he tried his approach on a couple of girls. But one day he came upon Rachel in the woods. She must have been pretending to be an animal, a doe from what I can judge she says on the tapes. She was bent over, eating a flower, or *pretending* to eat a flower, I couldn't tell which, when Marshall came sneaking up behind her and....

I just couldn't write it. When Diana came back from the cemetery some time later, saying that the work of chopping brush had been discouraging and that being alone in the cemetery had made her very nervous, I asked her to read my last attempt to tell about Marshall and Rachel. She read it and agreed that I wasn't doing such a good job of it. I half-jokingly suggested that it might help if we "acted out" that scene, but she didn't think this was funny, and in fact wasn't interested in sex at all, not then, and not the next day, and not the day after. She just wasn't having anything to do with sex, all of a sudden. I thought it might have something to do with the repulsiveness of Marshall's "affair" with Rachel, which became eventually a regular and wild sort of relationship, but it wasn't exactly this which accounted for Diana's sudden disinterest. In fact, I think that even this sordid business excited her. One afternoon she was sitting in her Adirondack chair beside me, listening to a playback of one of Rachel's terrible tapes, and her legs were crossed, and the foot of the top leg was swinging, swinging so steadily that it made her hips and thighs move. I figured at first it was just restlessness, or that kind of nervousness you see when girls are doing that while they're taking final exams or something in school, but there was also a distinct sexual quality about it which has led me to wonder if some girls can even masturbate by swinging their foot like that. Anyway, I asked her, offhand and casual, if she would like to make love, even though my fever seemed to be worse and I didn't really feel like it. "Oh, don't put yourself out," she said. It took me a moment for the pun to sink in, and when I got it I tried to laugh but couldn't. But as it turned out she didn't really want to make love. The next time she went off to the cemetery to cut brush, I sneaked a look in her purse and found out why. She was out of The Pill. The package had twenty-eight little empty holes. I wondered why she didn't want to tell me.

On November 20, a day of light snow, I became nineteen years old. I was still technically a "teenager," but it seemed to me that there is something special about being nineteen; it is the last year, the biggest year, of the teens; it is close to entering the twenties; it put me just two years away from the age Diana had been before her recent birthday; it made me feel, for one day at least, older and wiser and taller. But Diana, after all the trouble I'd gone to for *her* birthday, seemed to have forgotten mine, although she had clearly marked it on our calendar. I didn't want to remind her of it. I was really too ill to care, very much; I began to wonder if I had pneumonia or something. But what got me, more than her forgetting my birthday, was that she didn't even seem to care how ill I was, and she made me "work" hard that day, that is, she held a very long session, seven or eight hours, with the tape recorder and Daniel Lyam Montross. I thought how ironic it is to spend most of your birthday in a state of trance. She seemed to be in a hurry to get all the rest of his story out of him, which I thought was a good thing, although it made me very jealous to feel that on my birthday she had spent more time with *him* than with me. In bed that night I tried to snuggle up to her, but she turned her back to me. That stung me, so I came right out and told her that it was my birthday. She reminded me that I had insisted that she not buy me anything. All right, I said, but couldn't she just be affectionate, for a change? No, she said. Why not? I asked. I just can't, she said, and then she turned over toward me and said a very crude thing: Well, come on and I'll blow you, if you want.

I took a long walk. Without a lantern or flashlight. It was an extremely clear night sky, and the stars themselves provided nearly enough light to see by, although once I stumbled upon a family of resting deer and gave them a fright as bad as the one they gave me, leaping up and crashing off into the brush, a buck and two does and four or five fawns. I called out to them to come back, and was very sorry I had scared them.

I kept walking, my boots sometimes sinking ankle-deep in the new snow. Although I stopped now and then to study the spectacular star patterns, I seemed to be walking in a definite direction, I seemed to have some destination in mind. I've studied the stars quite a lot, and never failed to be impressed with the stupendous infinity of space and the thought of all the infinitude of possible galaxies and constellations and suns and worlds, but never until this night had the sky-spectacle had such an overwhelming effect on me, not necessarily obliterating my own problems but making me think of how unlimited are the problems of the universe, whole stars dying and exploding and worlds taking billions of years to reach perfection before being snuffed out like candles. I resolved that night to take up a closer study of astronomy; although I could recognize all the stars in the Pegasus constellation, the Andromeda constellation, and Cassiopeia, Pisces, Aries, Aquarius, and many others, I had a very vague notion of just how large and how far away each star was. But I knew that in the time it took for the light from any one of those stars to reach the earth, all the towns and cities of America had been born and would vanish. In all that empty space out there was more than enough room to harbor the transient souls of every creature who had ever lived in all the habitable worlds of the universe.

My walk took me, near midnight, to the fallen ruin of Gold Brook Chateau. Until I got there I had not been fully conscious that this was my destination. But as soon as I got there I knew it was. And I began yelling at once, "Henry! Henry! Henry??" My voice may have frightened night creatures. "Henry Fox!" I yelled. "Henry, where are you? I need you!" I waited and yelled louder, "Henry, I've got to talk to you!" There was never any answer. I felt no "presences." For all I knew, Henry Fox had been just an ignorant and even illiterate gold miner whose name I had read about in that article on the Five Corners gold mines, but I did not feel the least bit silly, yelling for him. I needed him, as much as Daniel Lyam Montross ever needed him. Sometimes I used to try to talk with God, but I've outgrown that. Being nineteen years old now, I could much more easily believe in Henry Fox than I could believe in God.

But like God, Henry Fox would not respond. So I began trying to "reach" Daniel. **He did, he began trying to reach me, although he should have known I won't ever come at his bidding.** Lately, when I thought of Daniel, it was not as if he were something *inside* me, inside my chest or head or elbow or little toe, but rather that he was something *around* me, exterior to me but always with me, around me, maybe just a fraction of an inch away from my skin, like—if you've ever seen photographs of the earth taken from outer space, you know how incredibly thin the layer of the atmosphere is around the earth—like that, like a very thin layer of something around me. **Now I reckon that's as good a way as any to tell it.** Anyway, I knew I couldn't hypnotize myself (I've tried it; it won't work; I've tried saying, "Go to sleep, Day" but only Diana can do that) and even if I could it wouldn't do me much good to try to talk to Daniel if I were in a trance. Still, I needed to contact him, even if he were nothing but a figment of myself. When I was younger, the minister of our church used to tell me that the reason God wouldn't talk to me was that I might not have had full faith in his existence, that possibly I could not "surrender" wholly to belief in Him. Well, this was my problem with Daniel too: there I was at the desuetude and desolation of Gold Brook Chateau trying to get in touch with a person who was nothing but the creation of my unconscious fantasy. Haven't you ever had an imaginary playmate? Well, that's what Daniel was (and Diana too, of course), but I desperately needed this imaginary playmate to tell me what was wrong with the other imaginary playmate so that the three of us could go on living in peace and harmony.

"Talk to me, Daniel," I said, almost in a whisper. "Henry's gone, Dan. He won't talk to me."

Then it seemed as though he I stood **stood** there **there** looking **looking** at **at** the **the** remains **remains** of **of** Gold **Gold** Brook **Brook** Chateau **Chateau** and **and** sorrowing **sorrowing** upon **upon** this **this** ravage **ravage** of **of** time **time**.

He was a great man.

"He was a great man," Daniel seemed to say then, of Henry Fox, who would not come to my bidding.

All I ever knew, I learned from him. But you don't need him, son. As I said in that poem, everything I learned boils down to knowing that learning's no good if the heart's in tow.

"What would he have told you," I asked, "if you had been me and were having the problems I've got with Diana?"

I had to laugh.

It was silent in the woods, there was no sound whatever from any night creature, but then I heard laughter, I clearly heard laughter, then realized that it was myself, that at least it was coming from me. Why was I laughing? Trying to make light of my problems? Embarrassed at myself for standing alone way off on that desolate mountainside and trying to talk to spirits? At any rate, there I was, laughing, and it had sort of a curative effect on me, I mean, it was the first time I had felt like laughing about anything in a long time, and it *did* make me feel a lot better.

Day, there're two or three things bothering that girl. One is the same thing that's bothering you: she's developing a dislike for my story, but, unlike you, she feels obliged to go on with it. Another thing bothering her is that you, with all your talk of living naturally and living off the land, have made her disinclined to go and have her pill prescription refilled, but she's left torn between letting nature take its course or, as she's been doing, abstaining. And finally, there's her "It jitters" again; she broods a lot about having no identity, except through you, except through me. That's why I let her believe that she's the author of my poem...and those to come. And maybe she is, in a way. As for you, you really ought to get to know her better. Despite all this time you've spent together, how much do you actually know of *her* story, of her childhood, of her *person*, of the things that have kept her from feeling that she has an It? That's just as important, I think, as your attempt to tell my story. The end of my story in Five Corners is tragic, and your premonition is correct that the end of *your* story in Five Corners is going to be pretty bad too, if not tragic. So you might as well skip the rest and get on with these endings.... And Day. One more thing. Happy birthday.

So I left that place and started back for camp. But I wasn't exactly feeling like laughing any more, I don't know why; I had the feeling that I knew something I hadn't known before, and it gave me a mixed feeling of determination and nervousness. When I got back to camp, in the wee hours of the morning, I discovered that Diana had waked up, or had never been asleep, and she gave me pure hell for going off and leaving her all alone like that in the middle of the night, and said she'd been scared nearly out of her mind, and that I had damn well better think twice before I ever did anythink like that again, and just what the hell did I mean, anyhow, was I trying to prove something? But I just crawled under the covers with her and held her until she hushed, and then I told her where I had been and what I had "learned." She chided me, saying I had made my fever worse, that I was very hot, that I should have had better sense than to take such a long walk on a cold night in the condition I was in. But she kissed me and said how sorry she was that she had ignored my birthday, and that she would make up for it, and that things were going to get better. Yes, I said, things always got better before they got worse. What do you mean by that? she asked. Something's going to happen to us, I said. Of course something's going to happen to us, she said; if it weren't, what would we have to live for? I decided not to say anything else about my premonition, but I still felt a sense of urgency, and knew that I could never possibly go to sleep, even though it was getting close to dawn.

Let's talk, I suggested. All right, she said, not feeling sleepy herself, What about? You, I said. I don't really know you. Tell me about your life. I don't know where to start, she said. Tell me about your father, I suggested. My father's a bastard, she said, And that's all I know to say about him. But I kept drawing her out, asking questions, and pretty soon she was telling me everything about her father, that bastard, and her mother, that meek, lost creature, and her childhood, uneventful, as it was, and her school experiences and her schoolteachers, and everything. I kept her talking until morning, when she got up and fetched for us a "breakfast" of raisins and nuts and apples and came and got back into our sleeping bag with me and we ate our breakfast while she went on telling me the story of her life, which took all morning, and left her feeling both happy for the chance to tell it and sad for how dull and uninteresting it was. Then after lunch, she declared, "That's all of my story. There isn't any more. That's all there is." And she took the axe and went once more to clear brush out of the Five Corners cemetery. I really had to admire her for her energy and determination in cleaning up that cemetery, and I lay there nursing my pneumonia and thinking what a wonderful person she was, and how much I loved her, and I lay there remembering parts of her story that she had finished telling me, I thought of her father and what a bastard he was, how he had been so busy trying to make his goddamn fortune that he never took much interest in his only daughter, that he thought he could discharge his duties as a father in terms of affection by occasionally permitting his lap to be sat upon or permitting his neck to be hugged—when of course it didn't inconvenience him.

And I thought of something else. I remembered her very words. "When I was six," she had said, "I made him a valentine. I don't remember making it, but years later he was cleaning out his study and I found it in the wastebasket. It wasn't too artistic, and rather trite, with hearts and flowers and all, you know. But I told him in the valentine that I loved him, and then I wrote on it a question: 'Daddy, do you think why I am me?'

"I'm still not sure," she had said, "just what I meant by that question. *'Do you think why I am me?'* But whatever it means, I've been asking it all my life."

And however long it takes, I determined, *I will help her find her answer.*

Oh, this is a story of—you know it, don't you?—a story not of ghost towns but of lost places in the heart, of vanished life in the hidden places of the soul, oh, this is not a story of actual places where actual people lived and dreamed and died but a story of lost lives and abandoned dreams and the dying of childhood, oh, a story of the great ghost villages of the mind, a story of untold stories, oh, of lost untellable stories, of a boy who loved a girl whose villages had been abandoned, of a boy who took a girl on a long outing to the town of lost dreams, of a boy who wanted to help her find her hidden It, oh,

a story of a boy who tried but then lost her.

But then I lost her. The goddamn gods or fates get all their kicks by plotting absurd ironies. Just at the point where I determined that I would help her find out why she was she, I lost her. She did not return from the cemetery. Late in the afternoon, I began to think admiringly that she must have a lot of perseverance and dedication, to be staying there and working alone in the cemetery so long. But then I began to get uneasy. I began to wonder if maybe she had cut herself badly with the axe. Or if her fear of the cemetery might have caused her to faint or something. As dusk started to settle on our woods, I knew I would have to go look for her. Was this what my premonition had been about? I got out of the sleeping bag and got dressed. When I stood up to put my trousers on, I felt dizzy and had to stop and hold on to the back of the chair for a while until my head cleared. Then I began shivering with a violent chill, until I could get my jacket on, but even with my jacket on I was still shivering, and not just from my sickness. It is less than a mile from our camp to the cemetery, but it is all uphill, and my breathing was terrible, I had to stop every fifty yards or so and get my breath back. I tried calling for her, but didn't have much voice. *Do you think why I am me?* Yes, I said aloud, I think why you are you. And I will know why you are you, I said aloud, to give me enough strength to get on up there to the cemetery.

Where I found her. Lying in the brush she had been cutting, the axe beside her, dropped into the snow. Beside the Allen family headstones. She was lying on her side, but with her face down. My first, strange thought was: "I have only dreamed you up, and now I am undreaming you." For I knew she must be dead. She lay so still. I knelt beside her. There was blood on the snow around her. I opened her wool jacket and saw the blood. All over her side. I wondered how she could have hit herself with the axe that far up on her body. But she had not hit herself. Somebody had shot her. Why? A goddamn stupid or drunk deer hunter who would shoot at anything that moved? Nobody had any *reason* for shooting her!

I was crying, I was sobbing, and at the sound of my sobs her eyes half-opened and she tried to look at me but could not raise her head. She tried to speak but couldn't. I tried to tell her it would be all right but I didn't know how. I had to do something. I had seen too many movies where somebody dies in somebody's arms, and I wasn't going to just kneel there and hold her while she died. What if I left her there and ran for help? But I couldn't run. And what if she were dead when I got back with help? I should have stayed with her. And if I couldn't run away, I ought to try to take her with me.

GODDAMN ALL YOU LOUSY "SPORTSMEN"!

First I had to find if she could be moved. If the bullet were lodged near her backbone I couldn't risk any moving of her that might hurt her spinal cord. I dabbed away some of the blood and found the hole where the bullet had gone in, just below her rib cage on the left side. I couldn't find anywhere where the bullet had come out in back. But there was blood all over her back too, maybe it had come out, or dribbled over there from the wound in front. I knew I had to try to get her out of there. I had learned in the Boy Scouts the "fireman's carry" but it wouldn't work; for one thing, the position of it would force more blood out of her. So I had to get her up on to me in a sort of modified piggyback carry: draped over my back with my arms under her knees, my hands grasping her hands over my chest to keep her from slipping. It was difficult. I didn't think I could do it. But I tried. I guess Daniel Lyam Montross must have been helping me, but I wasn't thinking of him, I didn't call on him or anything. The only thing I was thinking of, that might have helped me, was the awful beautiful question: *Do you think why I am me?* Out of the cemetery and down the hill I went staggering with her on my back, going downhill and thus letting gravity get us out of there, but still I slipped a couple of times, in the snow, and had to be careful how I fell so that she would not be hurt when I fell. I reached the road with her and soon passed our camp. I wished I had a drink of water or of cider; my mouth was dry as a bone, and burning, but I didn't stop. Down into Five Corners and across the bridge I went with her, my feet clattering on the wooden planks of the bridge like distant gunfire. I wondered if whoever had shot her had gone to find out what he had bagged and then ran off as fast as he could when he found that his game was a girl. Could I ever find him and kill him if she died? Was she, even now, still breathing? I couldn't tell. Her body was inert and lifeless upon me. I tried to remember which of the nearest houses, on the Hale Hollow Road into Bridgewater, still had people living in them, who might have cars. Most of them that were not completely abandoned seemed to be only summer places, no permanent residents. But there was one, freshly painted white, which I had passed whenever I had walked to Bridgewater, which I seemed to remember had people living in it. It was full dark now; I had to feel the road with my feet, to keep my feet steadily in the rut of a wheel track, my eyes straight ahead searching for the first sign of a light. It seemed I walked forever like that, blind in the rut, wondering how soon I would have to put her down because I could not bear the weight of her upon me much longer. Then I rounded a bend in the road and there, far down below, was a pinpoint of light. I stopped for just a moment or two, to do some deep breathing and get my lungs in shape again, and then I walked a little faster toward that light. But the harder I walked, the farther away that light seemed to be, and I wondered if it was only a star I was following. If it were, then I would follow that star into eternity. I went on and on. I began to think that maybe if I put her down now, gently, I could walk even faster and reach that light before the light went out. But I couldn't let go of her. I had to keep her. So I went on. Was the light a little brighter now? Was it a little closer? Now the light was not any longer round and clear, but blurred into a star-shape, with four cross-rays flaming out from it; I realized it was blurred because my eyes were full of water. The blur got bigger and bigger, and I knew I could reach it. But then suddenly the blur of light—or I—darkened and went out.

I recall a kind of dream I had: in the dream I was carrying her too, piggyback like this, and there was a man following us, who had been following us all along, but he was smiling at us, and she was alive, and laughing, and it was not nighttime but broad day, in some other place where we had finally gone, the Ozarks I guess it was, and not winter but springtime, and she was not hurt but whole, and the dogwood and redbud were blooming and the wind was warm and lifting her hair and her laughter, as I carried her piggyback through that strange and distant but magic woodland, some other place that seemed, in the dream, to be the right place.

When I woke up and came back from this pretty dream, I found that I was in a room, alone. The room was white, white tiles halfway up the walls, and instruments: I guessed it was a hospital; I hoped it was the right kind of hospital, not the funny farm. The walls and instruments had blurred shapes and I realized they were blurred because I was viewing them through the undulating plastic of an oxygen tent. In my delirium I imagined that there would be, somewhere, a button for my finger to press, in want of help, and I searched around the headboard of my bed until I imagined that I found a button to press, and imagined I pushed it, and imagined that because I pushed that button eventually a woman came in, a nurse. I imagined she said, I imagined her lips outside the oxygen tent saying, "Hi. How are you feeling?" and her imagined hand reached inside the tent and felt my brow and then felt for my pulse and took it. I wanted to ask her, "Where am I?" but that imagination would have sounded corny, like the movies. There was something much more important I had to imagine that I asked her:

"Where's Diana?"

"The girl?" I imagined the nurse saying. "She's in surgery."

"Will she be all right?"

"We hope so, of course," the nurse imaginatively said. "But it's much too early yet to know for sure." Then she asked me if there was anything that I imagined I needed. Did I imagine needing something to eat? I said no, but I imagined I needed a drink of water. She got an imaginary glass for me, and some imaginary pills, and told me to pretend that I was taking them. Then she said that she imagined a doctor would be coming in soon to see me, and meanwhile, if I needed anything, just to push the button. Then she vanished. Later a man seemed to materialize at the foot of my bed, and appeared to introduce himself. I did not hear his name, but it seemed to me, unless I was mistaken or confused, or both, or delirious, or all three, that he said his name was Doctor Henry Fox. Anyway, this Doctor Fox told me where I was, he said that I was in Woodstock Hospital, then he told me how I had come to be there, he said that I had collapsed with "the girl" (as he called her) on the doorstep of a farmhouse south of Bridgewater, and that the noise of my collapsing had roused the occupants from their TV set and they had driven us, "the girl" on the rear seat of their car, I on the floor, into Woodstock. Now, said this Dr. Fox, he needed to ask me a few questions. First, what was "the girl's" name? It seemed to me that I answered him by saying, Diana Whittacker. And it seemed he asked then, And what is your name? Day Whittacker, I think I replied. She's your sister? he seemed to ask. I'm almost sure I said, She's my wife. It seemed that he was giving me an unnecessarily long and skeptical look, but that he said simply, Oh. And then he asked, Do you carry Blue Cross-Blue Shield? I imagined successfully what the blue cross and shield were, and I said, Insurance, you mean? No, but don't worry about that. She's got—we've got—plenty of money. Then I imagined that he sat down in a chair beside my bed and in a friendly voice asked me to tell him about the accident. So I found myself imagining how it might have happened, that she had gone up to the cemetery to cut brush and when she didn't come back I had gone up there and found her. This doctor said that he imagined that it was rather late in the year to be out camping in the woods like that, but I just said that my wife and I imagined ourselves to be ardent and dedicated campers and naturalists. He appeared to be smiling. Then I took what I thought was a deep breath, and conceived a question which I conceived that I asked him: "Listen, tell me the truth: *is she going to live?*"

"I imagine so," he exhibited the semblance of saying, making an effort to sound gentle. Then he contrived to tell me that she was still in surgery, and that he, being *my* doctor, not *hers*, could not even tell me how long she would be in surgery. In addition to the severe wound, there was also apparently shock, which had delayed the surgery. All that he could permit himself to seem to say at the moment was, he said, that her condition appeared to be quite serious.

Then this Dr. Fox seemed to wave his hand and cause another woman to materialize. This one did not seem to be a nurse, although she was apparently dressed like one. Now, Dr. Fox seemed to be saying, We will have to fill out admission papers for you and your wife. Mrs. McLowery here [I thought he said] will ask you a few questions. I'll check back with you later. I stopped him as he appeared to be vanishing and asked him, When can I get out of bed? We'll have to see what can be seen, he said. Not for a while, it seems. Not for several days, I should imagine, he said. What seems to be wrong with me? I asked. Your temperature, apparently, is 103°, he said. You have suffered apparently from exposure, from what is thought to be fainting, from seeming overexertion and from God knows what else.

Both of your lungs appear to be inflamed. The doctor looked as if he were smiling, though. I think perhaps your brain is probably inflamed also, he said. He appeared to give my shoulder a gentle punch with his fist. See you later, he said.

The woman whom I had thought was introduced as Mrs. McLowery had some forms to fill out, and seemed to want to know our full names and our home address and a lot of other stuff. I had to do some quick thinking and use my imagination to fabricate most of it: changing the date of my birth so I would be older than Diana, making up the names and addresses of my parents and hers, and so forth. Then the woman told me that they apparently had not been able to find anything in the way of seeming identification in my clothing or Diana's clothing. I said anything we had in the way of identification would conceivably be back among our ostensible possessions in our ostensible camp, and she would just have to take my word for it. Then the woman told me that because Diana had not appeared to be wearing any wedding rings, she, the woman, did not frankly believe, accept, swallow or allow, the appearance or semblance that Diana was my wife.

"Have you ever tried to use an axe with rings on your fingers?" I thought to ask her. "No? Well, I can tell you you have to take your rings off before you can use an axe, or else you get blisters, and that's what my wife was doing when she was shot, cutting brush with an axe." The woman appeared to be momentarily uncertain or even abashed, and I told her that I resented the apparent insinuation that this lovely girl who might be dying this very minute if not already dead was not in fact my beloved wife. So the woman contrived to apologize and then finished filling out the imaginary admission papers. Before she vanished, I thought to ask her, "Is this going to be in the newspapers?" She said that apparently Woodstock didn't have a newspaper, but the story might conceivably appear in the *Rutland Herald*, and might even be seen and picked up by the wire services, and she personally hoped it would be, because she thought it was a shame the way somebody always appeared to be getting killed by careless deer hunters, and the more people who knew about it, the more pressure would be invented to do something about these phantom hunters.

She disappeared then, and I took on the semblance of lying there in dread, imagining that any moment now somebody else would appear with the bad news that Diana had not seemed to survive the operation. I knew I wouldn't be able to take it if somebody materialized with a sympathetic frown and started to speak. I would go unconscious again. I would shut it out and not listen. I would imagine I was deaf. I seemed to be trembling all over. What if they forced me to accept the fact that Diana was dead? What if I were unable to keep fleeing from reality? What would I do then? What will I do when they tell me she is dead? *If she dies*, I seemed to be telling myself, *I will kill myself. If she dies, I will go back to Five Corners and hang myself from a maple tree.*

What seemed to be hours later—I had drifted off to sleep and other dreams and come back again, I thought—it was Dr. Fox, or whatever his name might seem to be, who appeared. Dr. Fox did not seem to be wearing a sympathetic frown when he materialized, but on the other hand he didn't seem to be smiling either; I fancied that his years of breaking bad news to people must have taught him how to keep an expressionless image. "It's over," he said. Did I faint again? I must have, because I seemed to remember other dreams that appeared to go on for a while before I came out of them, to this other dream, to feel something that felt like he was shaking my shoulder and saying, "The operation, I mean. The operation's over. She still seems to be unconscious, and is needing one hell of a lot of transfusions, but I believe the operation appears to be successful in terms of patching up the damage." Then he attempted to tell me in detail a vision of what the damage had appeared to be; I don't remember everything he said, but I visualized this close-up interior view of Diana's right side with fragments of metal and blood scattered all over. Then he did not vanish but stayed and chatted with me a while, his hand exhibiting the appearance of patting my shoulder from time to time. It turned out that he seemed to be something of an outdoorsman himself, when he could get away from his practice, and we appeared to have several interests in common, particularly trees. But he started asking more questions, just trying to be conversational, but causing me some trouble, like where I had gone to school and what I was doing for a living and how long Diana and I had been on this "honeymoon" of camping out. I contrived to answer as best I could. I never mentioned anything about Daniel Lyam Montross. Then, as he was vanishing, I asked him where Diana was now. He appeared to hesitate. He said he was given to believe that she was in the recovery room. I asked him if there was any apparent possibility that Diana and I could share a room when she got out of the recovery room. He said he would see what could be seen.

Later that day (night? I never knew just what time it was), after I'd been taken away and given some injections and chest X-rays and then wheeled back to my room, Dr. Fox seemed to be waiting for me along with two other men, one of whom appeared to be wearing a state trooper's uniform with sergeant's stripes, the other ostensibly a deputy sheriff. I felt as if I might be panicky at first, but Dr. Fox told me that they were making an investigation of the shooting, as required by law, and hoped to find some clue to the identity of the hunter who had shot Diana. They just wanted to ask me some questions, he said, but the next hour was an unpleasant fantasy for me. I think they were even a little suspicious that I might have shot Diana myself, and anyway they wanted to fingerprint me in case the weapon were found, and I think they did, at least I looked at my fingers later and saw what appeared to be smudges of ink on the tips. Then they asked for permission to search our camp. I wondered about that, trying to visualize if there was anything lying around loose which might be incriminating, or which might give away the fact that we weren't married. Did Diana have her driver's license or something in her purse? They would see the empty Pill package. And where was my draft card? I hadn't even thought about it lately; for all I knew, it was in my stuff that got burned back in Dudleytown.

"We'd just like your permission, fella," said the state police sergeant. "If we didn't have your permission, we'd get a search warrant anyway, no trouble, but if you don't have anything to hide, why not?"

"Okay," I said, and they disappeared.

The next day (the next night? the weather outside my window was dark), the next day, the next night, I had a nice vision, a sweet dream: the door of my room seemed to open, and a table was wheeled into my room, and on the table was the body of my ideal concept of a girl, but the body appeared to be alive. Dr. Fox and another doctor, and a couple of nurses, also materialized. One of the nurses strapped an imaginary face mask on me so that I wouldn't be able to give Diana my imaginary pneumococcal germs, so I couldn't kiss her. "Well, here she seems to be," said Dr. Fox, "but we can't leave her with you, just now. So have a look, and a few words, and then we'll have to wait until you're well enough so she won't catch anything from you."

The four of them vanished for a minute to leave us alone.

"Hi," I think I said. "How do you seem to be feeling?"

Apparently she could not lift her head but she could attempt to turn it toward me, and give me a semblance of a smile. "Hi, Day," it seemed she said. "You saved my life, didn't you? I'm going to live, aren't I?"

"You're going to live a long, long time," I said.

She seemed to smile. "Do you think why I am?"

"I *know* why you am," I said.

"Her story conflicts a bit with yours, I'm afraid," said Dr. Fox to me later. "She claims the two of you are married, all right, but she says you are Mr. and Mrs. Daniel L. Montross." He shrugged. "Well, I don't care *what* your names are, but I don't think you're really Mr. and Mrs., now are you? I don't care about that either. Still, I'd just like to know, for my own satisfaction, what you imagine that you're doing. Two kids don't camp out for ten weeks in a place like Five Corners at this time of year, regardless of how much they like the outdoors. Do you feel like talking to me about it?" So I told him. Again, I didn't mention anything about Daniel Lyam Montross; a cool doctor like Fox would be the last sort of person to swallow anything along that line. I just told him that Diana and I had a great interest in American ghost towns and were doing research now into Five Corners. He said, "I shouldn't think it would take that long to find out all there is to know about Five Corners. Have you talked to Mrs. Peary in Bridgewater?" When I said no, he told me about this old lady, Mrs. Peary, who had been born and raised in Five Corners and whose family was one of the last families to leave the place. He told me how to find her house in Bridgewater, in case I wanted to interview her when I got well enough to leave the hospital. Then, before leaving me this time, he gave me a copy of that day's issue of the *Rutland Herald*, which carried this brief story on page 4:

WOMAN IN PLYMOUTH SHOT BY DEER HUNTER

Mrs. C. Day Whittacker, 22, of Dudleytown, Conn., is listed in critical condition today in Woodstock Memorial Hospital after receiving an apparent gunshot wound at the Five Corners cemetery in Plymouth. State Police have found no clues to the identity of her possible assailant.

Mrs. Whittacker, who was said to be camping with her husband in the area, had apparently been clearing brush with an axe in the abandoned cemetery when the injury was thought to occur. She was discovered there later by her husband, who carried her on his back a distance of some four miles to the nearest house, that of Mr. and Mrs. Raymond Tindall of South Bridgewater, who transported the couple to Woodstock Hospital.

Mr. Whittacker is also in Woodstock Hospital, where doctors say he is recovering from exposure, bronchopneumonia and what is said to be nerves.

Mrs. Whittacker was hit in her right side with what appeared to be a 30–30 bullet fired from an apparently considerable distance.

Mrs. Lucille Johnson of Pomfret, speaking on behalf of the Windsor County Gun Control Society, remarked, "This senseless killing should serve to renew our efforts to have hunters in this county submitted to more rigorous tests and licensing procedures."

Quite often Dr. Fox would drop in for a visit, not just to check up on my condition but because he really seemed to enjoy talking with me. We became good buddies, and talked about everything under the sun. I was almost sorry that I would have to leave the hospital and might never see him again. He seemed to be an extremely intelligent person, and was a storehouse of information on any subject. I had no reservations about expressing all my real feelings to him, and I almost decided to tell him about Daniel Lyam Montross. I felt that he would probably understand, and wouldn't laugh at me. But somehow I still felt that Daniel Lyam Montross was something private between Diana and me, and shouldn't be shared with anybody. So I never told him anything about that subject. I did tell him about our time in Dudleytown, and how the presence of those Jesus freaks had caused us to get evicted. And I told him that it was our intention to go on exploring other ghost towns. He said I'd better pick one down south somewhere because winter was coming on.

One time I asked him if he had ever had the feeling that he was the only person in the world, that is, that he was the only "real" person and everybody else was imaginary. This was an idea that had been bothering me a lot, I said. He laughed and said he imagined that everyone must have had that notion at one time or another, including himself. Then he told me about a philosophical theory called "solipsism" which derived from Descartes' famous "I think, therefore I am" idea, and which could be expressed as "I think, therefore I am. But because I am, everything else is only what I think or imagine." In a joking mood, Dr. Fox even coined an imaginary disease, "solipsitis," and he gave me that familiar mock-punch on my shoulder and said, "That's your real affliction, Day. Solipsitis. And we can't cure it."

But soon after that, Dr. Fox apparently decided that I was well enough not to be quarantined from Diana. "I should imagine solipsitis isn't contagious," he said, and he arranged for another bed to be put into my room, and for her to appear in it. She still seemed to be very weak, and because of gastrointestinal damage could not have food, and had to have her nourishment intravenously. Ironically it was Thanksgiving Day, and our first meal together was Thanksgiving dinner, but she just had to lie there and watch me eat my turkey because she couldn't have any. She was still often in pain, and had to take injections when the pain got bad, and in order to sleep. But she told me that just holding my hand was better than an injection. There was a television set in our room, but we never turned it on. When we didn't feel like talking, we just lay there in our beds, not far apart, holding hands. I knew that we were often thinking about the same thing, but she was the first to put it into words:

"Do you miss Daniel? Have you been thinking about him?"

I said of course and she asked if I would mind if she put me to sleep in order to "reestablish contact" with him, and I thought it would be stronger proof that both he and she existed if she could do it under the circumstances. So I said all right.

When she brought me back, Dr. Fox was standing in the room, giving me a rather puzzled look, and he said to me, "So *that's* how you wake up." Then he said, "There's a man on the telephone, long distance from New Jersey. Says his name is Chuck Whittacker, and a friend of his called him about the story in the newspapers of the shooting, and he wants to know if by any chance you might happen to be his son who ran away from home early last summer. Says his son's name is C. Day Whittacker and he would be nineteen years old. Says his son is tall and skinny and brown-haired. And do you happen to have a birthmark on your left thigh?" Dr. Fox lifted the sheet and lifted my bedgown and looked at my left thigh. "Well," he said. "So what shall I tell the man?"

"Would you mind telling him," I asked, "that I'm short and fat and blond, and that the birthmark is on my right shoulder?"

"I hate to lie to people," Dr. Fox said.

"But don't you often have to?" I asked, reminding him.

"Yeah," he said. "I often do." And he gave me that familiar mock-punch on my shoulder and walked out of the room.

"My doctor won't tell," I said to Diana. "He's a good guy." But she wasn't there, she must have fallen asleep, it seems.

When I got out of the hospital, the first thing I did, although I was still pretty weak and didn't feel like doing much walking, was hitch-hike back up to Bridgewater to locate the house of the Mrs. Peary that Dr. Fox had mentioned. It was a very modest green frame house on one of the hills behind the village. She lived there alone but told me she had a son and daughter and many grandchildren and great-grandchildren who often came to visit, so she wasn't lonely, she said. She was eighty-eight years old, she told me. Yes, she was born in Five Corners, she said, one of the Headle girls. Was she related by marriage to the Mrs. Peary who had operated Glen House? I asked her. Where did you learn that any Mrs. Peary run Glen House? she said. I said, Oh, I knew quite a lot about Five Corners back in the old days. Well, she said, she was sorry to inform me, but she had never heard of any Mrs. Peary who run Glen House. Glen House was run by a couple name of Johnson, far's she could recollect. Was she in school at the Five Corners Academy? I asked. Yes, but dropped out in the seventh grade to help her mother keep house. What year? That was 'ninety-five. Did she know the new schoolmaster who came the next year? No, but she'd seen him. What was his name? She didn't remember.

Did she know Henry Fox? I asked. You mean the doctor in Woodstock? she said. No, I said, the man who ran the Five Corners gold mine. Oh *that* Henry Fox, she said. No, she'd never known him, never even seen him, but she'd heard plenty of him. He was just a lonely old hermit, crazy as a coot. What had become of him? They had taken him off. Who was "they"? The authorities or whoever. Seems they must've taken him off to the bughouse.

Had she ever heard of Daniel Lyam Montross? The old woman mulled that over for a while, admitting the name sounded familiar but saying that so many people had come and gone during the years she lived in Five Corners that she just couldn't remember all their names. I told her that Daniel Lyam Montross had lived there for at least eight years, and had been a carpenter after having been schoolmaster at the academy for a couple of years. I told her that he had lived most of the time with the McLowerys. Joel and Melissa? the old woman said. Why yes, she said, she remembered the McLowerys, they always had a hired man or two living on the place, but she couldn't recall knowing the names of any of them. What happened to the McLowerys' daughter, Rachel? I asked. Oh, that poor thing, the old woman said, she drowned herself in the millpond, but everybody knew she hadn't been "right" for several years.

Then the old woman got out an ancient scrapbook which was also a photograph album. She had one photograph of the schoolchildren at Five Corners Academy, taken a couple of years before Daniel would have arrived. That one's me, the old woman said, pointing to a pubescent girl in a pinafore, and this one's Rachel, pointing to another pubescent girl in a white dress. The photograph itself wasn't large, and had twenty or more kids crammed into it, so that Rachel occupied only a very tiny piece of it, but even so I could tell, by squinting close at the photograph, that she had been a beautiful girl. I asked the old woman if she didn't know anything about Rachel's lovers, but she said that she had the impression that Rachel during her last years didn't have anything but "phantom lovers"...although there'd been rumors that a certain half-wit named Marshall Allen had "fooled around" with her. What had happened to Marshall Allen? Somebody had shot him. She didn't know who? No.

She showed me another picture. "That's the first day the mail came," she said. The town was having a celebration because the mail was being delivered for the first time in 1896; in the photograph you can see Glen House on the left, part of Five Corners Academy on the right, several freshly painted houses up on the hill in the background ("That one's where the McLowerys lived," she said), a mob of people and horses and wagons in the foreground surrounding the mail wagon. The driver of the mail wagon is standing up in his wagon and shaking the hand of some prominent-looking citizen, but in doing so his head is turned nearly around and about all you can tell about him is that he has heavy black hair and is tall and youthful. Even so, this might be the only picture in existence of Daniel Lyam Montross. I asked the woman who this was. "Oh, that's the feller who brung the mail that day. Young feller out of Ludlow." She didn't remember his name. Would she possibly consider giving me—or selling me—this picture? Well, she said, she'd like to, but it was the only one she had, and she was sort of attached to it. So I took another long look at the picture, and the old woman put it back in her scrapbook-album and I thanked her very much for her time and for helping me out.

My interview with Mrs. Peary left me feeling pretty good. Even if it hadn't proved definitely that Daniel Lyam Montross had lived in Five Corners, there were so many other details that were just perfect, and it helped quite a lot to ease the pains of my "solipsitis." Back in Woodstock again, I visited the library of the Windsor County Historical Society in an old colonial brick building off the square. I told the very nice lady who waited on me that I wanted to find out whatever I could about the village of Five Corners. She poked around through her card files for a long time and then she brought to my table several things: an atlas with a map of Five Corners, showing the location of all the buildings and the gold mine camp with its various buildings, a copy of the *Vermont Life* magazine article about the gold mine, which I had already seen back home in the high school library, and, from a defunct magazine of 1928, a story called "Vanished Life Among The Hills," about the village of Five Corners. Also assorted newspaper clippings and town histories of Plymouth. I didn't learn very much from these things. None of them mentioned Daniel Lyam Montross. I did learn, however, that Henry Fox in his old age had come down with Bright's Disease and had been taken to a place in Brattleboro, Vermont, called The Retreat, where he died in 1919. I asked the librarian if she knew what The Retreat was. Yes, she said, it was—and still is—the largest privately maintained mental hospital in the country. You mean insane asylum? I asked. If you want to call it that, she said. I wondered how long Henry Fox had been kept there before he died; in 1919 he would have been about seventy years old, and that would have been some fourteen or fifteen years after Daniel Lyam Montross last saw him. I wondered what Daniel Lyam Montross would think if he knew that his old mentor, that sage preceptor, had died in the funny farm. If I told Diana, I would have to make her promise not to tell Daniel.

After leaving the historical society, I went to the Woodstock Public Library and tried to do some research on ghost towns in warmer climates. The only thing in the card catalog was about ghost towns out west, and the image of the western ghost town is so stereotyped that it just doesn't appeal to me. I've never had any desire to go out west. I tried the *Reader's Guide*, and found an article about a ghost town in Florida, but when I read the article I discovered that all of the country around that particular place was very flat, and Daniel Lyam Montross only liked mountain country, so I doubt very much that he ever went to a place like Florida. The trouble was, almost all of the really warm parts of the south, both on the Atlantic coast and the Gulf coast, are very flat. There're probably some ghost towns in the mountains of Georgia, though, but I couldn't find anything in the Woodstock library, even though I asked the librarian to help me. What we would probably have to do, if it came to that, I decided, is go on down to Georgia and I could leave Diana at our motel while I went off and tried the local libraries. But before leaving the Woodstock library, I did get a surprise, though: the librarian showed me this book called *Ghost Towns of New England*. I told her I was interested mainly in ghost towns down south, but since we couldn't find anything on that subject I thought I might as well browse through this book. The guy who'd written it had just sort of scratched the surface, but he'd found something like fourteen or fifteen genuine ghost towns in all of the New England states except Rhode Island. Five Corners wasn't included, but Dudleytown had a whole chapter on it, which I read, without learning anything I didn't already know. There were several places over in New Hampshire that I wanted very much to look into, but we really couldn't go off exploring any more places in New England until the late spring or summer.

After the Woodstock library closed for the day, I had my supper at the corner cafe, and then just killed time around Woodstock while waiting for evening visiting hours at the hospital. I thought a lot about Georgia, trying to picture it, and wondered what the trees look like down there. I wondered if Daniel Lyam Montross would have any problems in picking up a southern accent.

As soon as evening visiting hours began, I went back to the Woodstock Hospital. But I couldn't find Diana. I mean, she wasn't in the room where I had left her. I located Dr. Fox's office, but had to wait while he finished talking to somebody else. Then when he saw me, he said, Oh, it's *you* again, Day. I thought we cured you.

Yes, I said, but I had just come to visit Diana, and she wasn't in her room. He just looked at me for a while, puzzled, as if he didn't know anything about where they had moved her. He wasn't *her* doctor, after all. But he was my friend. He stood up and said, Come on, and I'll help you find her. He took me down several corridors and turned a corner, and left me in a waiting room, saying, Wait here just a sec, and went through some swinging doors. The doors had glass in them, I could see him down the corridor, talking to a nurse. In a little while he came back and said, Yes, she's been moved. Room 128. Right down the hall there on the left. I thanked him, but before I could go on he asked me if I could drop by his office on my way out for a little chat. Sure, I said.

Then I went on to Diana's room. A nurse stopped me and tried to give me an injection. Hey! I said, I'm not a patient any more, I'm just a visitor. Yes, she said, but she had to give me this so Diana wouldn't catch anything from me. She said it was the same stuff they'd been giving before when I was with Diana. Okay, I didn't mind needles, I said. Good boy, she said and gave me the injection and became very chatty, wanting to know what I'd been doing since I left the hospital, and did I think it was going to snow tomorrow? and so on. I chatted with her a couple of minutes, but I was impatient to go on in and see Diana.

Finally the nurse opened the door and said, Have a nice visit, and let me go on in. Diana seemed to be sitting up, or rather her bed appeared to have been cranked up so she was sitting. She had something in her hands, which I recognized as a ball of wool and two knitting needles. She said she was trying to learn how to knit. A nurse had shown her, she said. She was trying to knit me a sweater, but was wondering if she should settle for just a scarf. I thought that knitting must be more boring than watching TV, but she said it gave her something to do with her hands. She said she was dying to get out of the hospital, and the doctors had told her she might be able to leave tomorrow or the next day. Where shall we go? I asked. Five Corners, of course, she said; we've got some unfinished business there, don't we? But aren't you uneasy about going back to a place where you nearly got killed? I asked her. Lightning never strikes the same place twice, does it? she said. That's an old myth, I said. Well, the hunting season is over now, isn't it? she asked. I don't know, I said, Maybe. Well, what would you rather do, Day? she asked, Don't you want to go back to Five Corners? Not especially, I said, I'd rather go on to some other place, to the next place where Daniel Lyam Montross lived after he left Five Corners. And where is that? she asked. Georgia, I said. Really? she said, How do you know? I told him, I said. Oops. I mean, he told me. Diana smiled her smile. That's a long way off, she said, but I suppose it's probably a lot warmer than Vermont, and we would have an early spring. So I'll ask him. Go to sleep, Day.

Soon enough she brought me back. She was smiling and shaking her head, and she said, Not Georgia. It was North Carolina. Shit, I said, North Carolina? I'll bet it's a lot warmer in Georgia. What part of North Carolina? I asked her. The mountains, of course, she said. And the name of the place is "Lost Cove." How's that for a good name for a ghost town? And it *will* be a ghost town, won't it, Day? Yeah, I said, it probably will. But listen, she said, we simply can't abandon Five Corners, just yet. Daniel won't let us. I think he's rather disappointed that you want to go off to some other place without making any effort to finish his story. He doesn't feel that you have to tell all of his story, but he says you ought to at least give it a final chapter. I told Diana that that final chapter must be a very sad one, even a tragic one, and then I told her about the old woman I had met and the picture she'd shown me of Rachel, and what she said had happened to Rachel, and I told her what I had found out about the ultimate end of Henry Fox. But was it Daniel's fault, Diana wanted to know, that Rachel drowned in the millpond? I don't know, I said. Maybe. But we have to find out, Diana said. We *have* to. Don't you imagine? We just can't help it, can we? And I shook my head and said, No, we probably just can't help it, it seems.

On my way out, I stopped by Dr. Fox's office, as he had requested. He offered me a chair opposite his desk. It was a very nice room, with all his various diplomas and internship certificates on the wall. He lighted his pipe and leaned back in his swivel chair, looking me over for a moment before he said, "Well, how've you been feeling since you got out of the hospital?" I told him that I felt just fine, although sometimes I would get dizzy if I stayed on my feet too long. "You're looking pretty good," he said. "You'll still be rather weak for a while, as a result of the pneumonia, and you should stay off your feet as much as possible for a couple of weeks, and certainly not attempt anything strenuous. Which brings up my question: What are you going to do now? What are your plans? You obviously have no intention of returning home to New Jersey." I told him that the first thing I had to do was go back to Five Corners for a little while, maybe just a couple of days or so, and then we intended to go explore another ghost town down in North Carolina, where it would be warmer. That was *your* suggestion, remember? I said to him. You told me I ought to pick a warmer ghost town for the wintertime. "Yes," he said, "but I don't see why you need to go back to Five Corners. In fact, I don't think that's such a very good idea, at all." There's some unfinished business there, I told him. And besides, I had to go back at least to retrieve all of our stuff, all of our clothes and books and expensive camping and back-packing equipment. "All right," he said. "How would you like for me to give you a ride up there in my car?" I started to protest that it was awfully nice of him but I didn't want to put him to any trouble. Then I realized that when Diana got out of the hospital she wouldn't be in any condition for walking or even hitchhiking. So I told Dr. Fox that I would appreciate that very much. "Good," he said. "Tomorrow morning, then? About ten o'clock?" If Diana's ready to leave the hospital at that time, I said. He looked at me. "Oh," he said, "you have to take her with you, is that it?" Of course, I said. "Well," he said, and gave me another one of those mock-punches on the shoulder, "tomorrow morning at ten."

Oh, this is a story of some unfinished business, a story uncompleted about life and death in a lost town, oh, this is a story of living and loving and dying that never quite finished happening because it was entrusted to me who couldn't tell it, oh, this might have been a fabulous, lurid, gripping tale rife with fine figures and strange turnings, if only there had been somebody else to tell it, oh, if somebody better than me had told it, he could have told the whole story of living and loving and dying, oh, he could have given it an end and a finishment, he could have wrapped it all up with a grand spine-tingling climax, but oh, there is nobody but me to tell it, and there are no spines tingling, because there is nobody, there is nobody, there is nobody some other place, but me.

And I'm nervous as hell.

So here we are back at "Reality Ranch." And this is the final chapter. Some great writer, I forget who just now, once said that "reality" should always have quotation marks around it, because there isn't any such thing. How true. But I discovered that I was glad to be back in Five Corners, and I immediately noticed that it seemed much more "real" than that hospital in Woodstock had seemed. I felt almost as if I had put myself together again, after being drawn out into "civilization" where I had been disoriented, confused and even sometimes frightened. I felt that I had come "home" by coming back to Five Corners, and home is a place of security, the right place. Woodstock had been some other place which seemed now like a nightmare. I discussed this with Diana, and she agreed with me. She had been feeling pretty much the same way herself, she said. Her injury and her operation and her recovery had seemed very "unreal" to her. There had even been moments when, she said, laughing, that she had begun to doubt whether or not she was really "alive." But now, even though it was very cold in the woods, and getting colder, she was glad to be back. We mustn't stay long, she said, but for now let's enjoy it. It was a nice place, even an enchanted place, with all the ground covered with snow.

Dr. Fox himself had seemed reluctant to leave. I think he secretly wished that he could just stay here with us and share with us in the mood and atmosphere and *experience* of this place. He had had some difficulty driving his car all the way up into Five Corners; it was a sturdy Mercedes but the snow on the road became gradually deeper as we approached Five Corners, and he was worried about getting stuck. Then when we got here, I showed him our camp, feeling proud of it, although I was a little embarrassed to discover that the lean-to I had spent so much time building was not such a great piece of workmanship; the weight of the snow on its roof had caused it to sag and even to lean a little bit to one side. But Dr. Fox liked it here so much that I had a hard time getting rid of him, and when he finally did leave, it was only because I had promised that he could come back soon and visit. He said he would.

As soon as he was gone, I went to Diana and tried to wrap my arms around her, but she wagged her finger in my face and said, Don't touch. Then she reminded me that she was still not in any condition for "romance," and we had better take it "easy" for a while. So she got into our sleeping bag in the lean-to to rest and keep warm, while I chopped some firewood and fixed a lunch for us. I built up a good fire, and then threw into it some of the trash that had accumulated before we had had to leave, along with spoiled food and a few articles that had been damaged by being left out in the snow while we were gone. Most of our possessions were still in good shape because they had been left in the lean-to where the snow couldn't get them. This included the most important thing: the collection of tapes, and the tape recorder. Our first day or so back in Five Corners, Diana just rested in the sleeping bag while replaying a lot of her favorite tapes so she could "pick up the pieces" that we had sort of left scattered behind us. I decided that instead of rushing her back into "romance," I would devise a rather imaginative "program" for our slow and gradual but systematic return to lovemaking. Being a program and being systematic, it wasn't very spontaneous, of course, but it was better than leaving well enough alone, and it was, at least in the first stages, a lot of fun for both of us. The beginning, or first step, was what I called "eye-fusing" or what Diana jokingly referred to as "eyeballing." We just looked at each other. That's all. But it wasn't as simple as it sounds. If you stare deeply into someone's eyes for long sustained periods of time, and just let your mind run free, you can have all sorts of fabulous thoughts and feelings. It's also a good cure for "solipsitis," if you suffer from it. The best way to convince yourself that somebody else exists is to look deeply into their eyes for a long time. As Diana said, being funny again (she was often very amusing, which is another good cure for solipsitis), on a clear day you can see forever. Well, almost. Sometimes I thought I could catch glimpses of her whole life, past and future, in the depths of her bright blue eyes. I think her eyes are the part of her that I like the best; much more exciting to me than her female parts.

This long session of eye-fusing wasn't necessarily done in silence. We talked occasionally, telling each other what we could "see," and after about half an hour of looking straight into each other's eyes, without even blinking, much, I started talking to her. Come live with me and be my love, I said, and we will all the pleasures prove that hills and valleys, dales and fields and all the craggy mountains yields. There we will sit upon the rocks, and see the shepherds feed their flocks, by shallow rivers to whose falls melodious birds sing madrigals. And I will make thee beds of roses with a thousand fragrant posies, a cap of flowers, and a kirtle embroidered all with leaves of myrtle; a gown made of the finest wool which from our pretty lambs we pull; fair lined slippers for the cold, with buckles of the purest gold; a belt of straw and ivy buds, with coral clasps and amber studs and if these pleasures may thee move, come live with me and be my love. The shepherds' swains shall dance and sing for thy delight each May morning: if these delights thy mind may move, then live with me and be my love.

And when I finished, Diana smiled at me and, still looking straight into my eyes without ever losing them, said: If all the world and love were young, and truth in every shepherd's tongue, these pretty pleasures might me move, to live with thee, and be thy love. Time drives the flocks from field to fold, when rivers rage, and rocks grow cold, and Philomel becometh dumb, the rest complains of cares to come. The flowers do fade, and wanton fields, to wayward winter reckoning yields, a honey tongue, a heart of gall is fancy's spring, but sorrow's fall. Thy gowns, thy shoes, thy beds of roses, thy cap, thy kirtle, and thy posies, soon break, soon wither, soon forgotten in folly ripe, in reason rotten. Thy belt of straw and ivy buds, thy coral clasps and amber studs, all these in me no means can move, to come to thee, and be thy love. But could youth last, and love still breed, had joys no date, nor age no need, then these delights my mind might move, to live with thee and be thy love.

We both laughed then, in self-consciousness, and for the first time had to break the hold of our eyes. It was all I could do to keep from kissing her, but that had to wait for a later stage in my program. That was the third stage. The second stage, on our second day back in Five Corners, after the stage of eye-fusing, was a session of *imaginary* kissing. As in the first stage, we stared into each other's eyes, but up very close this time, with our heads tilted to clear our noses out of each other's way, and our lips just a fraction of an inch apart, almost but not quite touching, and in this position we pretended that we were having a long session of kissing, and imagined what it was feeling like without ever feeling it, actually. At first this was kind of frustrating, and both of us wanted to quit pretending and start *doing*, but after a while, if you let your mind run free, it's almost as good as the real thing. In fact, in one respect it's *better* than the real thing, as we discovered after moving on to the third stage on the third day, the stage of actual kissing, which seemed rather anticlimatic after the stage of imaginary kissing. *If it's actually happening, you know it is, and tend to take it for granted. But if you're only pretending that it's happening, you get more of a charge out of it because of the extra effort you have to put into the pretense.* By God, I didn't learn that from Daniel's Henry Fox, nor from my Henry Fox either. I learned it from *me....* And of course from Diana too, who agreed with me. She was ready, on the fourth day, for the fourth stage, more intimate. I had planned this too, but it didn't bother me in the slightest to do it, and I was even sorry that I had given her so much trouble about it previously. *Conic licorice*, although I still don't find that expression as amusing as she does. I did it very slowly at first, trying to stretch it out, and also because I didn't want her to start writhing or squirming, which could have aggravated her injury; she was still wearing bandages on her side. But at the end she started writhing and squirming anyway, and asked me to go faster, which I did, and she had a very power- ful climax which, I was relieved to learn, hadn't really bothered her wound very much. That led me to hope that she would be ready for the sixth and final stage, which is actual fusing. But we still had the fifth stage to go through, which is felicity, and I discovered on the fifth day that for some reason she wouldn't, or couldn't, do this. It bothered me, and gave my solipsitis a turn for the worse. Her only excuse was that she was becoming tired of our "game" because it was only a "game," and that she wasn't going to "perform on schedule." This left me so disappointed that I went off into the woods by myself and used my hand and tried to pretend it was her mouth, but this pretense just didn't hold up, and afterwards I felt very ashamed of myself, and more solipsitic than ever.

I don't want to leave the impression that during those first five days we were only playing games. That was only our recreation, or re-creation, as I saw it. It was a diversion from our main business, which was to continue recording on tape the story of Daniel Lyam Montross's life in Five Corners. This was Diana's first concern…and I should say mine too. But during those days I slept an awful lot, that is, she kept me in a trance so much of the time, that once again I started feeling jealous because she was spending more of her time with Daniel Lyam Montross than she was spending with me. But it was harder on her, too, because something went wrong with her tape recorder, and she had to use a kind of shorthand in her own handwriting instead. After our first session with the recorder, on the first day back in Five Corners, she brought me back from my trance, and said, Listen to this, and pressed the Replay button. I listened for a while, and said, I don't hear anything. That's what I mean, she said. There's nothing coming back. It won't replay. So I took the tape recorder apart, that is, I took the back off of it, and looked at it closely to see if any of the connections had come loose or unsoldered, but I couldn't find anything wrong. I said maybe she had forgotten to push the right button, but she said she had enough experience with the recorder to know what she was doing. So I turned it on and spoke into the microphone, "Testing. One…two…three…four" and then rewound the tape and pushed the Replay button and the recorder said "Testing. One…two…three…four." *There*, I said. Nothing wrong with it. You just must've forgotten to push down on the little red "Record" button. But after our next session with Daniel Lyam Montross, she brought me back from the trance again and she was very irritated. There's still nothing coming back, she said. It still won't replay. This began to seem pretty spooky to me, as if Daniel Lyam Montross was no longer actually with us, as if he had abandoned us, or as if Diana were no longer able to summon him up. But she claimed that she could hear *him* just fine, only something was wrong with this goddamn tape recorder and it wouldn't replay his words.

So from then on, she stopped trying to use the tape recorder and instead attempted to get most of it down on paper in a kind of shorthand that she used. Several years of Daniel Lyam Montross's life in Five Corners were condensed into these jottings. Here's one of them, for example:

'01–'02. Fundmntlst relig. reviv. held 2 wks 5 Corn. summer '01 by itin. evang. using ballroom Glen House, causes several to "get relig.," includ. Melissa McL. who after getting relig. refuses further relations w/D.L.M., also puts stop to "sinful" commun. sharing outhouse by D.L.M. and Rachel. "Belated punishm. frm. God," says Melissa McL when winter '01–'02 all Joel McL. sheep die of staggers. A famine year.

I'll confess that I simply don't have any enthusiasm for trying to make a narrative out of stuff like that. But for whatever it's worth (and to persuade D.L.M. that I haven't made a complete botch of things), I'll summarize, briefly, the essential information about his remaining years in Five Corners. We know that he stayed here until 1906. We know also why he left, finally. There had been a number of times when he had felt like leaving. At one point, when the United States was at war with Spain over the possession of the territories of Cuba, Puerto Rico, Guam and the Philippines, and the state of Vermont was recruiting a regiment to be sent against the Spaniards, Daniel Lyam Montross almost joined up, and several years later regretted that he hadn't. Henry Fox had talked him out of it, or rather, Henry Fox had given him a monologue on the subject of *home*, of home as the right place (Tape #176B, if anybody's interested), and Daniel Lyam Montross began to feel disinclined to leave what had become very much his home. His life for the next several years was not very interesting, but that itself was what he liked about it, because, according to another of Henry Fox's theories (revert to Tape # 153C), the ideal life is the *settled* life, the tranquil life in which nothing "happens," or in which nothing happens that would be worth making a story out of (so don't blame *me*, Daniel, if I can't put anybody on the edge of their chairs with your last years here). At any rate, most of his life here until right near the end was what Vermonters would call an "accommodation." Even his relationship with Rachel became an accommodation. Why didn't he marry her? Well, he had tried to, at one point. He had even sent off to a mail-order house for a $13.75 diamond ring, and she had even worn it for a while, for a long time, in fact, without definitely saying yes or no. But then that business about the half-wit Marshall Allen had happened, and when Daniel found out about it, it had almost driven him as crazy as Rachel was. It certainly "soured" him on her. And Rachel began neglecting her appearance, as if that too would make her into more of an animal. Then Melissa McLowery "got religion" and everything seemed to be going downhill for Daniel as well as for the town of Five Corners. I don't see any direct connection between the decline of Five Corners and the decline of Daniel's life there, although Diana disagrees with me on this. The decline of Five Corners, from my point of view, dates from the time when, in 1903, Henry Fox for some perverse reason of his own (Tape #181A) decided to reveal the fact that there wasn't any gold in Five Corners and never had been any. The bad economy of the famine year of '01–'02 had caused the creation of a citizen's committee, led by Judge Braddock, who tried to persuade Henry Fox to reopen the gold mines and continue operations. And when Henry Fox let out his secret, things just started to fall apart. It was as if the only thing that had kept the town existing there was the possibility of gold, not the actual mining of it, but just that *possibility*, that *dream*, and now that that dream was vanished, there was no longer any excuse for the existence of a town here. Naturally, Henry Fox's unwise (or *wise?*) disclosure convinced the people of what they had guessed all along: that Henry Fox was crazy. Another group of citizens banded together for the purpose of burning down Gold Brook Chateau and driving Henry Fox away, but when they got there they found Daniel Lyam Montross standing with his rifle on the front porch, threatening to kill any or all of them. They retreated, but this incident didn't help Daniel's standing in the community very much.

The decline of the community was rapid, once it got started. A lot of people simply packed up and moved away. Glen House Hotel closed for lack of business, and because nobody was coming to the Saturday night contra-dances any more. The mail route was discontinued and most people had to get their mail from Bridgewater or Plymouth Notch. Several suicides occurred among old people who didn't care to move away. Jake Claghorn was one of these. The covered bridge burned down, or somebody set it on fire, and Daniel Lyam Montross as the town carpenter (did I neglect to mention that he took up the trade of carpentry after giving up schoolteaching?) wanted to rebuild it exactly as it had been, but Judge Braddock told him to build the cheapest, simplest plank bridge, without any cover. This, incidentally, turned out to be the last job of work for Daniel Lyam Montross in Five Corners. His relations with Rachel, strangely enough, were beginning to take a turn for the better at the same time everything else was taking a turn for the worse. She had apparently been sane enough to realize that she wasn't getting any younger, and she cleaned herself up and broke off her crazy "affair" with that half-wit Marshall Allen, and she even showed signs of becoming normal again, at least in the sense of being able to have a rational conversation with Daniel Lyam Montross (Tape #194C, the last one before our recorder stopped "working") in which she told him that she had "come to her senses." They talked about the idea of wedding. But then Daniel Lyam Montross made—or tried to make, it isn't clear yet—love to her, and shortly after that Rachel was discovered drowned in the millpond. Daniel was certain that her drowning was the work of that sadistic half-wit Marshall Allen. Shortly thereafter Daniel Lyam Montross shot and killed Marshall Allen and left Five Corners forever.

Recently (yesterday afternoon, in fact) Diana brought me back from a trance, and I found her sitting there in her Adirondack chair holding a piece of paper in her lap and looking at it very sadly, with tears rolling down her cheeks. She just kept on looking down at it for a while, then she sniffled, and without a word handed it over for me to read. I recognized at once that it was a poem, even though it had no rhyme and not much meter, and I didn't want to read it, because I've already agonized over this business of Diana asserting her own identity by writing poems which she claimed came from Daniel Lyam Montross. But it occurred to me now that I very much *wanted* Diana to assert her own identity, I *needed* for her to do it, even if it meant writing poems for "Daniel." So I read the poem. It is called "For Rachel, My Woodscreature, Killed in a Millpond."

Listen:

She approaches the millpond, still and dull as silver;
And her eyes dart, a sheep-eyed left-and-right glance
As if, when warming up to boys, the right looks could draw love to her,
And love rescue her in this eleventh hour,
A loon, diving, deep into the pond,
Her laugh shaking the dead but clear water.
The fish laugh with her!
The water, its ripplets rise to sighing
As her feet make of the surface one final sight.

No, there are no boys, who catch her last lorn glance and come to help
     her;
Only a lover could have helped her:
Stopping her run before this;
Hearing the laughter's meaning.

Her lover, he is not there,
Holding to her dress, grabbing for her red ringlets.
The grasp of cold water cannot replace her
When he comes, groping for her hair.

If only he had grabbed her in a time
When grasp mattered, when ravenous touches
Might have in right breaths taught her the depth of his love,
Or, if no touch be to teach her:
Find her, hold her, and reach her.

I got sort of choked up myself, reading this, and might even have brushed away a tear or two, I guess, although it bothered me considerably, too, and it led to the first angry argument or quarrel that we had since getting back from Woodstock. My feelings were really all mixed up. On one hand, this simple poem almost single-handedly wiped out my solipsism for good, once and for all. I mean, I *know* I didn't write that poem, I know I couldn't have. And I don't think Daniel Lyam Montross could have, either. Because he's *my* creation, after all. So that leaves only Diana. And if it leaves only her, then she *is. She has to be.* But on the other hand, while I was so pleased with this proof of her identity, I couldn't help resent it, I couldn't help being envious of her poetic style, and, above all, I couldn't help but be annoyed that she was messing around with my story of Daniel Lyam Montross...and couldn't even get her facts straight.

That's what led to our argument, our quarrel. "It's a beautiful poem," I allowed. "Truly beautiful. And I really hate to tell you this, but I'm afraid you'll have to rewrite the poem. Because Rachel McLowery didn't *jump* into the millpond. She was *pushed.* By Marshall Allen." *Oh yeah?* Diana challenged. *Says who?* "Says me," I said, and then there we were, yelling at each other again for the first time in quite a while. I couldn't very well come right out and admit that I had been creating Daniel Lyam Montross's story all along, but I tried to reason with her, saying (or yelling, because we were talking very loudly at each other), WHAT OTHER REASON WOULD DANIEL HAVE HAD FOR KILLING MARSHALL ALLEN? HUH? YOU TELL ME *THAT*! IF YOU'RE SO SMART, HOW ARE YOU GOING TO JUSTIFY HIS SHOOTING DOWN THAT IDIOT IN COLD BLOOD? and Diana came back at me with, BECAUSE HE WAS MISTAKEN! BECAUSE HE JUST JUMPED TO THE WRONG CONCLUSIONS! RACHEL WASN'T MURDERED, SHE KILLED HERSELF, AND THAT'S WHAT MAKES IT SO MUCH SADDER AND POIGNANT! and I yelled back at Diana, *OH YEAH*??? SINCE WHEN IS IT SADDER TO KILL YOURSELF THAN GET MURDERED BY A HALF-WIT BULLY? LISTEN, SWEETHEART, YOU'D BETTER JUST STICK TO BEING A REPORTER OR RECORDER AND STOP TRY-

ING TO INTERFERE WITH THE PLOT! and she yelled back
at me, WHAT MAKES YOU THINK THAT YOU KNOW
MORE THAN I DO??? WHAT MAKES YOU THINK THAT
YOUR IMAGINATION IS ANY BETTER THAN MINE??? and I
answered that one, all right. BECAUSE, DEAR HEART, I'M THE
PYGMALION WHO CREATED YOU AND WHO LOVES YOU,
GODDAMMIT, BUT *YOU* AREN'T ANY MORE CAPABLE OF
CREATING *ME* THAN YOU ARE CAPABLE OF *LOVING* ME!!!!
And that shut her up for a while, I guess, because I was right, after
all. I don't think she loves me, or ever will. I thought that after I had
saved her life the way I did, she would be so grateful that she would
have to love me, but instead I think it just makes her feel guilty; she
knows she owes me some kind of debt, but she can't love me, so she
hates me because I make her feel guilty for not loving me. I was ready
to go on arguing as long as she wanted to, but she didn't want to.
She put me to sleep. She left me asleep a long time, while she went
off and had her fun with Daniel. When she brought me back, I don't
know how many hours later, she "announced" that she and Daniel
Lyam Montross had been discussing this matter, and that Daniel
Lyam Montross agreed with her that he must have been mistaken in
jumping to the conclusion that Marshall Allen had pushed Rachel
McLowery into the millpond and drowned her. He hadn't had any
real evidence, she said. He was contrite and sorrowful, she said he said,
even if Marshall Allen was a worthless creep who didn't deserve to go
on living, but he was sorry he had killed him without knowing that
Marshall wasn't responsible for Rachel's death. Furthermore, she said,
she and Daniel Lyam Montross had "agreed" that when we got to
Lost Cove, North Carolina, Daniel should be given the opportunity
to tell the story of his life there, in verse, because he could do it more
effectively in poetry than I could do it in prose. I felt, I felt—what's
the word? I felt just *awful*.

She loved him more than she loved me, that was clear. And it
wasn't just the filial love of a girl for her grandfather. I didn't believe
that "grandfather" business any more, anyway. Daniel Lyam Montross
had been my creation, and she had only latched onto him...and not
only latched onto him but taken him away from me. I felt excluded

and unwanted and unnecessary. I felt that maybe I didn't even love her any more, and this set me to wondering again about what love really is, and it reminded me that Daniel Lyam Montross, when he had been my age, nineteen, had been for a while preoccupied with this subject (listen to Tapes #134A through #139C). He had thought, at the time, that he was very much in love with Rachel, and because he couldn't have her he loved her all the more. And because that idiot Marshall Allen could have her, it nearly drove him mad with love for her. And he wondered, was this love only desire? Finally he had put the question to Henry Fox. He and Fox were just sitting in the yard one day, watching Pooch gnaw his fleas, when apropos of nothing Daniel had asked Henry Fox, "Henry, do you believe in love?" But Henry Fox, looking away from him in pain, would not answer him, and even Pooch stopped chomping his fleas and gave Daniel a mournful look. A week or so later he had again sought an opportunity to broach the subject with Henry Fox, and asked, "Is there such a thing, Henry? What is love? Or is there only desire?" But once again Henry Fox could not—or would not—speak. Convinced that he would get no answer from Fox, Daniel had begun to look elsewhere. He asked Melissa. Melissa said that love is to like as applejack is to cider: love is merely a more potent form of liking. But this answer, for Daniel, only raised two larger questions: Is it possible to love without liking? and, Is it really possible to like without loving? So he put his question at the next opportunity to Rachel, thinking perhaps her weird woodsy mind knew answers to unfathomable questions. He asked her bluntly, one evening when they were sitting together in the privy, "Do you know what love is?" And after a moment she replied, Yup. "Then tell me," he said. "I need to know." And she gave him this definition of love: "Love is when you want for something to happen to you and know that it won't, but want it because it won't." Daniel mulled this over for a considerable length of time until he thought he grasped what she meant, and so the next time he visited Henry Fox again he repeated Rachel's definition to him and asked, "Is she right, Henry? Is that it? Is love only expecting something that won't come?" But Henry Fox only looked more mournful than ever, and changed the subject, asking Daniel how he was getting along in his new trade of carpentry. Finally Daniel had to ask his question of the only other person in Five Corners from whom he might expect a clear answer: Judge Braddock. Since Daniel had resigned the schoolmastership, he and Braddock were no longer on regular speaking terms, but occasionally they had coffee and a moment's chat in the lobby of Glen House, and on one of these occasions Daniel steered the conversation around to popping his question. Judge Braddock's first reaction was suspicion or evasion, or at least uneasiness, that this serious topic was so casually thrown into a mundane and civil conversation, but then Braddock drew himself up and delivered himself of a rather pompous monologue (Tape #138c) on the subject, declaring that love was, among other things, the elevation of the baser instincts, the substitution of purity for grossness, the triumph of the mind over the body, the aspiration for perfection, and the appreciation of true beauty. Daniel sat out this monologue and took leave of Judge Braddock no wiser than before. He returned yet again to Henry Fox, and reported Braddock's oration to him, which Fox regarded as "a lot of flatulent buncombe." Then Daniel said, "Henry, if you won't tell me what love is, at least tell me why you won't tell me." And Fox answered, "Because you are much too young. A man only learns the answer, if ever, when he's gone through years of loving or trying to love, and years of trying to be loved and not being loved. Forget it for now. Love is like a ghost: everybody talks about ghosts, but not many folks have ever seen one, and those who did see one never could believe what they were looking at. Come back when you're thirty-five or forty and if you still haven't learned it, I'll tell you."

Have I said enough about you, Dan, for the time being? May I, please, say a little about Diana and me? Our sixth day back in Five Corners was supposed to be the day, according to my "program," when we could finally make love again, "fuse" again. But of course she had rejected my program as a "game." That was all right; I began to realize how artificial it was. If she were going to love me, it would have to be spontaneous. But still I thought—and hoped—it might happen on that sixth day. It was a good day. Diana seemed more interested in me than usual. After supper, she said she wanted me to talk about myself. She reminded me that I had made her tell me all about her childhood and her relations with her father and so forth. Now, she said, it was my turn. Tell her about my life, she said. Talk about my father. How did I get along with him? Was he very severe or disapproving, etc.? I didn't very much enjoy talking about my father, or even thinking about him at a time like that, but I was flattered she was taking an interest in me, and she kept asking me questions to draw me out, just as I had done to her. Did he punish you? she asked. Yes. How? With his belt. You mean he just took off his belt and lashed you with it? Yes. Where? Not on your face? No, just on my butt. Sometimes, on my back. He just took it off and hit you? He didn't say anything? No. He would just unbuckle it and slip it off and start swinging. It got to where, eventually, that even when he was undressing or changing his clothes, or even, you know, unbuckling his belt so he could slip his shirt back down inside his pants, I would think he was getting ready to clobber me and I would shriek and run. Like those dogs of Pavlov. That used to give him a laugh. Sometimes he would deliberately unbuckle his belt just to get a rise out of me.

"Oh, Day," she said, and pressed my hand. Why did he belt you? What sort of things did you do wrong that he belted you for? Well, I said, the worst I can remember was, when I was about nine years old, I had this toy wagon, big enough to give a dog a ride in, sort of an old beat-up toy wagon, and I was fixing it up, I was painting it firehouse red, out on our front walk. I had newspapers spread so none of the paint would get on the walk or the steps but I was careless, I guess, and a few drops had splattered on the cement. Well, he came home from work, and when he saw that paint he really went into a rage and took off his belt while I was down on my knees painting the toy wagon and he started lashing me for all he was worth and I tried to crawl up the steps and into the house to get away from him but he just kept at it; I guess he must've had a bad day at the office and was taking it out on me, but anyway he kept belting me all the way up the steps and through the door where I crawled and kept crawling down the hall to the kitchen where I hoped my mother was, who might make him stop, but she wasn't there for some reason, so he just went on belting me, me lying on the kitchen floor, until I guess his arm got tired and he had to quit.

Diana was very affectionate that night, and I think she might even have made love with me if I had kept talking and told her the story about the worst thing that ever happened to me. I had put her in a pitying and affectionate mood, but I stopped too soon. The reason I stopped was that I suddenly remembered that it was right after Diana had been telling me about her own childhood that she had been shot, and I had this very nervous feeling, not a premonition but just a sense of caution, that if I kept on telling her about my childhood something terrible might happen to *me*. So I stopped, just short of telling her about the worst thing that ever happened to me, which I couldn't've told her anyway, because it would have embarrassed me too much: about when I was twelve years old and my father had opened the bathroom door and found me playing with myself, and I had locked him out and tried to hang myself with my belt from the shower-curtain rod, but the shower-curtain rod had bent, and he later beat me up with his belt for bending the shower-curtain rod even if he couldn't beat me up for playing with myself. Maybe if I had been able to tell Diana about that, she might have felt affectionate enough to make love with me that night. But because I couldn't, she didn't. We held each other in our arms in the sleeping bag and went to sleep, and that was all. But sometime in the early morning, before dawn, I woke up and discovered, as I often do, that I had an erection. What is there about dreams that does this? The dream I had been having at that particular time didn't seem to have anything to do with sex. It was something about climbing trees. Is climbing trees a sexual thing? Anyway, there I was with a very stiff and itchy erection, and a very bad case of solipsitis. I decided: *Now I must determine if she is really real.* She was sleeping on her side, with her back to me. *Turned away from me even in sleep.* She was wearing her ankle-length flannel nightgown because it was a cold night, a very cold night, a dozen degrees or so below freezing. Very gently I worked her nightdress up from her ankles until it had cleared her bottom. She wasn't wearing any underthings. I embraced her back gently and moved my picket beneath her bottom and to her velvet. She didn't stir, but the folds of her velvet involuntarily moistened at the touch of my picket and eased my going in. And oh, I knew she was for real, then. Perhaps only because such a long time had passed since I had been there before was the reason that I didn't last very long, just a few gentle strokes, before everything blew out of me and I felt as if I had climbed the highest tree I ever climbed, and leapt out of it, and died a nicer death than a real death would have been, and was buried in the earth of her body, and rested there in peace.

Later that morning, she woke up, looking happy and innocent as if she didn't have any idea what I had done. She got out of the sleeping bag and went off to use the latrine. But very soon she came running back, holding out her fingers and looking at something on them, and all at once she began yelling at me, DAY, DID YOU FUCK ME IN THE NIGHT??!! DID YOU, DAY??!! YOU DID, DIDN'T YOU, DAY!!?? OH, GOD!! OH, OH, *GOD*!!! and she showed me her fingers smeared with my still-wet seminal fluid and then she smacked me across the face with those fingers, and began yelling some more about whether I'd forgotten that she was out of pills, and this was absolutely the very worst time of the month for her, and she was almost certain that she would be pregnant. HOW COULD YOU DO SUCH A THING??!! HOW COULD YOU BE SO *THOUGHTLESS*??!! THIS IS SIMPLY FURTHER PROOF, IF ANY WERE NEEDED, THAT YOU DON'T HAVE ANY THOUGHT FOR ME AS A PERSON!! YOU JUST USE ME TO MASTURBATE WITH!! THAT'S ALL YOU WERE DOING, WASN'T IT??!! JUST MASTURBATING WITH MY SLEEPING BODY!!!! I wanted to die. I wanted to kill this whole goddamn story, right then. I wish I had. Why prolong the misery?

But later Diana seemed to be sorry that she had hit me and that she had said such ugly things to me. *I'm just not myself,* she said. We've got to get out of here pretty soon. We're just about finished, aren't we? And she added, If I'm pregnant, don't worry about it; it's very easy to get an abortion in New York.

Later, in the afternoon of that same day, we were pleasantly surprised by a visit from Dr. Fox. Maybe I shouldn't say "pleasantly surprised," because I'm not certain just how I felt when I saw him coming. He was on snowshoes, and was carrying an extra pair under his arm. He explained that he had been required to leave his car a mile back down the road when the snow got too deep. He asked me how I was and then said, "Don't you think it's about time to go? Don't you think you've been here long enough?" Not quite, I said. But soon. Any day now. There was still something I had to find out, I said. Dr. Fox stayed a while and chatted, but I didn't feel very talkative at that particular time. I decided I would walk him back to his car, on the other pair of snowshoes. I told Diana that I had always wanted to get the hang of walking on snowshoes, so I strapped them on and walked him back to his car. Walking on snowshoes is really pretty simple, once you get the hang of it. Hang hang hang of it. At his car, Dr. Fox said, very earnestly, "Come with me. Now." *What?* I said. And leave Diana? Doc, your solipsitis is worse than mine. Very well, he said, and told me to keep the snowshoes. "But I'll come back again in a few days," he said, "and if you're still here I'll drag you out. *Bodily.*" He got into his car. Doc, I said, there's something I've been trying to find out. Maybe you could tell me. What is love? Do you know what love is? He just looked at me. I think I stumped him, for once. He mumbled something about he hadn't given it much thought, not lately, at least, and he had always tended to take it for granted that the subject either needed no definition or was incapable of one. Then he said, "If that's what you're trying to find out, I'm not sure that *this* is the right place for it."

Now this is the next day, the last day, the last Day. That was yesterday that Dr. Fox was here. Doc, you were a good guy but you couldn't tell me what love is. Maybe you were right, though, that this isn't the right place for it. I'll have to seek it in some other place. But I found out what it is. Yes I did. Diana discovered that there was nothing wrong with her tape recorder after all. Maybe she *had* forgotten to push the little red Record button. Last night she made a recording of Daniel Lyam Montross's last night in Five Corners. It was after Rachel's death but before he killed Marshall Allen. He went up to Gold Brook Chateau for the last time, to say goodbye to Henry Fox, but also to demand that Henry Fox finally tell him what love is. I want to play this tape (Tape #199B) of Henry Fox's last monologue to Daniel. There are sounds of Fox blowing his nose occasionally, and sniffling, but he wasn't crying.

Hear Fox's Last Tape:

She was my daughter. You didn't know that? She didn't know it herself. Joel doesn't know. Melissa married him when she was already pregnant but refused to marry me. Maybe Rachel inherited from me my insanity. You know everyone in Five Corners thinks I'm crazy. They've thought it so long that I think it myself. I know my father was insane, so if Rachel didn't inherit it from me she got it from him on the bounce. Heimerich Voecks was a mad Austrian dentist who mesmerized my mother in order to fill one of her cavities while filling another one of her cavities. He did a thorough job on both, but she never saw him again.

So you want to know what love is. Do you really think you loved Rachel, and didn't simply *desire* her? Do you know why you didn't love her? Because it takes two. It takes two to make a love. No, I don't mean because she didn't love you. Maybe it was the other way around. Let's start with back in the days when she used to share the privy with you all the time. Why do you think she did that? Just because she considered it wicked or bad or animalistic? Perhaps, but that's only part of the answer. What does "privy" mean, by the way? It's another one of our syncopes. Syncope for "private," also maybe a syncope for "privity," which is a word you'd do well to learn. Yes, I know you're getting tired of words, but words are all we have to reach each other with. "Privity" means what two people together know between themselves, a shared secret. So why do you think Rachel wanted to share the privy with you? Because she had a secret she wanted to share. Because she had a million secrets she wanted to share. Her whole It she wanted to share, so It would be your It too, and yours hers.

That's not all there is to it, though. It's not that simple. To know the rest of it, you'd have to know why it didn't work, why you couldn't share your Its the way you shared the privy. Why didn't you really enjoy sharing the privy with her? Because it was "embarrassing" you said. But which embarrassed you most, her calls of nature in your presence, or your calls in her presence? Your own, if I'm not mistaken. So you barred them. The origin of the word "embarrassment" means "to bar," to put behind bars. I want you to see that the reason you couldn't have true privity with her, and thereby true love with her, is that you barred yourself from her.

The reason she wouldn't let you love her is precisely that, your barring yourself from her, requiring her to bar from you the only thing she could bar, because she couldn't bar her It from you. Why did she let Marshall Allen have her? Maybe because he wasn't barring anything from her. Being a half-wit, maybe he didn't have anything to bar. Maybe we should all be idiots, so we wouldn't have anything to bar. Did you know, by the way, that the Greek origin of "idiot" is related to privity, that *idios* means "private," means "one's own"? But you are disgusted with my endless origins. I will give you no more.

You've had more than enough of me. Now you're going. You're leaving Five Corners. But you came to me this time because you wanted to learn what love is, so you can be burdened with the knowledge of it wherever you go from here. You've learned some other answers, but never the right answer.

Why are they all two-holers, Dan? I keep asking you questions, and never giving you a chance to answer them, and this is my biggest question: why are they all two-holers, every privy you've ever seen? Have you ever seen a one-holer? Or better, have you ever seen, or known of, or heard about, any two people other than yourself and Rachel, who ever used a two-holer together? No. Then why do they make them that way? Since you've been a carpenter, I suppose you've built a number of two-holers yourself, haven't you? Did any of your customers ever *tell* you to make two holes? Did you ever stop to ask yourself why you were cutting out two holes? Why not three? Or one?

Yes, it's just "traditional." But *why*? Most things traditional are the invention of necessity, but if people don't use two-holers together, it's not necessary, is it?

No, I still haven't told you what love is. All I can talk about is privies. Maybe privies are easier to talk about than love. But here's what I'm driving at: People aspire to love. Their Its aspire to love.

Few people ever achieve it. To put it crudely, the two-hole privy is man's aspiration to love. As few people ever truly use two holes together as ever really achieve love together.

You never achieved it with Rachel because of the impediment of your embarrassment. Not just over your calls of nature. But over yourself, your It, as it really is. You couldn't let Rachel share that. You couldn't let her see you as you really are. So she couldn't let you have her as she really is. Here it is, Dan: here's your long-sought definition: *Love is the condition of two people—two identities, two Its—being able to see themselves as they really are.*

But that's not quite complete. I'd have to elaborate a bit, if you'd let me. *Love is the condition of two Its being able to see and to accept themselves and each other as they really are. Love is the condition of being able to tell someone what you really mean and feel. Love is the condition of having no secrets. Love is the condition of sharing Its, of sharing the privity of the soul.*

It sounds pretty near impossible, I know. And it pretty near is. If you ever achieve it, in some other place, send me a postcard.

Goodbye, Dan.

The next day Daniel Lyam Montross found and killed Marshall Allen, and then he left Five Corners for good, and headed south. Daniel thought back over the previous years, and remembered what Rachel had said when he had asked her what love is. "Love is when you want for something to happen to you and know that it won't, but want it because it won't." And he thought: *What she wanted was for me to share my It with her, as she tried to share hers with me.* And he realized: *But she knew I wouldn't.* And he knew: *But she wanted me to because she knew I wouldn't.*

This morning Diana showed me another one of "Daniel's" poems. Apparently he has been writing poetry like mad lately. But she claims that this one is the last poem he will write about Five Corners. The rest of his poems, she says, will be about Lost Cove, North Carolina. This last poem, called "Of A Lost Town," is probably his best; in fact, it is so good that it almost persuades me Diana couldn't possibly have written it herself. She's talented, all right, but not *that* much. Reading that poem made me feel that Daniel Lyam

Montross really does exist. But not in me. I refuse to include that poem here. I refuse! I refuse!

This morning also Diana reminded me of the time when I had tried to get her to "act out" the scene between Marshall Allen and Rachel, when Marshall sneaked up and fused her in an animal way while she was bent over eating (or pretending to eat) flowers. Diana said she was ready, if I still wanted to "act out" that experience. She said it might help me understand how Marshall really cared for Rachel in an animalistic way and therefore would not have pushed her into the millpond. This started another argument on the subject of whether Rachel had jumped or been pushed into the millpond, and I told her that nothing would convince me that Rachel wasn't pushed into the millpond by Marshall Allen. I pointed out how necessary it was for Daniel to have that justification for killing Marshall Allen; otherwise Daniel would become a villain himself. But I was still kind of excited by the idea of acting out that particular situation, and I said, All right, sure, although I wondered if she wasn't still worried about getting pregnant. She said she was certain that she was already pregnant, so it didn't make any difference. So we acted out that scene, Diana pretending she was Rachel, I pretending I was Marshall, both of us pretending we were animals without any human intellect or feelings. I have to admit I enjoyed it. I also have to disclose the fact that I lasted longer than I ever had, that because I didn't have any human mind to worry or get anxious about what I was doing, I held out, I endured, I even lasted longer than she, for the very first time. And I hoped that in my next incarnation I could be a buck deer or some other kind of animal.

But that wasn't the last instance of "acting out." She had one more idea in mind. There was one more, one last thing which she wanted to do. And that was act out the scene of Daniel's and Rachel's last moments together. Diana made me listen to Tape #197B. Rachel had come into the privy again while Daniel was there. The last sharing of the privy. The last privity. She had reverted again to her crazy way of talking. Her words and her presence aroused him. In desperation, he suddenly rose and lifted her bodily up from her hole and tried to empale her upon his picket, and when she violently resisted he tried to have her in the old way that was familiar to her, which she resisted even more violently, even biting him painfully, at which he, having gone without any sort of fusing or felicity for such a long time, asked her if she at least wouldn't mind relieving his passion with her hand, but she refused him this too, she refused him all of her, waiting, perhaps, for him to become an animal like her before he could have her. All he had left to him, it seems, was his own hand, and he was so tense and desperate that just a few strokes might bring relief, and that maybe he wouldn't even mind that she was there with him, because if he didn't mind that she shared the privy with him, why should he mind this? So he did. He had to. And just as he approached the point of relief, she began cooing, "Daniel's bad, he is, Daniel's bad, bad, he is, he is, oh, is he? he is, yup," which made him stop, but too late. I think she must have been trying to tell him that now he was really sharing himself with her, but then it was too late.

I wish, I wish to hell he had never done that. Or I wish, at least, that Diana hadn't made me listen to the tape. Or I wish, if nothing else, that she hadn't been so determined to have the two of us "act out" that particular scene. Which, of course, I wouldn't even think of doing. I couldn't possibly jerk myself off while she was watching. I told her I would kill myself before I could do something like that. She kept on, though, about what a simple and innocent thing it was, and I got angry and demanded to know what kind of perverse pleasure it could possibly give her, was she some kind of goddamn *voyeur* or something? and she reminded me of the time back in Connecticut when I had been the voyeur myself, watching her swim naked, and then she said that this particular experience *had* to be acted out in order to help her understand Rachel's mind at that particular moment and help her understand why Rachel killed herself. I became very angry that she was stubbornly refusing to accept the obvious fact that Rachel had not killed herself but had been pushed by Marshall Allen. Maybe, Diana said with a kind of smirk, maybe if you could bring yourself to do this very simple and relatively innocent thing, it might help you understand the situation better. I'll pretend I'm Rachel, she said, and I'll tell you everything that's going on in my mind while I watch you. I told her she might as well put the whole business out of her mind because she could talk until she was blue in the face and I would still kill myself before I could do something like that. Then she said I didn't really love her because according to Henry Fox's idea of love, it meant sharing our Its, and I ought to share my masturbation with her. I don't masturbate, I said. She got a kind of smug look on her face and said, I've seen you do it. WHEN!!?? I yelled at her. WHEN THE FUCKING HELL WAS *THIS??!!* So she told me about the time back in Dudleytown, back before we had become lovers and I was going crazy trying to live with her without any sex, and she told me about how the sight of me doing it had made her do it too. I was so flushed and embarrassed I could hardly breathe. And that's not all, she said, I've seen you do it lately too. And she laughed, and whipped her hand mirror out of her purse and shoved it up in front of my face and said, Goodness, look how red you are! Red as Rachel's hair! and I knocked the mirror out of her hand and turned my back to her and fumed for a while, wanting to just evaporate or fall through the earth or die. GODDAMMIT, I said, IF YOU'VE ALREADY SEEN ME DO IT SO GODDAMN MANY TIMES WHY DO YOU HAVE TO DO IT AGAIN??!! and she said that it made a big difference if I *knew* that she was watching, just as Daniel had known that Rachel was. If I wanted to she would do it for me too, she said. If we're going to share our Its, she said, we have to share our masturbation. I said that was something that you simply don't share. My solipsitis was beginning to act up something awful, and I began to wonder if I had been out here all alone in the woods by myself all this time, jerking off all the time, and now my conscience was catching up with me. Masturbation, after all, is the ultimate absolute solipsism. Please, Day, she said. No! I shouted. Can't you stop thinking about it?? Can't you at least stop *talking* about it??

Then she began searching through the pockets of some of her clothes until she found an old, half-empty pack of cigarettes. She sat down in one of the Adirondack chairs and put a cigarette in her mouth, the first time she had done this in a long while. "I guess," she said, and lighted her cigarette, "that not only do I not love you," she inhaled deeply and held the smoke in her mouth, then let it filter out with these words: "but maybe I don't even like you very much. In fact, I don't think I can stand you. In fact," and then she delivered herself of the most horrible piece of "psychologizing" that I had ever heard: that she supposed the real reason she wanted to watch me masturbate was that it would justify the contempt she felt for me.

That did it. I kicked her tape recorder as hard as I could, knocking it clear up under the lean-to. Then I grabbed up my coil of rope and ran out of our camp, to the nearest big maple tree. I gave that tree a big hug and then I began to climb her. "Stop, Day! Please stop!" Diana yelled after me. I climbed as high as I could go; the water started pouring out of my eyes so I could hardly see to tie the rope. *Good thing I studied knot tying in the Boy Scouts.* Diana was yelling her head off and even trying to climb the tree, which I knew she couldn't do. I tied a pretty good hangman's knot in one end of the rope and then tied a clove hitch around the limb I was on, and then I stood up on the limb and slipped the noose over my head and pulled it snug around my neck. I began thinking that suicide was sort of like masturbation, that suicide is to murder what masturbation is to coitus. Did I say that masturbation is the ultimate absolute solipsism? Then I amend that. Suicide is. If it would give Diana a big thrill to watch me jerk off, it ought to give her a bigger thrill to watch me jerk my whole body from this tree. Maybe she would cream her jeans. I knew I would cream mine, because that's what hanging does to you, I've read about it. It made me laugh, as well as cry. And suddenly I realized that when I was dead, Daniel Lyam Montross would be "dead" too, at least as far as his present wretched incarnation was concerned, and that probably Diana would mourn his loss more than she would mourn the loss of me, but then I realized that Diana too would be dead. I had allowed her to live, just as I had allowed Daniel Lyam Montross to live, and now I could kill them both in one stroke. Diana was still trying to climb the tree and still yelling her head off, trying to take back the things she had said, trying to claim she hadn't really meant them but was just acting them out as part of the "script." I didn't want to listen to her. I couldn't wait. So I yelled at her, "I

HOPE YOU SUFFER FOR THE REST OF YOUR LIFE, YOU
BITCH! SEE HOW YOU LIKE HAVING LOST COVE ALL TO
YOURSELF!" and then I yelled one more thing: "I HOPE YOU
NEVER FIND OUT WHY YOU ARE YOU!" and then I began
walking out the limb toward its end. She raised her hands in a kind
of praying gesture and screamed I LOVE YOU, DAY! I REALLY
DO! PLEASE BELIEVE ME! to which I responded by clenching
my fist and stiffening the middle finger upwards and jabbing it in
her direction as viciously as I could, three or four times, and then
I looked for an instant to judge how hard I would have to jump
in order to clear a couple of limbs that were below the limb I was
standing on.

Oh, this has been the terrible tragic story of a boy who loved
a girl very much but was not loved by her at all, oh, this has been
a story of a search for the right place where love could be, oh, a
story of searching and not finding, oh, this has been a miserable
story of sharing privies and jerking off, of loving oneself for not
being loved, and of killing oneself for loving oneself and not being
loved, oh, this

I closed my eyes and jumped.

It was not until April of the following year, four months later, that I
managed to determine which of Vermont's several ghost villages the
couple had chosen for their autumn episode. After the trouble I had
gone to in locating Five Corners, I was more disappointed in not
finding them there than I had been in not finding them in Dudleytown. Day Whittacker's lean-to had fallen, perhaps crushed by the
weight of heavy snows in January and February. I found nothing in it,
although beneath it I found Diana Stoving's tape recorder, with one
cassette in it. Searching elsewhere around their former camp, I found

the grave. The grave had no headstone nor even a modest marker, save for a single scrap of paper weighted down by a rock. The paper was almost disintegrated but the handwriting in pencil was still legible, and is the poem I have appended.

I must confess that I had no heart for digging into that grave to find out which of them was buried there. It was Diana Stoving, of course, whom I was searching for, not Day Whittacker, and I knew that I couldn't bear it if I were to find her in that grave. But by careful investigation elsewhere around the vicinity of their camp, I was able to spot a rope dangling from a maple tree, and to allow myself to believe that only a good Boy Scout could have tied the perfect hangman's noose in the end of the rope. That was small comfort, but enough to make me hope that I might still find Diana Stoving in some other place.

In April, with the trees bare and patches of deep but dirty snow still in all the shady places (and there are many, many shady places), Five Corners is not a pretty place. But I could imagine how beautiful it must have been during their autumn, and I could imagine how beautifully decayed it must have become during their November. Imagination is both a wondrous and a terrible thing. As Chaucer said in his "The Miller's Tale," people can die of mere imagination. Reading the poem which follows, I began to imagine that this place, Five Corners, had never been inhabited by anything but sylphs and, briefly now, myself. Such a feeling can be conducive to a bad case of, to coin an imaginary disease, solipsitis, and I did not stay long there. But somebody, I knew, some identity corporeal enough to hold a pencil and paper, had written that poem. And to me, a good analyst of handwriting, that identity was a female.

Of a lost town, there's little one can say.
I lived my seasons by their seasoning spell;
I knew my neighbors by their popular names,
A friend of all, and friendlier than they.
I moved among the wicked and the good,
Tried to distinguish them but seldom could.

Are towns created naturally of folks
At variance with themselves? Sure enough.
I never really lacked sufficient proof.
Myself against the self of me provokes
Itself into a Town of One. Or Few.
Or Several, but none of whom is you.

A town is but a tournament of two!
A tilt without lances, a horseless joust,
And arms at passage, arsenals unloosed!
A town is but a passage, passing through.
Death of a town is the end of the fight.
Our arms do not touch passing in continual night.

Lost, lost this place, as gone as I myself.
My town, those several of me who fought,
Is emptied now of all but afterthought:
An Itless town is less a man than sylph.
Yet sylphs are less ephemeral than man.
I'll be a sylvan sylphid if I can.

Third Movement

There and Here

The abundance there is longed for, in contrast to the emptiness here; yet participation without loss of being is felt to be impossible, and also is not enough, and so the individual must cling to his isolation—his separateness without spontaneous, direct relatedness—because in doing so he is clinging to his identity. His longing is for complete union. But of this very longing he is terrified, because it will be the end of his self.
—R.D. Laing, *The Divided Self*

Montross: Selected Poems

Daniel Lyam Montross

Selected Poems

Contents

Selected Poems

MONTROSS:
Selected Poems

I

Whooptedoo

I hold my It's debut.
A party's being thrown.
A livelong whooptedoo,
With favors for your own.
Refreshments frequently.
Get drunk on these with me.

It's not all fun and games.
Some speeches should be made,
Some highfalutin claims,
A screed, harangue, tirade.
You'll keep from being bored
By all the drink you've stored.

Why must a drinking bout
Accompany a fête
Such as my coming-out?
Because it may offset
The horrors of the sight
Of quenchless appetite.

Driving South in December

The migratory birds have gone
Ahead of them. They follow fast
On numbered highways close upon
Unperceived airways of the last.

The cold pursues them but the snow
Abandons them in Delaware
Thereafter all the way they go
The sky is clear and weather's fair.

The rising sun from off the sea
Shines on their left. Their lefts are gold.
This is the farthest south that he
Has wandered since my time of old.

Occasionally they traverse
Some trail or road I took before.
But seldom do they ask my course.
Such slights as this I can't ignore.

How can one's destination reach
Without advice? They seem to feel
Those migratory birds have each
Their own peculiar steering wheel.

Daniel Lyam Montross

Why Did I Go There?

Of all the places I have been,
It had enough to please:
The highest mountains I had seen,
The toweringest trees.

Was that enough to make me stop?
There's more some other place.
Yet there I had a surplus crop
Of extra breathing space.

Entity

Extreme, how often he thinks her but his fancy's
    figment
And grieves because he'll never know for sure.
O how terrible to feel she's only a segment
Of himself, who is so deeply insecure.

Little does he know she's just as daft as he is,
And catches herself disbelieving in him.
She thinks he's what a girl as silly as she is
Would fantasize, sweetly, on hysteric whim.

Faun and nymph sit in the wood so close together
They cannot see the forest for the trees,
Nor persons for their selves, and know not whether
Their vision is disorder or disease.

If it is true that one tree suffices to a woodland,
One person makes an entity, perhaps.
Therefore the burning question is: which one could
    stand
To let a vision of the other first collapse?

No Road

O my children the chagrin you felt when you got
    there
Or, rather, failed to get there in your car.
There never was a road for cars or anywhere
A way of ingress save for railroad car.
You had to leave the rented car there at Poplar,
And walk four miles to reach Lost Cove proper.

In Ought Six when first I found the Cove,
Leaving the Clinchfield train stalled in a grove,
The first few cars that people drove
Were on the market, but none would ever find
Access to that recess of humankind.

Getting There

Walking the trestle scared her.
High above the Toe River.
No handrail to hold to, and gaps
Between the ties. Oh! she gasped
And teetered, and he, holding, tottered.
The two swayed in the cold breeze.
Nights, blind, I used to skip along
This same trestle, and drunk to boot;
The river in its gorge roaring
As loud as I; nearly as liquid.
Care keeps us from dying.
Haste keeps us from caring.
The trestle is waiting, and daring.

On First Viewing the Place

The oblivescence came as no surprise.
This seasoned pair had learned not to expect.
And therefore they could not believe their eyes
On finding most of Love Cove still erect.

No house still stood with all its panes intact.
But still they stood. And <u>they</u> must stand and stare
Enrapturedly, and marvel at this fact:
The town exists without a person there.

If one could say a "town." It never had
A grocery store or such concessionaires
As drugstore, bar, cafe; and that is sad.
But twenty families called it theirs.

Now That We Are Here, Where Are We?

Close, Tennessee's east border,
Less than a mile in fact,
Or maybe even shorter,
I never paced it off.
A Yancey County quarter
Once but a water trough
In primitive disorder.

Steep, mountains are its warder,
Its solemn sentry mute.
Thick forests fast emborder
All corners of this glade,
Three-hundred-acre larder
Of air and sun and shade.
These elements transport her.

Rough path's a mean retarder,
A crooked climbing hike.
No access could be harder
To any town on earth.
And as the town's reporter,
I say for what it's worth:
It takes a perfect ardor.

Founding

Who cleared it? Some of it was clear
When Morgan Ailing came the year
Of eighteen forty, looking for
Some other place ulterior.
For years he'd been a mountaineer.
He knew he'd found the right place here.
But Indians had made a stop,
To fell the forest, plant a crop,
And call it home. This bothered him
Whenever he discovered grim
Reminders of their tenancy.
The land, his bride, could never be
A maiden lady any more.
Instead, she was, he thought, a whore.
And so he used her. All his sons,
Except the very youngest ones
(When twelve were born he lost his count),
Upon their father's whore would mount
And plant their seed. She took them each.
They stripped her far as they could reach.
Today her garments give the lie,
Reclaiming her virginity.

Housewarming

Touring, but hardly knowing which to choose,
They picked a house in fair repair to use.

It was a place that recent vandals spared,
The ancient Salter house of timbers squared.

The vandals must have brought along their girls,
Their rubbers left behind in twisted curls.

The walls were crudely crayoned with remarks
"Loretta sucks," and "Ethel's pussy barks."

Amused by all this evidence of sin,
Our couple warmed their house by joining in.

Post Coitum Triste

Charged hearts beat time in tune.
The quick caught breath unbends.
Light leaves the afternoon.
It cools these friends.

Such love of loving dulls,
As when a lengthy drought
Hits a small town and pulls
The people out.

The flesh dispeopled lies.
Before all else expire,
This emptied pair must rise
To light a fire.

II

First Sight

Young winter there was not as black or bleak
As in Vermont or in Connecticut.
The rhododendron, everywhere in glut
Of green, kept winter fresh week after week.

When I arrived, the first few folk I met
Were three young ladies washing clothing in
The waters of the creek. They were all wet
And cold, but customed to this discipline.

The youngest girl among this comely three,
A blue-eyed blonde, a charming specimen,
Was destined when she came of age to be
My love. I wish I'd known it even then.

Because if I had told her on the spot,
It would no doubt have overwhelmed her less
Than my mere coming did. I've n'er forgot
Her open-mouthed bedazzled bashfulness.

Instead of saying, as I did, "How are
Ya, gulls? How can I find the Ailing place?"
I should have said to her alone, "My star,
Your light has led me here; now let's embrace."

On Being a Furriner

A dark outlander rarely showed up there.
To be a stranger takes a certain style,
A mixture both of artlessness and guile,
Or else he's "fotched-on," native folk declare.

No move was made to make me feel apart
Nor welcome either. Like the weather, I
Was looked upon the way they scan the sky
To see what ill the elements would start.

They asked not what I did but what I could.
To be a stranger and a carpenter,
Gave them a choice of evils to prefer,
Unless their statements I misunderstood.

But Jotham Ailing left behind a will
Decreeing how he wished his coffin made.
If I my skimpy welcome overstayed,
They let a stranger show a useful skill.

Identity

By name and by byname the populace called
My presence among the close kin and the cohorts
    who keep tight breath,
As I walked through their midst in their hard blank
    gaze unenthralled,
Like some poor doomed convict marching to his
    death.

"The Yankee," first they called me when I came,
Or "Muntruss," they sounded the name of my clan,
Or then "MONTrust" or then "MintROST" their
    tongues would tease
my name.
Most just said "Him." Scarcely anyone knew me as
    "Dan."

Communication

Our difficulties sharply underline:
Their way of speech, or maybe it was mine.

I loved the lilt with which their voices sang.
Their ears were grated by my nasal twang.

My road as "rud," my four-syllable "cow"
Would make them snort and laugh, I don't see how.

"I wonder—" I would say in accents stiff,
Whereas those folks would sing, "I wonder me if."

"How are you?" was just "Hwarye?" on my tongue.
"Heigh-ho! God-proud to see ya!" they all sung.

My cow had "loo'ed"; a cow of theirs now "moo'ed."
But "Bossie" gave our tongues similitude.

The Curing

ONE

I "took down sick" the second week.
So early did I lose repute.
I lost my voice and couldn't speak
To boast I'd not been sick before.
What agony, that I was mute
And could not rail against death's door.
The nearest doctor miles away,
And no one cared to take me there.
If I had known that he was not
Their doctor anyhow, it may
Have eased my wretched mind a lot.
Days passed before they were aware
That I was sick. They seemed to think
Me idle. "Law," my hostess said,
"He don't git up to eat nor drink,
Jist lies the day long in that bed."
"A lazybones," her man replied,
"Molasses won't run down his laig."
I wonder if I would have died
Had not a neighbor lady found:
"I do believe he's got the plague."

TWO

Their ministrations failed to help.
I was beyond the reach of such
Poor remedies they dosed me with.

They shook their heads and spoke of "yarbs,"
Their medicine to me a myth.
"I reckon best we'd better fetch
Aunt Billie Ledyard right away."
They had the kindness to explain
That she could "doctor" me with "yarbs."
I was too weak to doubt them sane.
She came. Her face relieved my fears
A woman older than her years
But handsome nonetheless, and sage.
She plunged right in to treat my case.
There was no fever she could not assuage.
She said I'd live to ripe old age.

THREE

How right she was! I'll never know
Just what my diagnosis was.
She didn't say. Perhaps I had
Some malady indeed death-throe.
A dose of "yarbs" like magic does
The curing. Herbs she used on me
Were pennyroyal, creosote,
I think, and balm of Gilead,
And Jimson root and foxglove blue.
For days my head was kept abuzz.
My heart was kept ablaze because
She cared, and worked so hard for me,
This woman of good antidote.
All doctors should be given pause
By wondrous rural pharmacy.

The Outcast

Although Aunt Billie's herbs were welcome there,
I learned her husband wasn't on good terms
With any of the Lost Cove folks, who were
Displeased with what they thought his downright
    harms.

It seems he'd lighted up the woods to burn,
And not just once, though this was years before.
He'd only meant to clear off brush and fern
To graze his cattle on the forest floor.

The townsmen warned him twice to quit his ways.
But Carlisle Ledyard was a stubborn soul.
His third burn took off miles of trees for days.
They'd not forgive such lack of self-control.

Befriending. Brief Ending.

If they put Carlisle Ledyard on the shelf,
I stood in threat of banishment myself.

There's hidden meaning in the woods above:
The thing we both alike most lacked was love.

Reluctance was a sin I'd overcome,
To be his friend despite opprobrium.

But when I greeted him, he was, I fear,
Beyond the reach of sympathy or cheer.

Prospective friends to outcasts, do beware:
My good intentions led me to despair.

III

Relative

Both "towns" where they had lived before
Were swallowed up by wood.
A change it was, to have a door
In open neighborhood.

And yet these distances seclude
With loneliness diverse.
They wondered if such solitude
Was better or was worse.

Getting a Good Fire Going

Fires soon took much light toil from them, to find
A way to start them that they hadn't tried.
Pathetic, how indoors his woodsman's mind
Built bad-draught fires which sputtered, ebbed, and
    died.

Too long to learn to leave the fire alone:
Not to observe it closely while it's weak.
All hill folk know facts which were unbeknown
To them, who'd not give me a chance to speak.

We "Other-Sides" do not believe in ghosts,
But Flossie Salter "'peared" to them, and they,
Hearing her cry, who had become their hostess,
"A watched far won't burn!", turned their eyes away.

Additional Gratuitous Advice
from Mrs. Flossie Fay Salter
on Their Use of Her Hearth

Don't let the far burn out, by night
Or day! A far once lit keep bright
As long as you'ns intend to stay!
Bad luck, bad luck, to leave it lay
Untended! Shun the wood of peach
And sassafras! The fars of each
Could cause yore mothers both to die!
And Satan on the roof to lie!
If yore lit kindlin pops and cracks,
It means a snow will bear yore tracks!
And if the far should fry and sing,
You'll find yoreselfs a-quarrelling!

Cutting Her Water Off

Old Flossie ranted on.
The boy got up and fled.
Her Flossie turned to, "Hon,
Incline to me yore head:

"A private word to heed:
If monthly you require
Some rags for when you bleed,
Don't throw them in my far!

"It's turrible bad luck!"
The girl replied, "Don't fear.
I won't be monthly struck
As long as I am here."

The Ghost's Outrage

She'd been a Baptist, Primitive,
The hideboundedest kind who live.
(Although to say she's still "alive,"
Puts glosses on how souls survive.)
The way our couple misbehave
Has brought her running from the grave.
(If such a thing you can't conceive,
Then you, like they, must make believe.)
As doleful as a mourning dove,
She watched them make their frantic love.
(At all events, I think them brave
To choose a spot where ghosts might rave.)
Alas, if only he'd connive
At showing her he meant to wive.
(Do dead folk have much thought to give
On marriage as imperative?)

Two Reasons

Yes, I will grant it's rather odd
They'd met no ghosts in places past.
And Flossie, yes, is such a clod,
She leaves one numb if not aghast.

My theory is no jest or taunt
But uncontested fact, I vow:
A ghost desires a house to haunt,
And they'd not had a house till now.

Let's lift away the other gauze:
Your flying saucer seems a "ghost."
You "see" it. Is this not because
You see it when you need it most?

Strategy

O they had need of her!
To teach them country ways,
The use of juniper,
The meaning of the days.

As sharp-eyed as a hawk,
She was nobody's fool.
And when she spoke she'd talk
The hind leg off a mule.

Her meddling and her chat
Soon drove them up the walls.
They wished sometimes she'd scat,
At least when nighttime falls.

They found a plan unique,
So strange it made me laugh:
They asked that "I" should "speak"
To her on their behalf.

The Exorcism

"Flossie," I began, "it's me, Dan Montross, here.
I'd like a word or two with you, I beg."
"Eye Gawd a mighty! Dan! Pull up a cheer!"
Who'd think a ghost would hop on just one leg?

"How are ye, Floss? How's ever little thing?"
"Jist fine, jist fine," she said, but then she frowned.
"Exceptin <u>they</u> is always underwing,
And make it hard for me to git around."

She carried on: "Is this some kind of joke,
That they are livin here? It aint got rhyme
Nor reason! No, it's <u>my</u> own house!" I spoke:
"<u>It is your house, but it is not your time.</u>"

Then she was sad. "But tell you what," I said,
"It's Christmastime, almost; then you and I
Can visit here and share their board and bread."
She smiled, and bade the pair a fond goodbye.

Christmas Coming

He tried to get her to agree:
No presents by their Christmas tree.
Or else no presents bought with cash.
A festoon, garland, homemade crèche
Would do to brighten things a bit.
No spending for his benefit.
Some holly on the mantel shelf;
He'd go and pick the greens himself,
And bag a turkey with his sling.
But please, don't <u>buy</u> him anything.
She wouldn't buy this argument,
And all the way to Burnsville went
To shop the stores for him and her.
O gold! and frankincense! and myrrh!

To give is like to thieve, he thought,
Regarding all the things she'd bought.
The giving to the got transfers:
Her lavish presents make him hers.
And yet, he thought, by getting such,
What you get free may cost too much.

Mistletoe

Up overhead an oak where mistletoe was swishing.
He thought that finding it right in their yard was
    refreshing.
He climbed high up and got some of it; everything
    was meshing
To make of their Christmas a joyous and sightly show.

But nervously he understood that it was not just for
    kissing.
From such, the science of botany is missing.
On some dark cold Yule night when the fireplace was
    hot and hissing,
He'd lecture to her on the parasitic mistletoe.

IV

Hospitiful

My permanence showed through everyone's grin:
I was a stranger, and they "took me in."
And when Yuletide came and I was still their stranger,
A wonder that I wasn't made to sleep in a manger.

Presents. Presence.

The Day, the "younguns" think, to gift
Is on December twenty-fifth.
The oldsters feel that they should mix
The day of January six.
Although I cater to tradition,
I liked the young ones' definition.
And so I worked with that in mind.

That Day the children rose to find
Someone had come and left behind
Assorted wooden toys and things:
Doll houses, Shoo-Fly rockers, swings.
The younguns cheered; the oldsters stood smirking
Because they guessed who did this woodworking.

Virtue

Christlike, the carpenter who scatters his gifts,
Stays out all night walking in high snow drifts,
Hopes to ingratiate himself to his neighbors,
This point of such handsome Christlikeness belabors.

Enters

Now my Magdalene drags in with feet bare and
    palms which are
      clammy,
And stage-center stands with a look that would melt
    any heart,
A girl-child of twelve, the Ledyard's "leastun," named
    Ammey,
The one I had overlooked, distributing my art.

Had the Ledyard place been too far for me to walk
    on that mission?
True, he, when I'd sought his friendship, sent me
    away.
Was that it? Or was it a matter of precognition:
I knew already she'd become my Magadalene some
    day?

You Can't See Me, but I'm on My Knees

Forgive me, Ammey, had I known
That you were not already grown

But still a child despite your size,
I'd quickly go apologize.

What penance or amends could right
The wrongness of my oversight?

The giver was "unknown," you see.
Acknowledge anonymity?

So here, to cancel out my debts,
I send anonymous regrets.

Unverminous

If thus far I have given a whitewashed picture
Of Lost Cove folk, and not revealed the squalor,
It hasn't been from blindness or from stricture.
Like them, I disregard the almighty dollar.

There was no money there but stuff to barter,
And precious little stuff for even that.
The typical inhabitant was martyr
To poverty that wouldn't keep a rat.

To bear his miseries would take an Atlas.
Why bother throwing out the trash and litter
Except into the yard? He was not bitter
He had the solacement of being ratless.

Synopsis so Far

I drifted in like mistletoe:
Birds shit the seeds where'er they go.

A stranger, like a wolf, laments
The natives' false indifference.

I saw Death's face when I was sick.
My fever was the candlestick.

When well, if gratitude allows,
Befriend your nurse but not her spouse.

Some wood and labor sacrificed
At Christmas make you feel like Christ.

My gifts were hooks I wetly dipped.
The fish I prized the most I skipped.

V

A Ballit of Amenities

Old Flossie'd been their hostess, and now that she
  had left,
They felt relieved at evening, but mornings felt bereft.

Too lightly they had taken the wisdom of her years.
Too bad she comes so quickly, then disappears.

"In retrospect, I miss it," the girl would sigh anew.
"It <u>was</u> a thrill, her watching, when we lay down to
  screw."

Their fireplace has been mentioned, their other things
  have not.
There's more to daily living than keeping bodies hot.

The Salter house was cozy, because it was so small:
Two bedrooms, kitchen, parlor, four rooms in all.

The furniture they'd gathered, by "borrowing" around
From other empty houses, whatever still was sound.

They slept upon a mattress they'd found some other
  place.
'Twas filled with downy feathers, if not enough air
  space.

Few trips to town they'd taken, to stock up on
    supplies,
For "perishables" only; nothing else dies.

And then they'd finished shopping, returned to home,
    and O!
The thick wet flakes cascaded, and bound them in
    with snow.

A week he spent in chopping, to gather all their
    wood;
The seventh day he rested, and saw that it was good.

Content they spent their winter, no creature comforts
    missed,
Except perhaps a bathroom, and such did not exist.

There was a two-hole privy, they called their "country
    seat."
They often went together, to pool their body heat.

I smile to see them sitting, as I did years ago.
They share their isolation, their privity, their glow.

Problem

Of creature comforts I was quick to speak.
I meant those of the body, not the mind.
He had a healthy, excellent physique,
But felt that circumstance was so unkind.

Nightly or daily they engaged in sex,
As any two such people are like to do.
As like as not it left them nervous wrecks
For having their cake and eating it too.

On his part complication took a wry turn:
He had the strength to make great effort, but
He seldom lasted long enough for her.
This is the paradox, the unkind cut:
Release is what exertions finally earn.
He used all his exertions to defer.

Elements

From the woods came the spring, its waters erupting
    a fountain
Which coursed to a pool almost right beside their
    door.
They lived on the northern slope of Flat Top
    Mountain,
Altitude, 4,954.

The rarefied Air and the clear pure cold Water
Were the two basic elements most dear to know.
The Fire is only the Air's sultry daughter,
And Earth's all covered by Water's grandson, Snow.

Water and Air are the innate symbiotic pairing.
Like their lichen, whose pair uses a little of both.
As the atmosphere purifies by giving the Water an
    Airing,
Water gives Air its clouds, its mists, its vapors: its
    growth.

Daniel Lyam Montross

The Mistletoe Revisited Yet Again

But that's so much poetry. And the metaphor's ailing.
The lichen is outmoded, shopworn and bare.
One night when they'd finished their Christmas
    wassailing,
He plucked some old mistletoe out of her hair.

"Behold!" he exclaimed as if finding a spider,
And drunkenly started to lecture on how
An innocent tree gets this sponger inside her,
This free-loading guest who will drop in for chow.

This hanger-on may or may not be malignant.
So why is it license for lovers to kiss?
And "mistletoe's" origin leaves one indignant:
It comes from the Latin word meaning "to piss."

Turning It Around

She said, "I think a tree at least
Has some identity Its own,
And doesn't mind if that's increased
When spongers come and settle down.

"You're not a sponger anyway.
It's false, the way that you compare.
Reverse your precious figures, Day,
And see which selves we really are.

"The tree is you, the sponger I.
Your various selves are mighty boughs
To bear my slight identity.
The sponger has no earthly house."

The Wind, the Wind

Often they hear the wind
Howl, howl around the eaves
And 'twixt their timbers pierce.
Thinly and pregnably skinned,
They shiver in their sleeves
And listen long to hear
Horn, flute, pipe: winds so fierce.

Their house the instrument
Weather rehearses upon.
The fipples are the cracks
That all the timbers vent.
Windows with panes near gone
Become the vibrant reeds
The wintry blast attacks,
Like some bewailing prayer
That wheedles 'round their heads.
In the Sanskrit, nirvā: "blow."
Thus, a Nirvana's where
One's blown away from care.
This music wafts them off
Free, free in the whistling air.

What Do You Give a Ghost for Christmas?

Look now: in January he's using stuff
She gave him at Christmas, more than enough
To while hours of time when weather is rough.
—In the corner there Flossie sits dipping her snuff.

She gave him a fiddle, that is, violin,
Because I had said that a fiddler I'd been.
His terrible practicing makes such a din
—That poor Flossie is needing some aspirin.

And while he's preparing for his first concert,
He's casually wearing a fifty-dollar shirt
Of French velour, quite plush, the color is vert.
—And there's Flossie repining in homespun old skirt.

His cheeks are a-tingle with fragrant cologne,
Some after-shave lotion that playboys have known
On special occasions when oats are to be sown.
—And is Flossie's aroma entirely her own?

But the gift he most prizes is his girlfriend's dearness.
More treasured than gifts is the fact of her nearness.
And Flossie's content with what seems such a
    queerness:
—That the gift which they gave her was only her
    <u>hereness</u>.

Calendar: January

Now in this spare month they become
Surveyors of their journey. Months
Have passed since first they started out.
Eventually the venturesome
Have miles of days to gad about.

In our peculiar minds, the year
Is like a landscape, and our days
A journey through geography.
Into December, peaks uprear
On Calendar's topography.

But January's all plateau.
They stand and look behind them, down
Upon the slopes they steeply scaled:
A rugged trail where gaps still show,
A path less traveled than travailed.

Ahead of them the view's obscure,
The valley's hung with fog and mist.
And yet it leaves them unafraid.
They're comforted by being sure
That all the path is slow downgrade.

Idyll

Days are becoming longer but are still all too
    suddenly short.
The full night drops in before supper; they eat in half-
    dark,
And then have long hours to pass in some new game
    or sport.
My poetry's not enough to entertain them much, they
    remark.

I suggest that they put to use one of Flossie's oldest
    skills:
I remember how in the old days, hour upon evening
    hour,
She kept the children spellbound and breathless with
    scary tales:
Of spooks and ha'nts and specters white as flour.

It's marvelous enough that this young pair has had
    such travels,
Their idylls, treks and outings, north and south.
But how wondrous: they can listen as a long tale
    unravels,
A ghost story which comes right out of the horse's
    mouth.

Warming Up

Night after unearthly night,
She runs her repertoire:
The Cemetery War,
The Feud of Ancient Dead,
And How the Spirits Fight;
The Skeleton in Tree,
The Pool of Flaming Hair,
And Shades of Yesternight;
The Dog Without a Head,
The Spectral Jamboree,
And The Spotted Booger Mare,
The Critters of the Wild;
The Crying Baby Born
To Feebleminded Child;
The Succubus in Corn
Who Primes the Virgin Lad,
And What the Hermit Said,
And Many, Many More.
Each night, until their bed,
She told them all she knew.
And then she winked at me
(I think she winked, but he
Didn't notice). Anyway:
"Now listen, younguns, while
I git this tale acrost!
A tellin-story old,
The Tale of Dan Montrost."

The Ghost's Song
and Other Poems

I

Contents

"Sticks-out-of-sack!" she intoned, her incantation
Beginning each new sequence.
They thought such conjuration some witchery, but it
    was only
A self-charm, a private joke.

These magic wands,
Sticks in a sack, knapsack
I'd packed around with me,
Just to have something to fill it.

Selected Poems

Contents
(cont.)

Her knuckle-knobbed hands snapped the first stick.
Their ears if not their eyes perceived it.
Or was it just the crackling fire?
Dry, its pop splintered into kindling.

Now that stick, she commenced, were the carpinter.
And pinter! pinter! pinter! faded down the hall.
No use much fer carpinters hereabouts.
Sawyers, maybe. There wudn't nary bitty need
Fer a carpinter.
Is how come I bustid that'un.
Then she fetched from the sack a second.

Still-Hunt

This'un hyur now, she said of the second stick,
    this'un's
His rifle-gun. Crackerjack stick-out-of-sack!
Swear to Josh-way, he could crimp the tail of a
    razorback
At a hunurd yard or more!
Or shoot at a target from a hunurd feet
Six times and not leave but one hole!
How he kept body'n soul on speakin tarms them
    winter months
Was huntin was this hyur gun, fer squar'l and bar
And other beastes. Come time in the sprang
Fer the shootin-match, shootin fer the beef,
Couldn't nobody best him 'ceptin Walt Ailing.
And me, I 'spect Dan jist 'lowed Walter top shot
Fer a politeness
Because he was still The Stranger.
Dan's ways with a shootin-arn was what got
Him mixed up with the blockaders.
I won't break this stick yet, no.
But bye and bye I'm gonna.

Still-Fire

Third stick's a puny stave, aint it?
Fit for nought but burnin,
So I'll chunk it in the far.
Burns puny too, don't it?
That'un stands fer the far what lit the still,
The still fer bilin corn,
Fer cookin up the blockade brew,
The roastin-ear wine, ole mountain dew.
That's what Dan got into,
Shining the moon.
The moon on the hemlock screen
Where the still is hid,
And Dan all night on his knees,
Pokin sticks under the biler,
Keeping the far jist rat,
Jist rat.

Still-Life with Stallion

Call this stick, the fourth'un, a hitchin-post.
A sourwood saplin he ties his horse to.
Oh yessiree, he's got him a horse now.
A stallion black as a crow,
He swapped Mack Ailing twenty gallon for,
Out of his first big run of high wines.
Hear the stallion whinny?
He aint restless, nor hongry.
He jist caint tolerate the smell
Of the sour mash swill, the still-slop.
Cows'n pigs jist plumb crave the stuff
But horses do despise it.
Dan don't know this yet.
"Henry," says he (fer that's the name he give it),
"What's ailin you, anyhow?"
The stallion's nostrils quiver.

Strains in the Stillness

Two sticks she fetched together from the sack
And scraped one upon another beneath her chin,
Rolly trudum, trudum, trudum, rolly day!
She sang, stamping her foot.
Rang tang a-whaddle linky day!
Fifth stick and sixth'un, one'n'other,
Make up his fiddle and his bow.
Swapped a gallon to Philo English fer'em.
Sattidy nights he listens to them old-timey fiddlers
And watches their fingers, till he knows by heart
The tunes and timin and fingerin.
Th'other six nights of the week,
Alone at his watch at the still,
Keepin the far, he learns him his fiddle.
Folks tease him about it.
Say he'll give hisself away.

Stills in the Stereoscope

He give hisself away, he did. I mean that more ways
    than one.
The seventh stick she held out from her nose, like so,
And said, This hyur contraption, this thingumajig
    sortathing,
Fergit what he called it, a "Stars-Cup" or somethin.
Anyhow, see, you stick these double photygraphs in
    hyur,
And then you look through hyur, and it's real as day!
Makes you think you could walk rat through the
    pitcher!
Dan swapped a travelin pedlar half a gallon fer it.
And then he took it 'round, and showed us all
Faraway places, some other places, palaces and
    wondrous cities;
Didn't nobody even guess there ever was such places.
But now, younguns, stick yore eyes to this thing and
    I'll show ye
Pitchers that wasn't faraway but rat hyur at home.

Distilling the Sticky Installment

Now with that magic viewer,
Showing in three dimensions
Five more sticks, all but the last:
See them fellers in their khaki shirts
A-sneakin up the hill? Them's gov'ment men.
Long arm of the law.
Our eighth stick hyur's a long one, that long arm
Comin to raid Dan's still and git him.
But his horse warned him, and he lit out
Ahead of the law. I hid him.
Me, Flossie Fay Salter, I'm the ninth stick
Tall, thin and ugly stick.
In yan barn I hid him and his horse
Nigh on to two weeks afore the law cooled down.
Now look at this hyur pitcher:
That's my eldest darter, Frankie
A-fetchin Dan his vittles to the barn.
He got to teasin her and callin her
His "lick-wish stick." She's the tenth stick,
Tart as lickwish maybe, not as black.
See this next pitcher, the eleventh stick:
The cob pipe stuck in Swinn Brashear's mouth.
Never saw him without it. Years later,
Atter Frankie wedded up with him, she used to tell
As how he often wore his pipe to bed.
But Swinn, he was a goodern, and come to be
Dan's bestest friend, him who nearly stole his gal,
His Frankie, <u>my</u> Frankie.
They fought, Dan and Swinn. Dan won the fight,

But Swinn won Frankie anyway.
Twelfth stick was Dan's motto, learned it from
This fat man in this pitcher, our Pressy-dunt:
"Speak softly and carry a big stick."
There's not but one stick left.

Epistle to the Pestle

Some say thirteen is unlucky, and maybe it is,
Maybe it is. 'Pends on which way you like
Your luck to run. Thirteenth stick, last stick,
Thick stick, stout stalk of a stick.
Aint gon tell y'uns what it is, no.
Couldn't breathe it to save my soul.
But riddle ye, riddle ye: What would be
A man's, Dan's, mostest master stick?
To give him half of all his trouble
And half, leastways, of all his pleasure.
Now the bag is empty.

Still More

The magic sack had ejaculated
All its sticks, standing
For several years of my living
Until I was almost thirty,
And courted a girl named Frankie,
Not yet even knowing of Ammey
Except as a child still growing
Whom I greeted sometimes in passing
With a smile because she was pretty
But never got a word in return.
Who can say of any five years of his living
That the total images of his memories
Are any sharper than these sticks?

Yet she knew she'd left them bewildered
And casting screwed glances at one another
And wondering if she was touched in her telling
Or if they were touched in their believing.
So she said, Allrighty, you scoffers,
I'll dump all the sticks in a mixing,
And one of y'uns shet yore eyelids
And pick a stick at random,
And I'll take it as my text.

Girl, Still, on a Pedestal

Then Day, he shut his eyes, and groped to pick a stick
And Flossie cried, Eh, law! You got his bow, the sixth.
Caint fiddle with jist a bow, so leave it lay aside
And let yan other fiddlers play while Dan
Turns from the barn-stage to scan the crowd
And sees, knees wrapped 'round a stanchion, the girl,
The Ledyard's leastun, listening, but her eyes on Dan.

Forestalling

Knees shapely as geese,
Arms dangling their form,
Whole hanks of blonde hair outreaching,
Blue eyes of a size amazing,
Lips, lobes, bare toes,
Swells of a stung long hanging
Twined with herself,
Lone and drawn in upon herself
Only her eyes let outward
Where he could catch them
And take them as signals
For her hidden hands
Which he sought and found.

Still in the Sticks

I'll dance with you, my lady, Dan bowed before her.
Her curtsey was the step she took to flee.
She tripped, and headlong nearly fell, into his arms,
Who caught her up and laughing drew her
Out among the other dancers, who stopped
And watched, who tried, but couldn't
Remember the name of this humble girl.

II

Their Dance

The moonshine on his breath
Soon shared with her his fever
As if a whiff of death
Would chill but wouldn't grieve her.

They spun until the moon
Had dropped far out of sight,
The other dancers strewn
To homeward by starlight.

His arm around her waist
Would try to pull her nearer.
She shied before such haste
And wouldn't let him steer her.

But he was all she had
In all this world of harm,
And so she felt right glad
To hang upon his arm.

Fade-Out

He waltzed her home that e'en.
This thirty-year-old soak
With a girl just past sixteen,
Who never spoke.

Her mouth he tried to kiss
While she was unaware,
But dark caused him to miss
And get her hair.

He reached to find her face
But touched the empty air.
She'd slipped some other place
He found not where.

Bale and Woe

He has known this inevitable lonesome home-
     walking,
With only the wry face of the moon his fellow-
     traveler,
Between trees that say, We are anchored
And don't have to move with you in your homing
Nor swing our limbs to keep our balance.
Our drunkenness, the sap we suck, is extracted
Out of the same soil that holds our roots so firmly
And keeps us, unlike you, from awkwardly staggering.
Your sway is ours, your sweat is ours, your swearing
Is not unlike the soughing of our boughs
But your lament is of the girl who sends you
     homeward
While ours is of this race of men we share the earth
     with
Who walk between us without our sense of staying.

Double Take

He cursed the trees and stopped his walk, to curse.
They wrung their limbs in mock-fright at his oaths.
But one of them, among their lowest growths,
Mocked not, but beckoned, and that was worse.

Was she a tree? Or was this tree a her?
A sapling shrub, or second-growing brush,
In silhouette against the moon's cold hush,
As thin as any tree, but lithesomer.

Her limbs outstretched. And all her fingers splayed.
He couldn't help but rush toward that embrace
And soon perceive that this tree had a face
Whose lines were Ammey's, but were Ammey
    unafraid.

The Return

Why had she changed her mind?
Or had her mind changed her?
She still wouldn't speak, and he
Was too far past cheer to care.

They went back arm-in-arm
Along this trail he'd solo'd,
Back-tracking footprints of his
She'd steadfastly followed.

Until her house they reached,
Dark, and no one up,
And no one caring where
She took him, or let herself
Be taken. Yard, barn, shed, tree,
Any place would be her lair.

Words

Attempt at talk. Social preliminaries.
One last futile essay on behalf of humans
Who talk before or even in the process,
Who feel to pay these words for admission
Like gentling a cow while milking.
O hear me! O reply to my soothings.

She kissed him quick to close his rambling
And held him close to ramble his quickness
And quicked her clothes to kiss his ramble,
Give him a word! Any word! O wordless word!

Venue (Vulgar)

Pestle trying clumsily to find her vale…velvet…
Vault is the word, as pestle names his virile verge,
Which vibrated voraciously in search of home.
He had no view, in this light of Vesper,
But only feel, in these ventral places.
My verse deserts me in this wanting version.

Her parts were vague, and in his vertigo,
His pestle slipped away from her vestal vault,
Unto her void, that variant vent,
Some other place. The wrong place.

III

Audience

Diana whispered to Day,
Oh, see, that's my grandmother.
O see her! Just sixteen,
Loving our Dan at last,
Even if with the wrong place.
Day said, I see her. Now I
Want to <u>hear</u> her. She hasn't
Spoken a word, not one.

Negative

She was not mute. For a fact,
Beautiful was her tongue
Whenever she chose to speak.
But now there was only one
Word which she needed use
For all my questions: Does it
Hurt? Should I stop? Is this
Too fast? Or far? Do you
Not mind this kind of way?
To all these, her tongue behind
Her upper teeth, said, No.

Thought versus Sense

I studied for a while the strange new impressions.
Type of erotic meeting I'd never attempted.
Took me a while, took more than a taking,
To sort out the feelings, distinguish the differences:
Squirmings and nips
And interior squeezings.
Strokings unlike a vale can do.
But then I quit studying,
And that was the greatest difference:
That my study dissolved into feeling.
I was pure feeling only.

Emulation

Bright embers, in their fire,
Which make no crackling sound,
No sound at all but wind.
In silence look around,
Stare now at their desire,
They did. And now they grinned.

Their eyes eyed each other then.
No benefit of speech.
O they have copied me
Often enough, and each
Has often wanted to be
Myself, or <u>her</u>, again.

Even in this. Yes, <u>this</u>.
They sought to probe what proving
Or prove what probing could
Copy us, mime our coupling.
They sealed it with a kiss,
Rose, and joined hands.

The Summons

They went and hid
(Or thought they did)
From Flossie, so
She wouldn't see.

She waited long
Until they finished.
Anything wrong
Must take its time.

When they were done
And reappeared
She said, I'd feared
Y'uns'd plumb gone.

But now yo're here,
We've got a chore,
A small affair
These times require.

So Day must play
His fiddle. You

Must dance your dance.
I'll sing my song.

We three. And Dan.
Dan will call his story.
We'll hear him call,
But we'll be busy:

You in your dance.
Day on his strings.
Me with my voice.
To Dan's tune and tale.

IV

The Ghost's Song

ONE. THE OPENING

> Lo lee lo-oh, lo lee oh!
> Hearken to my sad, sad story.
> Lo oh lee-oh, lee oh lee lo!
> Of a love, and a brief glory.
> Oh lee oh, lo lee-oh, lee lo lee-oh lo!
> Of a girl of joy, who was the village
>   hoor.
> And the man she loved, a drunkard
>   sure.
> Lee lo, oh lo lee-oh, lo lee oh!

Ring of flesh, muscle-ring:
With this ring I thee wed,
To take me in and keep me
Even when I am limp,
To draw me, to pull me,
Swell me like a summer squash.
Ring a round a rosey.
She loves me like a locket.
Locked in liquored lacking,
Mired in more mere merriment,
I didn't know,
I didn't know she had a price.

Her father's notion,
Sad father, poor father,
Shiftless wretched son of a bitch,
Son of a bastard too.
Nobody had money.
But there was barter.

> I'm a human omen, Ammey,
> Aim at home and hominy,
> Ham omelets, ample amenities,
> Harmony and empathy,
> Images impossible.

> The first time you asked me
> For a gallon of my rakings of the hills,
> I thought you wanted it
> All for yourself
> And thought you were too young.

Now "nay" means no or neigh not nigh.
He who knows how to hoe the hay when high
Can keep his cap and cup caped in a coop,
But a dope who'll dip to such a depth is but a dupe.

> Amen. O Ammey, my Omega,
> Omphalos of my homing,
> Amaze me with your amber hair,
> Embarrass me among your emblems,
> Amuse me with your ample
>   impishness,
> Embower me in your ring's embrace.

Daniel Lyam Montross

But don't ask me for barter.

I think the old bastard
Had taught her himself,
Had told her,
That this way was safest,
Would keep her from bigging.
And keep them from begging.
Keep him in liquor,
Keep them in food.
Keep her incapable
Of bearing a child.

   I drank more than he did.
   Only once, by accident,
   I sobered up enough to learn
   Lost Cove was laughing at me.
   Too late.
   I was in love.

TWO. THERE AND HERE

   Oh lee lo-oh, lo lee oh!
   Oh see the pore thing, a-settin
   All by herself in yan meader,
   A-pluckin daisy petals, one by one,
   Lo oh lee-oh, lo lee-oh, lee lo lee oh!

He loves me,
He don't.
He'll have me,
He won't.
He would if he could,
But he can't.

> He said for me
> To run away
> With him and go
> Some other place.
> It scares me so
> To think of it,
> Of what's beyond
> These mountains, where
> No one is kin
> Nor blood of mine.

What's left of my life
Is here at home,
Is all I've known, or can.
This place is me.
I am this place.
Is what I had to say to Dan.
If my father says,
Go milk the cow,
It's all the same to me as when he says,
Go milk them men.
We do what we're told, to live.

But oh, there is a me
That's only his.
And he knows it.
The other of me
That opens for him.
More than one opening.

He knows a word he calls it.
It, he says. It's what he calls it
My heart I called it, or my soul.
A me that nobody's ever known.
I am Ammey. Am me. I am
Me alone.

Oh, to them other fellers
And their quick-shootin pestles,
I'm just a hole
Where they poke and squirt,
And pay, a chunk of pork,
A plucked chicken, or a turn of meal,
A bushel of corn, leastways,
Or at least a peck.
Ass, they call it,
Gettin all slaunch-eyed and drooling,
Up your sweet asshole honey-babe!
They don't last long, a minute.
A bushel of corn for a minute.

> But they are there,
> And him, he's here.
> In love of him I smile
> From ear to ear.
> He knows my heart,
> That names it It
> And seeks to find
> Its deepest part.
> I know his too.
> We tell, we share
> The thoughts we bear
> Until no wall
> Is left between.

He loves me,
He don't.
He'll have me,
He won't.
He would if he could,
But he can't.

THREE. THE ARRANGEMENT

> Lo oh lee-oh, lee oh lo lee!
> O many a year went by, went by,
> And many a day, lo lee oh!
> The drunkard he drank and didn't try.
> Oh lo oh lo oh lo oh lo oh lo lee-oh!
> He lost his gal to another man
> And she was sad it wasn't Dan.
> Oh Jesus Christ lo lee-oh!

Walt Ailing.
His wife died on him.
Worked to death, more than likely.
So he bargained with Carlisle Ledyard:
Corn and more corn, in perpetuity:
Get that girl off her ass:
Take her into my house:
Take her away from that drunkard:
Make her my second wife-woman, sort of:
Keep you in all the corn you need,
Fair deal?
And Carlisle Ledyard dealt her.
She cried.

> I held her.
> Rage held me.
> God help me.
> There's no God.
> Please, Ammey,
> Go with me,
> Is that worse
> Than living
> With Ailing?
> She said no.
> But going
> Is much worse
> Than staying.

She lived with him. But stayed by me. An odd policy.
Wedded we were, as much as man and wife. I was
  glad that
Ailing took her off the "streets." (There were no streets
Except those in her father's mind.) She was a wife
  now,
Not a whore. Though neither mine. Six children by
  him,
By his first wife, became hers. Were her hard labor.
He wouldn't give her one of her own. Even if he
  could.

> On hunts the squirrels mock me:
> Who are you? Stump? Stump?
> Not a stump? What the deuce!
> Lawk! the cuckold! Lawk the drunk!
> Run, run, run! Lawk, the booger-man!

He'd been a "customer," was how he knew of her.
And now he liked to take his pleasure whene'er he
  liked.
She didn't mind. He was just one. There were no
  more.
Except the one who was not one of them, but me.
I stayed her love. I kept that part of her
That Walt Ailing never knew. He never knew.
Until the end.

Ammey Ammey Ammey
My nice, my neat, my neither.
Oh me, oh my, Ammey,
There is no other, either.

FOUR. THE BIRTHING

Lo lee lee lee! Lee lo lee-oh lo!
That gal she bigged and bore,
Or tried to bear, you see.
Lo lee-oh, oh lo lee-oh lee!
Her own dear mother was midwife,
But her man was gone, and her love was
    drunk,
And she died to birth that girl-child.
Lo lee-oh lo-oh, oh lo, boo hoo boo hoo.

She tried to keep it hid from him. That swelling belly,
    beltless.
She told him she was only getting fat. He believed
    her.
Only her mother knew, and me. Her mother, the
    "yarb doctor,"
Aunt Billie, was called, to bring strong doses of hot
    pepper tea
To "fetch on the child-thing." And before the night
    was over,
Aunt Billie had used every herb she ever tried.
Nothing worked. (The village wags later said the pore
    creeter
Must've been tryin to git out the back way.)
Somebody came and told me, and I sobered up on
    black coffee
And rode ole Henry twenty miles at a hard gallop
To fetch a real doctor, and bring him back.

          He saved the baby,
          But not the mother.
          She lived just long enough
          To see it, and to name it
          Annette, or Annie.

I lived for months, drunk, beside her grave.
And then I sobered up, for good.

FIVE. THE DUEL

> Lo lee to-oh, lo lee oh!
> A year went by, and another year,
> While Walt got worse and worser,
> His grudge it festered in his heart
> Until he knew that Dan must die.
> Lo! Lee! Lo! Oh! Oh! Lo! Lee-oh!

He kept telling his friends it wasn't his fault.
He never lost a chance to tell anybody who'd listen
That he'd never been inside of Ammey's vault,
That in fact he'd not even known she had one.
Oh, he got himself a third "wife-woman," easy
    enough.
But he went on brooding. And giving me hard looks.
And he and his new wife-woman both mistreated the
    baby.

> In time it came to this:
> Get lost, or ready to die.
> All the Ailings backed him.
> He wouldn't take me on
> In a fight, man for man.
> But he still thought
> He could outshoot me.

I spent an hour at Ammey's grave before giving him
   "satisfaction."
And then I met him on the Clinchfield railroad tracks
On a straight stretch: the distance was three hundred
   yards.
Yes, we agreed on it: the distance had to be three
   hundred yards.
It takes a terrible keen eye just to see anything that
   far.
Swinn Brashear stood halfway and waved his red
   handkerchief.

> My first shot missed him.
> First time I'd ever missed.
> But his first shot missed.
> Whistled past my ear.
> His second shot missed too.
> Went through my shirt sleeve.
> I cried for Ammey and I aimed
> And hit him in his heart.

Old Woman's Last Words

To want to git some other place.
I know that wish.
Hit was lately Feb'wary, and winter done gone.
I ast'em, When d'you'uns reckon you'll be lightin out?
They'd a heap sight git a soon start, they tole.
I 'member me right well their last and final night:
Me tellin the last of the tale:
How Dan, after he kilt Walt with his rifle-gun,
Stole that girl-baby Annie and lit a rag
Fer some other mountains, some other place.
Didn't nobody never lay eyes on 'em again.
Then that gal, Diana, she called to me in despair,
I can't find Day! He's lost! Or gone! Or hiding!
Or maybe, says I, he wudn't never here to begin with
    anyhow.
Which sot her to cryin powerful miserable.
And so I said, Shush, chile, I was jist a-twittin ye.
Come, says I, I'll holp ye to fine him.
We looked and we looked, high and low, all over.
But I found him way out a-settin under a sourwood
    tree.
Jist settin thar kindly wishful-like.
We called him to home for their last night.
He said he'd jist been thinkin on how he'd done
Jist as good a job of tellin Dan's story
Back in the place they were before they come here.
Diana said, You did. I apologize, Day,
For thinking that these poems could do it better.
Dan's wrong. Maybe nobody can tell his story,

Least of all himself.
And then, afore they went to bed, I tole as how
I'd not see 'em, come day-bust, so we'd best say our
    goodbyes.
I tole as how I'd had a right smart of enjoyment.
They said the same.
Don't brood on Dan, says I. We didn't used to know
    nothin
Up hyur in these mountains…except that we was a-
    livin.
We warn't a town, jist a place, godforsaken.
Dan made us a town, for a little while.
And now, younguns, goodnight and far thee weel.
    Live long.
When they went to bed, I took Dan's second stick,
His rifle-gun, and broke it, chunked in the far.
All his sticks I chunked into the far.
Their last far, that last night, hit blazed and popped
Turrible loud and turrible hot. The sparks got out
Of hand, and lit the house. The house, my house
Commenced to burn. I cried and tried to
Wake them, but they were fast asleep,
And couldn't never hear me.
They must a been dreaming,
Deep dreams.

The Dreaming

We dream our lives, and live our sleep's extremes.
The one is to the other not as real.
We fabricate our future in our dreams.

The present moment isn't what it seems.
Experience is only what we feel.
Our lives are dreamt. In sleep we live extremes.

The past is prologue, as the Bard proclaims.
It made us what we are. Let's turn the deal
By fabricating future in our dreams.

Our night will wake to day from sound of screams.
But so our day will yearn for night to heal.
We dream our days, and live our night's extremes.

The future enters us in bits and gleams
In order that its brightness may reveal
How we can learn to make it in our dreams.

The past is history's. The present, schemes
Of chance or temporality can steal.
We dreamt our lives, and lived our sleep's extremes.
We'll fabricate our future in our dreams.

Fourth Movement

A Dream of a Small but Unlost Town

Happy are they who are happy; for there is no one to give them what they haven't got.
—The Second Beatitude of Daniel

✢ 1 ✢

I'll call you "G."

Let it stand for Gumshoe, for Guide, for Guru, for Gardener, for Guzzler, for Gallynipper, for whatever you like. I'm in a hurry; out of your respect for secrecy and my disinclination to cast about for some such ludicrous anagrammatization as "Danian Goldthorn" or "Hondio Grantland" or—in a hurry, I said—"Thorndolan Gandi," I'll simply call you "G."

When you were a little guy, oh five or so, you saw a movie, on one of the weekly Saturday afternoon trips when your uncle took you into the small county seat of "Jessup" [I have to shade all of them, don't I?], a movie about the capture of kidnappers by government men, and on the way home you announced to your uncle, self-importantly, that it was henceforth your intention to be a "G-man" when you grew up. Whenever your uncle saw you after that, he would grin and call you "G." The nickname stuck, replacing that auroral diminutive they'd all of them known you by, although, when you did manage to grow up, you never became anything remotely resembling a G-man.

But, just possibly, that sleuthing urge yet smolders in the wings, gratifying you when, for example, you discover from thin clues that a genre painting attributed to William Sidney Mount is actually the work of Frank Blackwell Mayer, even if not more than a dozen people will really care. Your credentials for the little job I've got for you are good enough: you have a knack for looking at the overlooked, a sharp art historian's eye, a hungering after truth…and a stagnancy of soul. The perfect devious devil's advocate. Besides which, you know the country almost by heart.

There's one other thing, G. [Those dulcet iambics of that last movement are a tough act to follow; but maybe this prose will come as a breath of fresh air…or a sip of strong French roast coffee after an oversweet gulp of Cointreau or Chartreuse.] That same uncle of yours—"Wick," I'll shade him—there was another vocal use Wick had for "G": when he was plowing or driving with his team of mules, Wick would say "Haw" to make them stop, and, to make them go, "Gee." So, hoss, *gee!* Go!

✝ 2 ✝

You will go. Your eye is the "I" briefly glimpsed in the Overture and then heard interviewing Felix G. Spofford near the end of the First Movement. But then, except for your brief sad appearance at the end of the Second Movement, you seem to lose the trail; at least we haven't caught another peep of you since then; although we've somehow had the feeling that you are still following us, closing in on us, about to catch us. It is as if you are deliberately hanging back, dawdling as it were, giving me a chance to get a good head start, all the more to dramatize the speed of your catching me. Now here you come.

How it all will happen: in January, during what they call "intersession" at the small New England liberal arts college where you work, while you will be teaching what you like to call an "intercourse" [you kill me, G], a small seminar, "George Caleb Bingham and Other Painters of The Frontier," the president's secretary will bring word that he would like for you to drop by his office at your earliest convenience. You will go at once. The president [since the first three letters of his name are the same as the first three letters of the college, no mean coincidence, and if I were to shade the college "Winfield," could I then shade him "Winston"?] President Winston is a friend of yours; he personally had hired you seven years ago; although you aren't drinking buddies or anything like that, you always speak to each other candidly, man to man, as if, like long friends, you understand fully each other's hearts, those hearts which are cold. His would be because the pressures of administration make him a businessman first, an academician second. Yours would be because…well, we've time enough later for that. You and President Winston never mince words or bother with pleasantries. He will tell you now to have a seat, a good twelve feet from him across his immense moon-shaped desk, necessitating that you make minor adjustments to the controls of your "aid," as the audiologists and salesmen would shade it.

Then he will say, in that voice which you have likened to the rattling of gravel in a tin can—or is it just your aid?—"Six years ago, G, after finishing your first year with us, you asked me to tell you if I'd caught any negative feedback from the students about your success as a teacher. Do you remember my answer?"

You will say: "You said, 'Don't worry, mister. I'll tell you the minute I hear anything, you'd better believe it.'"

"And I never have," he will say.

"And you never have," you will agree, then ask, "Why?"

"Because I never heard anything," he will say with impatient patience, as if explaining the obvious. But then will add: "Until lately."

"Oh," you will say, and on pretext of scratching your ribs give a slight turn to the volume control. "What have you been hearing?"

"*One,*" he will say and grab the thumb of his splayed hand, "that you *haven't* been hearing. The students say you can't hear them any more. Or, *two,*" he grabbed his index finger, "that you haven't been trying to. Because, perhaps, *three,*"—the middle finger—"you haven't been much interested in your students lately. Which could be the result of, *four,*"—the ring finger—"a loss of interest in your subject, or even in the business of teaching. Due to, I suppose, *five,*" —"some kind of disenchantment with yourself." He will make a fist of those enumerated fingers which have so neatly encapsulated you, and will bang the fist lightly on the papers atop his desk. "You're washed out, G."

"You can't fire me," you will remind him. "I have tenure."

He will laugh one of those devilish cackles for which he is so well noted, and fix upon you that sardonic eye so remarkably like that of the actor George C. Scott. "You know me a lot better than *that!*" he will say, and point a long finger at the door, or at the world *out there*, the cold Outside. "I could get you out of here so fast and so cleanly the A.A.U.P. couldn't find a trace of dirt left behind! You know it!"

You will have known it.

"But," he will hasten to add, "I'm not so hasty. I'm not thinking of throwing you out for good. You've been around as long as I have; you've become a kind of fixture. That's it. Fixtures don't *do* anything. They're just fixed there. Maybe you need a rest, a rejuvenation, is that it? What the hell are you teaching intersession for, anyway? Do you need the money?" He will pause, and when you don't say anything, he will ask, "Did you hear me? Is that thing turned up?"

"It's up," you will acknowledge, and say, "Yes, I need the money. My wife and kids have…they've left…for a while; they're out visiting my wife's mother in Arkansas, and it takes extra money to support them away from home. You know."

He will have known. The president himself not too long ago has undergone the unpleasantries of a protracted divorce proceeding. The eyebrow he lifts will be sympathetic. "Everything all right on the domestic front?" he will ask.

You will shrug. "That's for her to decide. I'll have to wait and see. But she said she didn't want to live with me any more."

The president will grimace as if to ward off further news of matters both painfully familiar and irrelevant. "Well, I'm sorry," he will say. "Maybe you should take it to a counselor or somebody. But couldn't it be related possibly to this other thing? You're a tired man, G. You smoke too much. The janitors tell me your ashtrays are overflowing. They also tell me you make an urn of coffee in your office every morning and drink most of it yourself. Ten or twelve cups a morning? Incidentally, the janitors have complained of the mess in the lavatory, when you clean the coffee maker and leave wet grounds in the wastebaskets. A minor detail, surely, but I'm the only one who will listen to their complaints. *And act upon them.* From the look of you, I'd hazard a guess the reason you need all that coffee is to sober up in the morning. Right? Okay, these things never get any better. My point is: your business is your business, but where it encroaches on this college, then it becomes my business. My advice is: take a rest. Get things in perspective. Straighten out your family problems, if you can. Get some help. See your doctor. Have a chest X-ray while you're at it. Get some exercise. Take up cross-country skiing. Or, better yet, get out of this snow for a while. Beachcomb the Bahamas. But *do something*, man!"

He will stand up, his signal that he has nothing further to say, except the terms: "You're on official leave of absence. All of the spring semester. At full pay." He will slap you on the back and usher you out the door.

✝ 3 ✝

So you will be cut loose and cast adrift, in the middle of the winter. The same cold nights that find us living it up in the splendid isolation of Lost Cove, endlessly entertained by the unearthly chatter of a spook named Flossie, these same nights will find you alone, at loose ends, incarcerated in the emptiness of that big white-brick New England colonial house of yours. You could not have left it; it is home; home is the right place, although you will think, wryly, of Frost's definition of home as "the place where, when you have to go there, / They have to take you in," and there will be nobody there but you to take you in. You will not begin talking to yourself...yet; that will come later. Mostly you will just drink and read books, trying to get caught up on all the unread volumes in that ostentatious library of yours. You will drink and read books. You will drink books and read the labels on your bottles. You will drink your labels and read your bottles. In time, whether from ennui or intoxication, you will discover that page after page of your reading has left not a line imprinted on your consciousness. You will try lighter reading, novels successively "easier," until you will be all the

437

way down to Harold Robbins, and when you cannot even follow him, you will resolve to quit. You never succeed in sticking to your resolutions, but you will stick to this one. You won't read another book for a long time.

As a diversion, to take your mind off the evil habit of bookreading, or at least to prevent you from holding a book in your hands, you will take up chair caning. It is difficult to learn, but, once mastered, relatively easy, and automatic. Your wife had several years previously purchased a set of six Thonet bentwood dining chairs, old and used, with all of their cane seats punctured or ruptured or torn. If you were to recane all of these seats, mightn't she come home? No, but it will be something to do. It will fill the hours. Several days of steady labor to cane one chair. Vocational therapy is it called? Your fingers will be nimble enough, dexterous enough, at least until the sixth or seventh bourbon and branch. But, in time, as a mnemonic device to aid you in the endless braiding or weaving of the cane, to remind your fingers to go over this strand and under that one, the involuntary phonograph of your mind will begin playing an old cigarette commercial: "Over! Under! Around! And Through! Pall Mall travels the smoke to you!" You will not be able to turn it off. There are several thousand over's and under's in the caning of any one chair, and this ditty will be like to driving you sane. Even though, eventually, you will try for diversion a German translation (*Über! Unten! Rundherum! Und Durch! Pall Mall reisen zu Ihnen der Rauch!*), the monotony will be enervating. Day by day, the integrity of the ditty will disintegrate into drivel (Hover! Hinder! Hound! And True! Pell Mellie's smelly smoke is blue!) until any ordinary mortal would have been soured on any cigarette, let alone Pall Malls, forever. Yet you will smoke more than ever, three packs a day (yes, Pall Malls), and keep on caning. Lover! Plunder! Unwound! And Toodle-oo! Paw's Maw unravels her joke's last clue!

At last you will recall President Winston's suggestion that you take up cross-country skiing. You will squander eighty dollars on a set of skis and poles and books and wax and torch and instruction book, and get out of your house, into your back yard. A shameful disaster. You will blame it on the weather (it *will* be only 10° above zero), but the real reason the mild acclivities of your back acres suddenly become steep mountain slopes is that you will be in such abominable condition: twenty or more pounds overweight, weak of lung, weaker of knee, bronchitic and asthmatic and possibly emphysematous. Less than twenty minutes after you will have started out, your cries for help will summon a neighbor lady on snowshoes to drag you home, your eyes blinded by their discharge, your beard and moustache caked with the discharge of your nose and mouth, your extremities all five frostbitten. You will be laid on the floor register of your antique coal furnace to thaw out.

You will make an immediate appointment with Dr. Ricardo Barto of Brattleboro [copyeditor: I let the shade slip, but leave it stand] and, longing for the balm of summertime and the peace of your lush vegetable patch, you will begin a premature indoor implantation of various seeds, in windowsill pots: tomatoes, lettuce, even corn, even muskmelons (!), even okra (!!) and black-eyed peas (!!!).

In time, the combination of cold, your foolhardiness, and fumes escaping from your antique coal furnace, will kill everything except the lettuce, which will struggle weakly on.

Dr. Barto will probe your various orifices, send you to the laboratory for nine X-rays of head and chest, and four blood tests, send you to an allergy specialist forty miles distant in another state for a full series of tests, and then send you to bed for a week to await the results. Your bed rest will be an incomplete imposture: you'll have to get up thrice a day to stoke the antique coal furnace, and, since you'll have no one to wait upon you, and have therefore set up your bed in the kitchen between the refrigerator and the stove, the one for your ice cubes and TV dinners, the other for heating the latter, you'll still have to get up to reach the sink faucets, not to mention the bathroom.

Loneliness and bed rest play grievous tricks upon one's perspective: you will bring to your land of counterpane little hills of family memorabilia: scrapbooks, photo albums, old letters and such; poring over these, you will systematically delude yourself into believing that your wife had never actually nagged you, or, if she had, that you deserved it; you will forget all the unkind things she has said to you; you will forget that she had been indifferent to your needs; you will even forget that she left you of her own accord. You will begin to miss her most miserably. Then you will begin to write to her, day by day, long eloquent endearing letters, showing her how wise and sound it would be if she were to come right on home. She will never answer.

✟ 4 ✟

"How old are you now?" the good Dr. Barto will ask, at the beginning of your return appointment. "Thirty-six, would it be?"

"Thirty-five," you will minutely correct him.

"Ah," he will say, and pretend to consult your folder while framing his next words in his mind. You will have known that he would be blunt; you admire him for his bluntness as you admire it in President Winston and others. And he will be blunt: "Dr. G," he will say, shaking his head slowly back and forth, "you are going to have a heart attack in the near future. If it fails to kill you, something else will. Pneumonia, possibly. Throat cancer. I won't discount tuberculosis. You need an operation on your sinuses. You need also to have removed two quite enlarged nasal polyps, as big as this—" he will show his meaty thumb-pad. "Also, the allergist reports that you have, I quote him, 'hit the jackpot.'"

"Jackpot negative or jackpot positive?" you will ask.

"Positive," the doctor will reply. "You are allergic to virtually everything. Dust. Mold. Weeds. *Trees*, even. Dogs and cats. Brunettes. Bookpaper. Bananas. Babies…."

You will interrupt, "Am I allergic to bourbon?"

He will consult his folder. "No, unfortunately," he will say. "But you must cut down. You *must*. I have said this before, and you have been deaf to me. Speaking of deafness, your hearing constantly deteriorates. The audiometer shows no hope. I have said this before, too: you will have to begin taking lessons in lipreading."

"Pardon me," you will say, "I didn't catch that."

Slowly and patiently, with exaggerated lip movements, the doctor will repeat himself. Then he will go on: "You must discipline yourself to an intensive program, a *mass*-ive program. You must take the lessons. You must cut down on destructive tastes and habits. You must dust-proof your house, particularly your bedroom. You must dry and de-mold your damp cellar."

"My damn what?" you will say. "My damn *salad*?"

"*Dampp cell-arr*," he will say. "Of your house. Your wet basement. You told me once you have frogs down there. They must go too. You must give up your mushroom culture. Avoid all spores."

"Sports? But you said I need exercise…."

"*Spo-errss*," he will enunciate. "As in mushrooms. But no, you must not avoid sports. You must find a sport, a strenuous sport, and you must cultivate it. You must give up the booze and the smokes. I mean it." Then he will become silent and stern.

After a while, you will ask, "Is that all?"

He will hold up an index finger. "You must diet."

"I know it," you will say. "I know I must die. It's why I drink and smoke and generally wreck myself."

"*Die-ittt*," he will correct you. "Get rid of your—" but then he will stop and study you quizzically for a long moment. Quietly and gently then he will ask: "Do you want to die?"

"Why not?" you will say. "It happens to the best of people, sooner or later."

"Would you perhaps be willing to consider the possibility," he will ask, "of having perhaps a small conversation or two with Dr. Sanderson or Dr. Fossett at The Retreat?"

"Psychiatrists?" you will say. "I couldn't afford it."

"The amount of their fee is commensurate with your ability to pay."

You will shake your head. "I don't need a shrink."

Gently he will ask, "What *do* you need, Dr. G?"

You will nearly blurt out the one word which is the only answer to such a question, but it would have cost you some embarrassment; he is only a medical doctor, after all, and what you need is not anything he could have written a prescription for, so instead of that word you will substitute another of the same number of letters "Rest," and then you will tell him that your college has put you on leave and that you hope to recuperate.

Then he will say that he hopes you would consider vigorous exercise a form of rest, and he will write you out two prescriptions, some green pills for your nose, some yellow ones for your lungs, and at his door he will say, "Don't forget the dust."

You will have misunderstood even that casual remark, but will nod, and go on home, idly wondering why you should not forget the toast. Had it been on his list of things to avoid? It doesn't matter. You could have just as easily given up toast as you could have given up "the booze and the smokes," which is to say that you could not have given up anything. The attic of your house is crammed with things that you cannot have given up. The attic of your mind is full to bursting with concepts, fixed ideas, delusions, that you cannot have given up. Your life is an omnium-gatherum of habits, routines, tastes, faults and follies, that you cannot have given up. It seems the only thing you will be willing to give up is, simply, your life itself.

In short, G, you will be like—I grope, I grovel, for the just-right metaphor—you will be like a town which is on the verge of becoming a ghost town.

✢ 5 ✢

By late February, after a blizzard which will dump three feet of new snow on top of four feet of old snow, you will have had enough: enough of yourself, if not quite enough to embolden the hand to

442

tie the knot in the rope on the beam in the attic; enough of that house, enough of bachelorhood, enough of listening to and talking to such a dull, vain, obnoxious fool as yourself. Your wife will not come home. Very well. But you will be missing your children, you will lack those three lovely little ladies, the oldest of whom, at ten, will seem to be the only person in the world who would answer your letters. Mightn't their mother be persuaded to permit you, perhaps, to spend a brief sweet moment or two in their company? You must see. You must go. To Arkansas.

Leaving an entrenched home requires not merely heart but also a head for attending to practical matters: you will have to have your Volvo checked and greased and oiled for the long trip; you will have to give the college secretaries a forwarding address; you will have to notify the post office and the milkman to stop deliveries; you will have to haul loads of garbage and trash to the town dump; and then a full day's labor will be required to close the house itself: shut off the electricity, close the flues, drain the pipes, put antifreeze in the toilets and drain traps, lock the windows. Kill the furnace.

At the close of the day you will be tired, covered with cobwebs and dust, and feeling both satisfied that the house is sealed in good hibernation and slightly dejected that you will have cut off its vital functions, when you will hear a knocking noise and wonder if you have overlooked one of the pipes or if the house itself is barking in protest against this abandonment. You will turn up your aid and try to locate the source of the knocking. It will occur to you that it might be coming from the door. The door? Who would knock upon the door? Nobody knocks upon your door.

You will open the door. There will be standing a student of yours, or, rather, a former student of yours, Cassandra Laigle, wearing her most gracious smile.

"Sorry to bother you, Dr. G," she will say. "But I guess you might've heard that Yellow House burned down yesterday."

"No," you will say. "I hadn't heard. Won't you come in."

She will come into your house, for the first time [rarely, if ever, would you condescend to invite students to your home], and will glance around her at the furnishings of the living room: the exposed ceiling beams, your works of art, your enormous bookcase, although, with the electricity shut off, these things perforce will be illuminated only by the pale light of dusk, which perhaps enhances them. "Beautiful," she will say. You will not offer her a chair; you will have no time for socializing at the moment. "Are you really living here all alone?" she will ask.

"I was," you will say.

"Well, the reason I asked," she will say, "was that, I mean, I don't have anywhere to stay. The dorms are all filled up, and Yellow House is just a shell, you ought to see it, I think they're just going to bulldoze it down. I was wondering if, you know, since you've got all this room, and nobody here but you, if you would consider letting me...I mean, I would pay you, if it's not too much, and I wouldn't be any trouble, just put me anywhere you like...."

Now, it happens that Cassandra Laigle is not at all a bad-looking girl, in fact quite pretty, breasts too small perhaps but otherwise most shapely, and more than once, in the past, G, you have coveted her in your fantasies. And the prospect that she will now be offering is fantastic. You are not a humorous man, G, rarely even smiling, but now you will laugh uproariously.

She will look at first puzzled, and then hurt. "Well, I was just wondering," she will protest. "I mean, I didn't know what you would think of the idea, and I certainly didn't mean to *intrude* on you or anything."

"No intrusion," you will say, controlling yourself and letting your laughter trickle off. "Forgive me. You see, Cass, it's just the irony. All day I've been working to close this place up, so I can get out of here. If you had come to me yesterday, or even this morning, I would have been more than happy to consider it. But now—"

"Oh," she will say. "You're leaving? Well, maybe...would you think about letting me keep your house for you while you're gone?"

"The house could keep you, but you couldn't keep the house. The furnace is impossible; I can't manage it myself. Part of the reason I'm leaving."

"Oh," she will say, looking forlorn and lost. You will nearly give in, G. You will very, very nearly decide to stay and have her live with you. Would she, in time, move into your bed? She would certainly be someone to talk with, the long nights. Cassandra is a bright girl; never less than B+ in your art history classes; and she is a senior, at least twenty-one. Oh, G, the book you might have written of her life with you! "I'm sorry," you will say. "Why don't you try the Huddlesons? I think they have a couple of spare rooms."

"Well," she will say, "all right," but it will be clear that she is disappointed; that she really *desires* to stay with you. You fool, G! Maybe Yellow House hasn't even burned down. Maybe she is just looking for an excuse to move in with you and cure your loneliness. Maybe she has had a secret crush on you all these years. Maybe—"Where are you going?" she will ask.

"Arkansas," you will say.

"Oh," she will say, and smile. "Are you going to write another book about it?"

You will smile; you will feel flattered; you will remember that Cassandra has been one of the very few students who has brought copies of your books to you for your autographs. "Maybe," you will say.

"Well, have a good time," she will say.

"The same to you, Cass. And I hope you find a place to stay. Try the Huddlesons." She will turn to go. "Oh, wait," you will say, and as she pauses, you will ask, "Would you like some lettuce?"

"Lettuce?" she will say.

"Yes, I've been growing lettuce in pots on my windowsill, and I hate to leave it. If you keep it watered, you might have some big crisp heads in a few more weeks."

"I don't have a windowsill...yet," she will say, almost apologetically, and once more you will waver in your resolve, but recover. "And no kitchens to fix salads in," she will add, looking beyond you toward your kitchen. "And I wouldn't much care to just munch on it plain. Thanks just the same."

You will leave the lettuce to wilt in the window.

Driving out of town that night, you will notice that, sure enough, Yellow House has been consumed in flames.

✢ 6 ✢

No, Cassandra, thanks just the same, but he isn't going home to write a book; that isn't what he is going home for; there will be no more flyleaves for him to ballpoint "For my dear student Cassandra, with fondest regards and best wishes, G." He is going home to die. You couldn't have saved him, Cassandra; you must never fault yourself, girl. The salmon at sea, when it feels the time is ripe, fights its way inland to its birthplace, there to spawn and die. But no, dear, he will not spawn another book.

It is merely a question of whether he will be able to wait long enough to let nature take its course, or will have to give nature a little boost, say, by selecting an acute replacement for his chronic suicide: he might drown himself in Lake Maumelle, as James Royal Slater did, or in the Arkansas River, as Margaret Austin tried to do, or he could gain some long-wanted notoriety by being the first to leap from one of Little Rock's new bank-building skyscrapers. The prophet without honor in his own country opts for dishonor instead.

Once, on his trip home, on the superhighway in western Tennessee, so close to the state line that he can already smell the muddy Mississippi, he will feel such a sudden and unusual tremor in his chest, a queer fibrillation, that he will have to pull the Volvo up quickly by the roadside and stop, and wonder if the final irony would be that he will die here in this alien state before being permitted to cross the state line into his homeland. But it will pass, and he will drive on, and cross the line. Even the squalid ugliness of flatland eastern Arkansas will seem lovely, lovely, to him.

You have wondered, Cass, why a man so infatuated with a rather backward and sparsely populated state that is too far north to be truly southern, too far south to be truly mid-western, and too far east to be truly southwestern, would have chosen to live, instead, in exile as it were, in a New England state so far removed from his homeland. I can't give you a good answer, but I, who have lived in four different communities in four different states for long periods each, and have pondered much longer than your Dr. G the question of a sense of home, a sense of the right place, can tell you this much, although I'd hate to trample on your tender young sensibilities: the *only* right place, the only home, for any of us, is that place from whence we originated: *nowhere*, namely, nonbeing, namely, death. That, perhaps, is what he is going home to. One is never disappointed in going there; one never feels disappointment there, or, for that matter, feels anything. I can tell you, Cass. I've been there. The only alternative to that right place is, for as long as you care to stay, some other place. And some other place is never home. Does that answer your question, child? And does it, please tell me, explain why so many of your generation killed themselves with drugs?

G will not have appreciated that I address these remarks to you, nor that, further, I revealed to you the depths of his lump-in-the-throat infatuation with that humble state, an infatuation which, more than anything else, will postpone the ultimate moment of his untimely demise. After a brief and tearful reunion with his three daughters, he will rent for himself, for one month, a room with closet-kitchen on the tenth floor of the Albert Pike Hotel, which had been the most elegant hostelry in Little Rock in the days of his boyhood, but will now, as the pittance he will pay for his room testifies, be faded into demidesuetude. Yet for him it will have its advantages: the enormous, high-ceilinged dining room still serves excellent southern food, and he will have it practically to himself; the elevator is not self-service but still patiently manned by Blacks in livery working their way through college and reading their algebra texts during the long, long waits for passengers, a friendly and most-accommodating assistant manager, Mr. Ruschmier, an ice-making machine right outside his door, full maid service, the morning *Arkansas Gazette* and the evening *Arkansas Democrat* delivered to his door, a convenient distance to the best of old Little Rock, that part of town which stubbornly refuses to follow the suburbs to the six-miles-away malls and plazas of the west end. The main public library is a short two blocks if he should ever choose to read a book again or seek inspiration for the writing of one. From his window he can see across the street the enormous Grecian temple of The Ancient and Accepted Scottish Rite of Freemasonry, dedicated to the memory of the same man the hotel is named for, that great Confederate general and humanist who is one of G's personal heroes.

He will live there a month, the month he will have paid for. The tenth floor is a suitable height for jumping out of, if the moment should ever have come. He will forestall that moment by reading carefully the morning and evening newspapers in search of anything interesting if not inspiring. He will spend as much time with his daughters as their mother will allow, taking them to the zoo, and for long drives in the country. Spring comes in March there, while his New England town is still buried beneath late snows. He will even take his wife to a movie, but it will be a John Cassavetes film that will bore them both to distraction with its ugly documentation of marital difficulties. He will invite his wife to the Albert Pike for a nightcap, but she will have to be in bed early to get up and take the girls for a dentist's appointment in the morning.

The days and evenings of that month, he will walk a lot, by himself, down the old streets, and back, and meditate, much, about mortality. But most of the time he will stay in his room, occasionally watching local programs and news on television, but usually reading the morning and the evening papers cover to back, with considerable interest, for the most trifling item of Arkansas news has never failed to satisfy him with its newsworthiness, its sense of being of and by and for his people, his own people, though he is sometimes astonished to realize how few, how pitifully few, of these people he has ever personally known.

I tell you these things, Cass, to help you understand why he will have rejected the utterly beautiful offer of your sharing his hearth and his heart, in order that he could go home. I hope you will have found suitable accommodation at the Huddlesons' house. If you are ever lonely or restless there, I will send to you this clipping, from one of the newspapers G will have been reading, to keep you company and whet your curiosity, until you have his ink on another flyleaf.

STOVING CASE CLOSED, NEW YORK POLICE REPORT

The search for Diana Stoving, 22, daughter of prominent Little Rock insurance executive, B.A. Stoving, has been discontinued by New York police officials, it was learned today by the Stoving family.

Miss Stoving, who disappeared shortly after her graduation from Sarah Lawrence College in June of last year, has not been in communication with her family or friends since that time.

New York police were asked to enter the case in September of last year, on the supposition that Miss Stoving may have taken up residence there.

The family also retained private detectives in the New York area, but without success. According to them, she was last seen, by her college roommate, in the New Jersey city of Garfield. From there, they were unable to trace her.

Miss Stoving, who grew up in Little Rock, was the only child of the President and Chairman of the Board of National Community Life Insurance Company, whose headquarters are in the Union Bank Building.

Keep in touch, Cassandra.

☩ 7 ☩

It will have been an excuse, G, for riding up the elevator in Little Rock's newest skyscraper, but now, sitting and waiting in a plush futuristic armchair in the opulent waiting room (Mr. Stoving is in conference, his secretary will say; you should have phoned for an appointment; but you are not able to use a telephone), you will begin to have misgivings. Would he laugh you out of his office? Or call the state asylum to come and get you? You have never had any dealings with gentlemen of his station, save perhaps a father or two briefly greeted on Parents' Day at the college. You will feel quite out of place in this room, in this building, the business world. You will have carefully donned your only good suit, but it is the big blue-with-yellow-striped tweed you'd picked up in Ireland and quite inappropriate to the business world. His secretary will have taken note of your suit, your long hair, your beard, your gold-rimmed glasses, the button stuck in your ear, and will have asked awkwardly, "What was it you wish to see Mr. Stoving about?" to which you will have mumbled cryptically, "It concerns his daughter."

You will have to wait for nearly thirty minutes, but even that will not be long enough for you to compose and rehearse your little pitch. When the big inner doors will finally open and out file a half dozen very expensively attired and groomed businessmen, and Miss Secretary will say, "You may go in now, Mr. G," you will want to say, "I've changed my mind. Cancel the appointment."

But you will go in, into the sumptuous sanctum as big as a dance hall and commanding a fine view of all Little Rock and environs, and when the man gives you his hand and then with the same hand wordlessly gestures you into a chair, you will sit, and size him up for a moment. He is the formidable epitome of Big Business; not even the sympathy you will be feeling for him can quite cleanse the reek of Mammon. He will sit in his own enormous spaceship chair, and will say, "What can I do for you, Mr. G? Or vice versa?"

You will clear your throat. "I know you're a businessman—I mean a *busy* man, Mr. Stoving, so I'll come right to the point. I saw the item in this morning's *Gazette* about your daughter missing. I'm a father myself, Mr. Stoving, three lovely little girls, and I asked myself, 'How would you feel if, when your daughters grew up, one of them disappeared like that?' And the answer was, I would feel pretty miserable. So I know how *you* must feel, Mr. Stoving. I've come to offer to find your daughter for you."

"Yes," Mr. Stoving will say, and begin giving his head a slow artificial nodding. He will take a Benson and Hedges cigarette from a package on his desk, tap the end of it on his wristwatch, put it in his mouth, then offer you one, but you will already have a Pall Mall burning between your fingers. "Yes," he will say again, and slowly raise his desk lighter to his cigarette. "I see." He will take a few puffs, inhale, and exhale: "How much do you propose to charge me?"

"I'm not interested in money, Mr. Stoving," you will say. This is a grave mistake, G; if you discount the profit motive, you are not speaking his language; you are arousing his suspicions.

"What are you interested in?" he will ask.

"I told you, I have daughters myself, and—"

"Yes, *three* of them, you said. An improvement. The last guy who offered to find my daughter for me only had *two* of them." Mr. Stoving will laugh at his wit, and say, "Now if I could only find somebody who has, say, *six* daughters, I might allow myself a little optimism. Ha! Yes, you said it, Mr. G, I'm a *busy* man, a *very* busy man, and I've already squandered untold hours of my time trying to find that girl. So now get your cards out on the table quickly, sir: who are you? Which agency are you from? What contract are you offering?"

"Mr. Stoving," you will say, somewhat apologetically, "I know you'll think this is most unusual, but I'm not from any agency or anything. I'm a free agent, you might say. I'm not even an ordinary detective as such, but I'd like to give it a try. I think I could find her. I'm not asking for any money because I don't really need it. I'm on leave all semester from my college, at full pay, and I've sort of been at loose ends, you know. I need something to do. I need to get *involved* in something. I need a *cause*, you might say."

"Have you considered the Peace Corps?" he will say. "Or the hospital volunteers?" Your eyes will sigh. "Which college?" he will ask you. You will tell him the name of the college, its location, what kind of school it is, the subject you teach. "How did you happen to be in Little Rock?" he will ask. You will explain that too. You will point out that both you and your wife are natives of Little Rock. Then you will boast,

"I've written three books about Arkansas. Maybe you've heard of them." And you will name your books.

"My wife reads," he will say, as if that explains or excuses anything. And then he will say, "I don't think you know what you're asking to get into, frankly, sir. And you strike me as rather presumptuous, if I may say so. You're saying, in effect, 'The New York police can't find her, and the best detective agency on the east coast can't find her, but *I* can find her.' And you don't even have any asparagus."

"*Asparagus?*" you will say.

He will look at you oddly. "Experience, I said."

"Oh," you will say, and brush back your hair to indicate the button in your ear. "I'm hard of hearing," you will point out.

Mr. Stoving's shoulders will slump. You should realize, G, although he will never have told you so, that he has persuaded himself, by this time, that you are part of a diabolical plot. That because you come from the east, from New England, you have some knowledge of his daughter's whereabouts, which you intend to keep secret until the appropriate moment when you can collect your big reward. He will decide that perhaps his only hope of seeing his daughter again would be to "play along with" your little deception about becoming a private detective.

So he will say, "Very well. I've got nothing to lose, have I? If you want to amuse yourself, playing 'I spy,' and if, as you say, you aren't even going to charge me anything...."

You will brighten. "Then you mean you'll let me do it?..."

"What if you *do* find her? Then, how much are you going to take me for?"

"Well," you will say, giving the matter some thought, "if you'd care just to reimburse my expenses or something, if I have any unusual expenses, or traveling expense, or like that...."

Mr. Stoving will grip his desk and lean abruptly toward you. "Listen. I'm a businessman. Let's not beat around the bush. Let's talk in round figures, sir. How much do you want? Let's put it down on paper. Fifty? A hundred? Two hundred?"

"Well, I suppose perhaps two hundred ought to cover the gas and oil."

"I was speaking in *thousands*, Mr. G."

"Oh," you will say. "Oh, good heavens, please, I told you, I don't want any profit...."

Mr. Stoving will push a button on his intercom and speak into it: "Louise. Bring your pad." Then he will turn to you and say, "Now I want my secretary to draw up a little document, which you will sign, and I will sign, and she will sign as a witness, and I want this little document to stipulate exactly and precisely the total amount of cash money that will be transferred from my hand to yours upon the successful completion of your little adventure."

"Dead or alive?" you will say. You will hate to be so blunt, but it is a minor technicality that has given you some thought.

He will stare at you. "If she's dead," he will say coldly, "forget it."

"Of course. Let me say, Mr. Stoving, that I hope very much to find her alive and in good health. I was only asking."

The secretary will come in and sit beside him. Mr. Stoving will begin to dictate a string of legal-sounding phrases which you will not be able to follow, catching only a random "party of the first part," "in good faith," "whereupon," "notwithstanding," "thereunto," and then he will pause in his dictation. "Now mush, Mr. G."

"Pardon?" you will say.

"How *much*?" he will say. "Name your figure."

"Well..." your mind will have been trying swiftly to calculate the number of miles, the number of meals, the number of motels you might conceivably need. "Would two thousand sound all right?"

He will laugh and swat his secretary on her shoulder. "Bargain basement, isn't he, Louise?" Then he will suggest to you, "Let's call it thirty."

"Dear me, no," you will protest. "What about five?"

"Twenty," he will say.

"Ten," you will say.

"Fifteen," he will say.

"It doesn't matter," you will say. "I really don't care."

To Louise he will say, "Make it fifteen."

When Louise will return to her desk to type up the document, you will point out, "There are some things I'll need to know. May I ask you a few questions?"

"Fire away," he will say. But then he will glance at his watch, and say, "No, wait. I've got a meeting in five minutes. Why don't you come to dinner tonight? I'm sure the little lady would be delighted to meet you too."

✝ 8 ✝

You will meet her that night, G; you will meet my Annie…although she will not be exactly delighted to meet you, or at least her reserve will not permit her to express whatever delight she might feel at meeting the man who is going to find her lost daughter. I suspect she will be more suspicious of you than Mr. Staving will have been. That's the way with ex-country girls: they have devoted so much of their energy to adapting themselves to city life's Proper Society that they have overdone it, have become even less tolerant than natural city people of anything remotely unconventional or outside their ordinary purview, and you, G, will certainly be the most unconventional dinner guest she has ever entertained in her home before.

Her home. It is on Edgehill Road, which gets its name from being the crest of the Heights, the upper crest/crust of the Pulaski Heights as one ascends the steep wind of Cantrell Road. It is an older part of the Heights, much closer to town than the spanking new suburbs, but still the most fashionable address in town, and it is old enough to have enormous trees and lush shrubs, with greenhouses and gardeners. The house itself is a tasteful and authentic reproduction of an antebellum southern plantation house, with high columns and verandas and all. You will wonder why a family with only one child would need that many bedrooms—eight in all. I wondered too, and was sorely inconvenienced, trying to find, in the middle of the night, which of the eight rooms the little girl-child was sleeping in.

Mrs. Stoving, you will discover, *does* read books, but she has not read yours, nor heard of you, and you will doubt that she really believes you are an author, because, as she will say, she has never entertained an author before, has in fact never met one, unless you count Agnes Roundtree Mazzarelli, the well-known Arkansas poetess, and you do not count Agnes Roundtree Mazzarelli. Mrs. Stoving will ask you to tell her what your books are about, but you will find them hard to describe. Upon learning that you and your wife are native Little Rockians, she will want to know what your father and your wife's father are *in*. Your father is in retirement; your wife's father is in his grave.

You will find her a rather charming woman, nonetheless. There would be a *fragility* about her which you will find curiously endearing; you will feel that her shell is so thin you could crack it with your fingernail. And she is a lovely woman, for her years: very light blonde hair just beginning to turn white, high cheekbones, pointed chin, deep-set hazel eyes which seem continually wistful and baffled, as if she is not at all certain just where she is, or how she has come to be there, or what is now or ever going to come of it.

From the beginning, you will recognize that she is Mr. Stoving's plaything, his pet, his slave. He dominates her completely. During the conversation at the dinner table, he will interrupt her so frequently and rudely that you will be tempted to cry in protest, "Please give her a chance to finish!" You will feel that you could learn more about what certain sort of person Diana Stoving had been if you got Mrs. Stoving's analysis. But you will never have the chance. As soon as the dinner is finished, Mr. Stoving will literally dismiss her, and draw you alone into his study, where the butler will serve you Cognac and Cuban cigars, and Mr. Stoving will say, "Well, what else do you need to know, Sherlock?" He has had four whiskey sours before dinner, much wine at dinner, and now the Cognac, which he will keep pouring. But you have not been exactly abstemious yourself, old Guzzler.

"Would you happen to have an extra grotophaff—photograph—of her, which I could keep?"

"Sure thing," he will say, and fetch a manila envelope from his desk. He will give you a 5 × 7 photograph. "That's her latest college picture."

You will study it, enraptured. "She's beautiful," you'll sigh.

"You bet," he will agree.

"May I ask, if it's not too personal, why she didn't have any brothers or sisters? If you'd rather not—"

"That's okay. Nothing special. Why overpopulate the country? I don't think Anne—my wife—needed to spend the best years of her life bringing up children. One's enough. Nothing personal intended; if you and your wife wanted *three*, that's your affair."

"Well then, my next personal question: did you know whether or not your daughter might have been taking any drugs?"

"All of 'em ask me that," he will say, shrugging. "It's the first thing they want to know. All I can say is, she never took any that I know of, when she was here at home. And she visited here sometimes for long periods. I mean, if you're hooked, you can't go without the stuff for long periods, can you?"

You will look at the photograph again. Her hair was not unusually long. "Would you say she was ever inclined to be a hippie-type, or do you know if she ever consorted with hippies?"

"Not Diana," he will say. "Not in Little Rock. And not in Bronxville, New York, either." When you will not pursue the point, he will ask, "Any more questions?" You will have the feeling that perhaps he is impatient to get you off his hands.

"Could you sort of fill me in on any information, however insignificant, that the other detectives managed to dig up?"

Mr. Stoving will sigh and pour himself another glass of Cognac. Then in a bored and businesslike way he will tell you all he knows. You will take careful notes in your indecipherable longhand on 3 by 5 index cards. He will conclude, "…so that's where the trail stops. Garfield, New Jersey. The service manager who fixed her car there said that she asked him how to find Passaic, or West Passaic, he couldn't remember which, and he told her how to find it, and that's the last anybody saw of her. It's like...it's like maybe a flying saucer swooped down and picked her up in Passaic or West Passaic and lifted her off the face of the earth. But you don't believe in flying saucers, do you, Professor?"

"No," you will say.

"Well, good luck," he will say, and will begin struggling to lift himself up out of his deep leather armchair.

You will motion for him to stay. "There's just one more question," you will tell him. "If you don't mind. Perhaps my most important question."

"Well—?" he will say, not really settling down into his chair again. "Ask it."

"Mr. Stoving, can you think of any reason, or reasons, why your daughter perhaps could be refusing to communicate with you, if she is alive somewhere?"

He will sink back into his chair, rub his hand over his eyes, and reach for the Cognac bottle again. He will pour and drink and begin talking, but he will not be talking to you; he will be mumbling, or grumbling, to himself. What little talent you have for lipreading will catch fragments of word formations on his muttering lips: "enough of this shit..." "more than a man can..." "how long am I..." "snotty little bitch...." Then he will stop for a long moment, and at length he will look up at you with glazed eyes, and will say, "That's one they haven't asked me." Then he will straighten his shoulders a bit and answer your question.

"Who knows?" he will say. "Ask *her* that, when you find her, will you? I'd like to know. I really would. Maybe she thinks she's too good for us. Maybe that thirty-thousand-dollar education she got at Sarah Lawrence put ideas into her head. It was her mother's notion, sending here there. Personally I don't see why the fucking hell she couldn't've gone to u. of a. or Hendrix or even goddamn U.A.L.R. Spoiled brat! But damn it all, it's not just *her*! No, *sir*! Not just my Diana! It's her whole fucking generation! By God, a man can't even pick up his newspaper these days without reading about some new stupid sonofabitching thing that these kids have done. They murder people for kicks, and don't give a blessed shit for society and institutions, or trying to earn a living or anything! No, I can tell you, mister, Diana was sure one girl who didn't need to earn a living! Oh boy, she was fixed for life! So now what do I read in the papers that these motherfucking psychiatrists are telling us? They're telling us that the problems of the younger generation are *our* fault! They say we haven't been strict enough, we haven't been firm enough, we haven't given our kids enough serious attention! Do you believe that bullshit? Do you? Not me, brother! I'm not buying that crap for one minute. Don't you try and lay that one on me! I was a *good* father, goddammit! A good father! All a girl could ask…." Mr. Stoving's shoulders will be shaking, his eyes will be wet, he will seem about to break down. He will begin mumbling to himself again. You will take leave of him now, G. You will thank him for the dinner, and tell him that you hope very much to be able to return his daughter to him in the near future. But as you are leaving, you will be thinking, *I don't really feel much sympathy for him.* Whatever sympathy you will be feeling will be entirely for Diana. And you will suddenly realize that you have no intention, if you do succeed in finding her, of returning her to this world that she came from.

✝ 9 ✝

I wish I could enrich the comedy of your gallant chase, G, by tapping you on the shoulder and lightly pointing out to you that on the same day you will go roaring off out of Arkansas to begin your great hunt, on that very same day we will be crossing *into* Arkansas on our way to our final town. But the dates won't coincide; there will be a gap of a week or so in between; we will already be settled in Arkansas before you will have first heard of Diana. As a little consolation, then, I'll play on my fiddle this robust rendition of the "William Tell Overture," as background music for your dauntless departure for places unknown. Tiddle-lump, tiddle-lump, tiddle lump lump LUMP!

First stop: Philadelphia, Pennsylvania. You will locate Miss Susan Trombley, working in the steno pool of a large law firm. You will offer to take her to lunch, but Miss Trombley, a pretty redhead, will be at first reluctant to accept your invitation. "Look," she will say, "I've told you guys all I know. I'm not hiding anything, really. I just don't have anything else to say about Diana."

"This is different," you will say, mysteriously. "I'm different. I'm not one of those guys." And you will take her to lunch, at a quiet and out-of-the-way coffee shop on Federal Street. During the meal, you will talk not about Diana but about yourselves. Upon learning that she had majored in printmaking at Sarah Lawrence, you will reveal that you are associate professor of art history at Winfield, and have done some printmaking yourself. You will discover that you are both admirers of the work of Antonio Frasconi; she will invite you to come up and see her wood engravings sometime. Then, over coffee after the meal, you will casually introduce your business: "I understand you were one of the last persons to see Diana before she disappeared."

Well, she will say, yes, she was the last of Diana's friends to see her after graduation. They were on the way home to Susan's parents' home in Ardmore, Pennsylvania, when Diana's new car developed a problem in the shock absorber and they had to stop in Garfield. Susan had been concerned about being late for a dinner-and-theatre date she had set up for herself and Diana with two Princeton men, so Diana had urged her to go on home alone on the bus while she waited to have her car repaired.

"She told me she might go home, meaning Little Rock, or she might go into New York to audition with a dance group. But I just *know* she didn't really want to do either one. Poor Diana. Maybe she *did* go into New York and maybe she got mixed up with some hippies and got murdered, for all I know. She was always an odd one. We were roommates the last year at Sarah Lawrence, and she was always doing funny little things, like going out on the lawn in the middle of the night to sit under a tree and 'commune with the night,' as she put it. The reason I know she didn't really want to go to New York and join a dance group is that once, when we were talking about what we'd *really* like to do after graduation, if we could do anything we wanted, she told me a very strange notion she'd had to spend a year or more just driving along old roads that weren't much used any more. She'd checked out this book from the Sarah Lawrence library, by J.R. Humphreys, I think it was called *The Lost Roads of America*, and she said she'd like to do something like that, traveling old roads."

You will inform Susan Trombley that Diana's father has mentioned to you that Susan had mentioned the book to the detectives from the agency he'd retained, and, at considerable expense, the agency has investigated the entire route described in the Humphreys book, from New Jersey to California, without finding anyone who had seen Diana or her car.

"Oh," Susan will say. "Well, I could have told them not to bother. Diana was too…well, she was too *original* just to duplicate what somebody else had already done. She would have had to find her own roads."

You will sigh, wondering which of the 132,796 roads of America Diana might be traveling on. But it is a lead, a slim lead, and you will have had no leads at all until now.

"Miss Trombley," you will say, "I'd like to go over with you, sort of reconstruct, if you can, that last afternoon when you were with Diana. She intended to go with you to your home in Ardmore, but at some point during that afternoon, she changed her mind. Do you have any idea why she changed her mind?"

"Well, I think getting her car repaired was more important to her. She was very proud of that car, and it was going to take a while to get the part that was needed and have it installed, and I was impatient to get on home."

"Were you with her constantly that whole afternoon?"

"Yes I was, until she left me at the bus station."

"You didn't see her speak to anyone, or do anything, while you were with her? I mean, she didn't meet anyone, or see something, that you didn't know about? I mean—I'm getting this kind of confused—but what I'm trying to find out is, for example, maybe while your back was turned, or, pardon me, you might have had to go to the Ladies' or something, maybe she met somebody who, let's say, asked her for a date or something."

"No, I don't think so. There was…yes, now that I think of it, there was a very brief period, ten minutes or so, while I left her in the waiting room to go and use the telephone. I wanted to call my friend Larry to tell him that we would be late. But I don't think Diana met anybody. She was just sitting there in the waiting room, reading."

"*What* was she reading, Miss Trombley?"

Miss Trombley will meditate a moment and say, "Oh, just a magazine or something. No, it wasn't; I think it was a newspaper."

"Please try to remember," you will say. "This could be important."

"Well, yes, I'm almost certain it was a newspaper."

"You don't know which newspaper?"

"No." Susan Trombley will shake her head, but then her eyes will light up and she will snap her finger and point it at you. "Hold on now! I don't know what newspaper she was reading, but I just remembered—maybe this is important—I just remembered that whatever newspaper she was reading, she must have seen something that startled her, or upset her, or, I mean, really *grabbed* her, because when I came back from my telephone call, she was sitting there holding that newspaper, and her face, her face looked like this—" Miss Trombley will ape an expression of astonishment—"and I remember asking her what she was reading and telling her she looked like she'd seen a ghost, but she just put me off, saying it was just a story about an accident or something. Hey! You know, maybe that's a clue. Why didn't I think to mention that to those other detectives? How did *you* get it out of me?"

"I'm different," you will say, and reach for the check.

Second stop: Garfield, New Jersey. At the Gillihan Porsche agency, you will identify yourself, state your business, and say you have only one question: would they happen to know what newspaper would have been in their waiting room on June 16 of the previous year? The dealers will consult one another and their secretary and their cashier and will conclude that, unless some customer had left behind some other newspaper, it was either the *New York Times* or the *Passaic Herald-Star*, or both. You will groan inwardly over the prospect of having to comb through a thick issue of the *New York Times* in search of some clue, but the cashier, a bright-eyed lass who probably never misplaces a nickel or penny, will save you from this ordeal by remembering, at the last moment, that their subscription to the *Times* had lapsed for a period of three weeks during that month.

You will drive then to the offices of the *Passaic Herald-Star* and ask to look at the back issue for June 16 of the previous year. You will spend almost an hour poring over it with the fine comb of your eye.

ELKS TO FÊTE WIVES WITH CHICKEN BARBECUE. Would Diana have developed a sudden craving, perhaps, for chicken barbecue, and have run afoul of an Elk? Unlikely.

PASSAIC COUPLE CELEBRATE FIFTIETH. Would she have wished to help Mr. and Mrs. Dominick Pastorello commemorate their golden anniversary, and have been abducted back to the Old Country by one of their sons? No.

"DEAR ABBY: Here's a new one for you. Every summer my husband and I take our kids for a two-week camping trip. My idea of camping is just to loaf around and enjoy the air and the sunshine, but my husband's idea is to take long hikes. The kids love to go with him, and I feel left behind, but try as I might, I can't work up the enthusiasm for hiking. Sign me, STUMPED." "Dear STUMPED You 'stumped' me too, because I'm the same way."

Did Diana, perhaps, develop a sudden desire to go camping or take a hike? Possibly, but you will remember, G, that Susan Trombley has said that whatever Diana had been reading left an expression of astonishment on her face.

YANKS STOP SOX IN SIXTH. NICKLAUS TIES TREVINO IN SECOND DAY. MOTORCYCLE WEEKEND PEACEFUL. RAINY WEEK AHEAD, FORECASTERS SAY. EAST PASSAIC HIGH GRADUATES 457. COUNCIL CHARGES

MAYOR TAKES KICKBACKS. ROTARIANS SCHEDULE STRAWBERRY COOK-OUT.

Good grief, you will think. *New Jersey!* Of all places to be stuck in....

E. PASSAIC MAN REVEALS AGE REGRESSION EXPERIMENTS.

✢ 10 ✢

"I've given it up," P.D. Sedgely will tell you. "It was taking up too much of my time; it was interfering with my job. I'm a schoolteacher, a simple schoolteacher, first and last. The day arrived when I realized that I could not go on, fooling around with the 'occult,' as it were, endlessly following up paths that led nowhere. I grew tired of trying to prove that any of my subjects had genuinely existed in previous incarnations. For a while I became more interested in teleportation—the ability of the mind to 'travel' to distant places—but that, too, was a time-consuming hobby. I have given it all up, sir. I have erased all my tapes. I have sold my tape recorder. I am a simple schoolteacher."

You will show him the photograph. "Did you ever meet this girl?"

He will study the photograph. He will not answer your question. He will ask you a question, "Are you a relative of hers?"

"No," you will say. You will smile. "Like yourself, I am a simple schoolteacher. This girl has been missing since last June. I told her father I would find her. I am trying to. Did you by any chance happen to meet her, last June?"

The man will look startled at your news, and then mumble to himself, "Day Whittacker...."

"Pardon me," you will say, and tap the earpiece of your aid.

"I am hard of hearing. Did you utter, perhaps, the expletive, 'Gee Whillicker' or something?"

"No," he will say. Then, "Yes," he will say, "I was just saying Gee Whittaker, I mean, I'm sorry to hear that some poor girl is missing. But no, I'm sorry, I never met her."

"I see," you will say. "I have simply been following up various leads, certain ideas that occurred to me. I am sorry to have bothered you. This girl, Miss Diana Stoving, was known to have been reading, on the day she disappeared, the June 16th issue of the *Passaic Herald-Star*, which, as you may recall, carried an item about yourself. It merely occurred to me that she might have read that item and become interested in you. She was a girl with a wide variety of interests, particularly in the offbeat and perhaps also in the occult. Of all the items in that issue of the newspaper which might have attracted her, the piece about you seemed, to my mind, the most promising. I am sorry if I have put you out."

"That's quite all right," he will say. "I understand. You say the poor girl has been missing ever since she was here? I mean, ever since that day in June of last year?"

"Yes. Her family, her poor father and mother, have heard not a word, have not laid eyes on the poor girl ever since."

"Too bad," he will say. "You haven't been able to find any trace of her?"

"I am a simple schoolteacher, like yourself. I am not a professional detective. The authorities have abandoned the search. I am the only hope." You will say these last words with dramatic emphasis, and then, with even more dramatic emphasis, you will add, "And you, Mr. Sedgely, are *my* only hope."

Clearly, you will have nonplussed him. "But I said—" he will begin to protest, but perhaps he is, as you will have surmised and gambled, a man of conscience. "Won't you come in?" he will invite.

"Gladly," you will say.

Yes, he will confess, Diana had been to see him. He will tell you as much as he can remember about her visits with him, but it will only be with considerable reluctance, after much probing on your part, that he will reveal the figure of, the identity of, Day Whittacker, who is not an expletive after all.

Perhaps because you will be playing the "simple schoolteacher" to the hilt, G, you will open up his locked closets. But all he can remember to tell about this "Daniel Lyam Montross" is that he had been born in the Connecticut village of Hadleytown or Bodleytown or Dudleytown—yes, it was, he thinks, *Dudley*town—and that he had met a violent end some seventy-odd years later out in some western state, Oklahoma or Missouri or one of those, he can't remember which. But his tapes are erased. His tape recorder has been sold. He cannot play back for you the recording he had made of Day Whittacker as this "Montross" being questioned by Diana Stoving. He is sorry that he had ever fooled around with the matter. He is even sorrier that he had given Diana Stoving the power to put Day Whittacker into a hypnotic trance simply by telling him to go to sleep. He has been disappointed, and even slightly hurt, that they had been so ungrateful to him as to disappear without any further communication. They could at least have sent him a postcard occasionally, couldn't they? But no, he does not feel any guilt. "Blame me, if you wish," he will conclude, "for having rediscovered Montross in the first place in the person of Day Whittacker, but I can hardly be blamed for whatever two impetuous young people take it upon themselves to do with their lives."

You will glance at your wristwatch. It will be getting close to suppertime. "May I take you to dinner?" you will ask him. He would be delighted. You will take him to dinner, at a good Passaic restaurant, and you will say to him, "Tell me all you know about reincarnation."

You are by nature a doubting man, G, given to detachment and mistrust; a proper intellectual, you hold with Euripides that man's most valuable trait is a judicious sense of what not to believe. But although you are so thoroughly the ungullible skeptic, you are not close-minded or intolerant. Your first reaction to the staggering possibility of my metempsychosed reexistence within the bones and brain of Day Whittacker will not be incredulity but impartial curiosity and an unwillingness to dismiss, out of hand, the sheer possibility of it all. It will be as if, after hearing about flying saucers for years, you have finally caught a glimpse of one yourself; instead of rushing to have your eyes examined, you begin taking notes and drawing diagrams. The modestly doubting scholar's approach.

What will disturb you much more than the supposition of my transmigration is the sudden intrusion of this kid, Whittacker, into what you will have begun to conceive as a private matter between Miss Stoving and yourself. For days now, you will have had her photograph; it will have been the last thing you look at before turning out the light in various motels between Arkansas and New Jersey; you have, in a way, you will tell yourself, come to fall in love with her, and come to see yourself as her White Knight riding to the rescue. Now, suddenly, you will have to reckon with this upstart adolescent.

Although you and P.D. Sedgely will have hit it off so well together, getting along splendidly like the brotherly simple-school-teachers that you are, you will not get along very well, at all, with Mr. and Mrs. Charles J. Whittacker. Your tweedy, seedy appearance has persuaded Sedgely that you are indeed a simple schoolteacher like himself. Your tweedy, seedy appearance will give Mr. and Mrs. Whittacker to think you some kind of nut. The last thing they could accept is that you are a detective, but you will seem to hint that you might possibly be able to find out something about the whereabouts of their boy, and Mrs. Whittacker, at least, will be interested; Mr. Whittacker, it will seem, couldn't care less; he has convinced himself that the boy is a no-good thankless bum, or, worse, a draft-dodger, and has all but written him off.

Mrs. Whittacker will be even more interested when you show her the picture of Diana, for then she will remember that Diana, in the guise of a *Life* reporter, had appeared at their home just a day or two before poor Day disappeared, although it had never occurred to her to make any connection. Had this girl, who was, after all, a "grown-up" ("I mean she was a college graduate?" Mrs. Whittacker will say/ask), lured her poor boy off into a life of sin or something?

Her poor boy certainly wouldn't have done any harm to the girl? He was a kind and gentle boy....

Mrs. Whittacker will show you the one communication they have had from Day since his disappearance, the postcard, postmarked in July from Torrington, Connecticut. The Whittackers had been in touch with the chief of police of Torrington, but he couldn't find anything, so they had surmised that Day had simply mailed the card there on his way to some other place. Also, Mrs. Whittacker will inform you, a friend of theirs had sent them a clipping from the Rutland, Vermont, *Herald* in November, about a woman whose name was given as Mrs. C. Day Whittacker who had been shot in the woods and was in Woodstock Hospital, and "Chuck, my husband, called them up there at the hospital to try and find out if the woman's husband might possibly be our Day, but this doctor he spoke to said it wasn't?"

Mr. Whittacker will interrupt in disgust, "Jane, what're you wasting your time with this guy for? He doesn't give a damn about Day. He's only interested in that girl." And he will stalk out of the room to get himself a beer in the kitchen.

Alone with her, you will say apologetically, "I'm sorry if I'm wasting your time, Mrs. Whittacker, but—"

"Oh, that's all right?" she will say wearily.

You will ask her to tell you about Day, what sort of person he was. You will get a rather glowing picture of what a nice and kind and talented boy he had been. Had he ever taken drugs? Certainly not. Had he ever been in trouble? No. Never arrested? No. Ever had any emotional problems? No, well, there was only one time, when he was twelve years old, that he had tried to hang himself in the bathroom. Hang himself in the bathroom? Why? Figure it out for yourself. His father had barged in on him, and he pushed his father out and locked the door and tried to hang himself from the shower-curtain rod with his belt, but the curtain rod broke and his father busted down the door and let that boy know in no uncertain terms that he had better think twice before pulling a stunt like that again. And they had never had any more trouble with him along that line. In fact, Day was such a good boy that he paid for a new shower-curtain rod out of his own earnings as an odd-job boy for the neighbors.

"Mrs. Whittacker, would it be all right, would it inconvenience you too much, if I asked to have a look at Day's things?"

"His things?" she will say.

"Yes, his room, his possessions, his notebooks or whatever...."

"Well—" she will hesitate. It will be clear she is reluctant to let this grown-up beatnik character go prying around in her boy's stuff, and she will wish her husband hadn't gone off like that and left her to make her have to be the one to deny your request. "He hasn't got so awful much?" she will offer as an excuse, but when you assure her, Anything, anything at all, she will relent and take you back to the room which had been Day's. She will not leave you alone with it, but stand in the doorway, as if guarding so you will not steal any of this humble junk or otherwise desecrate it.

Quickly, like the art historian plunging through the Fogg Library in search of the one essential fact, you will examine his things: his high school yearbooks, his scrapbook, his small library, his clothing and Scouting equipment, his odds and ends, his miscellany of memorabilia. A typical New Jersey teenager, you will think at first, you who have been teaching them for years in your Winfield classes. But then you will begin to piece together an image of a kid who is not all *that* typical, after all; a young man of unusual interests, of stronger desires, of different chemistry, of, perhaps, deeper loneliness.

You will find nothing related to reincarnation, no trace of "Daniel Lyam Montross," nothing about hypnosis. Almost all of his stuff is oriented around The Great Outdoors: camping and back-packing and woodcraft. And about trees: his collection of bark samples, his scrapbooks of leaves, his books on forestry and woods management.

There is only one thing which will really catch your eye: in an issue of his high school literary magazine, *Reflections*, there is an article which he had written, in the tenth or eleventh grade: "A Visit

To A New Jersey Ghost Town," which begins, "Most kids think of ghost towns as false-fronted old saloons and such out in the Wide West mining areas, but do you know that we've got at least three authentic ghost towns right here in New Jersey? Last weekend, I had a very interesting overnight camp-out, all by myself, in one of them, the village of Tavistock, which isn't really *completely* a ghost town, because according to the last census there are a grand total of ten (10) people somewhere within the incorporated township (although I didn't see any of them). The history of this town-that-is-no-more-a-town is interesting...." The article goes on to give a brief history of Tavistock, followed by an hour-by-hour record of Day's short sojourn there, his interests focused mainly on identifying old trees rather than old buildings, and concludes, "Spending the night in a ghost town isn't as scary as spending the night in a cemetery (and I've done both). A ghost town isn't really dead. It's just sort of gone some other place for a while."

Well well, you will think. If a wealthy girl who is interested in old roads meets a Boy Scout who is interested in old towns, then you've got a real combination...even if she's three years older.

But *why*, you will be wondering, was she so interested in this "Daniel Lyam Montross"? Was he just a "vehicle"?

✝ 11 ✝

See our hawk-eyed Gumshoe tippy-toeing (yes, G, you will be wearing crepe-soled boots) through the woods, down the old Dark Entry Road, his one good ear straining, his aid turned up so high that were a fly to alight upon it and let a fart, it would sound like unto, verily, a thunderclap. The woods, late in March, will yet have patches of snow in shady places; nothing yet will be in bloom and the birds will not have come back from the south. Dudleytown will be as still and quiet as death.

It will be your intention to take them by surprise, to give them no chance of escape, to seize, at least, the girl, and fight off the boy, if need be. You will have a photograph of him too now; you will know that he is tall, but not as tall as you; in hand to hand combat, if it comes to that, your weak lungs and your damaged heart might be able to hold out long enough to subdue him, and if not…well, you would have tried.

You will poke around in the various cellar holes, you will visit the old dam with thin ice still on the edges of the millpond, you will sneak around the old leaning shanty, Dudleytown's one remaining building, you will follow the Appalachian Trail as far as the rock which I had styled the Landlocked Whale, you will creep up and down the length of Dudleytown Road, scanning the woods and the walls and the old cellar holes. Dr. Barto would have admired you for all the exercise you will be getting, exploring every path and trail and glade.

You won't see a soul.

And all you will find, as evidence that *any*body had ever been there, except for the cellar holes and stone walls and the shanty, is, in a glade filled with some kind of evergreen shrub (the laurel will not whitely bloom for a good while yet, G, and you know nothing about plant identification, anyway), what appears to be the dark remains of some kind of campfire, or some kind of fire. You will poke about among the ashes and find a small fragment of what appears to be burned cloth of some kind, yellow, some kind of yellow canvas, or duck perhaps, somebody had burned their knapsack, perhaps, or something. From the looks of it, the fire has not been lit for many months.

And you will get out quickly, before dusk, because, as you will say to yourself, the place "gives you the creeps." The villager in Cornwall Bridge you had interviewed, Miss Mary Elizabeth Evans, an old spinster, who had briefly met Day when he'd been trying to find Dudleytown, will have told you all about the infamous "Curse of Dudleytown," and you will have no inclination to dawdle longer than necessary, to tempt or disturb any ghosts or presences or whatever, to bring any further bad luck upon yourself. As soon

as you are convinced that there is no one in Dudleytown, you will
return to your Volvo and drive away.

You won't have found my father's grave either.

But you will be more thorough than Day or Diana had been,
in attempting to document the existence of my family in Dudleytown. You will visit the Cornwall Town Clerk and the Cornwall
Library, where the librarian will be only too happy to give you access
to all her material. You will look to her like a genuine scholar, which
you are. You will find, alas, no mention of any Montrosses. There
will be a "McRoss" or two, but not in Dudleytown proper. You will
find records of a family referred to as "Monti Rosso," but, judging
from the various given names, they were all of Mediterranean origin.
Ditto the Monterazzis. The Manterussels were apparently Flemish
in origin. The Montrusches were German. At last, with a cry of
elation which will cause the librarian to put her index finger to her
lips, you will discover a "Daniela Latham Mountrose," but, upon
further investigation, will find that she was only an old weaver who
had lived in West Cornwall, not Dudleytown, and died in 1834 at
the age of eighty. Still, you will think, possibly the descendants of
this "Mountrose" changed the spelling of the name, as frequently
happens, and moved into Dudleytown. You won't be able to discount
the possibility. But neither will you be able to prove it. There are no
records of any Montrosses or Mountroses in Dudleytown.

And now you will be left with a bigger question: Why had
Diana and Day left Dudleytown? And where had they gone? You
will make casual inquiries around the village of Cornwall Bridge,
asking if anyone had seen them. This is how you will meet Felix
G. Spofford, the man who had participated in, and will report to
you on, the eviction of the "Jesus freaks" from Dudleytown. But
no, he won't have any idea where they might have gone. To hell,
he hopes.

This is where we will last catch sight of the eye of your "I,"
G. Would you like to have your eye back, your "I" back, G? Would
you use it properly? What is more, would you use it *honestly*? I'm
afraid, G, that if I were to give you your "I" back, you might very
well do something sneaky, such as having Day killed or disabled

during the riot and eviction of the Jesus freaks from Dudleytown, so that you could have Diana all to yourself. That will not do. That will not do at all.

So you will go on. You will continue the search, following your "hunch," which will be based, albeit weakly, on that information Mrs. Whittacker has given you about the false lead of gun-wounded "Mrs. C. Day Whittacker" in the Woodstock Hospital. You will assume, for the moment, that Diana *could* have been that victim, and you will surmise that the couple had chosen, or stumbled upon, a ghost town in Vermont somewhere in the vicinity of Woodstock. You are, I must admit, quite familiar with the state of Vermont. You know it has an abundance of ghost *villages*, if not ghost *towns*, and you will now be faced with the relatively easy task of making a map of these in order to determine which one of them is closest to Woodstock. Their very names are poetry to you: Green River, Halifax Center, Concord Corner, Goose Green, Greenbank Hollow, Waitsfield Common…and Five Corners. When your research is completed, you will discover that Five Corners is much closer to Woodstock than any of the others.

Early April will find you, at last, driving your Volvo merrily up Hale Hollow Road into the place where five little roads come together to mark the spot of a bygone community. But in early April, if the snows have gone (and they won't all have), the back roads of Vermont become quagmires, and you will bog your Volvo hopelessly in the center of what had been the Main Street of Five Corners, right out in front of where Glen House Hotel had stood. Undaunted, you will abandon your car and set out on foot to find our couple. Your disappointment in not finding them there will somehow be greater than your disappointment in not having found them in Dudleytown. It will be as if all your knowledge of Vermont ghost villages is for nothing. You will find Day's lean-to, collapsed beneath the snows of yestermonths, on the slope of the McLowerys' back yard. You will find other evidence that they, or *somebody*, had indeed been there and gone: their campfire (you will sift nothing of consequence from its ashes), the trench of their latrine, their clothesline still stretched between two trees. You will take note of their ecological consciousness: they didn't litter, they didn't leave any trash behind. You will get down on your knees and peer underneath the collapsed lean-to. It is dark under there. You will strike a match. Back in one corner you will see something. You will fetch a long stick and rake it out. It will be a portable cassette tape recorder, with one tape in it. The floor of the lean-to has sheltered it from the winter snows, and its batteries are still fresh. You will push a button, and listen, fiddling with the controls of your hearing aid; but without the benefit of lips to read, you won't be able to make out the meaning of the words. It will be a man's voice, though, you can tell. Not a boy's voice. An older man's voice.

And then, searching further around the camp, you will find the mound of earth. Obviously, from the shape of it, a grave. Obviously, from the looks of the dirt, rather freshly dug. You will not have any digging tools with you. Even if you were to have a shovel, you will not be able to dig into that grave. You will not have the nerve. If your Volvo weren't stuck in the mud, you could rush right back to Woodstock and notify the authorities, and have one of *them* excavate this grave. But even if your Volvo weren't stuck, you'll not be able to do this. You will be afraid to. You will not be able to face up to reality if it should develop that the body buried in that grave is your beloved Diana.

Staggering farther around the camp, in near-panic and despair, you will come across the long rope dangling from a maple tree, one end of it tied to the uppermost branches, the other end tied neatly in a hangman's noose. Only a good Boy Scout could have tied such a knot. And unless he had tied it for the unlikely purpose of hanging *her* with it, he must have used it on himself. He'd tried to hang himself once before, remember? Perversely almost, G, you will rejoice at this thought. Day is dead and buried, and Diana is yours. If only you can find her.

You will keep the tape recorder and take it back to your car, wanting to get out of there and find someone who will listen to the tape for you and tell you what it says, in hopes of finding further clues. The penciled-on-paper poem you will have found resting on the grave is interesting, but offers no clue. *I'll be a sylphan sylphid if I can.* All right, but where? Where has your sylvan sylphid gone?

You will heave and strain your bulk against the car's fender, with the wheels in gear and spinning, trying to get it out of the mud. You will fetch large flat rocks and jam them under the tires of the car, and manage to inch the car a foot or so backwards, but, even so, you will begin to see that it is hopeless. In a last expenditure of desperate energy, you will take a deep breath and thrust your back up against the front grill of the car and push for all you are worth. Suddenly something will give…in your back: a sharp pain in your spinal column. You idiot, G; why must you always be attempting tasks that are too great for you? Now you will not only be without the use of your car but also without the use of your spine. It will pain you to move. Night will be coming on; you will not be able to walk three or four miles to the nearest house. You will have to spend the night in Five Corners.

An awful night. A terrible night. You will recline the seat of your Volvo as far as it would recline, not quite horizontal, and you will ease your ruptured back into it. You will lay there and smoke your Pall Malls and take sips from your flask of Old Grand-Dad, until the flask, a pint, is empty, but you will not be drugged enough to sleep or even to ease the pain in your back. You will make sure that all the doors of the car are locked from inside. You will leave your aid turned on, so high it sometimes will whistle in feedback and snap you out of your long reveries. You will grow cold and have to turn on the engine to heat the car, apologizing to the Things of the Night for the noise. And when you turn off the engine, the tinnitus in your ear will keep roaring.

Will you sleep at all that night, G? You must, because the dreams you will have are too strange to be the dreams of non-REM sleep…odd jumbled images: a schoolhouse stove, a two-hole privy, a Hermit at a Mine, Red Hair in the Water of a Pond. At the first peep of dawn your swollen bladder will force you out of the car.

During the night the mud will have frozen, the quagmire hardened, and you will find that it is relatively easy to back your Volvo out of it and make your getaway from that god-forsaken place. Your first pressing business will be to have your back attended to.

You will return to Woodstock and, after breakfast, you will wait for the Woodstock Clinic to open for the day. There you will be treated by the good Dr. Henry Fox [copyeditor: again the shade slips, but doctors are hard to libel], who will have you X-rayed, examine the X-ray, and declare that you have a slipped shade—I mean, a slipped *disk*. He will ask you how you have slipped it. You will tell him. You will tell him that you were trying to find a couple of lost kids in Five Corners. He will smile. The nature of his smile will cause you to ask him if he is familiar with Five Corners. Oh yes, he will say, he knows of the place. "You wouldn't happen to know anything about these kids?" you will ask, and show him the two photographs. The doctor will hesitate, long enough for you to guess that he does know something about the kids, but all he will say is, evasively, "Well, I *may* have met them." You will press him further, but he will say, "I'd rather not talk about it." "All right," you will say, "just tell me if you have any idea, any idea at all, of where either of them might have gone, north, west, east, south." "South," he will say. You will press him. "I don't remember exactly," he will say. "There was a time when the boy had been thinking about going south during the cold weather. Virginia, perhaps, or the Carolinas. But that was before—" "Before?" you will say, "before *what*?" He will change the subject. "Your slipped disk, Mr. G, needs attention. You must take care of it. You must stay off your feet as much as possible until it mends and stops aching."

Since, as you well know, your own home is merely a drive of less than two hours from Woodstock, you will decide, albeit reluctantly, just to "drop in and check on things." So you will go home. The house will be as you had left it, in fine disorder, sealed in snug but cold hibernation. Despite your aching back, you will find yourself lighting a fire in the fireplace. You will discover yourself hauling a bucket of water from the cistern in the cellar, because the plumbing is disconnected. You will not reconnect the plumbing. But you will stay.

"I'm just going around in circles," you will say to yourself. "I'm right back where I started from."

✢ 12 ✢

My dictionary is an old one, and well worn; it was one of only three books I owned in my last years in my final town; there were a number of words I had never learned from Henry Fox [not your Woodstock physician, G; it must be a common name; and, as you'll discover, I had my own Henry Fox] and there is a word which I had never heard, much less learned, from him:

tin·ni·tus/te-nīt-es/*n* [L. ringing, tinnitus, fr. *tinnitus*, pp. of *tinnire*, to ring, of imit. origin]: a sensation of noise (as a ringing or roaring) that is purely subjective.

Purely subjective, yes, G, but nonetheless audible, distinct, constant, and maddening. Yours had begun when meningococcal meningitis, contracted from an unwashed peach, had burned out your auditory nerves at the age of twelve, but then the tinnitus had been a not altogether unpleasant chorus of crickets, cicadas, katydids, tree frogs, and occasionally a distant cowbell; these still remain, but now are cacophonously overlaid by a wild contrapuntal syncopation of throbbing instruments without earthly comparison, which, as the search for Diana Stoving has intensified, have become faster and louder and more urgent, a demented choir and brass band of devils each playing or singing in his own feverish tempo to drive you loose from reality…or to drive you to the end of your long, long search.

It is a wonder to me that you will have managed to keep your cool and to remain, so many weeks, throughout the month of April, alone in that house again. You will not resume chair caning, to give the devils the words of a commercial to accompany their music. One of the first little things you will do is weigh yourself, on the bathroom scale, and smile to see that you have shed six pounds already, down now to 219, where you haven't been for years. The next thing you will do is make three copies of a letter: "Gentlemen: In preparation for an investigation I have been making into the whereabouts of certain American ghost towns and ghost villages, I would very much appreciate being informed if there are any of these located in your state." You will mail these three copies to the Departments of Conservation and Development in the Commonwealth of Virginia, the State of North Carolina, and the State of South Carolina.

Your ruptured back will gradually mend. You will take up a kind of primitive living, not in emulation of Diana and Day but out of your reluctance to relight your antique furnace, reconnect the plumbing and electricity, and restore the house to its former functions. You will be tempted, for a while, to see if Cassandra Laigle is living at the Huddlesons', and to invite her to move in with you if she wishes, or at least to ask her to listen to your tape recording for you and tell what it says. But you will be able to share neither your house nor your tape recording with anyone.

Eventually you will receive replies to two of your three letters. South Carolina will not answer. Perhaps they have no ghost towns. The Commonwealth of Virginia will appear to be offended that you would think such a progressive state might harbor any ghost towns, but they will inform you of one—"not to mention, of course, Jamestown itself"—the old city of Warwick, on the James River, once the rival of Richmond as Virginia's largest town, but now passed utterly into oblivion. It will sound like an interesting place, you will think, but it had obviously been a tidewater town, that is, a *flat*land town, and you will suspect that this "Daniel Lyam Montross," or at least whichever of the two was following him around, had been a lover of hills, and thus would have eschewed the flatlands. How right you are, G. So you will turn to the other, the last, letter.

Which is from the State of North Carolina. "Dear Dr. G: In response to your letter of April 9, I am enclosing material describing Lost Cove, a mountain settlement near Burnsville, North Carolina, which is now unpopulated. I know of no other such communities in this state which would be suitable for your investigation. Most of the dwellings of Lost Cove are still standing, although I learned, only last week, that one of these dwellings burned recently, perhaps struck by lightning or ignited by vandals. Thank you for your interest in North Carolina." Enclosed will be Xerox copies of various newspaper clippings about my beloved mountain aerie.

How very curious, G, that you will never go there! I think you would have liked it. I'm sure the four-mile hike along the Clinchfield railroad line to reach the place would have been good exercise for you, although in your physical condition the final mile up the mountain could have severely winded you, could probably have given you a heart attack.

Is that why you will not go there? Do you have some premonition that the great effort of trying to reach the place will kill you?

Or is your "excuse" simply a recognition that Lost Cove, if you would have failed to find either one of our couple there, will be your third strike? Three strikes and you're out, is that it? Or have you managed to see a "pattern" emerging in what is actually only a coincidence: the seasonal migration of our couple: summer in Dudleytown, autumn in Five Corners, winter in Lost Cove, and now spring in—? It will be spring now; Lost Cove will be empty; after all the effort you would have to make to reach that place, even if it didn't give you a fatal heart attack, you would have been defeated to find no one there.

Or will you decide that you do not *want* Lost Cove to be the place where you will find Diana, that it isn't the right place, that you must look for her in some other place? I do not know why you will not go to Lost Cove; I am not, after all, merely your puppeteer (although I'll confess to being in a hurry, now that you will be so close to finding me).

The real reason, perhaps, why you will not go to Lost Cove will be based on another one of your "hunches": you will sense that the burned-down house referred to in that letter might have been the house she had been living in, and you will be thinking: *If she was brave enough to go all alone to Lost Cove, and her house burned down on her, where would she go? Wouldn't she be tired by now of all this trouble and traveling? Wouldn't she be lonely? Wouldn't she regain her senses and possibly even go home to Arkansas?* For all you will know, G, during these weeks you will have been searching and agonizing, she might have already returned to Arkansas, safe if not sound in the welcoming arms of her parents.

To Arkansas?

Yes, G, there are ghost towns in Arkansas too. And as you will recall, Mr. Sedgely has mentioned something to the effect that I met my violent end eventually in "Oklahoma or Missouri or one of those places." Could one of those places have been Arkansas? There are plenty of ghost towns in Arkansas, if that is what "Daniel Lyam Montross" (or Diana) was looking for. You will not need to write to the Arkansas Department of Conservation and Development to learn their names. You could take down from the shelves of your library various books which describe them; you could consult your maps, your old state maps and your topographic maps. But you will not even need to do that; you know already most of the names by heart beginning with Arkansas Post itself, the first settlement of the state, now extinct, and running through those places whose sounds are not exactly poetry to your ears, but romantic all the same: Aberdeen, Cabin Creek, Fair Play, George Town, Harrington, Hix Ferry, Jacksonport, Iceledo, Norriston, Napoleon, Paraclifta, Plum Orchard, Rome, Rough and Ready, Rush, and St— but yes, there will be that need of yours, that pressing need of yours, for secrecy.

I have played around with several possible pseudonyms for your town, *my* town, our final town: I like the alliterative "Linger Longer," although it has an unwieldy clang, like cowbells. "Bide Awhile" is crisper, but sounds like a summer tourist's cottage. "Tarry Further" has a nice purr to it but sounds too much like a man's name. And none of these has the proper Ozarkian rustication. So, to maintain the invitational tone of the real name, that name which beckons one not to leave but to stay more, even though it sounds less beseeching than demanding, I'll call our town, our final town, "Stick Around"…the last stick out of my sack.

Do you like it, G?

☩ 13 ☩

Conductor, could we have a little swell of background music, please? It will only be the tinnitus in G's ear, of course, but the devils will be banished and in their stead will be sweet strings, violins, *fiddles* if you will (I'll play one of them myself; I can do the lively John Playford dances perfectly, although I might have a little trouble with the *Pastorals* of Beethoven and Vaughan Williams). Here we are, friends, in Ozarkadia; it is a fine morning in May; the wildflowers are everywhere; the birds threaten to drown out my fiddle.

Do you like it, G? Aren't you pleasantly, even blissfully, surprised? Do you understand now why I've chosen *you* for this job? You'll forgive me for putting you to such bother and agony before springing my happy surprise on you. Would it flatter you, would it boost your crumbling ego, your shattered It, if I told you that the reason I settled ultimately in Stick Around was that this was the right place for eventually meeting *you*? Believe that if you want to; it's just as good, just as plausible as the actual reason, which was simply that I wandered into it, just as I had wandered into Five Corners and into Lost Cove, without design or destination, and I liked it, and wanted to stay, wanted to *stick around*. In 1932, when I first came here, it was a bustling, even a thriving, village, in contrast to the previous places I had lived. There were several stores, a bank, a small hotel, a physician, druggist, dentist, two churches, even an industry, "Orvil Blackshire's" tomato-canning factory; the place seemed to be practically a metropolis compared with Dudleytown, Five Corners, and Lost Cove: But now look at it. The countryside around it hasn't changed much; it was then, as now, the remotest, wildest part of the Ozarks, the headwaters of the beautiful Buffalo River country, with a branch of the Little Buffalo flowing right through the center of Stick Around. One thing, perhaps, that drew me to this country was that it seemed to recapitulate the diverse topographies of Dudleytown, Five Corners, and Lost Cove a little like each of them, enough, my "hills of Vaucluse," to remind me of my past.

You will leave the paved state highway in the town of "Jessup," county seat of "Isaac" County, and follow a dirt and gravel road some ten miles to reach Stick Around. You've been on this road often enough, but never before done the driving yourself, and you'll have to shift the Volvo from "Drive" into "Low" several times to get up those hills. After passing through the village of "Acropolis" [I hate to shade that one, its real name is so much prettier], south of Jessup, the road winds steeply up Blackshire Mountain for several miles before dropping down into the high valley of Stick Around. Unlike the Greek Acropolis, whose parthenon is the highest spot in town, the village of Acropolis is actually much lower, in elevation, than Stick Around; hence it always sounded a bit odd when Stick Around people had spoken of going "up" to Acropolis; the "up" had meant only *north*, that on a map, Acropolis would be north of Stick Around. Today, you will notice, Acropolis itself is practically a ghost town, although it still has its post office, which Stick Around lost to it thirty years ago.

You'll prepare yourself for another surprise, G: Stick Around isn't a ghost town. Not yet. And maybe not ever; I don't think it will ever die. Although the village proper is deserted, there are still plenty of families living within the township, on the outskirts of the village. As you come in on the Acropolis road, some of these people will see you and wave at you, although they don't know (or remember) you from Adam. It's a friendly habit of ours that won't ever die: we wave at friends and strangers alike. You will wave back at them. But then, as you drive closer to the village proper, you won't see any more people.

Although there are still several inhabited houses along the Acropolis road north of Stick Around, and several productive farms still operating to the westward, toward "Roxey," and the Roxey road is in fairly good repair, the road southward, to "Squire" and "Hankstown," has years before been given up to the forest and is not even passable by jeep, while the road eastward, to "Drayton," is passable only by logging trucks. Thus, there is only one way into Stick Around, the broad dirt and gravel road from Acropolis, and one way out of Stick Around, the narrow dirt road to Roxey.

Outside the village, you will stop briefly at the white church-house and drive into the churchyard and park. You will go into the modest wooden frame building, its door unlocked. The interior is unchanged, its rostrum still in place, its twelve long wooden benches still in neat rows…but covered with thick dust. On the thick wooden door of the church, generations of children and teens have written or carved their names, including your own, and recently someone [not me, G, I swear; but there's more than one of us Over Here] has written

JICK
   clue
      word
         to
          me!!!
1519–1972

I live on & on
   &
                        on
                            &
                              on
                                 ;

You will puzzle over this, and file away the word "Jick" in your memory, in case you should ever be called upon to use it as a clue word [you never will be; and in time you will wonder if some other writer is encroaching on your territory], then you will walk down the steps and out into the church's graveyard. The names on the headstones are familiar to you: "Buchanan," "Breedlove," "McArtor," "Truett," "Ramey," "Madewell," "Prudden," "McKinstry," "Black-shire," and "Hansell." You will not find any "Montross." That sacred burial ground was for good Christians only.

The church is not the only unused-but-still-standing build-ing in Stick Around. In the village proper, where you will next stop your car, there is a building very special to you: you know it will be abandoned, and it is: the windows broken and boarded up, the signs removed except for two or three faded tin advertisements for "Royal Crown Cola," "Vicks VapoRub" and "Camels." Once there had also been a "Drink Coca-Cola" sign with the information: "U.S. POST OFFICE, Stick Around, Ark." This sign is gone. You will find it inside the store, propped against a wall, covered with dust. There is little else inside the store: a broken showcase, empty nail kegs, collage of advertisements for Bull Durham, Day's Work, Garrett Snuff, Lydia Pinkham Remedies, Putnam Dyes, an official white printed sign KINDLY DO NOT EXPECTORATE UPON THE FLOOR discolored by stains of tobacco juice, and, beneath this sign, the rack of post office boxes, each with a glass door, and a fragment of a WANTED poster with front and side photo of some desperado wanted for kidnapping years ago. The little glass doors of the post office boxes are all covered with dust. All except two of them: you will notice that the dust has been wiped off of Nos. 47 and 28, and you will rightly wonder why.

This store-and-post-office, which had also been the home of "Lara Burns," is very special to you, but it is not your destination. Your destination, and your destiny, is on up the road a piece, more than a mile in fact, along the "Banner Creek" road, the road that used to be one of the cutoffs of the main road to Drayton, but now is a dead end. The house itself is set back from the road, a hundred feet up the west slope of "Lingerfelt" Mountain, the green woods all around it, to set off the yellow I had painted it. What will bring you here? You will be thinking, *If I had to pick a house, of all the abandoned houses of Stick Around, I would, more than likely, have picked this one.*

But before you tiptoe up the steps on those crepe-soled boots, you will please pause for a moment to admire, or at least to notice, with your knowledge of American domestic architecture, the handiwork of my last piece of carpentry: the house itself. The yellow paint is faded from all the boards except those on the front of the house sheltered by the porch roof from the washing rain; but notice the little touches, the mild "Carpenter Gothic" as some have called it: the cheerful balusters of the railing on the porch; the jigsaw work of the window shutters; the trim of the eaves, the bargeboards: I was proud of that structure, which is, I think, the only physical evidence of myself which has managed to survive. Not a large house by any means, and yet one of only three or four two-story houses in the whole township; I wanted a second story to elevate the two bedrooms, one for myself, the other for young Annie; we caught the night breezes up there. That window on the left was mine; I stood there in the mornings to greet the day; how often I—

But you will be growing tired of me, G, and now, at the climax of your long search, with 5691 miles added to the odometer of your Volvo, you will have no time to linger over the architecture of my house. All right, this moment will be yours, after all; you will have earned it. I will fade off; I'll retire the "eye" of my I from you for a while, but I'll be back. Especially will I be back, in a flash, if you try anything tricky.

✟ 14 ✟

You will not knock. You will try the door, and finding it unlocked, you will burst in upon the house with a jubilant exclamation of "Doctor Livingstone, I presume!" But your poor wit will be thrown back in your face. Dr. Livingstone won't be there. And neither will be Diana.

The ultimate despair could have overwhelmed you now. You might well be thinking, *How could I possibly have hoped to find her here? What vanity, to think that this was the right place.* But you will soon discover that someone is indeed making current use of the house for living purposes. There are fresh wild flowers in vases. Cooking smells coming from the kitchen. You will holler up the stairway "HELL-O?" and turn up your aid to listen for a reply, but you will get none. Had she seen you coming, and gone into hiding?

You will go out through the kitchen door and down into the back yard. There is no one around. The forest woods encroach from every side but you will notice that there is a small pig lot with small but live pigs in it, and that a sizable plot of ground is being kept in tilth, for a garden patch, and you, old Gardener, will not be able to resist stepping out among the rows to examine and evaluate this horticulture. A good garden, a lush garden…but the head lettuce is planted a little too close together, you will think; good heads won't form if they're that close. And the collard greens ought to be picked before the leaves get so large. The pea vines have finished their harvest and ought to be pulled out, for a second planting of lettuce, or a row of snap beans. The corn is—

You won't see her. She will come up behind you and could have tapped you on the shoulder before you will know she is with you. You will straighten up from bending over to examine the corn, and there she will be, *there* in reality, looking you in the eye with those beautiful blue eyes, which, you will realize, are so much like her mother's, with that same vaguely wistful or baffled look, as if she were not at all certain just where she is, or how she came to be here, or what is now or ever going to come of it. Now the Dr. Livingstone greeting will be a stale joke on your tongue, and your first words to her will be, "You ought to hill your corn."

"Hill it?" will be her hello.

"Yes, it's high enough now that unless you hoe some dirt up around the base of the stalks, a good strong wind could blow the corn down. And also—" You will be struck then with the absurdity of your opening words, so mundane in the momentousness of this occasion.

"Is that your car out front?" she will ask. When you nod, she will say, "Vermont plates. That's a long way off."

"Yes," you will agree. "I've come a long way."

Oh, she is beautiful. These months of living close to nature have tanned her skin and put rich color in it. The photograph doesn't do her justice…although she seems to be, as you will be so disturbed to notice, in a family way, swollen around the abdomen, about four or five months pregnant. No matter. She is still lovelier than you have ever dreamed. And you will know that you would never never be able to return her to her father.

What? She will have just said something, which you will have missed. You will be reluctant to reveal to her that you are anything less than a whole and perfect man by telling her you are hard of hearing. But what had she just said? "I blew the wood"? "I threw you good"? "It's true you should"? You misunderstood. "I'm sorry," you will say, and reluctantly brush back your hair to reveal the earpiece. "I don't hear very well. What did you say?"

"I said," she will say, "'I knew you would.'"

"What? Knew I would *what*?"

"Come a long way," she will say.

You will stare at her. How had she known it? Has she been at last in touch with her father, and he has tipped her off that you are looking for her? Or has she merely expected that somebody, anybody, would finally catch up with her? Have your Vermont plates tipped her off? Had she done something in Vermont—broken a law or *buried a body*—and expected somebody from Vermont to catch up with her? "Do you know who I am?" you will ask her.

She will nod, smiling her wonderful beautiful lovely smile.

"But how—?" you will plead.

"I've read your books," she will declare. "All of them. I recognized you from the jacket photos. I read *The Cerise Stone* when I was a freshman in college, and, being from Little Rock myself, you see, I thought it was a wonderful evocation of that crazy old town. And, just recently, when I happened to be in North Carolina, in the public library at Burnsville I came across a copy of *Firefly*, and I just loved it. It made me so interested in this part of the Ozarks that—" She will stop. Noticing the astounded expression on your face, she will ask, "You are him, aren't you? I mean, aren't you the author?"

You will manage to nod your head, and begin looking around for a place to sit. You will not want to collapse upon her cornstalks.

"What's the matter?" she will ask solicitously. You will have reached out unconsciously and gripped her arm to steady yourself.

"Let's sit on the porch," she will suggest, and guide you around the house to the shade of the front porch. She will put you in the rocking chair and sit beside you in a rush-seat straight-back chair. "Do you like it?" she will ask, gesturing at the porch and its furniture. "I think it suggests the mood of the porch of Lara's store in *Firefly*. Don't you think? The chairs, at least. I found them at an antique shop in Harrison. And look at that porch swing. I'm sorry, are you ill? Can I get you anything? A glass of water? Or something stronger? There's dandelion wine, and homemade beer, and...yes! guess what, Mr. G, I've got a jug of your authentic old Stick Around moonshine! Would you care for a taste? It's the 'pure quill,' as you put it. I bought it from one of Lothar Chisholm's sons, up on the mountain." She will jump up and go into the house, and return with two glasses and a genuine old stoneware jug, and will pour a generous dollop of the colorless liquid into both glasses. "I'm sorry there's no ice. Do you like it 'neat,' Mr. G? Or shall I get you some water?" You will shake your head, and she will clank her glass against yours and say, "Well, here's to your happy 'homecoming,' Mr. G!" She will take a sip, and then go on, "I half expected to see you show up, eventually. That is, I said to myself that you hadn't been back to the Ozarks in a long time, and you were probably getting restless to come back again, and that I wouldn't be at all surprised if you just came driving up the road some day. And now look, here you are!" But then her delight will cloud over, and she will ask, concernedly, "Is something wrong? What is it?"

"It's nothing," you will say. "I'm somewhat flabbergasted, is all. Except for a precious few of my students at college, nobody ever mentions my books to me. I've never met anybody in Little Rock who's even heard of them." [You will almost slip, here, G, you will almost add: "Not even your own mother, who reads so much."]

She will laugh. "I'll bet you're wondering what I'm doing here. You must have realized when you first saw me that I'm not a native of the Ozarks, despite this house and these clothes." She will indicate her attire, a simple summer dress of flower-print pattern like those that Ozark girls had worn in the thirties and forties...except that it is a maternity dress. "Even though I'm a native of Arkansas, I'd never been very much interested in the Ozarks until I read *Firefly*, and until…oh, it's a long, long story, Mr. G, and I very much doubt that even *you* would believe it. I've thought sometimes of trying to write the story myself, but I doubt anyone would believe me. Are you looking for story material, Mr. G? Isn't that part of the reason why you've come back to Stick Around? Would you like to hear the most marvelous story? Perhaps you could write it, so that it would be believed…."

And she will begin to tell you a most marvelous story, commencing on an afternoon in June of the previous year, in the waiting room of a Porsche dealer in Garfield, New Jersey. You will listen carefully and with great interest, interrupting her gently at times when you do not hear her or when you misunderstand what she is saying. Yes, you will begin to think, it is a story for a book. A fairytale book, maybe, but still….

"Wait!" you will interrupt her, early in her narrative. "Now hold on just a minute, and let me get this straight. I have one big question: *Why* were you so interested in this 'Daniel Lyam Montross'?"

"I was getting to that," she will protest, a little petulantly, "I was simply trying to 'pace' my story, in the same way that you do, Mr. G. Well, here it is: you see, Daniel Lyam Montross was my grandfather."

"*What*?!" you will exclaim. "No! Oh, come now, Miss Stoving, you can't expect anyone to believe *that*!"

It will be she, now, who is looking astonished. Her mouth will gape open, and then in a tiny little voice she will say, "Mr. G…?"

"Yes?" you will say.

"Mr. G," she will say in almost a hoarse whisper, "you called me 'Miss Stoving' just now. Why did you call me that? How did you know what my name is?"

"Well…" you will extemporize. "Some people down the road. I was asking them who lived in this house now, and they told me your name."

"But I haven't told anyone around here what my real name is."

"You haven't? Are you sure?"

"I'm *very* sure, Mr. G. Please, *please* tell me how you knew my name."

"Well, Diana—may I call you Diana?—I have a little story of my own to tell you." By this time, G, the very last thing you will care to mention to her is her father. You will not tell her that you are, as it were, in her father's employ; you will merely tell her that you had happened to see in the *Arkansas Gazette* a news item to the effect that she had disappeared, and that, because you were at loose ends and needed something to do, you had decided to test your sleuthing powers by trying to find her. She will be very much flattered; she will be completely awed at the masterful way you had managed to trace her from Susan Trombley to P.D. Sedgely and thence to Dudleytown, and thence to Five Corners. You will even confess how deeply *involved* with her you had come to feel. You will not tell her that you have fallen in love with the thought of her; not yet, at least; that might come later. But you will say to her, after telling her how you traced her to Five Corners, "You can't imagine how relieved I was to be able to deduce, from various clues, that it was not you but *he* who was buried in that grave."

Again her jaw will hang slack as she stares at you with awe. "Buried?" she will say. "*Grave?*" she will say. And a long moment will pass before her laughter (nervous is it, G?) and her next words: "Oh, *that.*"

"Yes," you will say. "*That.* But don't misunderstand me. I was sorry, too. I wasn't *entirely* relieved. My elation and sadness were all mixed together. I sensed that you and the boy must have spent enough time together to become rather, well, shall we say *attached* to one another, and therefore his suicide must have been a shock to you, regardless of his—"

"Mr. G," she will interrupt, and ask you a matter-of-fact question "How long can you stay?"

"Pardon?" you will not have understood exactly her question.

"How long can you stay? How long do you plan to stick around in Stick Around? Now that you've found me, after so much trouble, you didn't intend to rush right off, did you?"

"Oh, no," you will say. "I can stay as long as you wish. I can stick around forever, if you want me to."

"Good," she will say. "Not forever, but long enough to hear all my story, to learn all of Day's story, and to learn as much as you can of Daniel Lyam Montross's story. It might take a while. There's an extra bedroom upstairs. In fact, it was Daniel Lyam Montross's own bedroom, and I think he would have been very happy to know that you came and stayed in it, and that you might even give him the immortality he deserves by writing a book about him some day. So, will you stay?"

"I'd love to," you will say, at a loss for better words to express your complete delight and anticipation.

"Fine," she will say. "Maybe even, if you stay long enough, you might get to meet Day. He's gone…some other place…for a while. You see—and I'd rather wait and tell this at the appropriate time in the story—but recently we have reached that part of Daniel Lyam Montross's life where he will leave Stick Around for a period of two weeks in order to go to Little Rock and—no, I won't tell you, just yet, what he went to Little Rock for; all I can tell you is that it concerns *me*, when I was a little girl. Well, anyway, Day decided to go off by himself during this two-week period that Daniel is gone to Little Rock, partly because Daniel doesn't want me to know about it. But there's another reason, which is Day's own idea: that maybe we've been getting tired of each other, seeing so much of each other all the time for months and months. So, just as a little "experiment," we have separated for two weeks, to see if 'absence makes the heart grow fonder.' I think Day has built himself a little hut off in the woods, up the mountain, somewhere—he won't tell me where it is; that's part of the experiment, you see. But he'll be back. Oh, yes, he'll be back! And we write letters to each other every day, isn't that sweet?"

You will be concentrating intently on her words, as if trying to detect any indication that she might really be as demented as you are beginning to think she is. She will sound perfectly rational, and even truthful. But you will not be able to accept it. You cannot join her in her illusions. *One* of you has to keep fingers wrapped tightly around reality, or all is lost. The only response you can make to her "explanation" is to say: "You write *letters*?"

"Yes, and we 'mail' them, too. We take them down to the store, that empty building which used to be the Stick Around post office, *you* know, and we just leave them for each other in the old boxes. My box number is 47 and his box number is 28. Every day we write to each other! I wish I could let you read his letters! *Then* you'd believe me! But his letters are rather *personal*, you know, and besides, I don't think he would want me to show them to you."

"But the grave," you will protest, "the grave in Five Corners.... *Who* is buried there?"

She will smile and say, "Both of us."

You will reel dizzily for a moment, G, and begin to feel that your aggravated case of solipsism has driven you loose from whatever semblance of reality still remains of this "world."

But then she will laugh at your perplexity, and will say, "You do this yourself, G. In your own fictions, you sometimes play maddening tricks with reality. In order to build up suspense, is it? All right, are you suspended? Do you want to hear our story? Shall I continue? Very well. It was a Sunday morning in June when we left New Jersey and drove northeastward toward Dudleytown. Before we got there, it began to rain very hard...."

☦ 15 ☦

It will be already late afternoon before you manage to get away with the excuse that you need to pick up a carton of Pall Malls, and to drive into the square of the small county seat, Jessup; you will park in front of Buford's Hardware Store and go in. Old Clovis Buford is still running the place himself, you will be pleased to see. He does not recognize nor remember you. You will not tell him your name. You will ask him, "Would you send a telegram for me?"

"This aint Western Union, mister," he will say. "But fer twenty cents cash money, I'll let ye use my phone to call up Harrison way and send yore tellygram."

You will explain that you are hard of hearing and unable to use the telephone. You will give him twenty cents and ask him if he would kindly make the call for you. He will phone into the operator at Harrison, and you will dictate your message:

B.A. STOVING
UNION BANK BUILDING
LITTLE ROCK
PLEASE ADVISE NAME DIANA'S GRANDFATHER
SOONEST IMPORTANT STOP

G
C/O BUFORD'S HARDWARE
STORE
JESSUP, ARKANSAS

And then there will be nothing to do but hang around and wait for a reply. "Hot day, aint it?" Clovis Buford will say. "Awful hot fer this time a May. Don't look to rain, neither." He will putter around in your vicinity, stacking up his merchandise. "What-all kind of car is that you got out there, mister?" You will tell him that it is a Volvo, of Swedish manufacture. "Don't 'low as how I ever heerd tell a that kind afore," he will say. "You git good mileage on her?" You will tell him that the mileage is pretty good. He will amble over to his window for a better look at it, and to see if he can see your license plates. He will come back and say, "*Ver*-mont! Where in thunderation is *Ver*-mont at?" You will explain that Ver-*mont* is a New England state, east of upper New York State. "Git kinda cold, winters, up yonder?" he will ask. Pretty cold, you will tell him. Much snow. He will ponder your strange bearded face closely and say, "I aint seen you hereabouts before, have I? You got any folks, this part a the country?" And you will want very much to say, "Mr. Buford, do you remember a little boy who came in here one day, oh about thirty years ago, and asked you if you carried any spare tongues for toy wagons? Well, that was me." But you won't tell him this. You will say: "No, I'm sorry to say, but I don't have any folks around here. Not any more."

Finally, the phone will ring, and Mr. Buford will scribble on a scrap of wrapping paper your answer:

G
C/O BUFORD'S HARDWARE STORE
JESSUP, ARKANSAS
NAME DIANA'S GRANDFATHER RICHARD ARTHUR
STOVING THE THIRD
STOP QUERY WHY STOP

                                    B.A. STOVING

"Could you phone another telegram for me?" you will ask Mr. Buford.

"You got the money, I got the time, heh, heh," he will say.

You will glance at your watch. It will be ten minutes until five o'clock. "Let's hurry," you will say.

Mr. Buford will have a little difficulty reaching the operator in Harrison this time, but your telegram will be placed through shortly before five.

B.A. STOVING
UNION BANK BUILDING
LITTLE ROCK
HER OTHER REPEAT OTHER GRANDFATHER STOP
THAT IS COMMA HER
MATERNAL GRANDFATHER HER MOTHER'S
FATHER STOP HIS NAME PLEASE STOP

                                              G

"Operator says you owe me three dollars and twenty-two cents fer them two telly-grams," Mr. Buford will say. You will pay him, and out of gratitude for his making the calls for you, you will wonder if there is anything in his store which you might buy from him. Any hardware? A gift for Diana, perhaps? What might she need? How about this electric mixer? But she doesn't have electricity. Do *you* need *any*thing, G? A knife? A fishing pole? A *gun* perhaps? Yes, you might care to do some quail hunting. Perhaps a good but inexpensive rifle. Mr. Buford will show you his stock of .22's. Longrifle twelve-shot automatic. Good for birds. Mr. Buford is happy to sell you the rifle. He hasn't made very many sales this day.

"Who's this hyere 'grandfather' feller yo're so interested in?" Mr. Buford will ask, and then apologize, "Don't mean to be nosey, no."

Oh, just a fellow you were trying to locate, you will say. And then you will decide to ask him, "Mr. Buford, have you ever heard of anybody named Daniel Lyam Montross?"

He will scratch his head, and hem and haw. "Sounds kinda familiar. But cain't say as how I have," he will say. "Whereabouts does he live at?"

"He used to live up beyond Stick Around," you will say.

"Hhmmm, now. What's he do?"

"He's dead," you will say, but will add, "I think."

"Daniel Lyam Montross, huh? I wush Fern was still here. She had a better head for names than me. But she passed on last summer. Had breast complaints fer a time, and was laid up at the sanertarium down to Booneville. Brought her home, and she seemed to perk up, but then took a turn fer the worse again. Had to rush her up to Harrison in the middle of the night. Doctors said—"

Mr. Buford will give you a long history of his late wife's diseases, and then begin discussing a few of his own ailments. He will describe in detail the symptoms of one recent disorder, and ask you what you would prescribe. You will tell him that you haven't the slightest idea, and will discover that he has been mistaking you for a doctor. Perhaps because of your appearance. You will feel a little flattered, and will point out to him that you *are* a doctor, but not a medical doctor. You will try to explain to him what a Ph.D. is. He will appear to understand, but then he will have great difficulty understanding what art history is. In fact, he will not be able to understand at all what art history is.

An hour will pass and no reply will come to your second telegram. Probably, you will realize, it had failed to reach Stoving before his office closed. You will wonder if you should send a duplicate of it to his home address. But you will have already put Mr. Buford to such bother, making your phone calls for you, and now he will be acting kind of fidgety, and will say to you, "Gener'ly I have to close up store long about now and go eat my supper." It is after six o'clock. You will not ask him to keep his store open any longer. The matter can wait. There is no hurry. You will have all the time in the world.

All the time in the world, G, and on your return to Stick Around that evening, you will drive slowly, observing the beauty of the countryside, and reflecting that in this world of Ozarkadia there is no place for an art historian. *Why did I ever leave?* you will be wondering, forgetting why you left. *And now that I'm here, why don't I just stay?*

You will permit yourself a pleasant dream of your future, fabricating your future life in Stick Around, with lovely Diana at the center of that life…if only you carefully and successfully are able to help her weather the grave crisis of relinquishing her delusion that Day Whittacker still exists. And your first big task will be to prove it to yourself.

You will stop again at the old abandoned post office, just for a few minutes, just long enough to set a "trap": from the glove compartment of your car you will take a small whisk broom and then go into the post office. You will sweep the dust on the floor until it has accumulated in a thick layer in front of the post office boxes. There now. Anybody coming to the post office boxes will leave their footprints in that dust.

Then you will go on "home," to an excellent dinner of catfish fried in cornmeal. Diana will claim she caught the fish herself, in Banner Creek.

After the meal, she will resume telling the story of her

Dudleytown adventure. First she will offer you a postprandial glass of the moonshine. But you will fetch from the Volvo your own half-gallon of Old Grand-Dad.

"What an appropriate name!" she will laugh, and share it with you.

✝ 16 ✝

You will wake up late the next morning in a bed in the room which had been mine, and at first you will not be able to recall where you are or how you came here. You will lie in bed for half an hour nursing your splitting hangover and trying to piece together the evening before. As the evening progressed and you listened to more and more of her story about Dudleytown, you will have consumed more than enough bourbon, more than even you, old Guzzler, usually drank. Possibly the reason we lost the eye of your "I" in the First Movement was that that eye was befuddled by the booze. At any rate, you can't remember an awful lot of her story, and after she will have begun telling of their move to Vermont you will lose the track entirely. All you will hear is that strange new tinnitus in your ear: that sound of a fiddle playing one of the eight John Playford dances, so real, so audible, that it will seem to have been coming from right outside the window of my house.

Still fully clothed (except for your shoes, which she will have removed), you do not need to get up and dress; you will merely need to get up. You will rise and put on your shoes and stagger down the stairs and to the kitchen, where you will find her shelling peas into a bowl. "Good morning," you will say. "Where can I wash up?" She will indicate the sink in the kitchen and the pail of water beside it. She will ask how you like your eggs, and you will reply, Scrambled.

While you are having your breakfast, she will say, politely, "I hope you slept well."

"Like a log," you will say. "Deeply and without a single dream. How much did I drink last night?"

"Oh, about half of your bottle."

"My bottle's a half-gallon. That means a quart. I hope I behaved myself."

"Well..." she will hesitate. "Toward the end, you *did* get a little bit...well, *frisky*, let's say."

"I hope I didn't...*molest* you or anything."

"No. Well, you just kissed me, once. And you asked me to sleep with you. But you passed out as soon as your head touched the pillow. I wasn't exactly sober myself. But I remember, toward the end, asking you why you were drinking so much, and you said it was because my story is so *sad*. But I don't think it's very sad, G, really; I think it's a very happy story, with a very happy ending. Why did you think it was sad?"

"Ignore what I say when I'm stoned, Diana. When I'm stoned, I reduce myself in my own eyes to nothing, and therefore nothing I say can matter. But tell me, you said your story has a 'happy ending.' Do you mean your story has already ended?"

"Well, yes, in a way. I mean, we've found the right place and we're settled now, and it's almost time for what you might call the very last chapter in Daniel Lyam Montross's life. Just as soon as Day comes back—"

"And *when*, may I ask, will that be?"

"I told you, I don't know. It's up to him. Listen, would you like to walk down to the post office with me and see if today's letter from him has arrived? Maybe it will say when he's coming."

"I'll drive you in my car," you will offer.

"No," she will say. "It's just a mile. And you need the exercise, don't you? Last night, when you were pretty far gone, you started telling me about what your doctors had said. Are you *really* dying, G? Don't you think that if you got a lot of exercise, and took off some weight, and stopped drinking and smoking so much, and—"

"Please, Diana," you will protest. "I *know* that. It's etched in acid on my heart. But all right, I don't mind walking to your 'post office' with you." So then the two of you will set out on your hike to the post office, this fine May morning with wild flowers all along the way and the singing of birds you cannot hear because of the tinnitus of fiddles, real or imagined, playing one of the eight John Playford dances. You will notice the letter she is carrying, her reply to the "letter" she's supposedly got from him the day before, and you will say, "I should think that two people who have been seeing as much of each other as you and Day have supposedly been doing would eventually run out of things to say to each other."

"Oh, no!" she will protest. "That isn't true at all! I wish I could let you read one of his letters; then you'd see what I mean. One of the things Daniel Lyam Montross learned when he was a young man, from that Henry Fox I was telling you about when you were getting so woozy last night—maybe you don't remember, but one of the characteristics of love is that two people will share themselves completely and therefore never run out of things to say. Does your mind ever run out of things to *think* about, G? No, I didn't think it *could*. Day tells me everything that's on his mind, and it's always interesting."

"And you?" you will ask. "Do you tell 'him' everything that's on your mind?"

"Well, I don't think—and I'm not just trying to be modest—but I don't think my mind is anywhere near as interesting as his. But yes, I try to tell him everything. At least, I never keep anything from him."

"In other words," you will attempt a clarification, "you would consider yourself to be genuinely in love with 'him,' according to Henry Fox's definition?"

"Of course!" she will say, as if you didn't even need to state something so obvious. You cannot help feeling madly jealous, and you will feel that it is even worse to be so jealous of someone who doesn't exist. And you will realize that it isn't going to be as easy as you thought to get "him" off her mind.

You will arrive at the post office, and go into the building with her, watching her as she puts her letter into Box 28. The first thing you will notice is that there are no footprints in the dust except her own, the small prints of her canvas sneakers. But now she will open Box 47 and find there a "letter" which, you will notice, is enclosed in an envelope identical with the one she has put into the other box. You will crane your neck to observe the handwriting on the envelope, which will seem very similar to the handwriting on the other envelope. "Busybody!" she will say, laughing, and move away from you to open her "letter" and "read" it. Several passages of the "letter" will cause her to laugh, but she will not pretend to share them with you. For a moment, you will even feel jealous again of "him" for making her laugh. You will be tempted to snatch the letter from her and look at it yourself, but you are afraid that you won't know quite what to say to her if the paper proved to be blank.

"Well," she will report at length, "he doesn't say when he's coming back, definitely, but he says he doesn't think he can stand to miss me so, very much longer. And he's nearly finished seeding the mountain."

"Doing what, pardon me?"

"Seeding the mountain. He's carrying on some work that Daniel started but couldn't finish before his death. You see, or maybe you *know*, don't you?—that the loggers back in the thirties and forties brutally cut the timber out of the forests around here and never bothered to plant seedlings to replace it, so that a lot of scrub wood took over the forests. It's the first thing that Day noticed when we got here, how ugly these woods are in contrast to the magnificent forests of North Carolina. It made him sorry that we had left Lost Cove. But Daniel had felt the same way, and, instead of brooding about it, he got busy and started cutting out the scrub woods and transplanting seedlings of pine and such. Almost all of the thirty-year-old pines that you'll find on Lingerfelt Mountain are ones that he planted. But there was a piece of about forty acres that he never finished before he was killed, so Day has been finishing that piece for him."

"Good boy," you will comment, but again feeling green with jealousy as well as feeling the absurdity of envying someone who doesn't exist. "I'm most eager to meet him. Do you happen to know when he usually brings his letters to the post office?"

"Are you thinking of trying to waylay him?" she will ask with a smile. "I don't know, really. Every morning I've been coming here at just about this same time, and his letter is always there waiting for me. But I don't know whether he comes before me, in the morning, or after me, in the afternoon. Or at night, for that matter."

Diana will retrieve the letter she has posted in "his" box and ask you for a pencil. You will give her your ballpoint. The envelope is sealed, but she will write something on the back of the envelope and then show it to you to read: "P.S. He says he is 'most eager' to meet you. So hurry, darling, please. And don't forget the tablets." She will return it to Box 28.

"Is he taking medicine?" you will ask. "What are these 'tablets'?"

"Oh, those are his writing-tablets, the notebooks he kept when we were living in Five Corners, Vermont. In the letter, I told him that we ought to let you read it. It's much better written than my diary."

"You kept a diary?" you will ask.

"Yes, and ever since you arrived yesterday I've been debating with myself whether or not I ought to let you read it. If you're really serious about doing a book about me—about *us*, I mean—then you ought to read it. Of course, some of it is *very* personal. But it might help you understand my point of view. Are you interested?"

"Am I *interested*?" you will exclaim. "I'm perishing with interest!"

"Oh, really?" she will say skeptically. "But last night when I was trying to tell you my story, you got drunk and I don't think you were even listening, or trying to listen, most of the time."

"I'm sorry. But don't you think that in your telling of the story you were inclined to, shall we say, *censor* a bit? I mean, after all, a boy and girl alone together in the woods...."

Diana will laugh. "Oh, *I* get it!" she will say. "I left out the sex, is that it? Well, I'm afraid my diary doesn't tell everything. Day's notebooks are 'hotter' than my diary. But if you want the real spice about Daniel, you'll have to hear the tapes and poems."

"Tapes and poems!" you will exclaim. "Good lord, we've got quite an archive on our hands, haven't we? Incidentally, if you've been missing one of your tapes, I'm returning it to you. I found it underneath your lean-to at Five Corners."

"Oh bless your heart! That must be Henry Fox's 'love' tape. Did you listen to it?"

"Unfortunately, I can't hear well enough to listen to a tape recorder. I was hoping you could be my 'ears' for me."

"I will! Oh, I'm *so* glad you found that tape. It's our most important tape, Henry Fox's *last* tape, and I wondered what had happened to it. It was one of our last tapes in Five Corners, before—"

"Yes, before?" you will prod. "Before *what*?"

"Before we had to leave."

"Why did you have to leave?"

"Well, that part of the story was finished anyway. Daniel Lyam Montross himself left Five Corners right after hearing that last monologue from Henry Fox. Get the tape. I'll read it for you."

You will fetch from the car the cassette recorder with the tape in it, and she will play it, stopping it after each sentence to repeat back to you my version of Henry Fox's last great sermon in definition of love. How the sharing of privies leads to love. You have wanted to know for years, G, what love is, so that you could better understand why you've never had any. If that is all you will have wanted to know, your search will now be over.

"Beautiful," you will say when she finishes. "That privy metaphor of Fox's is positively enchanting. But tell me, if you and 'Day' have actually attained a state of love that fits Henry Fox's definition, why don't you share your privy?"

"How do you know we don't?"

"Forgive me, but I couldn't help but notice that your privy, Diana, has only *one* hole."

She will laugh, and say, "Oh, my." She will sigh and say, "You really *are* a detective, aren't you? What am I going to do? At this rate, you'll know all of my secrets pretty soon."

"The sooner the better," you will say.

"It's still going to take a while," she will declare.

⚜ 17 ⚜

It will take a while, all right, G, more than a while, before you will learn the whole story. The sheer size of her archives will overwhelm you: her thick diaries, Day's tablets, my collected poems, not to mention the voluminous aural documentation, her collection of over one thousand hours of cassette tape recordings. She will offer to select the more important ones, and, since you cannot hear them, she will offer to listen to them herself and then speak slowly to you so you can understand her, as she repeats my words recorded on the tapes, beginning with my childhood and boyhood in Dudleytown. These tapes will indeed be "spicy" enough for you, and the novelty of hearing my bawdy words on the lovely lips of this girl will be an erotic entertainment such as you have never experienced before. What a delightful evening you will have! My first "priming" with Violate Parmenter will arouse you so much that you will be tempted to ask Diana if she would like to reenact the scene with you, but, since you will have promised her that you won't drink quite so much this evening, in order to be more attentive to the story, you won't have the nerve the drink would have given you. Nor will you, when bedtime comes, have either the nerve to invite her to join you in bed or sufficient drowsiness to enable you to sleep. Your evening routines, old Groove, had long since fixed themselves into such a pattern: no drink, no sex; no sex, no sleep; no sleep, much drink; much drink, no sex. When she will yawn and announce that it is past her bedtime, all you could do will be to explain that you can't sleep without another drink or two. You will hope, of course, that she will suggest an alternative soporific, but she won't. All she will say is, "Well, as long as you're staying up, you might as well have something to read." And she will give you the first volume of her diary. And peck you a quick wet kiss on your forehead before running off to bed.

Old Gullet will keep company with Old Grand-Dad and the young confessions for the next two hours. Her diary does not, as she has said, contain much sex. She seemed often to be more interested in what she had to eat. Obviously, during the latter stages of the Dudleytown episode, she and this Day Whittacker had frequent sexual relations, and, as she confessed to the diary, she had shared herself with the hippies or Jesus freaks or whatever they were, which disturbed you greatly, old Grudge, but, by giving you a picture of a girl who was "mixed up" enough to do such things, prepared you in advance for the far more muddled happenings in Five Corners, the oral things, the voyeuristic things, culminating in this strange and disoriented entry:

December 4

Now why did he have to go and do that?? Oh what a horrible child I've been! But oh how immature and impulsive he was! I don't know which was worse, my shameful self-centered wickedness which drove him to it, or his self-pitying melodramatic overreaction to my badness. Was it such a terrible request for me to make? Just to watch him play with himself? Is that so abominable? I'm so confused I don't have any values lately; I can't judge how wrong or innocent something is. I think perhaps he really wanted to kill Daniel; that's what he was trying to do. But the funny thing is that he couldn't, and didn't, kill Daniel. Daniel is still very much alive, and *with* me, and I had a long long talk with him, in which I told him I'd love to write his poems for him in Lost Cove. I want to get to Lost Cove as soon as I can. This place has driven me crazy. I've been here too long. It's time to go some other place.

You will close the diary then, and close your eyes for a moment, fighting off an involuntary shudder, and with the help of another belt of Old Grand-Dad you will formulate your Great Guess: poor self-pitying Day Whittacker had indeed hanged himself, unable to cope with the rich skeins of Diana's efflorescent personality, and she, poor thing, had been totally unable to accept the fact of his death, and had, despite burying him in Five Corners, gone on believing that he still exists. She had gone on alone to Lost Cove, the very place itself symbolic of her lost and deluded state, and now has come to Stick Around, still alone, but waiting, waiting for Day's resurrection. In time she will realize, perhaps, that such a resurrection is never going to occur, and *then*, G, you could take his place, and have her for your own, and help her find her way out of all the lost places of her mind.

How ironic that you will no longer be bent on proving whether or not *I* ever existed, but instead determined to help her realize that Day Whittacker no longer exists.

Now it is late, and that fiddle music in your ear will be giving you trouble. It will be too late to listen to another one of the eight Playford dances. Before going to bed, you will stand for a moment in the doorway of Diana's room, peering through the darkness at the form of her body curled into sleep. You will want very much to go and touch her belly, to find out if there really is a solid bulge of flesh there, if she really is pregnant, or if she hasn't simply been wearing a pillow or something beneath her dress. But you will know that even a solid bulge of flesh would not necessarily prove anything; you know of the phenomenon called "false or imaginary pregnancy" in which women actually swell up psychosomatically in their conviction of being pregnant. So you will not touch her, now. But you will feel a great wave of compassion for that poor, lonely, confused creature, and it will be all you can do to force yourself to go to your own bed. "I'll take care of you," you will mumble aloud before falling asleep.

It will be late, as usual, when you will wake up, and find that the house is empty. She will not be in the garden or yard either. You will be pleased to notice, in the kitchen, that she has left for you, on the warming shelf of the old iron cookstove, a plate of scrambled eggs and bacon with a slice of toast, and there is a pot of coffee on the stove. While you have your breakfast, you will uneasily reflect that it, the breakfast, might be her parting gift for you, that she might have fled, that she might have had misgivings about letting you read her incriminating diary, or that she might be afraid that you are going to get all of her secrets out of her.

After breakfast, you will set out, on foot, for the post office. That will be your intention, your destination, anyway, to see that there are no new footprints in the dust by the boxes and to see, and possibly open, any new "letter" from "him." You will be a bit surprised, then, to meet her on the road, coming from that direction.

"Where have you been?" you will ask her.

She will show you the bouquet in her hand. "Oh, just out picking wild flowers along the road," she will say.

"You haven't been to the post office?"

"Not yet," she will say, but something in the tone of her voice will make you believe she is lying. Then she will ask you, "Where are you going?"

"Oh, I was just looking for you," you will say, and reflect, *Here we are, brazenly deceiving each other already.*

"Well, shall we walk to the post office?" she will ask. "First, I'll have to go and fetch my letter at the house and put these flowers in a vase. But you walk on, and I'll catch up with you."

So you will walk on, at a fast clip, but she, young thing, will soon catch up with you, and, showing you her envelope, which is not yet sealed, will say, "I've decided that if I can let you read my diary I might as well let you read my letters…if you'd care to."

And you will care to.

Dearsomest, darlingsomest Day-O,

Boy, you'd better come on back, P.D.Q. I miss you, I do, I do. Our little "experiment" has gone on long enough, don't you think? You miss me, I miss you, we miss us, us miss we, so let's cut out all this missing, hey love? Besides, I'm beginning to suspect that G thinks you don't even exist.

You *do*, don't you? Sometimes I wonder. Your letter yesterday was wonderful, and I'm tickled to pieces to hear about that raccoon you found, but sometimes it seems as if your letters come from another world. Sometimes I find myself disbelieving that you really are just *somewhere* around here in the woods. Where are you, Day? Please at least tell me that, just so I can think, when I think of you (as I do all the time, you know it, old Love), just so I can think of *where* you are. Lingerfelt Mountain? Hardscrapple Mountain? South Bench? Butterchurn Holler? I promise I won't go and try to find you, if you don't want.

Kiss that adorable raccoon for me. What are you going to name him, or her, or it?

love love love O infinite love,
Diana

p.s. My new friend G is a very lonely person, a very sad person. You know what Daniel tells us, in his Seventh Beatitude, that the true peacemakers are those who never close themselves off from their kindred. And G *is* our kindred. I think what he's really looking for is love. And you won't mind, will you? Remember the Fifth and Sixth Beatitudes.

Reading this letter, old Grasper, will give you a mixture of feelings: at first, you will feel covetous of those sweet endearments she addresses "him" with, but then you will become gradually certain that this letter is not really addressed to "him" but to you (after all, as she says, she has "decided" to let you read it), and it is her indirect way of letting you know that she herself is willing to admit the possibility of Day's nonexistence, and that furthermore she is getting ready to accept you as her lover but will have to "clear" it first with her conscience in the form of this dearsomest Day-O.

"What are these Beatitudes?" you will ask her.

"You haven't noticed the walls of your room?" she will ask you. When you shake your head, she will tell you, "Well, next time you're up there, take a close look at the walls. That was *his* room, as I told you, Daniel Lyam Montross's room, and during his last days he wrote on the—" she will pause, and resume, "On second thought, *don't* look at the walls. Not yet, anyway. You've got to hear the rest of the story first, and read—Oh, look what we've got here!"

You will have arrived at the post office, and she will now "find," stuffed into her box so that its door won't close, a roll of notebooks, soft-cover spiral-bound notebooks of the kind used by your college students. "They're Day's tablets," she will exclaim. "He sent them, after all! I didn't think he would!"

You will notice again there are no footprints in the dust except her own. *So that,* you will tell yourself, *explains her absence from the house this morning. She had to come down here to "plant" Day's notebooks, and also, probably, another "letter" from "him."*

"Here," she will say, giving you the notebooks. "These are for you. And this is for me"—she will indicate the "letter" which, you notice again, is in the same kind of envelope as those she sends her letters in. She will begin "reading" it to herself, keeping her distance from you so that you can't pry, and giggling occasionally (rather falsely, you will detect) at the "contents" of the "letter."

When she has finished and refolded the letter and reinserted it in its envelope, you will protest, "Why won't you let me read his letters if you'll let me read yours?"

"I can't share *every*thing with you," she will say, laughing. "There are some things that are simply *too* personal. But I can tell you most of what he said. He said that he's glad you're here; he thinks it's just what Daniel Lyam Montross is looking for, that is, your coming here is just what we need. And therefore Day is glad to be of any help, and he sends you his tablets with his compliments, his best respects, and his doubts that 'such a great writer,' as he calls you, would find his style very attractive, but he adds a caution that in reading his tablets you should refrain from judging him too harshly, or judging me too harshly, until you've heard all of the rest of the story, and, although he would love to meet you, he is not going to come back until you've heard *all* of the story, and are prepared to acknowledge two things, first, that he and I have done nothing 'wrong,' in your opinion, and second, that you believe with all of your heart in Daniel Lyam Montross."

A clever and inventive girl! you will reflect, admiring her for the swiftness of her mind that can concoct *ad libitum* such fanciful but plausible contingencies. But your own swift mind, old Gambiter, will detect the Queen's sly maneuver to put you in check, and will make your Knight forestall her.

"That sounds almost like a kind of blackmail," you will point out. "What you're saying is, in effect, that he will never appear *unless* I meet those two conditions. And what if I can't?"

"Don't be so pessimistic," she will say. "And there, you have his notebooks. So get busy and read them, and, as he says, don't be too quick to judge either one of us."

You are not a fast reader, and it will take you most of the day to read the notebooks. You will be deliberately reading slower than usual, trying to understand all the circumstances leading up to the hanging. For a shady reading spot, you will pick a secluded thicket across the road from the post office, a spot where the Squires Creek Bank and Trust Company had stood before it was taken apart so that its stones could be piled along the road edge to hold back the waters of the occasionally flooding Squires Creek. From this shady thicket, you can spy on the post office, in case Diana comes again to "plant" another letter or to retrieve her own letter. But, absent from the Ozarks for such a long time, you will have forgotten that thickets such as this one you are hiding in are likely to be infested with chiggers and ticks. When you will begin to scratch, in the late afternoon, you will think that it is nervous scratching brought upon you by Day's story of their unhappy life in Five Corners.

Your feelings toward Day Whittacker, while reading his story, will be ambivalent, to put it mildly. You will feel that Day wasn't able to understand Diana very well, that often the age difference between them became an age gap. You will wish that it had been *you* who had lived with her in Five Corners. But then you will realize that the foundation for such a wish lay in the fact that you and Day Whittacker are very much alike. You will remember yourself at the age of nineteen. There will be times when you will find yourself not only scratching but brushing away a tear or two from your eyes. When was the last time you were ever able to weep while reading anything? Go ahead. It will be good for you. It will help you believe.

In time, although you will realize that your tears are real, you will become aware that your scratching is not produced by the same source; you will remember that there are such things as ticks and chiggers, and you will quickly if belatedly get out of that secluded thicket. Before returning to Diana's house, you will check the post office and find that her letter to "Day" is gone. Had she used the back door of the post office to retrieve it? The footprints in the dust are the same, only hers. But she has not, you will be pleased to notice, "planted" another "letter" from "him." A good omen? Is she getting ready to give him up?

When you see her again, at suppertime, you will say, "Well, I've finished his notebooks. And naturally, I'm left with a few questions, if you don't mind."

She won't mind.

"My most important question," you will point out, "assuming that I am expected to write this whole story, and make it plausible, is simply this: If Day Whittacker hanged himself in Five Corners, why, for God's sake, *why* must you go on with this pretense that he still exists?"

"That's simple," she will say. "I hate to spoil whatever illusions *you* would like to have, G, but the fact is that he didn't succeed. He must have forgotten about 'Fox's Law,' one of the most important things that Henry Fox ever taught to Daniel. I'll play the tape for you if you'd care to hear it. Anyway, the essence of Fox's Law is that there is an inverse ratio between how much one wants or expects something to happen and how likely it is *to* happen. In other words, if you expect something, you won't get it. If you get something, you didn't expect it. I guess I must have forgotten it myself, because I should have known that as long as I actually expected him to...to...well, you know why he tried to hang himself, don't you? because I...I had this selfish whim to watch him play...well, you *read* that awful part, didn't you? I should have known that since I wanted and expected him to do it, he would never, never do it.

And when he climbed that tree, I expected that he wouldn't do it, he wouldn't jump. And because I expected he wouldn't, he *did*. Yes, he jumped. But, don't you see, Fox's Law was operating on him too. He fully *expected* to kill himself. He was quite confident he could do it. Confidence breeds expectation. He knew he was quite skilled at climbing trees. Even more was he skilled at tying knots. He had every expectation of success. And for that reason he failed. Don't you see?"

No, G, you will not see. A clever job of backing and filling, yes, but obviously another *ad libitum* concoction. "How do you mean, he 'failed'?" you will ask. "What happened?"

"Oh, it was pathetic. When he jumped, he sort of tripped, and fell only about eight or ten feet, down to another limb, and got all tangled up in his rope. It took me nearly an hour to climb up there and help him get loose. And even then he was in a state of shock, and couldn't, or *wouldn't*, talk to me. But Daniel would still talk to me. What's the matter? Don't you believe me?"

"There remain a couple of other questions. One of these I have asked you before: *Who*, then, is buried in that grave?"

"And you remember what I answered last time you asked it, that *both* of us are. That's the end of *your* story. I died of a gunshot wound in Woodstock Hospital, and Day buried me in Five Corners and then hanged himself, and Dr. Fox came back and buried Day in the same grave with me. Isn't that beautiful?"

"You're aggravating my solipsism something awful."

"Is that why you're scratching yourself so much? Is your solipsism itching you, or do you scratch just to prove that your flesh still exists?"

"No, they're chigger bites."

"But, 'I itch, therefore I am,' right? As long as you itch, you know that you *are*. But you've got to let me, and Day, and Daniel exist too. Because *we are*. That 'grave' you found was nothing but a trench that Day dug to bury our stuff in. Dr. Fox left us only one pair of snowshoes, and in order to get out of that place, Day had to carry me. As Dr. Fox told him, jokingly, if he could carry me four miles when I was shot he could carry me one or two miles when I was well. But anyway we couldn't carry all of our stuff with us—you can't imagine how much junk will accumulate in a few months—so Day, who's such an ecologist, you know, decided to bury it. Call it, if you want to, the symbolic burying of ourselves, the awful selves that we were in Five Corners before we resolvd our 'It Jitters.' That's why I put a copy of Daniel's poem, 'Of a Lost Town,' on top of that 'grave.' I thought of it as appropriate to the symbolism."

"But there's one more little detail," you will point out. "That poem was obviously in your handwriting. I recognized that at that time. But answer me this: why are the last pages of Day's notebook, the part about his hanging, which he obviously couldn't have written himself if he hanged himself, why are those pages in the same handwriting, that is, *your* handwriting?"

"Well, don't you see?" she will offer, somewhat desperately, you will detect, "I had to finish it myself. Can't you understand? Poor Day was...well, I mean, after all, at that particular time, he wasn't in any condition for doing any more writing himself...."

That "*condition*," you will be certain now, was death.

✠ 18 ✠

"Are you ready for the poems?" she will ask after supper, and there will ensue this cozy domestic scene: the two of you at the table on either side of the old kerosene lantern, you holding in your lap the three-ring binder of my collected cadences and doggerel, Diana holding in her lap her knitting; she will be knitting, in anticipation of autumn chill (four months off, but underlining her optimism and her forethought), a sweater for "Day," a sweater which, you will be happy to notice, is large enough for your own frame, provided you succeed in shedding the rest of your surplus avoirdupois.

Although it will happen that you will hear fiddle music, seeming to come from right outside the window, fiddle music in the tinnitus of your ear playing one of eight Playford dances to the tune of the iambic measure to help you scan my verse, you will not read my rhymes and songs for any appreciation of their rhythms and figures; you will read them in search of further clues that Day is dead, and you will find plenty of these clues, beginning with the very fact that no mention whatever is made of his "recuperation" or "recovery." The poems seem to take it for granted that he "exists" without bothering to explain how he has suddenly surfaced from a state of death or of supposed shock. He hanged himself in the end of the notebooks, and now suddenly we find him making love to Diana on the floor of the deserted Salter house. But of course! Since he is only a figment of her imagination, or, as the early poem entitled "Entity" puts it, "She thinks he's what a girl as silly as she is / Would fantasize, sweetly, on hysteric whim," she felt no need to justify his "recovery" by wasting any other poems on the subject of his existence, although that poem called "The Curing," which details my own recovery with the help of Aunt Billie's herbs, will seem to you an allusion to Day's recovery.

And what about this "Flossie"? This *ghost*? Unquestionable proof, if any were needed, that Day did not exist. One person, one very deluded person, might very well imagine seeing a ghost, and Diana in her pitiful isolation and loneliness would certainly be prone to such illusions. But *two* persons? No, two persons together would not agree upon seeing a ghost.

You will mention this to Diana. Although you are not really interested in the thread of continuity which the poems have, you cannot help but chuckle, once, at the antics of Flossie, and to challenge Diana, "Oh, come now! Did you *really* see this ghost?"

Diana, remembering Flossie, will laugh too, and say, "That old dear! I wish I could send her a postcard or something just to let her know that we're okay, but *where* would I mail it to, for heaven's sake?…Goodness, G, those chigger bites are really getting worse, aren't they? You're scratching yourself to pieces. Maybe you'd better let me put something on them."

"But a ghost, Diana, a *ghost*…."

"What's a ghost town without a ghost?" she will say, and put down her knitting and fetch some stuff to put on your chigger bites. "First let's try this—" a cotton swab soaked in kerosene "—and then this—" a tube of some kind of ointment.

You will be somewhat reluctant to expose *all* of the locations of your chigger bites; whatever you are, old Grandstander, you aren't an exhibitionist. But she will be persistent and thorough. "They bit Day *there* too," she will say.

Her ministrations will arouse you, but you will remain cool enough to say, "Diana, I'm afraid that nobody is going to believe in this Flossie character. In rewriting the poems, you ought to make it clear that she was just your imagination, or—perhaps better—she was an actual, real-live old character, some old recluse who lived in Lost Cove."

"You sound like a college writing teacher," she will say, dabbing at your nether regions with the ointment. "Which reminds me, do you know Kynan Harris, or have you read his work?"

"An insufferable buffoon," you will remark. "His novels are meaningless."

"Well, anyway, he was my writing teacher at Sarah Lawrence, and he told me that all of my stories were 'pedestrian.' I guess they were. But what do you think of these poems? Are they pedestrian?"

"Not at all."

"Do you think they're publishable?" she will ask, and the ointment she is stroking onto your chigger bites is persuasive.

"Most of them. As I say, with some revision, to make the characters more credible...."

"But I can't revise them!" she will protest. "Because I didn't write them."

"All of this handwriting is obviously yours," you will point out.

"Of course!" she will say and give one of your chigger bites a light pinch. "Can't you get it through your head that *I* was the only one who could take up pencil and paper and put the words down?"

"*Where was Day?*" you will shoot at her.

She will stop ointmenting your bites. "He was…well, don't you understand? he had to be *put to sleep*."

"Yes, 'put to sleep' is the apt euphemism."

She will stare at you. "Oh, darn you," she will say, but she will resume searching for chigger bites and dabbing ointment on them.

Her attentions will be deliberate and intimate. Not to lose touch with the subject, you will say, "After all, Sylvia Plath was about your age when she wrote some of her best work."

Diana will sigh. "You flatter me enormously, G. But I swear, I don't have the least bit of talent for verse." And her fingers will not stop with the small swellings of your chigger bites; they will find a larger swelling.

"Now look what you've done," you will tease her, but she will not blush.

"Well, do they still itch?" she will ask.

"Not they," you will say. "*It*." She will laugh, but you, still clinging to the subject, will go on, "Maybe you think you have no talent for verse, but have you ever heard of 'automatic writing'? The opening of the gates to the unconscious? If you would like to publish these poems, I'd be happy to recommend them to my agent. But of course, you'll just have to face up to the necessity for revision, to take this 'ghost' out.…"

"Oh, darn you!" she will say. "Darn you!" And she will run off to bed, leaving you alone with your bottle of booze and your itch, the Itch of your It. *I itch, therefore I am.* And apparently, you will decide, she intends for you to pay a price for the relief of that itch. The price of your belief. Belief before relief.

You will leaf through the poems again, not skimming and skipping in search of clues, as you will have done during your first reading, and you will, for the sake of your itch, finally persuade yourself that Diana could not have written the poems, that even if she *had* written them, through some kind of automatic writing, they are inspired by, imbued with, a *presence* that is beyond Diana. I appreciate that, G. I'm rewarded that you'll make such an effort, even out of ulterior motive. To show my gratitude, I'll permit you to satisfy, in part at least, that ulterior motive. But not tonight. This night is your penultimate one, and Diana is already fast asleep, fabricating a splendid future in her dreams. You will have one more night in Stick Around after this one.

✛ 19 ✛

And two more days. You will wake late, on your penultimate day, with your last hangover, to discover Diana in distress. She will have already been to the post office, not waiting for you to wake, and will report that there is no letter from "Day." "I can't understand it," she will say. "He's never missed a single day so far."

"Perhaps," you will suggest, "your last letter offended 'him.' You might have hurt his feelings by asking his permission for you and I to—"

"I wasn't asking his permission," she will correct you. "As usual, you don't understand. Day is an even firmer believer than I am in the Beatitudes of Daniel, and if you really believe them, you can't feel such petty emotions as jealousy or envy, or have any conventional notions of 'morality.' So I *know* that isn't the reason. There must be something else." She will suddenly give you a narrow-eyed look, and say, "*You* wouldn't possibly have *purloined* his letter, would you?" You will swear up and down that you wouldn't do such a thing. You wouldn't, *would* you? No. You will be convinced, now, that the real reason there is no "letter" from "him" today is that she is on the verge of giving up the pretense; today is a transitional phase: she is getting ready to face reality, to accept the fact that there will never be any more "letters" from "him." And the time has come, you will decide, for you to help her rid her mind of the illusion completely.

How can you prove that Day Whittacker exists?

"Well, here are some of his clothes." She will open a dresser to show you the pile of shirts, sweaters, socks, handkerchiefs, etc., which doesn't mean anything at all. She could have kept his clothes after burying him.

How can you prove that Day Whittacker exists?

"Well, here are some of his books." In the bookcase, several books on forestry, woods management, plant pathology, and astronomy. Ditto, she could have kept his books after burying him.

How can you prove that Day Whittacker exists?

"Well, here is his garden and his pigpen and there are his free-ranging chickens. I'm just taking care of them while he's gone. He planted the garden. It was one of the first things he did. He planted some of it too early, and we had a late frost on April third which killed it, and so he had to plant it again. I don't know anything about gardening. He just taught me how to identify the weeds so I can keep the weeds out. And I love these Poland China piglets, which he got from a farmer over on the Roxey Road, but I don't know how to raise pigs." You will like that allusion to death and resurrection in the killing of "his" garden by the frost, and his "replanting" of it, but the existence of the garden and pigs is no proof at all of "his" existence.

How can you prove that Day Whittacker exists?

"Well, here is his voice on my tapes. Listen. Can't you hear well enough to tell that it's his voice? Well, not really *his*.... I mean, this is Daniel Lyam Montross talking. You can't hear what he's saying? But you can hear the tone of the voice, can't you? It doesn't sound anything like *my* voice, does it?" But her voice is, at times, you will have noticed, inclined to be rather husky, and she could easily imitate a male voice, especially in her eagerness to go on believing that this male still exists.

How can you prove that Day Whittacker exists?

"Well, why don't you go up on the mountain and see if you can find the pine seedlings he planted? I don't know where they are, but they're up *there* somewhere, thousands of them. You might even come across Day himself. But if you do, don't bother him. I mean, as he says, he doesn't even want to see you until you've come to believe in Daniel Lyam Montross, and that's important to him. But if you see him, would you ask him why he didn't write—No, I think the best thing, if you see him, is just to wave at him or something, and go the other way, without speaking...."

You will go hunting that afternoon, old Gunner. Yes, you would look for "his" pine seedlings, you would even look for "him," but your main excuse for hiking up the mountain will be to hunt for quail. The meals Diana has been serving will have been getting a little monotonous, the main course being nothing but the fish that she catches in Banner Creek, and you, old Gourmet, will think that a few fowl might relieve the monotony. She will not go with you. She has an aversion to firearms. Understandable. Besides, she has a long letter to write. So you will go alone.

You know these woods of Lingerfelt Mountain. You had been lost in them at the age of five. You won't get lost in them now. The cedars that were small when you were small are now large enough to be cut into clothes closets. The pawpaws and chinquapins are still plentiful, but somebody obviously has been cutting down the scrub trees and hardwood "weeds," and, sure enough, replanting the forest floor with pine seedlings. But anyone could have done that. This part of Stick Around is right on the edge of the Ozark National Forest, and probably the government had undertaken this reseeding program, which is, you will notice as you go farther and farther up the mountain, quite extensive, certainly not a one-man operation.

You will follow an old logging trail which is familiar to you; it had been the road you'd taken to get out of the woods when you were lost at the age of five. It comes to an end in a ferny glen where there is a waterfall and evidence of ancient Indian inhabitation: tiny burial mounds and rock shelters with shards of old pottery in them. This glen of the waterfall had been the place where you had met that strange old hermit, the man who'd told you how to find your way out of these woods. You aren't lost now.

You won't flush any quail. Nor will you flush any Day. You will fire your .22 several times at a tree, just for target practice, and then you will go on back down the mountain.

⚜ 20 ⚜

"Well, we might as well get on with the story, if there's nothing better to do," you will say to her that evening.

"There isn't any more," she will say.

"*What?*" you will exclaim.

"Not much, any way. There's very little remaining, and we'll have that when Day comes back."

You will stare at her, incredulous that she, having carried the life of Daniel Lyam Montross all the way through "his poems," all the way from Dudleytown to Five Corners to Lost Cove to Stick Around, would suddenly drop the effort. "But," you will protest, "I presume that 'he' *did* come to Stick Around, did he not? And lived here for twenty years or more, did he not?"

She will nod. "Oh, yes," she will say.

"But *nothing* happened to him here?" you will demand.

Again she will nod. "Nothing except his eventual death. But that's the beauty of it. That's why this was *the right place* for him, don't you see? It wasn't nearly as pretty a place as Lost Cove, I can tell you, or even Five Corners, for that matter, but it was a place where he could live and be happy without anything happening to him." Your open-mouthed incredulity, old Goggle-eyes, will cause her to laugh, and say, "You novelists." She will laugh again and go on, "You novelists have to have a lot of incidents and happenings and episodes to keep you in business. But don't you know that all of those occurrences or experiences or adventures usually involve some pain or strife or anguish? They're *aberrations*—any conflict is an aberration, and Daniel Lyam Montross had no further conflicts until the very end of his life. But without conflicts, you don't have a story, do you?"

"Now see here, young lady," you will object. "I won't be made a fool of. You aren't going to sit there and ask me to believe—"

"You don't believe anyway!" she will assert. "Do you? You don't believe in Daniel Lyam Montross. You think he's just something I made up, as an excuse for all this traveling." When you will not answer her positively or negatively, she will go on, nodding her head, "Yes, you're just like I was, when I first got involved in this whole business. In the beginning, I wasn't 'buying' any of it. I told Day, right off the bat I said to him, 'I don't really believe in reincarnation, not for one minute, and I don't believe in hypnosis either, and I certainly don't believe you're my grandfather.' I told him that and let it sink in, and then I said, 'But I would like to believe. I would like to find out. Wouldn't that be marvelous, to be able to believe'?"

"And now," you will ask, cynically, "do you believe?"

"With all of my heart," she will say. "And you're just like I was, G, you don't believe in anything. That's your spiritual deadness. You need something to believe in. And I'm offering it to you. Wouldn't you like to have something to believe in?"

"Yes, but you aren't helping matters by trying to persuade me that his life suddenly stopped being eventful after he came to Stick Around."

She will take your hand. "Come with me," she will say. She will take you into the room where she keeps her tape recorder and her tapes. She will indicate a stack of about three hundred or so tapes. "Those," she will say, "were the Dudleytown tapes and the Five Corners tapes, with a few from Lost Cove. And these—" she will indicate the much larger balance of tapes, seven or eight hundred "—*these* are the Stick Around tapes."

"But why so many?" you will ask, "if nothing happened to him...."

"Oh, several of these tapes are about him, and we still have to make our last tape. But most of these tapes are not about what happened to him, but what happened to Stick Around. It's a nearly complete chronicle of the history of this village and everybody in it between 1932 and his death in 1953, by which time the village was nearly dead also. There are some fabulous stories here, all of the incidents and happenings and episodes and adventures that you could ever hope for, but they are not things that happened to him."

"Good Lord!" you will exclaim, for you will suddenly be

not unmindful of what a novelist might be able to do with such a treasure trove. "You wouldn't be joking by any chance?"

"Listen," she will say, turning on the recorder. "Or listen to me while I repeat what the tapes say. Just a few samples. First, here's a typical tape *about* Daniel Lyam Montross, when I was trying to find out what happened to him here, and when I discovered that practically nothing did. I was just picking dates at random and asking him. Listen—"

The day is June 15, 1934. Has anything interesting happened to you today?

I read a nice poem by John Donne....

Today is April 15, 1938. What did you do today?

I taught Annie how to distinguish the oaks and ashes....

This is March 15, 1933. What did you accomplish today?

I meditated on the difference in sound and meaning between the "brook" of Connecticut and Vermont, and the "creek" of North Carolina and Arkansas.

November 15, 1944. What was today worth to you?

I heard Rupe Blackshire tell an interesting story about a coon hunt.

Now it's July 15, 1950. What happened today?

I meditated on the subject of envy, and decided that envy is the most despicable of all emotions.

Today is February 15, 1937. Anything today?

I had a nice remembrance-having of Ammey.

Today is August 15, 1939. What did you do today?

I helped find a lost—

Diana will push the Rewind button. "That goes on like that for another hour," she will say. "And there's not one single date on which anything happens to him that would be worth mentioning in a novel." She will remove the tape, and put in a different cassette. "But listen to me recite this one for you. This one's an example of his 'Stick Around Chronicles,' his retellings of what he heard from other people."

And Diana will begin repeating for you a most interesting story about a hunter of wild hogs. You will not realize it at the moment, G, but eventually you will employ this very story as a central part of a future novel which will be called *Razorback*.

"Or listen to this," Diana will say, putting on another tape, and again, although you will not be aware of it just now, you will hear a story that will serve you some day as the wellspring for your sixth novel, *The Architecture of the Arkansas Ozarks*.

"Or this." And there in genesis will be the outrageous outlines of what will become *The Scarlet Whickerbill*. "Or this one. Or this one. Or this one." And as the evening passes, there will open up for you a bountiful storehouse of incipient fictions.

"Holy Moses!" you will cry, shaking your head at the sheer plentitude of it all. "What I wouldn't give to have those tapes!"

"Yes?" Diana will say, moving closer to you and becoming serious. "*What wouldn't you give?* Would you give *anything*?" Do you want to bargain? I'll 'sell' you these tapes, G, but not for cash. One thing I learned from my stupid old father was how to make a deal. And I'll make you a deal."

You will be reluctant, G, out of fear that it would be some price or penalty you couldn't pay. But you will want those tapes. Desperately. "Well," you will say. "What is it, then?"

"Your soul."

You will chuckle, but nervously, and say, "Mephistopheles!"

"I *knew* you would say that," she will say, "but, as usual, you are too quick to leap to conclusions. Mephistopheles would consider your soul a bad trade. *Your* soul, G, is moribund and suicidal. My tapes wouldn't be of any use to you, because you aren't going to live long enough to use them."

"How right you are!" you will say with sarcasm. "So it's a pointless trade anyway, isn't it?"

"No," she will say. "Not if you relinquish that sordid soul. What I have in mind isn't so much a swap as a trade-in. Not my tapes for your old soul. But my tapes for a new soul that will live long enough to use the tapes and make them live too."

"How do I acquire this 'new soul'?"

"First you've got to be *willing*. You've got to be willing to believe in Daniel Lyam Montross."

"Oh, I believe!" you will admit. "I *do*. After all, you couldn't possibly have 'imagined' or 'invented' all of these Stick Around stories all by yourself."

She will offer you her hand. "Is it a deal, then, G?"

"It's a deal," you will say.

She will shake your hand, but after you have shaken hands, she will not remove her hand from yours. She will hold your hand tightly in hers, and say, "Now we start trading in that old soul. Tell me: how does this feel?"

"How does what feel?"

"I'm holding your hand."

"Oh yes, I see," you will say, looking at your hand being held tightly in the embrace of her hand.

"Well, this is nice," you will allow, offhand.

"Really?" she will doubt you. "When was the last time you actually felt any real pleasure at the touch of someone's hand?"

"Offhand, I don't remember."

"You wouldn't," she will say. She will stand up, still holding your hand, and she will tug that hand. "Come on," she will say, and with her other hand she will lift the kerosene lantern from the table, and conduct you up the stairs. You will wonder what she has in mind.

You will be thinking, *Well, she seems to have eliminated Day Whittacker at last.*

She will lead you into your bedroom, never letting go of your hand, and she will hold the lantern high against one wall. "You've never bothered to read these walls yet, have you?" she will ask, and when you shake your head, she will say, "Then look up there. Look up there and see what that says."

She will hold the lantern high against the wall; it is a spot that only a tall man could have reached (*or a girl standing on a chair,* you will think, briefly, but you will dismiss that thought quickly from your mind, because you will want very much to believe). The handwriting, in old pencil, nearly faded, on the white plaster of the wall, does not seem to be a script that a girl could imitate. And it says:

> Only the lordly are imperative. So I can't and won't command you. So this isn't my supreme commandment but my supreme and only pre-scription: embrace: cling: touch: hug: enfold: cuddle: squeeze: hold! Hold!

"Well," she will say to you, "do you believe *that*?" Then she will blow out her lantern and set it aside. Then she will hold you. You will embrace her. She will cling to you. You will touch her. She will hug you. You will enfold her. She will cuddle you. You will squeeze her. To my prescription. Then you will go to bed, but you will not "make love." Yes, it will be a great wonderful love that you will make, but you will not "make love." That would have seemed, somehow, superfluous. Which is what I meant. The ultimate cure for solipsism, G, is not the orgasm, which requires no partner, after all, but the caress. All over. A last word from my dictionary [goodbye, Henry; we're finished, old friend]: *polymorphous*. The whole body. You never guessed, did you, G, that there are so many different ways just to *hold* someone?

In the tightness of your embrace, the hard metal corner of your hearing aid will mash against her breast, and she will ask you why you don't take it off. You will say you want to be able to hear her.

"But I don't have anything more to say, for now," she will say.

"But there's one thing I've been wondering about," you will say. "Your Daniel Lyam Montross is beginning to seem very real to me, and I think I really do believe in him. But, you know, I used to live in Stick Around myself; when I was a young boy, every summer I visited here and lived with my aunt and uncle all summer long. That was back in the late thirties. If Daniel Lyam Montross was living here at that time, why didn't I ever meet him?"

She will increase the pressure of her embrace, and her lips, so close to yours, will say, "You did."

And then she will say one thing more: "Go to sleep, G."

✦ 21 ✦

Had it been the power of suggestion? Had you identified so closely with Day Whittacker in those episodes where she had used her "magic words" on him, that now, when she used them on you, they had "worked?" Or had you been genuinely sleepy? Or had you yearned for some brief return to those happy days? Whatever the case, it will be full morning when you wake, without a hangover for the first time in ages, and you will remember your dream:

The porch of Lara Burns' store, the Stick Around post office, one hot morning in July: the daily assemblage of townspeople coming to get their mail, exchange gossip, buy little things at the store, and loaf around, out of the heat of the sun. All of the chairs of the porch are occupied, and upended nail kegs do service for extra sitting places. The children and teens sit on the porch rail or stand in the yard, but your traditional, appropriated sitting-place, little Guy, is the porch swing, although this morning you must share it with two women, one of them your Aunt Josie.

Although it is a hot morning, a mild breeze comes down Squires Creek, bearing the faint sound of the machinery in the canning factory, and the acid smell of boiling tomatoes. Old Herman Blackshire is keeping the boiler running; it makes him mad that he has to miss the morning assembly at Lara's store.

The others take advantage of his absence to tell tales about him. Quent Buchanan tells how old Herman was up at Jessup the other day bragging that he'd drunk whiskey every day for seventy years and never been harmed by it, when one of those temperance fellers up there interrupted him and said, "Yeah, but how old are you?" and when old Herman says he's eighty-five, that temperance feller said, "Well, if you hadn't drunk all that liquor, you might be a hundred by this time." And poor old Herman got kind of bothered, thinking about that, and couldn't come up with any answer.

Doc Squires, one of the best tellers of tales, knows a better one about old Herman. Doc says he saw old Herman out driving his one-horse wagon the other day when he'd had a little too much to drink. The old mare slipped on a "road-apple" and fell right down in the shafts. Old Herman stood up in the wagon and started cursing the mare, but the mare wouldn't get up. Old Herman slapped her with the lines and hollered, "You damned old fool! If you don't get up, I'm gonna drive right over you!"

They run out of stories to tell on old Herman and begin to look around to see if anybody else is missing that they can tell stories on.

Your Aunt Josie says to you, "Show Doc Squires your finger, boy." And she says to Doc Squires, "Lookee here at this boy's finger, Doc. They aint no trace left of that there wart what was on it yestiddy."

Doc Squires examines your finger and says, "Sure 'nough, it's clean as a whistle." And then all of them begin to talk about that bearded old feller who'd come here yesterday at this time, and who, when Lara had mentioned to him your wart, which they said you'd got from handling toadfrogs, had borrowed a thaw of tobacco from one of the men, and, after masticating it, had spat a drop onto your wart, and rubbed it in, and said "What I see increase, What I rub decrease," and pretty soon had gone on his way. You'd seen him once or twice before; his clothes were the same as everybody else's: blue denim overalls and cotton shirt; but he wore a broad-brimmed black hat that seemed bigger than most people's hats, and his black and gray hair came nearly to his shoulders, and he had a beard, although the beard wasn't long and was neatly trimmed. Your wart was gone completely when you woke this morning.

"He aint a warlock or he-witch, I reckon not," somebody says, "but I'll swear if he aint the best wart-taker in this county."

"Many a time I seen him do it. Aint ne'er failed yet."

"I don't put no stock by them spells he uses, but I got to admit he must be doin somethin right."

"Wonder what he does fer a livin. He aint never worked over to the fact'ry, has he?"

"Him? Aw, he jest keeps a few chickens and pigs and a gyarden patch up thar at that fancy yaller house of his'n."

"Must be eight, nine year since he built that yaller house. Where'd he come from, anyway?"

"He don't say. He aint one to talk about hisself. I heerd, though, that he come from east Tennessee or Care-liner some'ers."

"Wal, I heerd rumors he was a 'scaped con-vict, runnin from the law. Some folks say he must a murdered somebody over there."

"Wal, I also heerd, some time back, that he was a runaway bank embezzler and had a pile of money hidden some'ers."

"Yeah, that was three, four years ago. Me and some of them Buchanan boys snuck up to that yaller house wunst when he weren't around, and we turned that place plum upside down, but couldn't find a danged cent. He aint got no money."

"Don't he never buy nuthin hyere at the store?"

"Naw, and he don't mail no letters neither, and I've never knowed him to git a letter from nobody."

"But he aint what you'd call a real hermit. He don't avoid folks. I've had many a long chitchat with him myself."

"Me too. But gener'ly he lets me do all the talkin. He don't say much."

"You ever seen that gal of his? Annie he calls 'er. Reckon she's his daughter, aint but about ten year old, but a real pretty-un."

"She don't go to the schoolhouse. Ast him wunst about 'er, how come he don't send 'er to the school, and he claims he's edjercatin her hisself."

"Some folks say he must have some kind of peculiar religion, all his own, and maybe he don't want that gal to git any wrong notions from the rest a the world."

"You ever heerd him fiddle? Why, that feller could fiddle the cob outen a jug! They tried wunst to git 'im to fiddle fer the squar dances up at Acropolis, but he wouldn't. Says there's too many fights gits started at squar dances and he'd done had enough fights to last him the rest a his life. But I've known him to play fer a weddin or two."

"I bet he caint fiddle near so good as he fingers a shootin-arn. I run into him one day up near Butterchurn Holler, shootin squarl, and I

declare, I never seen such a shot in all my life. Why, he could hit a squarl
from a half a mile off."

"Fact he aint got a womern makes some folks say he must've been
disappointed in love. Or else that gal's maw got killed or died or somethin."

"Mighty peculiar feller. But I aint heerd nobody say one bad word
about him. Nor tell e'er a funny tale on him, neither."

"Me neither."

When all of the people have left the store porch, and you are alone
with your Lara again, you show her the place on your finger where the
wart was and is no more, and you ask her, "Lara, what's that feller's
name?"

✦ 22 ✦

You will have wanted your dream to stick around, you will have
hoped that that recapturing of the bright unlonely past would stay
more, a little while, long enough for you to talk with your beloved
firefly Lara again, but that dream, like all dreams, will pass away,
and you will be left lying in bed remembering what will seem to
have been, even more, a dream: the pressures and touches of Diana's
arms and hands, the wrapping of the back of your neck in the crook
of her elbow, the way her fingertips had clutched the small of your
back, the clasp of her armpits on your shoulder and ribs, the clench
of her clavicle on your throat....

You will spring out of bed, full of zest for the new day (not
knowing, I'm sorry, that this will be your last day), and first you
will search the wall to reassure yourself that my supreme prescription had not been a dream. Yes, it is still there in the daylight, that
old-fashioned hand scrawling that injunction to embrace and cling
and touch and hug and enfold and cuddle and squeeze and hold.

Then you will notice (why has it taken you so long to notice my walls, old Gimlet-eye?) that all four of the white plaster walls are covered with pencilings: aphorisms, epigrams, sententious graffiti: observations on nature and on human nature, mottoes, reminders, lists: an old man talking to himself on his walls.

I'm not certain you will be quite ready for it, just then, but since it is your last day, you will find my nine beatitudes:

Montross, His Blessings

1. Happy are they who need no god beyond themselves; for theirs is the kindom of It.
2. Happy are they who are happy; for there is no one to give them what they haven't got.
3. Happy are the unhumble, the openly honestly unmodest; for only they can endure the custody of Earth.
4. Happy are they who've lost their expectation; for they shall not be disappointed.
5. Happy are they who tender love to another; for the offering expects no return.
6. Happy are they who know their hearts aren't pure; for they shall see their It.
7. Happy are they who never close themselves to another; for they are the true peacemakers.
8. Happy are they who never cause another's guilt; for their Its have made peace with their own.
9. Happy above all are they who can remove their minds from their body's business; for their reward is the fullness of feeling.

A pair of hands will come up from behind you and cover your eyes and a voice you can't hear will say "Guess who?" and you will smile and say "Diana?" and the hands will uncover your eyes and you will turn around and there she will be; her mouth will be moving but you are deaf. You will get your hearing aid and plug yourself in, and hear what she is saying: that you aren't "ready," yet, to be reading what comes after these beatitudes. But she will be smiling, and only half-serious, and she will not try to cover your eyes again when you turn back to the wall to read the rest of it. The original Beatitudeanist had stopped with His nine, but I had added nine others:

Montross, His Damnings

1. Wretched are they who chase after beauty; for the end of the chase is the end of the beauty.
2. Wretched are they who work for wages; for the one is never equal to the other.
3. Wretched are the passive; for they who wait shall have only their waiting.
4. Wretched are they who are dead while living; for the one is never equal to the other.
5. Wretched are the envious; for equality is impossible.
6. Wretched are they who think themselves only male or only female; for the one is not equal to the other.
7. Wretched are they who are wronged, or who think they are; for they have no feeling of right.
8. Wretched are they who want more than they have; for the one is never equal to the other.
9. Wretched are they who think themselves wretched; for thought is all they have.

"The old boy got kind of sour in his dotage, didn't he?" you will remark.

"Sour?" she will say. "I don't think that's the right word, at all. There's nothing cynical or bitter about those writings. Pragmatic, maybe, but not pessimistic. If you think they're sour, that's what I meant when I said you aren't ready for them. Because they're addressed to *you*."

"Oh, I *see*," you will say with some sarcasm. "I suppose he knew that I was going to come along some day and see them."

"Don't scoff," she will say. "At least he knew that *I* was going to come along some day and see them, and they're addressed to me too."

"What makes you think that he knew you were going to come along and see them? At the time he wrote them, I mean?"

"At the time he wrote them," she will tell you, "I was here."

"*What?*" You will adjust the volume wheel on your aid.

"I was here," she will repeat. "I haven't told you this, G, because I was saving it for later, for our last chapter, after you've heard the story of how his daughter Annie left him, and left Stick Around, or, rather, was taken away, or eloped, or—I want you to hear the story soon—but anyway, you see, his daughter Annie, who was my mother, was discovered by Burton Stoving, who was an army captain on maneuvers in the Ozarks during the war, and he, my father, took her away and married her. But Daniel Lyam Montross made her promise—" Diana will shake her head and complain, "Oh, I wish you could hear the whole story, but anyway, what happened was, when I was three years old, Daniel Lyam Montross came to Little Rock and 'borrowed' me—*kidnapped* me is what they called it—he intended to return me when I was grown up, but *they* didn't know that—anyway, he brought me here to Stick Around, and I lived with him in this house for a week before they came and—" Diana will make a gesture in imitation of tearing out her hair at the futility of trying to tell it, and then she will sigh and say, "That was why Day is gone, don't you see? The two weeks he is gone represent the two weeks that Daniel was gone from Stick Around when he went to Little Rock to 'borrow' me. He refuses to tell me about that part. Anyway, the point is: these writings on the wall, these blessings and damnings of his, were the last things he wrote. And he told me—I was just three years old, of course, and couldn't remember, but Day and I have already 'recaptured' this particular part—he told me that someday I would come back again and see these writings, and that these writings expressed in a nutshell the kind of life he had wanted me to have, full of that happiness and bare of that wretchedness, and—" You apparently will be staring at her so disbelievingly that she will be unconsciously raising the volume of her voice, as if to get through to you, "Don't you *SEE*? HE HAD WANTED, BY *KIDNAPPING ME*, TO BRING ME UP *RIGHT* AND KEEP ME FROM GETTING THE *HOR-*

RIBLE TWISTED PERSONALITY I GOT! HE WANTED ME
TO BE *HAPPY!* HE WANTED TO TEACH ME HOW TO BE
UNLIKE OTHER PEOPLE! AND HE COULDN'T! *BECAUSE
THEY KILLED HIM!*"

She will fall against you, then, and you will hold her tightly,
and while you hold her, feeling genuine pity and compassion for
her, you will begin to see, at last, what you think is "The True Picture," the "real" justification for all of this long and strange story.
There have been times when you, in trying to justify her reasons for
inventing me, will have toyed with the theory of Spoiled-Rich-Girl-
in-Search-of-Kicks, but now, you will realize, it is more serious, and
more sad, than that. The money was a factor, but only secondary.
Given the kind of parents and environment she had, she might
well have grown up wretched, might in fact have grown up *more*
wretched, if they had lived in poverty. Blessed (or damned) with
an uncommon intelligence, but lacking any sense of identity (you
will remember that beautiful but poignant "Do you think why I am
me?"), she had needed to invent her personal saviour: a substitute
father, or, in this case, *grand*father, a wise and kind old man with
much experience, well traveled, whose own sins would make him
quick to forgive those she bore with guilt, whose powerful identity
would compensate for her lack of one, whose native intellect, mother
wit, and acquired intellectuality could come up with such handy,
sententious beatitudes to give her something to live *by*, and *for*. It
is a magnificent creation, a stunning concoction, but you will be
sorry to realize that not even you, old Genius, would be able to
write the story of it.

And you will know that you must not be too quick to attempt
to disabuse her of her strange illusions. You would have to be patient,
and play along with her little game, and in time...well, apparently
she is already approaching the point of her story where her grandfather gets killed, and then, perhaps, she would allow him to "stay
dead," and would have nobody, then, but you.

I appreciate that, old Goodheart, I really do. I'm glad you will
decide not to "de-fabricate" me in her sensitive, delicate mind. You
will allow me to stick around, while you concentrate on eliminating

that other pathetic delusion of hers, that nineteen-year-old Jersey jerk who'd been unworthy of her, and, being unworthy, had killed himself in despair.

"Shall we go to the post office?" you will gently suggest.

She will shake her head, and hug you tighter.

Gently you will pry her apart from you, and ask, "Don't you want to see if a 'letter' has come for you today?"

Again she will shake her head. "I'm afraid to look," she will say. "I'm afraid of finding nothing there."

Understandable. But she must be brave. "You must," you will say. "You have to face up to realities."

She will look at you with hesitant, yet beseeching eyes, eyes which seem to ask you to let her hold on to her delusion a little while longer, and yet, at the same time, seem to ask you to speed her away from it. "Come on," you will say. "It'll take just a minute. We'll go in my car."

She will allow you to lead her, unresisting, out of the house and into your Volvo. But then you can't find your ignition key. Had you left it in your other trousers? But you are wearing the same pair you had on yesterday. "I can't find my key," you'll tell her. "I'll go look in my room."

You will look in your room. You will search the stairs, the whole house. You will come back to the car and search the floor of the car. "Damn," you will say. "I was going to drive into Jessup today to get some more cigarettes and bourbon." And also to see if a telegram has ever arrived for you. "You wouldn't happen to have any cigarettes, would you?" you will ask. She will shake her head. "You wouldn't happen to have seen my car key, would you?" you will ask. She will shake her head and turn her eyes from you. "Well, I guess we'll just have to walk. To the post office, I mean. If the key doesn't show up, I'll just have to hitchhike or walk into Jessup later on."

At the post office, she will hold back, still reluctant to face reality. She won't go into that deserted old building. So you will go in for her. You will notice, first thing, that there still aren't any footprints in the dust other than yours and her own. But then you will be very unhappy to notice that there is an envelope in her box.

How long does she have to continue this self-deceit? You will want to rip open the envelope and confront her with the blankness of the contents. But you have *some* principles, after all, so you will take it out and give it to her, unopened.

Her face will beam and she will eagerly take the envelope from you with a little squeal of pleasure, and open it, and begin "reading" it to herself, with obvious pleasure. *Did I do something wrong?* you will be asking yourself. *Did I say or do the wrong thing, that she has decided to continue her belief in "him" after being so close to getting over it?*

"Oh, he's coming back!" she will exclaim. "He doesn't say when, but he's coming back!"

"Let me see the 'letter,' Diana," you will insist.

"Oh, *no!*" she will object. "Not *this* one. I couldn't even tell you—"

You will snatch the letter from her and run. Down the Squires Creek road you will run.

"You bastard!" she will holler, coming after you. "Give that back!"

You will run on, determined to outrun her and find some secret place where you can stop long enough to look at this "letter," to prove that it is empty. But unfortunately, old Gasper, you are in no condition to be doing any running, and she is right on your heels, clawing at your back. You should have known better than to attempt to increase the pace of your running.

You will stop abruptly and crumple up with your first heart attack.

How ironic: I have created you for the purpose of keeping Diana alive, she who was doing such a poor job of keeping herself alive. I thought you could keep her alive, if not forever at least long enough to get my story told. I should have picked someone whose heart is in better condition than yours, but you are my only logical choice. Now, will you die on us yourself?

When you fall, she will grab at the letter in your hand, and tear it away from you, leaving you clutching a mere fragment of one corner. You will hold this to your heart and groan, "My heart—"

"Serves you right, you Grabber!" she will say, but her tone will not be entirely hostile; she will become solicitous for your condition, and kneel beside you. Your florid face and heaving chest will alarm her. "I'll go get your car and drive you to a doctor," she will suggest.

"No key," you will gasp.

"I—" she will hesitate. "Maybe I can find it. Keep calm. I'll be right back." She will run off toward home.

You would have preferred that she stay with you, holding your hand, while you died. To die alone, in the middle of this dirt road in this dying old town…. Well, on second thought, it does have a certain appropriateness. Except that you will not be actually dying. When she returns, in less than ten minutes, driving your car, you will be sitting up, your respiration and pulse will be nearly normal, and you will have had time to study the fragment of letter you'd torn away, which says only "Remember the pool at Marcella Falls?" The script is not identical to hers, but, you will be relieved to observe, it is very similar to hers: the "e"s and "o"s are formed like hers.

You will return this fragment to her. "I'm sorry," you will apologize. "I shouldn't have stolen your letter like that. But my curiosity was killing me. And it nearly *did*, you might say, *kill* me."

"Are you all right?" she will ask. "I was very worried…."

"I should have gone into training for that run," you will remark lightly. "I'm just in rotten condition. Where did you find my car key?"

"Oh, it was on the—" she will pause, and decide not to lie. "It was hidden on the rotten condition. I hid it. If you're going to Jessup for more cigarettes and whiskey, you'll have to walk. Nobody's going to pick you up." And she will take the key out of the ignition and run away with it. But she will not run far. She will stop, and wait, as if challenging you to catch her. You will leave your car abandoned there on the Squires Creek road, and start out after her. You will jog a while, then walk a while.

"Starting right now!" she will yell at you, backing off as you near her. "Starting right now, we get you into good condition!"

♱ 23 ♱

Running, jogging, trotting, walking, you will begin on this day to get into condition. This is both your end and your beginning. The finish line at a race track is in the same place as the starting line, is it not? You do not know it, then, but this is to be your last day in Stick Around. And you do not know it then either, but this running will be the beginning of your long, long race. You will never stop, old Greyhound, but I pleasantly picture you disburdened and disembarrassed of that potbelly, trim of limb and long of gait and full of wind. Sprint on, old Gee!

How many miles will you cover that day? With her beside you, or ahead of you, as your pacer, you will cover every road and trail into and out of and across Stick Around. You wouldn't have smoked a cigarette if you had one. Hiking and hastening and heaving, you will hurry to cover all the odds and ends that still stick around in your mind.

Why has "Day" decided to start writing to you again, after skipping yesterday?

He was "out of town" yesterday. He had to go all the way down to Russellville to be interviewed by the National Forestry Service. And guess what, he got the job! Starting next month, he'll be a forest ranger in the Ozark National Forest.

And then "he" will go live by himself in some forest tower?

Maybe, but I hope he can just stay here in Stick Around.

Do you intend to stay here in Stick Around?

Of course!

Forever?

Well, I can't say *that*. But I can tell you, I've had enough of traveling; I've discovered, as Daniel Lyam Montross finally did, that traveling creates instability and insecurity, and that even if Stick Around isn't as nice as some other places I've been, it's *home*, and home creates stability and security.

But won't you ever get lonely?

Not if you're here.

Pardon? I didn't catch that.

I said, not for a year. You see, I've had a lot of experience with being lonely, but I've decided that I simply will not be lonely, for at least a year. That is, I'll give it a year, and if at the end of that year I *want* to, then I'll feel lonely. Stick Around isn't *completely* a ghost town, you know. There are still several families living up there in the hills and valleys outside of town, and Day and I have already made some friends.

Tell me, if you don't mind, why your privy has only one hole.

Well, don't you see? after Daniel Lyam Montross's daughter left him, he was alone, and when his original privy got kind of old and worn out, he built a new one, and since there was nobody but him, he didn't need more than one hole.

But your "Day" didn't feel the need to remedy that situation? After all, in your story so much emphasis was laid on sharing....

You have a scatological mind, G. But if you must know, neither of us has ever used that outhouse. If you live in the woods as long as we have, you prefer the woods.

Will you marry me?

No.

Tell me, what is the meaning of the reference to the pool at Marcella Falls in "his" latest "letter." I couldn't resist reading that piece that tore off, the end of his letter, and it said, "Remember the pool at Marcella Falls?"

Oh, that's just an allusion to the subject of voyeurism. If I told you what it really means, you would understand why I can't let you read his letter, and that is *precisely* the reason I can't let you. But, as you've remarked, there are different kinds of voyeurism in the various sections of our story. In the first section was the pool at Marcella Falls where Day spied on me the first time I was taking a bath there myself, and later watched me when I took a skinny dip with those Jesus freaks. Then of course, in the second section, there was that awful business about voyeurism in relation to masturbation, which was indirectly responsible for Day's trying to hang himself. In the third section, there was the situation wherein Flossie sometimes watched us when we were making love. Now, in the fourth section, there is also another kind of voyeurism. That's what Day was referring to, because it harks back to the pool at Marcella Falls.

The fourth section? What is the fourth section?

This is the fourth section. Right now. We're in it.

Oh. Are you suggesting that we're being watched? By a voyeur? Who is watching us?

Daniel, of course, is watching us. He's responsible for our being here, after all. He's in charge of the whole show. I don't know if he's getting any voyeuristic pleasure out of it, but I *do* know that he's watching.

You're making me self-conscious. Are you insinuating that he created us?

Of course he did! Neither of us would be here, right now, if it hadn't been for him, would we? He not only created us, but he is also re-creating us: giving us something to live for.

But he won't let me marry you?

No.

Why did he create me, then?

To tell his story, when all the rest of us have tried and failed. And to tell *our* story.

But he seems to be doing all of the storytelling by himself.

In our "solipsism," as you call it, all of us invent each other for various reasons, to fill various needs. Day, if you wish, invented Daniel Lyam Montross as a father substitute, a kindly protector, and he invented me for my companionship and love, if not my money, just as I invented him for his practical knowledge of living in the woods. Daniel Lyam Montross invented Day as a reincarnation-in-disguise for himself, and he invented me as a catalyst to take Day to these various towns, concluding with Stick Around, and he invented you to tell the story of it. But the very important thing is, you see, that while we in our solipsism have all invented each other for various reasons, *nobody* invented Daniel Lyam Montross except *himself.* He existed long before any of us.

And there is no hope that he could be persuaded to let me marry you?

I'm sorry, no.

Please list the volumes in Daniel Lyam Montross's library.

He wasn't an intellectual, not what you would think of as a reading man. There were only three books: the Holy Bible, an anthology of Elizabethan poetry, and an unabridged dictionary. He read the first for humor, the second for music, and the third for drama.

And he was never bored? Or lonely? What about his sex life? Was he suddenly celibate during those twenty-odd years here in Stick Around?

The sex of the sections, as you have remarked, was sequential: the first, coital; the second, oral; the third, anal. This is the fourth section. The sex of the sections was sequential and the fourth is sequestered.

Sequestered? Do you mean solitary? Masturbatory?

No. Not necessarily. Sequestered in the sense of separated, isolated, withdrawn. You recall his ninth beatitude, which implies that the supreme happiness comes from being able to exclude the mind from the body's business, as for example in sex. That exclusion, or seclusion, is the sequestering. It is, incidentally, how Daniel "cured" our sexual maladjustments: by taking our minds off of it during the act, Day was able to last longer while I—But I can't dwell on it, because it's sequestered, don't you see? Your mind and mine are not permitted to perceive it.

Are you and I going to make love, ever?

Not if it can be perceived by any mind.

What?

Neither of us would be happy doing it if our minds or anyone else's minds saw us doing it.

Who?

Anyone. We are being observed, as I told you.

Why?

To see which place we wind up in, some other place or the right place.

Where?

The right place.

How?

Through wretchedness to happiness, through damnation to blessedness.

When?

Soon.

I'm running out of questions, and my feet are killing me. But there's just one question left. All these days and months, why haven't you ever written to your father and mother?

How do you know I haven't?

✢ 24 ✢

Naturally I can't let you marry her, old Groom, even if you weren't already wed. Nor can I let the sequence of sex in these sections be upset by any unsequestered love at this point. But, just as I've permitted you the joy of that one soul-renewing night of holding and embracing, I'm happy to give you, on this your last afternoon in Stick Around, that innocent but wanton happening you've always wanted: the experience of a refreshing sharing of a swim, the two of you rinsing the sweats of your running and hiking by a quick naked plunge into that secluded pool of Banner Creek known as Old Bottomless. The picture is not quite of pastoral beauty, for both of you are paunchy, she with child, and you, old Gut, with gut, but I must observe that without her dress on she looks even less swollen than usual, somehow, while your vigorous race has already removed perhaps an inch from your waistline and you can, by expanding your chest and holding your breath, shrink the other inches. The occasion is, as I say, both innocent and wanton, chaste but frolicsome: you would love, wouldn't you? for it to develop into something sequestered, but I am watching you, for now, and as long as I choose to watch you, you are not sequestered. So, enjoy yourself, for now. And soak your feet well. Because when this half-hour is up, you'll have to do some more walking.

☩ 25 ☩

It will have been a stupid question; you will realize this too late. Most of your questions have been sharp, even clever, but this one will be showing your hand. How could you possibly have known that she had not corresponded with her parents unless you had been in touch with them? Unless you are, as she will quickly guess, hired by her father to find her?

"How much did my father offer to pay you?" she will ask.

You will tell her.

She will say, "I'll give you twice that much if you promise not to tell him where I am. I'll give you three times that much."

You will shake your head. You will tell her that you had never been interested in money, in the first place.

"Are you going to tell him where I am?" she will ask.

"I don't know," you will equivocate. "You still haven't answered my question. Why haven't you written to your parents? Even to let them know that you're still alive."

"I won't write to my father because I detest him," she will say. "Do you know, in all the years that I was away at school, at Margaret Hall and then at Sarah Lawrence, I got a total of maybe six or seven letters from him, all of them little short things dictated to his secretary. 'Be a good girl and work hard.' 'Be a good girl and stay out of trouble.' He never seemed to care about any of the specific problems that I might have been having. He thought money would take care of any problem."

"But couldn't you write to your mother instead?"

"No. I want her to see how it feels to have your only daughter abandon you. Because that's what she did. She abandoned Daniel Lyam Montross, after he'd spent so many years trying to bring her up to be a person and have an It and be able to see it. Why couldn't she have stayed here in Stick Around and married one of the local boys? Why did she have to go off and marry that absolute louse Burton Stoving and become a society girl? Why couldn't—"

Now, old Goodfriend, if it will help your faith and understanding any, I'll take you into my confidence and tell you of certain matters which not even Diana herself has been told, for good reason. She is, as you have seen, an intelligent girl, and she seems lately to have resolved most of her "It jitters," but there are some things that she is still simply too young and too sensitive to know. One of these is the story, involving intrigue and stealth, of how I "kidnapped" her. I refused her request to "re-create" this story. It is exciting, but immaterial, even irrelevant. She wanted, in effect, to "age-regress" herself to her third year, and pretend to be in Little Rock, and have me come and kidnap her. I had to refuse. That entire two-week episode is sequestered from her. There's nothing to be gained by repeating the episode. The child was frightened, of course, at first. She didn't know who I was or what I intended to do with her. And because she was only three years old, I had trouble getting her to understand. Perhaps I should have waited until she was older. But by then it would have been too late. Already, perhaps, it was too late....

Just as, in the case of Annie herself, it had been too late. When I took her away from Walt Ailing and fled from Lost Cove in search of some other place where I could raise her, the nature of her It had already been fixed by her earliest years as Walt Ailing's child; I couldn't erase whatever wretchedness she'd suffered during those years; I couldn't remove the It that had already been formed before I got ahold of her. For example, I couldn't do very much about her meekness, the most ingrained and terrible of her qualities. She grew up as meek as ever. I think the life she lived in Stick Around was far happier than those lives of most girls her age, but my experiment, if you want to call it that, wasn't a complete success.

My own life in Stick Around wasn't solitary, you know; I never thought of myself as a hermit, and in any case my hermitism or withdrawal or isolation wasn't sudden but gradual; it kept pace with the decline of the old rural life, the decline not just of Stick Around but of all Ozarkadia, the advancement and encroachment of this century's so-called progress. I was never successful in persuading Annie that there were certain aspects of our country life which must be preserved against the encroachment of "civilization." Burton Stoving, when he appeared, was a symbol to me of the very worst element of this encroachment: he was the Military, an army captain at the time; he was the Urban Life, a member of the big city's society; he was Money, he was Progress, he was Civilization. But these very qualities that made him repugnant to me made him desirable to Annie.

That, in itself, says more about my failure in raising and rearing and fostering her than anything else. So I lost Annie to him. I didn't try to stop her. I thought, *If everything I've helped you learn doesn't make you see what a mess you're getting into if you marry this fellow, then there's nothing I can say now to stop you.* She was nearly twenty at the time, and already pregnant.

But I told her that when this child was born, I wanted to "borrow" that child. I wanted this one last opportunity to "experiment," if you want to keep on calling it that. I was an old man, nearly seventy, but I knew I could live long enough to finish this work, long enough to take one human creature and show him or her all of the possibilities of the human It, to protect him or her from all the trammelings and warpings and frustrations of society, to reveal to him or her the grand world of nature and the way he or she belonged to it. That was my bargain with Annie.

But she reneged. The baby was born, and I waited three years, which was perhaps too long. If I had acted earlier...but the question is speculative anyway, since my end might have been the same in any case. By the end of those three years I wasn't ready to wait any longer, and I acted. I knew, of course, that Annie would guess who had taken the child. But if they followed, and found us, I had any number of escape routes carefully plotted, and I knew the fastness of these forests better than any man alive.... Or better, at least, than all but one man. He's another story.

Will you stay to hear it, G? Or shall I send you off now? By telling you that it was only after I had "borrowed" the child and brought her here to Stick Around, that I finally learned her mother's reason for not letting me have her: that Diana was her only child, that she couldn't let me have her only child, that she couldn't have any more children. Because Burton Stoving was sterile.

Diana is not, would you say? *defective.* Somewhat strange, yes, in an altogether charming way. But you wouldn't think there's anything wrong with her genes.

I'd rather whisper, G, but you wouldn't hear me. So turn up that aid and listen to me very, very carefully, because I'm not going to repeat myself; and if you repeat me to a soul, let alone Diana, I'll come back once again and hound you to your grave.

She was my daughter.

✣ 26 ✣

But the story of that, like the end of your sweet naked hour in the cool water of Old Bottomless, is sequestered.

✣ 27 ✣

Let us hurry, now, through a desequestering. Could we have a crescendo of background music, please, Conductor? Fiddles sawed for all they're worth, in a swelling climax of sound. Thank you.

You will hear it in your tinnitus, G, but when you climb out of the pool and retrieve your clothing, and plug your hearing aid back in, you will seem to think that it is not *merely* tinnitus, this grand finale of fiddling that sounds like all eight of the Playford dances mixed together. No, it isn't tinnitus. When Diana comes out of the pool, you will ask her if she doesn't think she can hear this tempestuous fiddling, and she will smile and say, Yes, she believes she can hear it too.

You will look all around you, now, and find the fiddler. He is sitting on a rock within full view of what you thought was your secluded bathing place. A local youth? A spying farmboy? He is a gangling, dark-tanned fellow, in his late teens, dressed in faded blue overalls, chambray work-shirt, a straw hat and—to complete the picture of rusticity—a stalk of Johnson grass gripped between his grinning teeth.

When he sees that you have spotted him, he will stop fiddling, but in your ear the grand crescendo-climax of strings will continue. "Howdy," he will say, cordially. The brim of his straw hat is casting the upper part of his face in shadow, but there will be something disturbingly familiar about him. Have you seen perhaps a photograph of him somewhere?

Diana will see him too. She will cry out, "Day! You've come back!" and she will run toward him. He will rise and come to meet her, and they will embrace. And they will kiss. And you will want to evaporate from the face of the earth. Diana will break loose from his embrace and say to him happily, "Well, you old voyeur, you, are we even now?" He will nod, and then she will bring him to you.

"Day," she will say, "I want you to meet G. G, this is Day. Day, G. Gee, Day!"

He will offer his hand and you will take it. "Mighty proud to meet you," he will say. "I've been hearin a right smart about you, feller."

"I've been hearin a right smart about you too, feller," you'll say to him.

Diana will explain to you, "Day has been trying to learn the Ozark dialect. Do you think he sounds authentic?"

"Purty good, I'd say," you'll say in the same saying, "fer a Jersey furriner. I tuk ye fer a local boy at fust."

"Aw, gosh dawg, I'm not *that* good, yet," he will protest. Then he will ask you, "Wal, you fixin to light out, directly?"

"Yeah. Reckon I'd best be gittin on." Sadly.

"Come go home with us. Light and hitch. Set a spell."

"Caint stop long."

"Stay more and eat you some supper with us. No sense rushin off." The three of you, the four of us, will head for home.

Diana will tell him, "We've been running all afternoon, G and I, just as you suggested. But now my feet are dead. Carry me, Day. Carry me!"

And she will climb up on his back, and he will carry her on down the road toward home. You will follow. With a smile, you'll remember the time he had carried her out of Five Corners when she was shot, and you'll remember the dream he had when he passed out after carrying her four miles to safety

> *...in the dream I was carrying her too, piggyback like this, and there was a man following us, who had been following us all along, but he was smiling at us, and she was alive, and laughing, and it was not nighttime but broad day, in some other place where we had finally gone, and not winter but springtime, and she was not hurt but whole, and the dogwood and redbud were blooming and the wind was warm and lifting her hair and her laughter, as I carried her piggyback through that strange and distant but magic woodland, some other place that seemed, in the dream, to be the right place....*

So you will understand what I meant: we fabricate our future in our dreams. But our dreams have a nice habit of often coming true. And you won't be entirely sad, will you, G? I won't let you.

When you reach my yellow house, you will sit, in the late afternoon, before supper, on the porch, in the chairs that are so much like those of Lara's store-porch. Diana will be excited. This will be a moment that she has long waited for. She can hardly wait. As soon as you are settled in your chairs, she will look at Day and ask him,

"Now? Okay?" He will smile and nod his head. "Go to sleep, Day," she will say.

We will meet again at last, G.

"We meet again at last, G," I say. "Our third meeting, isn't it?"

You look puzzled. "When was the second time?"

"You don't remember?" I say. "Surely you remember."

You remember. "Yes, I'd forgotten about that," you say. "Probably I was keeping it out of my mind, because I don't really want to believe in you."

"I can understand that," I say.

"That time," you say, "you told me to go away. You sent me off, out into the world. And now I've tried to come back again. And you're going to make me go away again, aren't you?"

"Not just yet," I say. "Stick around, for a little while. I'm not due to die until nearly dusk. You know this is the last day, don't you? They're after us, G. They're coming to get us. But we have a little time left." I turn to Diana and ask her, "Do you think you ran him enough today to make him sleepy? Do you think you got him tired enough so that we could put him to sleep for a while?"

"Let me get my tape recorder first," she says.

✝ 28 ✝

I found you, little Guy, in the dark glen of the waterfall. The hound was with you, but he seemed to be just as lost as you. The both of you were reclining on the ground, moping, beside the pool of the falls. The hound barked at me as I approached, and you looked up, fear in your eyes.

"Howdy there, sonny," I said, as friendly as I could. Your dog snarled but I gave him my palm to sniff, and he knew my scent.

"Howdy," you said, and sat up, not quite as frightened as you'd been at first. You recognized me. "Aren't you that magician who cured my wart?"

I nodded. "That I am," I said, "but I'm not any magician. How's the wart?"

"It's gone," you said, and showed me. "When I woke up the day after, I couldn't find no trace of it."

"Good," I said. "I'm right glad to hear that."

"How'd you do it?" you asked. "What made it work? Was it just that tobacco juice you spitted on it?"

"Well, no," I said. "That was just a gimmick. What made it work was that you believed it would work. And if you believe anything hard enough, it's bound to."

You thought about this, turning the thought over in your almost six-year-old head, and you shook your head. "That's not true. Because I'm lost, right now. And even if I believed I wasn't lost, it wouldn't help. I'd still be lost."

"You're not lost," I pointed out to you. "Because I've found you, haven't I?"

You thought about that one, and decided that I must be right. Another little miracle of this old magician. But then you thought of something else, and frowned. "Do you mean you're going to take me home?"

"If you want me to," I said.

"I'll git a lickin'," you protested. "They'll really clobber me, this time."

"Probably," I said, remembering my own boyhood, and then I told you of it. "When I was just about your age, five or so, I climbed up a tree in the back yard to hide from my folks, but my dad found me and started up the tree after me. I had a fool notion that I could just flap my arms like this—" I flapped my arms for you, and you giggled "—and just go flying off through the air, to get away. But naturally I discovered pretty quick that people can't fly, and I fell down out of that tree, almost to the ground, but that old tree saved me; she put out one of her limbs and kept me from hittin the ground. Then I got up and run away, and just like you, I hid out in the woods all night. But they found me the next day and clobbered me black and blue."

You nodded, understanding, and said, "So what can I do? I don't want to go back and git clobbered."

"I don't blame you," I said. "I think a grown-up person who'd hit a little kid that couldn't hit back is pretty low."

"Haven't you ever hit any kids?" you asked.

"Not since I've been grown."

"Didn't you never even spank your daughter?"

"How'd you know I got a daughter?" I asked.

"I heerd people down to Lara's store talkin about you."

"Well, no, I never punished her. What's the point, anyhow, in punishing other people?"

"Didn't she never do anything bad?"

"What does 'bad' mean?"

"Didn't she never tell a lie or do something you told her not to?"

"What good is spankin going to do, if she did?"

"It's supposed to keep her from doing it again," you explained, a little pedantically, I thought; this little spadger explaining the facts of human nature to this old man who never learned anything.

"I see," I said. "Well, tell me. What did you get punished for?"

"I told a lie," you said. "I wanted to spend the night with Lara, but the only way I could do that was tell my Aunt Josie that Lara was throwin a bunkin party for us kids, and when my Aunt Josie found out there was no bunkin party, she really beat me up, but I still wouldn't tell her what I'd done, and she kept on beatin me. So I run away."

"Well, you see what I mean," I said. "Her punishment of you wouldn't make you tell the truth. No amount of beating is going to find the truth. So what's the point of the punishment?"

You thought about that for a while, and decided that I must be right. Abruptly you asked me, "Can I go and live with you?"

I'm sorry I laughed. I'm even sorrier that I didn't give it more thought; but I don't think it would have worked. My laughing put a hurt frown on your face, so I said, "I'd be right glad to have you, son. But it would be mighty hard to keep you hidden. Folks would find you, soon enough, and drag you on home. And they'd probably be turned against me for trying to keep you."

You cradled your chin in your hands and sighed. "But I cain't go back," you said. "Even if they didn't clobber me. Because Lara's got that *feller Everett Dahl now, and she loves him now, and probably she don't even care if I'm lost or not."*

"Tell me about it," I requested, and you told me then that story which, one day, you would try to tell again, in a book called Firefly, *the story of a lonely, longing, lovely woman who was the spinster postmistress of Stick Around and whose only love was this tousle-haired little whippersnapper, five going on six, who kept her company all the time...until, just recently, a man from her past returned to her.*

"So you've lost her," I said when you'd finished, and laid a hand on your shoulder in sympathy. "I know how you must feel, son. I've lost a few myself." And in return for your story, I told you some stories of my own, about a brunette in a place called Dudleytown, and a redhead in a place called Five Corners, and a blonde in a place called Lost Cove.

You listened, captured; you thought I was nearly as good a storyteller as your beloved Lara had been. And when I finished, you asked me, "Is my life going to be like that when I get growed up?"

"Not just like that," I said. "Happier, I hope. But like me, you're going to have to do a lot of searching."

"What do I have to search for?"

"Love," I told you.

"Will I ever find it?"

"I don't know. I wish I could tell you that you will. But I just don't know." I stood up then, and took your hand. "Come on, son. It's time to go." I led you out of the glen of the waterfall, and down the mountain to a place where the logging trails begin. "If you ever do find it," I said, "come back and tell me about it. Or send me a postcard."

And then I showed you the division of the trail, the diverging paths. "That fork," I said, pointing, "goes to Stick Around." I pointed at the other path. "And that fork," I said, "goes to some other place. It isn't the right place either, and it's a long, long road."

"Thanks, mister," you said. "Though still I wish I could just stay with you. But I will come back and tell you if I ever find it." You turned to go. But then you turned back for a moment and said, "I never even learned your name."

⚜ 29 ⚜

Time for only a few more words before we go. That glen of the waterfall will serve us, G, for one more set. And it's nearly time. I can't hold out, in this house, against these lawmen. The sheriff has gone back to Jessup, probably to phone the state police for more help. Soon I'll have to take this girl and strike out up the mountain. That glen of the waterfall, which I might never have known about if I hadn't been searching for you there years ago, will make a perfect place to hide for the night.

I shake your hand, old Gentleman, and thank you for the pains you've taken. It has been worth your while, hasn't it? You've got a story, haven't you? Even if you've never found what you really came here looking for, which is love. You found it, but it wasn't yours. And finding it without being able to have it will keep you searching for it, in some other place. I'm glad of that, G; you're a good searcher; you'll go on searching. I leave you again with my First Damnation: the end of the search is the end of the beauty.

Now I've got to go. But you stop me long enough to say, "I hope, Dan, that you're planning to 'stay dead' this time around, that you'll be leaving these kids alone."

I can't help but laugh at your concern, and I rush to set your mind at ease on that score. "Oh yes, that's part of the plan. Besides, I'm tired. I've had all I wanted. I'm going to sleep a long time."

"Good," you say. "Then there's just one question. Nothing important. Just an inconsequential dangling end I'd like to sew up. In my notes, I've got the different regional variations on your bywords for sexual terms. For example, a penis in Dudleytown was a "perkin," in Five Corners a "picket," in Lost Cove a "pestle." What was it in Stick Around?"

Old Gross, to the end! I laugh and slap you on the shoulder. "'Private,'" I say. "Sequestered."

"And," you continue, "vale...velvet...vault...?"

"Sequestered too," I say. "'Veil.'"

Now, G, when Day "comes back," you shake his hand too, and tell him you're sorry you can't stay longer, and tell him how much you envy him. He reminds you of my Fifth Damnation, that envy is the worst of emotions. In that case, you ask him, does he not envy or resent your hour in the pool with Diana? Of course not, he says, and adds, "That was part of the script."

And you say to him in conclusion, as you have said to me, "There's just one question. Nothing very important. Just an inconsequential dangling end I'd like to sew up. But could you please explain to me how you put letters in Diana's box without leaving any footprints? You see, I set this little 'trap' of piling up some dust in front of the boxes—"

"In front of the boxes, yes," he says. "But didn't you realize there's a back side to the boxes, behind the counter? Haven't you ever been on The Other Side of the counter?"

Don't go just yet. There is Diana to say goodbye to, and her request to listen to. How would you like, G, to join them in their final "masque," their last acting-out? They can use you, even if you don't exactly relish the "rôle" they have in mind for you, that of the state trooper who shot me. But you possess a rifle, which will lend a semblance of "reality" to their "masque."

Diana shows you an old newspaper clipping, supposedly taken from a 1953 edition of the local weekly, the *Jessup Record*; you consider, for just one brief moment, the possibility that she could have had this newspaper clipping printed for her at her expense on a sheet of old and yellowed newsprint. But you dismiss such a petty thought from your mind, and you read the clipping:

TROOPER WINS STICK AROUND SHOOT-OUT
WITH OLD KIDNAPPER; CHILD IS SAFE

State Police Corp. Sugrue "Sog" Ellen was credited today with finding the hide-out of the "Stick Around Hermit" who kidnapped the three-year-old child, Diane

Staving, daughter of prominent Little Rock family, last week.

Corp. Ellen, or "Sog" as he is known to chums in Stick Around, where he was born and reared, is familiar with the woods of Lingerfelt Mountain, and said he had a "hunch" where to look. Finding the hermit-kidnapper by a waterfall in one of the mountain's hollers, Corp. Ellen demanded he lay down his arms and surrender. When the man refused, Corp. Ellen, making sure the child was not in line of fire, shot and killed the man.

The child was promptly returned to her happy parents, and was found to be unharmed.

The dead man, about 70 years of age, known, to Stick Around friends only as "Dan," had lived in the area for about twenty years, they said. A search of his dwelling, located near Stick Around village, failed to furnish further identification.

His motive for kidnapping the child was unknown. It was speculated that the man, being penniless, had hoped to collect ransom.

State Police Headquarters in Russellville said Corp. Ellen will probably be decorated.

"It's a lie," Diana says to you. "That trooper didn't ask Daniel to surrender. Daniel didn't even see him. But that trooper wasn't taking any chances. Daniel had already wounded three sheriff's deputies and two state troopers, escaping with me from this house. He wasn't trying to kill them; he was such a good shot that he could hit them just where he wanted, just enough to disable them so we could make a getaway from this house and go hide up on the mountain. But that Corporal Ellen wasn't taking any chances. All the officers were under orders to try to take Daniel alive, if possible, or just to wound him, not kill him. But Corporal Ellen sneaked up on us in the glen of the waterfall and without any warning he shot Daniel twice. It was bad shooting too, which didn't kill him instantly. It took him a while to die."

On the mountain behind my house, in a grove of cedars, Diana shows you one more thing, one last thing: my grave. She readily admits that the headstone is not "authentic," that is, not original; she has purchased it recently herself, has had it cut to order out of Arkansas granite by a stonecutter in Harrison. They had buried me here, on my own property, in my own woods, without much of a marker, just a temporary metal stake. Diana has seen fit to leave something more permanent:

DANIEL LYAM MONTROSS
June 17, 1880–May 26, 1953
The last Montross of Dudleytown
The only Montross of Stick Around
"We dream our lives, and live our sleep's extremes."

Now it is time for her to be taken to the glen of the waterfall. She has her last fresh tape ready in her tape recorder. You must follow after, with your rifle. You must sneak into the glen of the waterfall and "shoot" me, twice, and then, as Sugrue Ellen had done, turn and go without a word. He had turned and left, not even bothering to take or comfort the child, in order to summon his fellow officers. You will turn and leave, and go, to leave us alone together in these our last moments.

"But you'll come back?" Diana says to you, and gives you a kiss. "Someday you'll come back?"

"I'll come back," you say.

✝ 30 ✝

This is all I know of my last hour unto some other place.

I'll sleep my first true sleep. We've found our true kindred; the elements care for us. Aeolus wafts a gust to dance the leaves around our heads. I am shot. Blood and being trickle off my skin. My killer's gone back down the hill to get some help. I'm blind to all the woods and world except her face. I gaze into her eyes, and feel her grace. The waterfall roars above the roar of death. Before it quits, I'll slip away to sleep.

Look, child, into my eyes. Speech is all I lack. Solemn and silent. But in my solemn eyes you'll catch a glimpse of time, and know a proof of me, that will still your trembling. You mustn't be afraid; you know I'll live. In the mirror of my eyes you'll see creation.

It doesn't help to cry. You'll learn that tears are only for yourself. Lay your head against my chest, child, and listen:

I live, I draw the breath of life. Hear this tone, this tune, this time. Hear these driftings and quivers, these settlings and stirrings, these dronings and burbles, these ripples and thrummings, these hummings and coursings: these humors in this clod, this chunk of flesh, this body knowing weight and gravity, lying quietly and waiting.

Now take your head away, child. Lift your chin and smile for me. There will be no sound. No sounds are heard in death, no winds in the leaves, no humors coursing through the flesh. The roar of the waterfall will cease. Death is a quiet woman.

Before she takes me to her breast, I'll show you the Indian shelters and their little burial mounds in this glen of the waterfall. People lived here once. I was an Indian once, and so were you; our people lived here. We might live here again. Time is but the shadow of the world thrown against the screen of eternity; that shadow passes over us, and passes on, but circles and returns. And while it's gone, we see the light.

Death is a silent woman, but not a dark one: all emblazoned and bespangled with timeless radiance she blinds my eyes before she takes me to her breast. And in my blinded eyes you'll catch a glimpse of the shadow of time that's moving over you, to give you a life you'll see enough of the life you'll have to help you dream its future. I had wanted to help you dream it, but like everything else I've tried to do, I failed again.

Bright Death repells me with her light only because I know I lived a failure. But this will be my one success: letting her take me to her breast.

I've known her before, without the blinding light; I've known her for a third of my life, in sleep. We pass a third of our lives in her embrace while we dream of the rest that comes before our final rest.

I don't fear her, as she reaches to take me to her breast. But maybe I fear that pang, that explosion, that orgasmic climax. Which is fear of myself, not of her. I'll last a while before I come.

Life is a duration, a passing of the shadow of time over us. Death is a timeless eternity. The orgasm is an instant.

And after that instant, she will possess all my habits and desires, and pleasures and afflictions. But not my ideas, which will roam through time in search of some other place.

Before she takes me to her breast, I remember the reading I got at my birth from my sister: *Our birth is but a sleep and a forgetting.* And our death is but a waking and a remembering. I will remember it all in the instant of that climax.

Child, if I close my eyes, don't be frightened. I close my eyes to see my way to reach her dazzling breast.

And if you hear me cry out, don't be alarmed. I'm singing the short song of my last instant's ecstasy.

Finale

Putney, Vt.
June 5

Mr. B.A. Stoving
Union Bank Building
Little Rock, Arkansas

Dear Mr. Stoving

After a three-month investigation, involving some 6000 miles of travel, I was able to locate your daughter. You will be happy to know that she is very much alive, and well, and quite contented.

After finding her and hearing her story, I debated with myself for some time before reaching the conclusion that I should respect her wishes by not divulging to you her present whereabouts.

However, I can tell you this much about her: she is deeply in love with a most remarkable young man who would be the envy of any girl searching for a strong, practicable and entertaining male who offers much promise as a life's companion. The fact that he is making his career in forest work, and has no college education, does not detract from his stature as one of the most interesting young men I've ever met.

She expects to bear his child in August. I hope that, after the baby is born, she will want to be in touch with you at last, to send you pictures of your grandchild. If she does not, it will be only because she feels she has her own good reasons for not writing to you.

Perhaps you will feel that a permanently missing daughter is no better than a dead one. But I'm writing to you because I thought it might be some comfort to you to know that she has found the right place in life, after a long search.

Yours sincerely,
G.

P.S. Please do not feel that you are obliged to me in any way, financial or otherwise, for this information.

Stick Around, Ark.
p.o.: Acropolis, Ark.
August 30

Dear G,

    Just a few words to serve in place of birth announcement and enclose this Polaroid snapshot of the *three* of us.

    We have named him Daniel G. (after *you*, old Godfather) Stoving-Whittacker.

    If you're such a great art historian, do you recognize the "pose" of this photograph? Give up? It's Giorgione's "Tempest"! The "soldier" on the left is Day, and the "gypsy" on the right nursing her baby is me (and little Dan).

    Guess who was on the other side of the camera? Who *took* the picture? I know it will give you a sleepless night, and the answer isn't even important, but you'll appreciate my devious cleverness in making a mystery of it, the same way that *you* make a mystery of everything.

    Everything is wonderful here, and all of us are blissfully happy. Stick Around can get terribly hot in August, but, as you know, Daniel built this house with a kind of natural air-conditioning, and the bedrooms on the second floor are always cool.

    Day and I were very pleased to hear about the progress on your book, although we have a few reservations about that title, *There Was Another Place Which Was The Right Place*. Why burden the book with something so unwieldy and unmemorable? Why not simply call it *Some Other Place. The Right Place.*?

    I was glad to learn that your wife and daughters have returned home, and that your garden is so productive this year. And I was simply amazed to hear that you've lost twenty pounds. Is that what I started, on that day?

    Incidentally, did you know that you went off and left your rifle? If you'll forgive this last example of my "psychologizing," whenever somebody goes off and leaves something behind, it means they want to stay, or they want to come back again. So please do.

Love,
Diana

About the Author

Donald Harington

Although he was born and raised in Little Rock, Donald Harington spent nearly all of his early summers in the Ozark mountain hamlet of Drakes Creek, his mother's hometown, where his grandparents operated the general store and post office. There, before he lost his hearing to meningitis at the age of twelve, he listened carefully to the vanishing Ozark folk language and the old tales told by storytellers.

His academic career is in art and art history and he has taught art history at a variety of colleges, including his alma mater, the University of Arkansas, Fayetteville, where he has been lecturing for fifteen years. He lives in Fayetteville with his wife Kim.

His first novel, *The Cherry Pit*, was published by Random House in 1965, and since then he has published eleven other novels, most of them set in the Ozark hamlet of his own creation, Stay More, based loosely upon Drakes Creek. He has also written books about artists.

He won the Robert Penn Warren Award in 2003, the Porter Prize in 1987, the Heasley Prize at Lyon College in 1998, was inducted into the Arkansas Writers' Hall of Fame in 1999 and that same year won the Arkansas Fiction Award of the Arkansas Library Association. He has been called "an undiscovered continent" (Fred Chappell) and "America's Greatest Unknown Novelist" (Entertainment Weekly).

The fonts used in this book are from the Garamond family